Pause

By: Vatalini Sahar

First published by AX Creative 2025

This novel is entirely a work of fiction. The names, characters and incidents portrayed in it are the work of the author's imagination. Any resemblance to actual persons, living or dead, events or localities is entirely coincidental.
Vatalini Sahar asserts the moral right to be identified as the author of this work.
Vatalini Sahar has no responsibility for the persistence or accuracy of URLs for external or third-party Internet Websites referred to in this publication and does not guarantee that any content on such Websites is, or will remain, accurate or appropriate.

Designations used by companies to distinguish their products are often claimed as trademarks All brand names and product names used in this book and on its cover are trade names, service marks, trademarks and registered trademarks of their respective owners. The publishers and the book are not associated with any product or vendor mentioned in this book. None of the companies referenced within the book have endorsed the book.

Vatalini Sahar is a pen name. All rights and legal responsibilities pertaining to this work are held by the author writing under this name.
This work was written and edited by a human author. No generative AI tools were used to write or co-author the narrative.

This is a work of fiction. Any resemblance to actual persons, living or dead, or actual events is purely coincidental.

First edition
Cover art by Jessica Boeschinger
Editing by Jennifer Fink

Print ISBN: 979-8-218-73932-4

This novel includes emotionally intense material that may be difficult for some readers, including themes of grief, substance use, complicated family dynamics, explicit intimacy, and scenes involving blurred and self-destructive sexual consent.

Please take care while reading.
— Vatalini Sahar

To my husband, my constant muse.
Everynight, our adventures become a new story.
I love you.

Chapter 1

His frustration was growing while waiting for her. He sat at the bar with low hums of conversations surrounding him. His usual pour of bourbon was not mellowing his angst. He motioned to the bartender to upgrade his drink to a double pour of its sister brand, hoping the older age would settle the tension throughout his body. His mind wandered back to his latest puzzle on his living room table; a gradient of white to black. A small but challenging puzzle with only one hundred pieces created a calm meditative state for him to relax. He had become unsettled. He had become distracted—an unideal time to become distracted.

He returned week after week to indulge and watch his beautiful distraction. Tonight, seated across the restaurant, she dined with a man. Laughing, smiling, and gently caressing the arm of who she was with. A noted signature move on her part. He felt jealousy? He needed to end this fixation and introduce himself. What was this attraction to a woman he didn't know?

Over the past few weeks, they had shared glances of acknowledgment with each other, but neither had spoken one word. There was an understanding placed in their nonverbal exchange. He would have to make the first move. Not often placed in that position, it was a refreshing game, and tonight, he would make his introduction.

First, if the ritual remained the same, she would have to finish her night with a trip upstairs, then return to the restaurant's bar and order a cheeseburger with a glass of red wine. Like his affinity for puzzles, he was caught pulling together the details of what he witnessed. He wasn't sure he liked what the pieces were alluding to but couldn't declare with absolute certainty that his assumption was correct.

He lifted his glass, letting the ice swirl in the golden liquid, continuing to wait. He glanced over as she stood from her seat; she smoothed her hands over her ample thighs hidden beneath the sheer fabric of her long black dress. She looked over to the bar to where he sat. Was this another nonverbal exchange with him? A small smile spread across her lips, not to him but to the bartender watching her.

He tried not to stare as she and her date moved about the restaurant. Her long black hair gently waved with the power of her walk. She was tall, taller than the man she was with, but he was sure not taller than him. Her curvaceous figure entranced him. Her dress though modest, left little to the imagination of what softness was beneath that fabric. Her guest guided her out of the restaurant, Clark tensed, watching, until she was out of sight in the direction of the elevator's banks in the hotel lobby.

It was just before nine. The dinner rush of the evening was beginning to depart, creating a more ambient vibe. He clenched his jaw—hoping to avoid his thoughts drifting into what could be happening upstairs. He reached into his jacket and pulled out a small notebook and pen. He opened his last bookmarked page and concentrated on reviewing his notes.

Flipping back a few sheets, he found the page dated from the night he first saw her. He had written at the bottom of the page—under the shorthand of his business dinner at Prime. *Ask Patrick about the woman at the bar*. He closed the journal, recalling the first night he saw her.

That night Clark had been trying to focus on his dinner guests. The day had been full of meetings with prospective companies that needed investors. Each company had been more mismanaged than the last, with ideas that were either cheater brands or antiquated.

He was tired; his head ached as he listened to the continuous chatter of two lackluster entrepreneurs who had been explaining their product for two hours too long. An app that could let you control the music of collegiate sporting venues. Despite how ludicrous it sounded, they had funding from *other investors*, which meant family and friends with money.

Readying himself to speak, he was caught off guard as her soft laugh floated through the air. Clark immediately noticed, watching as she leaned into her dining partner and gently stroked his cheek. A burning feeling struck him. He furrowed his eyebrows at the sensation. Why had that action jolted him? He had seen beautiful women, maybe even more beautiful women than her before. None, however, had sparked energy from across the room. He focused back on his dinner and guests but couldn't help the occasional peek toward her table. When she had finally left, Clark at first felt relieved, followed by a curiosity about who she was. Perhaps he was misinterpreting the emotions for familiarity. Did he already know her?

As Clark's dinner was ending, she returned to the restaurant. This time directly to the bar. Clark watched as she smiled gratefully at the bartender, who slid her a glass of red wine as if it was routine. She accepted it and exchanged a few words while swirling the glass.

"Clark?" His attention was brought back to his table. "Do you have anything else?" He looked over at his colleague Adam.

Taking his attention away from the mysterious woman, he spoke. "We went through a lot today—your enthusiasm about your company and needs haven't gone unnoticed." He moved his napkin from his lap and lightly tossed it over his plate. "We have everything we need. Adam will be back in touch." Clark made one last mark in the notebook to the side of his plate and turned it over.

Clark continued to glance over to the bar as Adam walked their dining guests out of the restaurant. Clark was sure he didn't know her. Feeling tight, he stood from the table as Adam walked back toward him, carrying a usual all-knowing smirk. Clark ignored his friend and finished his drink.

"It wasn't horrible." Adam offered, standing next to Clark at the side of the table. He stood close to Clark's height but had a much thinner build. He removed his black-framed glasses, setting them on the table as he rubbed his much bragged-about baby blue eyes.

"I would hire them for sales," Clark dryly commented. "Where did you even find these guys?" Before Adam could answer, Clark continued, "I cannot sit through these much longer." He pinched the bridge of his nose.

"The day wasn't totally wasted—I like the idea of the app funneling money back into the school. I bet I can find a loophole in their pattern, and we can get this done in like six months." Adam laughed. "Our Tech group could mimic this easily." He pulled out a chair and put his glasses back on. "Sit back down."

Clark obliged, listening as Adam continued to speak about the app's potential. His attention drifted back to the bar. His mystery woman beamed a large smile as her food was brought to her. She reached into her purse and brought out her phone, leaning it against a decorative candle. She pushed back her hair, slipping in one airpod at a time, and greedily situated the plate in front of her. She quickly tied her hair up to a high bun and began eating, one fry at a time.

Noticing silence next to him, Clark refocused back on Adam.

"I just wanted us to be different. I wanted to change the landscape of startups. I want to find the ones no one knows about; I want to find entrepreneurs with kids, startup leaders who look like me and think there is no hope. That was the goal of all this. Otherwise, why are we here?"

"I am here because you asked me to be. I wanted to retire in Belize." Adam reminded Clark.

"Your wife didn't want to go." Clark smartly replied. "You are stuck with me."

"Be that as it may. We are here; we are in it. It will sort out." Adam flippantly responded. "Amanda is upstairs. I told her I would be back before midnight."

"You're fine to leave. I am going to head out soon too." Adam hesitated. "Is everything okay?" Clark asked. "You guys okay?" He repeated.

"She wants to settle down, and after everything I have put her through, I have to give in. Her sister just got pregnant; we are still trying." Adam exhaled heavily. "You know me. This is hard—really accepting the 'suburb family life.' She deserves this."

"I think it will suit you more than you think," Clark encouraged.

"Maybe," Adam looked at his watch. "I could squeeze in a nightcap." Clark looked over to Adam's glass on the table. Tonic water and lime. His wine was untouched. "They have a nice non-alcoholic whiskey at the bar. Patrick brought it in a few months ago." Adam was close to celebrating a year of sobriety.

Meeting in college, Clark and Adam quickly realized how well they worked together. Their talents and personalities balanced for a successful duo. They became business partners in multiple failed endeavors until their last company became an overwhelming success, leading them to be bought out less than two years ago. It had left Clark unprepared for what to do next. He never thought he would sell a business that finally became successful, but it was an offer even he couldn't refuse.

While Adam immediately began traveling the world with his new wife, Clark struggled to figure out his next steps. He knew he wanted to give back. He wanted to be a presence in his community and his city and figure out the best way he could utilize his money and skill and help others rise up to their potential. Then it came to him.

Cottage Growth, CG for short. A play on a major thoroughfare in Clark's former southside neighborhood.

A venture capital community where startups could work under their protection with salary, benefits, on-site childcare, and relocation expenses. It was unheard of. It was an idea ahead of its time. It was one Clark felt passionate about pursuing.

He pitched the idea to Adam, who initially laughed it off, insisting Clark do some traveling of his own. Clark was able to sway Adam's opinion by adding that if CG became successful and a staple of the Chicago business community, perhaps Adam could get a park named after him and rival the Pritzker name. Adam quickly agreed. After much convincing of their shared financial manager, Marcus. Clark extracted enough for half the startup cost. This meant Adam had to begin a fundraising campaign to find other investors to support this venture capital (VC). Clark hated the idea of asking for money again. He wanted complete control, but he knew Marcus wouldn't let him go broke if this venture failed. So he had to settle with 51%.

"What was the name of the whiskey you mentioned?" Clark glanced over to the bar again. Adam turned in his seat to look at what had been keeping Clark's attention.

"You haven't stopped staring at that woman all night." Clark quickly glanced toward Adam. "Must have had quite the workout upstairs." Adam chuckled.

"You don't know that." Clark glared over at his friend.

"No, I don't know for sure—but then again, you could go talk to her and find out." Adam reached into his wallet and threw down a few hundred dollars. "My treat," Adam grinned, leaving Clark alone at the table.

There was an attraction toward her; he couldn't deny it. She was beautiful, yes, but when she walked back in, he felt his vision play tricks on him, slowing down time as she took her seat. He left his table and walked toward the washroom at the back of the restaurant.

He pushed the thick mahogany door of the bathroom open and stood in front of the sink. He sighed heavily at his reflection. Placing his hands on the cold black marble, Clark declined the steamed white towel in the attendant's hand. Smiling tightly, he dropped a few dollars in the jar. The attendant returned to his post, leaving Clark to indulge in a private moment; splashing cold water on his face, he studied his appearance. His eyes were dark from strain and lack of sleep, but the line of his beard and hair were perfectly shaped as he had been able to see his barber today. His chocolate complexion blended in with his short, black, trimmed beard. His full lips were chapped—an old habit of chewing on them. Patting his face dry, he leaned back over the sink again, turning his neck from side to side. He steadied his mind, pausing to focus on the water droplets racing down the drain.

He pushed himself back up, looking at his reflection and smoothing the sides of his suit coat. He stood broad as he did tall. His height had often caused intimidation when he entered a room, but his frame fit the bill for handling the stress and complexities of his world. His stature made wearing suits a favorable task. He inhaled deeply, taking in one last breath, ready to head toward the bar. Exiting the bathroom, he heard his name.

"Clark! I was hoping to catch you before you left." The familiar voice called for him. "How was your dinner?" Patrick, General Manager of Prime, lightly jogged toward Clark.

"Everything was great as usual." Clark greeted him with a friendly fist bump.

"Heading to the bar? Let me buy you a drink." Patrick offered.

Clark looked over to see that his mystery woman was gone. Back up to the room? Or did she leave the hotel? He didn't know. His lingering headache had intensified by this point. "It has been a long day. I will take you up on it another time." Patrick patted his back, leading Clark out of the restaurant as staff continued to clean up for the night.

"I'll walk you out." Both men began walking toward the exit. "Looks like you and Adam are working on something?" A busboy quickly approached them, handing Clark his journal that had been left on the table.

"Always. I will share more when I can." Clark extended a thank you to the young man and flipped the pages of his journal under his thumb. He looked back to his last notation and then toward Patrick. "Did you know that woman who was here?" Clark motioned toward the bar. He noticed his question caught the bartender's attention as well.

"Bar was packed tonight. Lots of women showed up." Patrick quickly replied.

"Everyone saw this woman," Clark smirked. "You did too."

"If we are talking about the same woman, then yeah, I know her. She is here often."

"How often?" Clark noticed Patrick's hesitation while searching for an answer that would satisfy both of them.

"As often as you, I suppose ." Patrick ran his hand through his slicked-back black hair. His suit coat fabric relaxed from a full evening. "When did you start looking at blondes?" Patrick cocked his head.

Clark tried to gauge his tone. "She wasn't blonde." Clark correct-ed, realizing he wasn't going to get any information from Patrick tonight.

"Oh, then sorry, man, I guess I missed who you are talking about." Patrick continued to walk with Clark throughout the restaurant on his way out. "Are you sure you don't want one nightcap before you go?"

Clark nodded, watching the bartender reach for the red lip-stained wine glass where she sat as he set it off to the side.

Clark would come back but would she?

Chapter 2

She did. The same night the following week. Clark had convinced himself he just happened to be back at Prime to enjoy the lounge. Designed as a dark and warm environment, he snagged his favorite spot next to the window facing out toward LaSalle Street, which gave a perfect view of the comings and goings on the busy street and inside the LaSalle Street Hotel.

Settling at his table, he placed an order with his server, flipped his phone over with the screen face down on the table, and stretched his palms out before him. Clark rubbed his thumb across the condensation of the water glass before him when he caught her familiar laugh floating through the air. Clark casually leaned over in his seat and glanced at the main dining room. There she was, with another man, or maybe the same one? He couldn't tell as he couldn't see them well. Her back was toward him, but he could still recognize her. Her hair, shape, and what was now deemed her signature move.

Was she doing this weekly? Daily? Clark frequented Prime enough that he would have seen her before last week. This woman had eluded his thoughts. Clark leaned into a few fantasy moments, but he hadn't thought he'd see her again so soon. Reaching for his drink with the top of his fingers, he brought it closer. He kept his gaze across the restaurant, slowly savoring his first sip.

She was led out of the restaurant toward the elevator bank. She stiffened her composure when her companion placed his hand on her back. She was either very new to this or didn't want to be there.

His eyes followed her until she disappeared past his ability to see. Would she come back down again? Indulge in dinner this time? He had to know—he wanted to know. His curiosity was getting the best of him.

He had no choice but to wait. He reached for his phone, flipping the screen side up. Having nothing else planned for the evening, he motioned for his server again, adding dinner to his tab. Opening his Economist app beneath his thumb, he tried to focus on the article before him.

He read the same sentence four times, realizing he would not be able to focus on the achievement of two environmental-focused investors being voted onto the ExxonMobil board. Still, instead, his imagination cruelly created images of what she was doing upstairs.

Why would she be doing it? Did she need money? He had money; she could work for him instead. The thought entertained Clark in a devious manner. Even in his private moment, that wasn't what he initially meant.

Time progressed slowly. He finished his dinner and nursed his third drink of the night. The main dining floor was closed with a semi-full lounge. Clark was about to call it for the night when she finally made her appearance back at the bar. Clark did not attempt to talk to her. He wasn't ready to acknowledge any truths. Simply put—he wasn't prepared to speak to her. Instead, he watched her cautiously, observing her beautiful appearance from his closer vantage point.

She was sad. Her smile for the wine was bright upon receipt of the glass but did not seem genuine. Her eyes were not radiantly sparkling as before while she conversed with the bartender, but instead, she nodded gently, her lips pressed tightly together.

Once alone, she swiveled the deep red liquid around the glass before taking her first and only drink. Clark held his breath as she drank all of her wine. A small dribble escaped from the crook of her rouge-stained pout. She caught the excess with her middle finger and gently slid the remaining wine across her bottom lip. She held the empty glass in her hand. She studied it intensely, lightly twirl-ing the stemware loosely in her hand. She stood up from her seat and closed her eyes before slamming the delicate glassware on the marble bar.

The bar went silent. Clark impulsively stood up from his seat, fighting his urge to help. The bartender hurried toward her; she gripped the shattered glass in her hand. Patrick rushed over to her side, taking the towel the bartender had been trying to put on her hand and seating her back down. People politely turned away but couldn't help but peek back over as more employees surrounded her.

Clark sat back down but did not look away. Her expression was sullen. Her eyes were fixated on the mixture of blood and glass in her hand. She held the glass in her palm tighter and tighter, en-couraging the glass to penetrate deeper into her. Patrick leaned in, very close to her, whispering into her ear, confirming to Clark that Patrick knew her well. Patrick placed his hand on her wrist and forcefully squeezed his hand, causing her to release her grip.

As the last remnants of glass fell from her hand, she locked eyes with Clark. He didn't break the gaze, holding it with her until she tilted her head softly, raising her eyebrows with a nervous smile. She was the first to break contact, finally looking up at Patrick and nodding. Patrick pulled her up to her feet and led her out of the restaurant.

Clark's mind was racing. Had she been hurt? Where was the man from earlier? He wanted to press Patrick about her. He wanted to know what had happened. Leaving the restaurant that night, he walked home, unable to get her image out of his head. Her sitting and holding the glass so painfully. It was almost symbolic of how Clark thought she felt. Then her gaze at him. Her eyes took his breath away from a distance. How would he react closer to her? He wanted to know. He needed to know.

Clark returned the following week; he had only caught her on her way out carrying a white take-out bag. He stopped, seeing her wrap herself tighter in her coat before venturing outside. He turned and looked at the bar and then back out to the sidewalk intersec-tion, where she stood waiting for a light. He took a chance. He retraced her steps and left the lobby doors, hesitating about twenty feet from her. She held the bag in her right hand, as he observed she was still favoring her left which was lifted to rest slightly higher against her hips. The wind played with her hair sweeping dramatically around her face.

As he was ready to take a step toward her, the light changed; she looked out toward the traffic and then back in Clark's direction. She saw him again; she began walking ahead with another tilt of her head and a soft smile. Clark reached deep into his pocket for the security of his cigarettes. Pulling one quickly out toward his lips, he couldn't find his lighter. She crossed the street and continued to walk. He leaned back against the wall of the building.

The impulse to follow her tempted him, but that was crazy. *That* was being a stalker. Clark laughed inwardly. Did she not dine with any other man tonight? Did she not go upstairs to a room? Had Clark confused a situation that had a seemingly simple answer? It was all becoming too much. Next week, if she were back, he would approach her. He would start with an introduction and work his way to finding out all the answers he sought.

Chapter 3

Tonight was the night. Clark put his journal back into his jacket pocket, shaking the memories of their past few encounters. The bar was quiet, with only a handful of tables occupied.

An elevator bell caught his attention, and she returned. No moonlight escapade tonight. She had been gone less than ten minutes. The bartender who had been serving him grabbed a wine glass and began to pour from the Silver Oak Cabernet bottle.

"She likes it to breathe for a few minutes." The bartender grinned as he placed it to the side.

Clark made no reaction. He hadn't intended to be obvious, but she matched her schedule with the same bartender. Clark wondered if there was a deeper connection between them. He hadn't seen Patrick on the floor tonight, but that didn't mean he wasn't around. She sat across the bar from him and exchanged pleasantries with their shared bartender.

It was time to make his introduction.

She avoided his gaze as she made her way to the bar smiling inwardly as she took her regular seat. Her dark stranger had come back and was waiting for her. She noticed him earlier in the night and quickly dismissed the excitement she felt, focusing on the man she was with, forcing her mind not to wander off in fantasy with her dark stranger contently watching her from afar. Her date that evening did not go beyond dinner. As she had let the hotel room door close behind her, she calmed her steps down, heading toward the elevator and back to Prime.

Seated at the bar tonight, he made his presence known. After the wine glass incident, she was surprised to see him return. A sensation fluttered through her, a familiar one that she didn't think possible to feel again. The memory of his gaze, the warmth of his eyes when she held the shattered wine glass in her hand there was no judgment; she unknowingly felt safe in his eyes. A man she didn't know. Yet now, as he sat across the bar, she knew. He was here for her.

A whiskey glass slid next to her arm. Her nerves tingled with excitement. Finally.

"May I join you?" His voice was low, vibrations dancing above Simi's skin. She looked up into the eyes of her dark stranger, raising her eyebrows in curiosity. She waved her hand lightly at the chair next to her. As he took his seat next to her, she paused, bringing out the emulation of herself she wanted to present him with tonight— sexy, strong, secure, . . . sane.

"I'm Clark." He extended his hand out to her. She enclosed her hand around his, clenching her teeth at the sensation.

"Simi." Her throat caught immediately; she pulled back her hand abruptly. His gaze was curious toward her, "My name is Simi." She confirmed.

"Beautiful name."

"Thank you," Simi felt her heart pounding. She refocused herself and leaned in closer to him. "I am glad you finally decided to introduce yourself."

"Why is that?" He played along.

"I was thinking of billing you for voyeurism." She smiled in achievement, winning a laugh from him.

"I haven't been too subtle with my lead to talk to you. The bartender called me out too." Clark didn't break her gaze.

"I understand. I am exceptionally beautiful. It takes courage to talk to someone like me." Simi adjusted in her seat.

"You are nervous," Clark stated. Her bravado had failed as a defense.

"No," she lied. She was nervous. Her entire body fighting against her. She placed her hand on Clark's arm and leaned in, her lips just inches away from his shoulder. She danced her fingers up his sleeve.

"What should I be nervous about? You seem very nice."

"Do I?"

"Yes, though a bit shy."

"Observant." Clark leaned in. "I am anything but shy."

Simi made no reaction. She held his gaze, taking the opportunity to study his features, and view him from the close vantage point he had finally reached.

"Observe anything interesting?" Simi smiled brightly; her hand went back to resting on his arm.

"Definitely." Clark lifted her hand off his arm; he turned in his seat, positioning himself to sit face-to-face with her. He reached for her left hand. "Are you okay?" His thumb ran over the bandage on her palm. She instinctively wanted to pull her hand away until his touch encapsulated her. She exhaled slowly.

"I'm . . ." Her voice trembled. "I'm fine." His hand was enclosed around hers before releasing his grip. "I thought I would have scared you off after that."

"Takes a lot more than a broken glass to scare me."

"Two glasses then?" Simi twirled her wine.

"Maybe three. Then I would know you're a masochist, which could work for me." Clark chided.

"A voyeur and a masochist. Seems like a decent pairing."

"You can't call me out as a voyeur just because I frequent the same bar as you. It has a completely different meaning."

"Do you prefer stalker?"

"Clark would work just as well."

"Right," Simi motioned playfully. "Clark."

She was determined to keep the conversation light and entertaining. She was in control despite how her body responded to him. She knew what she was doing and would not waiver, no matter how secure he made her feel. Recent feedback informed Simi that she didn't do inauthenticity well, but she was trying to improve. Even if it meant losing her entire true self in the process, she was prepared and eager to do that. Simi tugged at the watch on her wrist, finding a source of comfort to relax her.

"So Clark, are you staying here tonight?" Simi was baiting him.

"No, I live here." Clark held in a smile, his fingers tapping on the side of his glass.

"That doesn't mean you aren't staying here tonight." Simi rested her hand on his shoulder; she turned to press her leg against his.

"Actually, it does." Clark reached for her hand keeping it still in his grasp. "I just wanted to talk to you." Simi felt her cheeks flush with embarrassment. Self-realization was fighting to take over her mental state. "Is that okay?"

"Why?" She hadn't meant to say it out loud. She quickly covered her lips with her fingertips, shaking her head with a nervous laugh.

"Sometimes it's just nice to sit at a bar and have a conversation with someone new." Clark was trying to break her façade. He was succeeding. "How lucky am I to have selected the most beautiful woman in the room."

"Exceptionally beautiful." Simi corrected, trying to find a balance in her personality. He was being genuine, and she felt inclined to return the gesture. She would tread softly, keeping her sexy, strong, secure, and sane self in the forefront.

"Exceptionally beautiful. My mistake."

They were interrupted as their shared bartender Bradley, stood in front of them before placing two cheeseburgers on the bar. "I figured you wouldn't want to eat alone." Bradley smiled, placing two cheeseburgers in front of Clark and Simi. "Can I refresh your drinks?"

"Please," Clark answered for them, and he smiled in her direction.

Simi turned to Clark. "Join me for dinner?"

"Absolutely." Clark handed her a rolled white napkin filled with utensils. Simi rolled out the napkin across her lap. "I've never had the cheeseburger before."

"It's my weekly treat. I have a thing for cheeseburgers, and they do not disappoint." Simi turned away from him, picked up her burger, and took a large bite. Some pieces spilled out on the side of her mouth as she continued to chew. Feeling his gaze, she grabbed her napkin and wiped her mouth. Clark held an amused smile.

"It's not bad." Clark agreed after taking his first bite. "Is this your favorite burger in the city?"

"Yep." The hum from Clark prompted Simi to inquire. "What?"

"You are new to Chicago. It's a good burger, don't get me wrong. Not the best. A local would know that."

"Quite the detective."

"Observer." Clark corrected.

A comfortable quietness fell between them as they ate. Simi was trying to handle her thoughts, what actions or things she could say to keep him close, but not too close.

"Where does the name Simi originate?" He broke the silence, pushing his plate off to the side.

"It's Persian," Simi used her napkin to wipe at the sides of her mouth.

"I assumed you were somewhere from that region," Clark waved his hand in a circular motion around her face. "You have that look."

Simi raised an eyebrow. "What does that mean?"

"A bit exotic, a bit tribal." Clark continued to explain.

"Tribal? You have a way with words." Simi laughed. "I don't think anyone has ever called me tribal before."

"Take it as a compliment. It's a very attractive look." Clark emphasized. "Much better than exceptionally beautiful."

"Seems to have gotten your attention."

"Did you want my attention, Simi?" She didn't dare meet his gaze. The tone of his words shocked her senses. She kept her eyes low as she folded her napkin until it was a neat rectangle. She was feeling exposed.

"Thank you for dining with me tonight." She tipped her glass with his. She finished the last of her wine, gently set the glass down, and pushed her plate away. She waved for Bradley's attention.

"Are you leaving?" Clark's forwardness had spooked Simi, and a sudden urge to flee was all she could think to do. "You didn't finish."

"Drank the wine too fast; probably best if I go." Bradley came over with her slip, waiting for her signature.

"Please, I insist," he pulled his wallet out.

"I umm," Simi paused, trying to find the right words. "I have like a tab here. It's not a big thing."

"A tab?" Clark chuckled.

"Yeah. It's billed to me later." Her answer was short. She was not providing Clark with any sort of explanation.

"So either you own the place or do enough business here that a tab would make sense?" Clark inquired; he rubbed the bottom of his chin with his fingers. He didn't wait for an answer; knowing he wouldn't get one, he continued. "I come here a lot, and I have only recently seen you."

"Maybe you weren't ready to see me yet." Simi offered. "I've been around."

"I'm not sure how I could have missed you."

Simi tilted her head to the side at Clark's comment. "Well, I am not always this glammed up."

"Just on Thursdays," Clark stated flatly. Not yet ready to concede the night. "I will walk you home."

It wasn't an ask. He had declined her invitation earlier, which indicated Clark only wanted to make sure she got home safely. Simi was still unsure of his true intention with her, but at this point, she was enjoying his company. She accepted his offer and excused herself to the coat check. Slipping on her black trench coat, she tied her belt around her waist as Clark talked to Bradley.

"I am ready," Simi announced. Clark looked over, acknowledging her, and wrapped up his conversation. She waved a kiss back to Bradley as Clark guided her out of the restaurant and hotel lobby. "What was that about?"

"I was asking if I could get a hook-up with a tab too." Clark teased in the patio area of the restaurant. Simi held in a smile. "Seeing how you dine here weekly, and I will join you, I think it makes the most sense."

"I don't remember inviting you to dinner every Thursday."

"No, you just invited me upstairs. I invited myself to dinner next week." Clark grinned, pushing the boundaries of their banter.

Simi shot him a sharp glare; he didn't know how thick her skin was. "Unfortunately for you, I don't do dinners without being invited upstairs. Tonight, was an introduction."

"Maybe." His tone was playful, "or tonight was a revelation."

"A revelation of what?"

"That you just want to have dinner." Clark extended his arm out. "Ready to go?" Simi hesitated; his familiarity was palpable. "It's just a walk, Simi." She looked at Clark; he was being sincere. Simi secured her arm around his. They began to walk silently, with only the sound of her heels tapping on the pavement. "Did you see Patrick tonight?"

Simi shook her head. "No." She answered casually, seeing a smile form across Clark's face. "What?"

"The owner of Prime would know who Patrick is." He chuckled, causing Simi to break the tension with laughter herself.

Simi was still smiling. She liked his humor. "Your logic doesn't make sense. You know Patrick. Do you own Prime?"

"No, but if I did, I would know about exceptionally beautiful women having a—"

"Exceptionally beautiful tribal women," Simi interrupted.

"Correct, having a tab system." Clark leaned his head over. "Caveat being, they wouldn't need one. It would just be free."

"Then you would have no restaurant."

"Do I get to keep the exceptionally beautiful tribal woman?" Clark asked, looking ahead, waiting for Simi to answer. After a few moments, Clark shared. "I've known Patrick for a long time. I followed him from the worst bars, when he was slinging back cheap PBRs under the table to now, ensuring all my money for entertainment." Simi nodded, realizing there was a long history between them and how that could affect her. "These are my favorite types of nights." Clark prompted.

"Mine too." She inhaled a deep breath. "It does get too cold for me sometimes. I was told Chicago summers were the best, so looking forward to a change soon. I feel like I need a warm escape."

"Where do you want to go?"

"Some place hot, like Vegas. The sun hits just right in Vegas. Maybe, Palm Desert?" Simi began to rattle off. She would answer home if she could step foot in that house again. "Though the idea of an island sounds nice too."

"I don't think I have been to Palm Desert yet." Clark shared. "Seems too hot."

"Deserts are like that." She remarked. "Palm Desert is nice; it's quiet. I enjoyed it there a lot." She turned to him. "I would recommend it but stay away during Coachella. Unless you are into festivals."

"Not my thing. Probably been to Lollapalooza twice? Both times against my will." He shared. "Though, . . ." Clark chuckled.

"What is it?"

"I am a sucker for a good baseline. In the right headspace, I can really get in the groove." Clark shared. "Why don't you like music festivals?"

"Don't get me wrong, I love live music. I went to Coachella once to see Hans Zimmer. He didn't disappoint. He was amazing. As soon as he was done, I left too." Simi smiled at the memory. "Festivals are just a lot."

"Well, given it is April, we will probably have snow again before May, so if you decide to fly to Palm Desert, we can meet there for our next dinner. You can show me around." She smiled to herself. He was warm, and he was familiar.

"It is not going to snow again. It was in the 70s today."

"You are new to Chicago." Clark laughed. "Even if it doesn't, I love the snow; I love when it's so cold that your lungs hurt. I can see myself doing something reckless like buying a house in Alaska."

"Alaska? That seems random."

"Do you have a better suggestion?"

"Norway? Switzer . . ." Simi stopped short of finishing the word. She quickly clenched her teeth together. She was talking too much with him.

"You okay?" Clark stopped next to her.

"Yep." She released her arm from Clark's, kneeling as she played with her shoe. She needed to recalibrate the ease of the conversation. The familiarity was beginning to trigger her? Her hair cascaded around her face, giving her privacy as she squeezed her eyes closed. Ready, she stood back up. "Loose strap."

Clark offered his arm back to her, and she accepted as the quietness fell back between them. She looked up at him. He did not meet her gaze but instead focused on their walk ahead. A feeling deep inside tugged at her. One she hadn't felt in a very long time. She realized she had looked too long when he began to grin.

"Is there something on my cheek?" Simi shook her head, too shy to admit she admired the sharp line of his beard. Only a straight blade was able to be that clean. He either had a steady hand or a brown barber. "I am not too far from here. I didn't realize they built anything residential in this area, it's mostly hotels and offices," Clark commented as they came up to another hotel.

"This is me." Simi stopped in front of the hotel. Clark shifted back into his stance, looking at another nice five-star luxury hotel.

"Are you just visiting Chicago?" Clark asked curiously.

"Not visiting per se." Simi looked away toward the water of Lake Michigan.

"I don't know what that means."

"Neither do I."

"If you are some Persian Heiress hiding in Chicago, I'd like a heads up." Simi covered her hand over her mouth at the intensity of her laugh.

"What an imagination you have. I suppose it's better than the former assumption of me?"

"Which would be?" Clark challenged.

Simi ignored his question. "It was a nice evening. Thank you, Clark." Clark reached for her hand and softly kissed the crook of her thumb and pointer finger. His kiss warmed Simi from the tip of her fingers to the bottom of her toes. The subtle scratches of his beard against her skin lit her nerves on fire. She held her breath, her body excitedly responding to him.

"I hope to see you next week for dinner." Clark tempted. Simi smiled softly and turned for the door. She took half a step before she turned to him. She looked deep into his eyes, bringing a vulnerability to the surface of Clark.

"What is the motive here?" Simi stepped back. "What are you looking for? What do you want? Because you have told me what you don't want."

"I just want to get to know you, Simi," Clark revealed. "No motive. It's been a fun game of glances this past month. Don't you want to find out why? Don't you want to get to know me?" His confidence amused Simi. She was not green with this type of man. In fact—she was drawn to it.

"I'll bite Clark. Next week would be nice. Maybe we could meet at a proper time for dinner?" She tilted her head slightly with her question. The city lights illuminated behind her.

"What's a proper time for you?" Clark was unsure if he was finding himself in an unspoken booking arrangement.

"I prefer to eat later, maybe like nine, when the crowd dies down?" She suggested. Clark couldn't help but smile.

"Nine works. Pick you up here first?"

"No, I will meet you there." She shook out a slight chill. "Thank you again for the walk, for the entire evening." Simi pressed her lips together, beginning to turn away from Clark.

"Can I ask you something?" His hand touched her shoulder. She looked back at him, nervous about the question.

"Okay?" Simi held her breath—was he being coy this entire time? Did he want what he knew she would provide? He knew where she was staying now too. Her stomach tightened until she saw a smile spread across his face. He removed his hand and slid his tongue across his teeth.

"Is Simi your real name?" Simi tried to hide her smile and nodded. Clark teased her with a suspicious look. "What is it short for ?"

"Simurgh." Simi shared. "It's a mythical bird in ancient Persian Mythology. Similar to what you may know is the Phoenix." She smiled at the memory that played across her mind. "My mom was deep into our culture and poetry."

"I am going to want to know more about all of that." Clark raised his eyebrow in curiosity. "Be ready to teach me everything next week."

"Yeah, we'll see." Simi smiled tightly, attempting to hide her amusement. She caught his gaze one last time before she walked back toward her hotel doors.

Clark watched as she disappeared from the glass. There was a lingering scent in the air that Clark had been trying to place all night. It was subtle but familiar, taking him back to a memory during his travels in the Middle East. He couldn't recall what it was, but he liked it. Clark smiled, looking out to the lake and deciding to extend his walk back home.

Chapter 4

Oh, Simi, Simi, what are you doing now? Simi sighed to herself. She leaned back against the wall of the elevator and turned slightly to look at her gaze, her own gaze. She felt her hand still tingling from his kiss. She brought her hand to her lips, slowly rubbing them across where he had left his mark. *Fuck, fuck, fuck*, she softly hissed. Exiting the elevator, she walked down the quiet hallway until she reached double doors. Simi walked into the expansive suite she had been calling home. She headed straight into the bedroom and slipped off her shoes and dress. Simi carefully removed her watch and placed it on the bed stand. Catching her reflection and began to study her appearance. She traced her fingers over old, faded scars and up over her breasts.

Simi sighed heavily as she walked toward the window and looked down. Clark was walking across the bridge. Simi had become able to easily identify him. The moonlight glistened over the river as the water traveled out to the lake. She continued to watch him as he leaned over the side of the bridge and looked out to the lake. She let out a long exhale after noticing she had been holding her breath. He was different but familiar; a tinge of pain soared across her heart.

Simi's thoughts betrayed her as her memories fluttered to his lips, his hands, and her touching his arm. She stepped back from the window and fell into her bed. Once more, rubbing her hands over her breasts, she continued down her torso and stopped above her lace underwear. She took a deep breath; her mind was racing.

She was fighting with her mind to focus on the end of her evening and keep her prior dinner blocked. She had perfected disappearing during times with her dinner dates, but she was not evading those memories with ease tonight. She frowned, covering her hands over her eyes. Memories were racing, and she couldn't stop them.

Good, bad, and painful memories. Memories that were no longer kind to her. She heard a familiar voice whisper her name softly, a memory flashing across with the audio. Again, she heard him softly say her name, as he used to do when she couldn't sleep. She caught her sob in her throat, eyes watering, unable to stop. She immediately removed her hands from her body and ran to the bathroom. She blasted the water on cold. She kept her lingerie on and sat on the marble floor of the shower. She was holding it in, keeping the tears and sadness at bay. Her past was gone. This is what her life was going to be now. This was a decision she firmly made. She was not broken. She was in complete control. The water was so cold that it felt like sharp blades against her skin. She reached up, turning the dial off. Her body began to shiver. She clenched her teeth and hands tightly. Repeating a familiar poem in Persian, she would often use it to soothe herself. Stepping out of the shower, she reached for a towel and returned to her bedroom. She pulled back the covers and lay on the bed. She continued to repeat the comforting poem until sleep accepted her.

The following day Simi woke up uncomfortably wrapped in her covers. The alarm of her phone was blaring out of her jacket. She struggled to find her coat in the living area to turn off the painful sound. Reaching into her pockets, she finally found the device and silenced it. Rubbing her eyes, she noticed the time.

Shit.

She rushed back into the bedroom and grabbed a pair of jeans and a sweater, putting them over her now-dry lingerie. She ran to the bathroom, drenching a washcloth in cold water. Returning to her bedroom, she grabbed her bag and quickly rushed out of the room. She continued to wipe last night's makeup off of her face in the elevator and raced toward the lobby exit, hoping she would make it in time to avoid an additional lecture on 'scheduling for healing.'

"You are late." The woman held the door open for Simi.

She didn't respond immediately, dropped her bag to the floor, and took her seat. "I overslept." Simi reached for a water bottle on the table in front of her.

"Lucky for you, my next appointment was canceled, so not only do you get your full hour but thirty minutes more. Just for you."

"Lucky me." Simi gulped the water down quickly. She fought the urge to wretch. She needed food but opted for a lecture instead.

The room was dimly lit. Calming aromatics of lavender filled the air. Simi sat diagonally across from Jane, a trendy older woman in her early 60s and her therapist. Jane had short white hair and always wore fun bright-colored framed eyeglasses. She was a rebel in her past life. Hidden remnants of cheetah print tattoos peeked through her professional attire. Simi felt a connection to her. She had a life before becoming a psychologist—real-life experience and knowledge not obtained through academic studies, but personally lived struggle and hardship. Jane was the type of therapist Simi knew she needed even when she didn't want it.

"Did you self-medicate to sleep last night?" Jane asked, opening her journal. She leaned back into her chair and crossed her legs. Simi stayed silent. "Have you asked them to stop refilling the mini-bar with alcohol?" Simi shook her head no. "Why not?"

"I don't have a drinking problem. Last night was just very hard." Simi shared.

"Yes, the past few Thursday nights have been awful, I'd imagine." Jane countered back.

"That isn't what I meant." Simi wasn't ready to talk about the reality of her Thursday nights yet. "I met someone last night. After." Simi's gaze wandered around the room, looking at the artwork and messages of inspiration as a distraction. "It was normal and nice." She boasted.

"So, before you met him, the same thing?".

Simi shook her head. "Actually, no. It was just dinner. He didn't want anything else."

"This was someone new last night?"

"No, I have only had dinner with this one man. He never wants more than that. He is a recent widow."

"Is that why you continue to meet with him? Are you connecting with him in loss?" Simi shook her head no.

"Defeats the point of what I am doing if I am being true to myself?"

"Oh yes, the famed Persia, was it?" Jane replied shortly. "What about the man from two weeks ago? What has happened to him?" Simi shifted uncomfortably in her chair.

"I don't know if I can do that again. Every encounter tends to get a bit more." Simi frowned. "I think there can be better clients for me than him. I have others who are interested."

"Simi, you are here to heal. You were doing great. You were openly talking about what had happened. You were ready to go back home. You began discussing plans for the future, and then you completely pivoted to something extremely harmful to you. What happened? I would rather be treating you for alcoholism than this." Jane shared. "We need to have these sessions to get you to stop."

"You aren't treating me for either. I am here for grief counseling." Simi corrected.

"Amongst everything else." Jane quickly shot back. "Have you asked yourself why you are doing this?"

"We know why. Today, I don't want to go into it."

"When do you want to discuss how you are hurting yourself? This is a pressing issue that we need to work on, Simi."

"I am not hurting myself. I am finally taking steps to prevent myself from being hurt. I know what I am doing." Simi firmly defended, her hand squeezing the bottle of water. The plastic collapsing under her palm echoed throughout the office.

"How long do you plan on doing this?"

"As long as it takes," Simi answered.

"Takes to do what?" Jane pushed.

Simi swallowed hard; tears brimmed in her eyes. Simi fantasized about screaming it out and just opening her lips and letting out everything tightly held inside. She pictured herself in the meadow behind her house. Standing alone, in the sun amongst the flowers, shouting, screaming, wailing. It was a release she was desperately seeking but too scared to do. She instead chooses to mute the pain.

"Let it out, Simi, cry and let it out." Jane urged. "He—"

"Stop." Simi cut her off.

"He doesn't want—"

Simi cut her off again and stood up. "Jane, I said stop it!" She held her breath for a moment. "Not yet." Simi's heart ached, and her stomach was in knots. She ran her hands through her hair, gently massaging her temples, attempting to find any source of comfort.

Minutes went by as Jane let Simi sit in her silence.

"Did your brother arrive yet?" Simi had almost forgotten that her younger brother was on his way to visit. She was hiding so much from him, so much she wanted to share with him. She knew how much he could handle and, right now, everything she was doing would be too much for him.

"No, in a few days."

"What do you think you will do while he is here?"

"I don't know. Maybe go somewhere? I didn't mean to have him come here. I had a momentary lapse of judgment after my little mishap." Simi waved her injured hand. "I should have him cancel. I know he won't."

"Maybe you can take him home? Maybe with his support, you are ready to go back home?"

"No. I am not ready." Simi admitted. "Can we move on from this?"

"Do you want to leave your session?" Jane asked. Simi shook her head no. "Do you want to talk to me about who you met last night?" Simi thought about Clark, his smile, the muscle she felt beneath his sports coat.

"He was nice." She shared in a whisper. "I agreed to go out with him next week."

"Okay. When do you see him?" Jane asked.

"Next Thursday."

"Simi!" Jane frustratedly closed her book.

"No, it's not like that. It isn't." Simi quickly explained. "It's not from the website. I met him normally. He approached me at the bar after. Actually," Simi mustered a smile, "We have seen each other often at the bar, but he didn't approach me until last night." Jane still donned a severe look of concern. "I even gave him my real name, which is good, right? I tried to stay in Persia's mindset, but," Simi exhaled, "It was jarring, Jane." She looked down at her shoes, trying to find the words. She wanted to tell Jane about the familiar comfort that Clark provided her. The similar humor and cadence when he spoke.

"Simi, what was jarring?"

"Nothing."

Jane was frustrated with Simi. "Okay, how have your dreams been? Anything you want to share about them?"

"They come and go. They haven't been as bad since we started talking through them."

"Good. I am glad to hear that much." Jane leaned back into her chair. She crossed her leg over her knee and rotated her red patent bootie in a circular motion. "Simi, we have to talk about these Persia dinner dates. I can't tell you what to do, but I am strongly suggesting that you stop them." Simi looked off to the side, focusing on the steam emitting from the air purifier. "After your wine glass accident, I was confident you would reevaluate and realize what you're doing isn't healthy or good for you. You shared with me how you felt after that incident. You held a glass in your hand so tightly that it had to be pried out. You have stitches."

"I wouldn't call these stitches." Simi defended.

"Then you still met with someone else last night? Okay, it didn't end up with sex, but what if it did? Were you going to participate in that again? Is this who you want to be now?"

"It is who I have to be." Simi sighed.

"Look at your hand; your body had a response to what you are doing to yourself." Jane pressed. "Simi, you are not well. You went from depression to a delusional state." Jane frowned.

"I am not delusional. I am just . . ."Simi searched for words. "I just am trying to heal the best way I can."

"This is the wrong way, Simi." Simi clenched her teeth; being called delusional hurt. She had control; she was in control.

"I don't know what else to do, Jane. It hurts so bad. I wake up, and my body hurts. My heart hurts. I sit up from the bed, and it just hurts, Jane. It's a chronic, heavy, painful feeling that weighs on me daily. On Thursday, I put on a little makeup and a new persona. I can escape the pain of my reality for a few hours. I am not hurting anyone."

"Except yourself," Jane noted.

"There is nothing left of me anyway." Simi barely finished her sentence. "He took me with him, yet, I am still here."

"He didn't take you with him, Simi, and you are very much here." Jane flipped back the pages in her journal. "You have goals, wants, ambitions. You can still do everything you want to do." Jane stopped on a page. "Shaadi's? Am I staying it right?" Jane asked. Simi swallowed hard. She gripped the top of the chair she stood behind. "He might not be here to see your dreams come to fruition, but he wanted you to succeed in them. The best thing we can do for those we lost is honor them. Like how you were going to do with Shaadi."

Hearing her mother's name repeated took the limited breath out of Simi's lungs. She felt light-headed; circling the chair, she sat back down, leaning forward, resting her elbows on her knees.

"How about this? What if while your brother is here, take a trip. It doesn't have to be home, but go somewhere you feel happy. Why don't you try just to be Simi for a little bit? Can you pause from these date nights? If you feel like you truly miss them, we can talk about how you can safely continue on this new journey." Simi squirmed in her seat, debating Jane's request in her head. "This only works if you want the help."

"I am here, aren't I? I am trying to talk with you." Simi defended. "I come; I don't miss any appointments. What do you want from me!"

"Progress," Jane stated.

Simi stayed quiet, holding Jane's gaze. She counted her breaths, managing her temper, her rage and pain escaping her lips.

"I don't think this is going to work between us anymore. I am not feeling the support I need from you." Simi slowly responded, attempting to inflict pain on Jane.

"I am sorry to hear that you feel this way. Perhaps, you should find another therapist who will indulge your delusional state."

"I am not delusional."

"Okay."

"I am not delusional," Simi repeated slower this time. She quickly stood up from her seat. "You sit there knowing. You have sat there for months, knowing the pain inside me! You know this is helping me. You won't admit it! You are judging it instead of seeing the promise of it!" Simi's voice cracked slightly at the end of her impassioned speech.

Jane remained motionless, raising her eyebrows toward Simi, silently challenging her to stay. To open up and talk about the pain instead of masking it. Simi didn't take the bait.

"Well, I guess there is nothing left to say then," Simi whispered raspy, holding her emotions in the middle of her throat.

Before reaching the door, Jane finally said, "Be safe, Simi."

The plea in Jane's voice imprinted into Simi's consciousness, leaving an additional level of disappointment within herself. She slammed the door shut in one last act of defiance against Jane.

***

It was three days before Simi decided she wanted to leave her bed. As if she wasn't lonely enough, she had walked out on the only person she had in this city. Rolling over on her side, she looked out the window, the sunshine peering through. She was wounded. The fatal blow of her reality wasn't getting easier to face. To walk out of Jane's was a stupid and impulsive decision. Simi wasn't ready to admit that to herself yet. The sun reflected on her watch resting on the nightstand. She danced her fingers lightly over it. Deeply inhaling, she rolled on her back, squeezing her eyes shut. She began reciting her poem, suppressing the urge to release the sob bubbling in her throat. Time was not making this easier. The sessions and advice were not making her reality livable, just more complicated.

There was a faint knock at the door. Simi pulled the covers over her head. She hadn't moved the do not disturb sign in weeks, but today wouldn't be the first time they cleaned around her. She heard the click of the door open in the living room and snuggled deeper into her pillow, hoping they would clean everything but the bedroom this time.

"Abji joon." Her brother's voice permeated the air. She winced at the nickname before she opened her eyes and scrambled out of bed to the bedroom door. He stood in front of the dining table, picking up Simi's practice sheets. Her language books were in disarray around the table with a tray of untouched room service.

"Daroush!" Simi quickly wiped at her face. "What are you doing here?" She ran to him, holding him tightly. The chill of his clothes was cold against her skin. She had never been happier holding her baby brother.

"Simi, you stink." Daroush chuckled, gently pulling back from his sister. "What is all this? What language is this? Are you not eating?"

"It's practice sheets, and I am eating." Daroush sat his bag down on the chair. "I told them to give you your room."

"They did. Your phone was off. It's been off since before I left Paris." Daroush reached for his sister. "Simi, you scared the hell out of me. I didn't know what I was opening the door to today." Simi looked deep into his green eyes. She clenched her jaw, refusing to let him see her cry.

"I didn't mean to scare you. I lost track of time." Simi admitted. Daroush looked lovingly at his sister. Though relieved to see her alive, he was very concerned about what he saw.

Daroush was younger than her by five years. Handsome as he was, he was still a boy in her eyes. Same height as Simi, with a thick mop of jet-black hair. He stayed clean-shaven. He hated facial hair, though Simi always encouraged him to grow it out. He had hit the genetic lottery by getting green eyes. Simi was always jealous of his looks.

Daroush lifted the paper toward her. "Are you learning a new language?" Simi took the paper from Daroush and put it on the table.

"I had started Japanese lessons before I left my job. Then, you know, he wanted to pick it up last year. It was something to focus on and do." Simi nervously collected the books around her, compiling them neatly on the coffee table. Daroush nodded, understanding that if she had been studying a language for the past six months, she was fluent by now. She had always been able to grasp languages easier than him, despite being trilingual.

"No more art gallery? You are going to be a linguist?" Daroush looked at her and felt crushed. The sadness swept through her eyes. "How about you go take a shower and clean up? They put me across the hall. Come into my room when you are done. We can grab something to eat? You need to eat Simi." He put his hands around her waist. "Let's go to that place. What is it called? The burger spot you love?"

"In and Out." Simi chuckled.

"Yeah, let's go there."

"They don't have any here."

Daroush teasingly gasped. "Simurgh lives where there is no In and Out? This explains so much!"

"Cute, Daroush. Go to your room. I will be there shortly." Simi rolled her eyes at her brother's antics. "Thank you for coming." She kissed Daroush on the cheek and walked back into the bedroom.

Daroush looked around the room. Despite her language books and practice sheets, it was as he assumed it would be, tidy with no outward signs of distress. He walked toward a long low cabinet where he found the minibar. It was fully stocked. Listening to the shower begin, he quietly peeked above the garbage cans. He looked around curiously before pulling the bottom drawer of the dresser in the bedroom. His stomach dropped, finding all the empty minibar bottles hidden. He exhaled heavily and closed the drawer. He had waited too long to come back and check on her. If he had waited longer, he was sure his worst nightmare would have come true. His sister was unwell, and he had a responsibility to her.

"She is okay." Daroush closed the door behind him, speaking to Patrick, who had been outside in the hall waiting for him.

When Simi hadn't answered her phone, Daroush was terrified of what he would find. When he was last in Chicago, they went to Prime every night. It was where she wanted to be. Knowing his sister, he proactively connected with Patrick, who checked on her often. He needed some sort of assurance that she was safe.

"I gotta tell you, when you walked in, my heart stopped until I heard the conversation." Patrick admitted. "She needs to get out of here. This isn't healthy."

Daroush nodded, looking over to Patrick, pressing his palms over his exhausted blue eyes. Daroush noted that Patrick looked more stressed than he remembered when he was last in Chicago. He wasn't entirely sure if it was caused by Simi. Patrick exhaled, shaking himself awake, uncomfortably scratching at his jaw, the stubble of the day not yet shaved off before work.

"That's the goal. When was she at your place last?" Daroush asked as he fumbled with the hotel keycard in his hand.

"She is in about every Thursday. I wasn't there last Thursday, but I have a good bartender who watches out for her when I am not there."

"Is she talking to people?"

"She would come in pretty sad looking. Then recently, she has been dressing up, yeah, talking to people a lot more." Patrick gently described. "I think she comes back for some kind of connection. It does get busy, but we always make sure she gets home."

"I appreciate everything you have been doing for her. I do. I am forever in your debt." Daroush shook his hand.

"It's a non-issue. Debt will be cleared when I come to Paris," Patrick joked. "I am sure I will see you guys this week." Patrick began heading down to the elevators.

"I wouldn't be surprised." Remarked Daroush as Patrick left.

Daroush walked toward the door across the hall from his sister's room. He waved the hotel key across the lock and walked in. His heartbeat was still racing. He had to calm down. The adrenaline was still raw, rushing through him. He opened the minibar and grabbed water, quickly gulping the bottle down. He squeezed the bottle in his hand, providing some sense of relief from his frustration. He wanted to yell. She looked pale and empty inside. Her natural radiance was nowhere to be seen. She looked like a shell of who she was to him. He was going to get her out of this hotel.

Daroush was sitting on his bed when Simi knocked on the door. He opened it, happy to see a refreshed and recognizable sister looking back at him.

"Come in, come in." Daroush guided his sister. "You smell so much better, Abji." Simi laughed.

"I am sorry about how you arrived. I would never want you to see me like that. It just has been a hard few days." Simi urged on. "You are here now. Everything is better."

"Everything is hardly better." Daroush reached for her hand. "What happened?" Though Patrick didn't share much about Simi's activities, they had spoken after her broken wine glass episode at the bar.

"It was an accident." Daroush held his breath, waiting to see if his sister would lie to him. "I was at the bar, and something just took over me. I just wanted to smash it." Simi's eyes were low as she spoke. She paced around his room. "I didn't intend for it to happen in real life. I thought I imagined it, but suddenly, Patrick and Bradley are wrapping a towel around me." Simi explained. "You remember them?" Daroush nodded, relieved to see his sister still honest with him.

"I am very worried about you. Maman is too. We want you to come back to Paris." Daroush shared. Simi became visibly uncomfortable at the suggestion.

"Do you think, just maybe for a little bit, you and I can be in this bubble where we don't talk about anything other than simple, pleasant things?"

"What does that mean?"

"Just for a bit, can we just not talk about all the things we need to talk about and hang out?" Simi was sincere in her ask.

"Of course. Abji, yes. Whatever you want to do."

"Are you tired? Do you want to sleep?"

"I am, but let's at least share a meal before I adjust to the time zone." Daroush paused. "But outside, and not at Prime. Let's see the sunshine. I think I saw some sidewalk seating." Simi chuckled.

"Okay, sure." Simi walked over and tussled her fingers through her brother's hair. "I will be back in a few minutes. Are you comfortable here? Do you have everything you need?"

"I am fine, Abji. Hungry and tired. Hurry, please." Simi nodded and left Daroush alone in his room.

Daroush knew what had to be done. He was not going to leave her here again. No matter how hard she fought him, he would ensure she left this city and went home. If she refused, he would be forced to do the unthinkable and bring Maman to Chicago and drag her back to Paris against her will.

Chapter 5

Clark stared out the window of the empty office space. He listened to the agent list the details to Adam and himself but could not keep focus. Simi had preoccupied his mind the entire week. His anticipation for their dinner had been surprising even for him. Just in their small interaction, she had captured his interest quite effortlessly. He slid his hand against the white wall of the conference room and looked over at Adam with a hard-pass gesture. This wasn't the space. Adam nodded, taking the cue. He was ready to leave.

Clark held the door for a young woman exchanging a smile as they began walking on the street.

"Man, the world is your oyster." Adam kept his eye on the woman as she walked out of site.

"Dating is exhausting."

"Marriage is exhausting." Adam corrected. Clark glanced over to his friend.

"Something happened?" He asked. Adam reached into his pocket to pull out his phone and opened his text messages.

"No, just it's hard sometimes." Clark didn't press more. Adam was the type to share when he was ready. "Evan's office is around here. I said we could meet for drinks after or like maybe a coffee?" Clark frowned at Adam.

"Thanks, but no thanks," Clark answered. "I didn't know you guys were hanging out again." After what had happened before Adam's wedding, he had hoped they both would never see Evan again.

"I am in control if that is what you are suggesting," Adam quickly snapped. "We bumped into each other at a Cubs game. Reconnected . . .it's not a big thing."

"This is why I don't go to Cubs games. No one goes to Sox games." They stopped at a red light in Daley Plaza. Still unseasonably cool for the day, the plaza was full of small vendors as kids shrieked with delight sliding down the Picasso statue.

"You're still sour about the charity thing."

Clark shot over a glance. "Seriously, Adam?" Adam knew better, but he wasn't in the mood to bring up the real reason they didn't see eye to eye. "Anyway, thanks for the invite, but I am having dinner with the woman from Prime tonight." Adam gave a hearty chuckle as they passed through the crowd bustling in the plaza.

"Oh, you are serious?" Adam clicked his tongue. "Have fun with all that." Adam felt Clark's hesitation and attempted to soothe the tension regarding Evan. "It's just a catch-up. It's Thursday. How crazy can tonight get?" Adam patted Clark on the shoulder and headed to his meeting spot.

As Clark began walking back home, a feeling of unease rushed through him. He had become protective of Adam as the years progressed in his friendship. Nothing good ever came from Evan, and Clark was convinced the trend would only continue.

Clark reflected on how tight-lipped Adam had recently been about his investor meetings ensuring Clark's money would be raised. Clark knew how hard funding was in general. Funding for this project was probably near impossible, but if Adam said he could do it, he would. Finding capital was never Clark's forte. Adam could get through any door with his personality and network.

That wasn't Clark. When they started, he had no connections, and his personality was too harsh for most people. He had difficulty pretending to care about frivolous things and a short fuse when hearing incorrect information. Clark had been told most of his life that he lacked compassion and empathy, but it was how he had to be. Emotion was too complex for him to process and understand. He enjoyed logic, and if there was a problem, there was a solution. If there were a problem and emotion mixed with it—it was a waste of everyone's time. Logic then didn't exist, and there was no winning. Ever.

This made for a more private life for him. Growing up in Chicago, he exposed himself to as much as he could absorb. He was lucky to live in a diverse city but quickly learned that the landscape would be more difficult to navigate than Adam would experience. Living through it and learning how to survive it emboldened his hope for what Cottage Growth could accomplish for his community and his entire city. He wanted to see diversity where there hadn't been, open doors and change the landscape of opportunities.

Clark arrived at Prime a few minutes before their scheduled time. He stepped off to the side of the lobby in the hotel, pulled out his small notebook, and began writing a note to himself.

"Is that Japanese?" Her voice came from beside him. "Do you know the language?" Her eyes were bright as she glided her hand over his arm, looking down at his notebook. He flipped the book over.

"It's a Hobonichi Techno journal. It's a perfect size and has grids on the page. I love these, but no, I don't know Japanese." Clark brushed his thumb across the Japanese characters on the bottom of the page.

"Interesting." Her eyes softened, losing a bit of her excitement. "I didn't mean to interrupt." She began to pull back her hand, but he quickly placed his over hers.

"I was just finished." He brought her hand up to his lips, softly kissing her knuckles. "So nice to see you." She smiled shyly. "I was thinking, I eat here often, and it seems so do you. What if we went someplace else?" Clark offered. He wanted to ensure that Simi knew he was only interested in dinner tonight.

Simi looked toward the restaurant for a moment, then down at her shoes. She had been excited to wear a pair of taller heels but was still adjusting to walking in them. "How far is it?"

"Not too far. Happy to grab a cab, though."

Simi shook her head. "No need for a cab. I can make it. Let's try something else out," Simi agreed.

There was a warm breeze flowing throughout the city as the evening cooled down. Streets were still active, with the impending hope of the cold weather being over. Side by side, Simi held on to Clark's arm as they walked across the bridge over the Chicago River.

Clark appreciated that she accepted the silence between them.

Too often, he found women unable to understand a quiet moment. Their constant need to talk always felt like insecurity to him. As if a moment of pause would cause them to reveal who they were. He had yet to find someone as comfortable in silence as he was. Simi walked alongside him in her thoughts as she viewed the city with her eyes, smiling slightly when she caught his gaze. This was different. She got it.

"I hope you like Cuban food." Clark pulled the door open to a small restaurant. Simi entered with Clark following her from behind. The restaurant was 1940s art-deco-themed and romantically dark.

The bar was packed, but the noise died down further into the dining area as Simi and Clark were seated in a far back booth. Simi removed her jacket, revealing another long-sleeved black dress that hugged her proportionately well. Her hair was cascaded over one side, and a large gold necklace hung from her neck. Clark tried not to stare, attempting to figure out the emblem hanging from the chain as she was handed the menu. Simi's watch caught Clark's attention.

"Okay, you will have to explain that watch to me." Simi looked down at her wrist. She smiled but didn't say anything. "Well?"

"Mmm?" Simi looked from her menu curiously at Clark.

"The watch? It's beautiful and looks vintage, but it's evident that you are wearing a man's watch. Was it your fathers?" Simi seemed startled by the question. "Grandfathers?" Clark asked again, fighting the playful urge to ask if it was stolen.

"I uh, you know." Simi searched for something. "I found it at a street shop somewhere. I just liked it," she lied.

"May I see?" Clark asked. Simi hesitated only for a moment before unlocking it. Clark took the piece into his hand. "Wow, heavy. Simi, this is"—Clark looked closely at the watch—"this is a Patek Philippe."

"Yeah, so it says." Simi went back to looking through the menu.

"This is a nice watch. Where did you say you found this?" Clark reached for his phone. Simi took the watch from his hand and slid it back on her wrist. He was sure she was casually wearing a watch that cost as much as his condo down payment.

"So long ago, you know, I don't remember." Clark wasn't buying this act. She knew exactly what she was wearing. "What do you recommend here?" She asked, hoping to avoid him searching on his phone. Clark looked up, noticing her discomfort, and set the phone down.

He offered his recommendations, gauging what dishes seemed to evoke a response from her. She nodded as he continued to offer suggestions, wondering if he should have opted for a burger spot. Simi smiled and closed the menu. She invited him to order for her so she could sample his favorites together.

Clark had never been asked to order for someone else. Is this something she would do regularly? Or was this a test for him? Taking her request, he chose his two favorite entrees with two small plates, finishing off with a pitcher of Mojitos, to which Simi requested a glass of red sangria.

"I don't know what you have planned for tonight, but I like it," Clark quipped. Simi laughed, feeling slightly embarrassed. "There you are. I wasn't sure if I left you at the other restaurant," commentating on her quiet demeanor.

"I am sorry. I guess I'm nervous. I haven't done this in a while."

"Done what?" Clark wanted confirmation.

"Oof, a date?" She frowned at her word choice. "Or hanging out with someone new?" Simi admitted. The drinks arrived at the table, and Clark took the lead in pouring two glasses of Mojitos while Simi tasted her sangria. He pressed a bit more.

"You seem to converse fairly well." Simi knew what he was implying. He had been watching while she had her dinners.

She hadn't intentionally meant to be quiet. Since Daroush had been with her, she felt more and more like herself. The ask of Jane to just be Simi was happening intentionally whether she wanted to or not. She had not been ready to tell Daroush about tonight, so she kept him active all day, taking him around the city to ensure he would want an early night in. True to her baby brother's habits, he did, and was asleep with enough time for Simi to get dressed and meet Clark.

"I started listening to Hans Zimmer." Clark broke her thoughts.

"Yeah?" Simi smiled. "Did you not know who he was?"

"No, I didn't. No idea what to expect." Clark relaxed as Simi re-engaged with him.

"What did you think?"

"Well, first, I had to adjust that you listen to the first three minutes at max volume, then need to turn it down immediately." Simi laughed in agreement. "I didn't realize he was behind so many soundtracks."

"Yeah, he is like that. How special that is." Simi complimented.

"What is special?"

"To hear his music for the first time. I can never do that again. I am a bit jealous."

"He will put out new music," Clark assured her.

"Right, but like I know him. I have a general idea of what it will sound like. You heard it for the first time." Clark hadn't appreciated what she was saying until she explained it further. "Think about that moment. You had no idea what to expect, and then it starts quiet, builds and builds, then there is a swell of emotion and excitement flowing through your ears. You are listening and processing what is playing and what is going to happen next until it's over. The journey of the song is completed, and you just have to sit back and digest it."

"Wow," was all Clark was able to say. The passion in which she invoked her explanation stopped him in his tracks.

"Sorry." Simi realized she had become overexcited and shyly apologized, reaching for the comfort of her sangria.

"No, don't be; that was beautiful. Are you a musician?"

"No, art is more my thing." Simi placed her glass down, grateful for the small plates arriving.

Silence again fell between them as they both indulged in their first bites. Simi felt Clark's eyes on her, knowing he was trying to keep the conversation pace steady. She wasn't being helpful with her quick-to-end sentences.

"So, how long have you visiting Chicago?"

His goal tonight was to get to know her, with no ulterior motive. He felt he scored a few points with the earlier conversation and wanted to keep the momentum.

"Just before Thanksgiving. It was supposed to be a short trip, but

I ended up staying.”

“This city is easy to fall in love with.”

“This city broke my heart,” Simi slipped out and quickly re-buffed. “I have been told if you stick it out in the trenches, you can find daybreak again.”

“I like that,” Clark commented. “So, you are here to find daylight?”

Simi pursed her lips. “It’s silly. Just trying some new stuff out, I guess. Seeing what sticks.” She rattled off. Simi found herself nervous, trying to extract the sexy allure of Persia for Clark, but she delivered an inauthentic version of herself. “So, have you been to Cuba?” Her transition was rushed. “You know traveling is the best.” She attempted to move the conversation off of herself.

Clark took the cue and found himself taking over the conversation, sharing his experiences abroad and people he had met. She had been as masterful as he was, able to ask the right questions to keep him talking most of the night. As the food arrived, he continued to share stories from his time in Cuba. He loved the ability to go to a country and truly be disconnected from the world. It was like walking into a time warp. He held a special place in his heart for Cuba and the Cuban culture.

While Simi had never been, she was fascinated by how Clark spoke of his time there. For most of the night, he could transcend the conversation to make her feel in the moment with him. She found herself awakening to his comfort and masculine qualities. He didn’t share the same anecdotal hyperbole men usually had stashed for nights out. The content he delivered to her required thought and care, and she genuinely felt an attraction to his uniqueness.

The server came and set down the bill between them. Simi went to reach into her purse.

“Now, I know you aren’t going to argue with me about the check.” Simi smiled, pulling out a lip balm. Clark laughed. “Nice save. I wasn’t sure if you would play some ‘tab’ line on me again.”

“I guess you will never know.” Simi glided the balm over her lips as he tried to figure out simple math for the bill. She kept smiling as she continued to play with her pout salaciously. The conversation, the meal, and the drinks had Simi feeling enticed.

"I am pretty sure I paid for the meal twice." He folded the bill and pushed it to the side of the table.

"So easily distracted." She was tipsy, possibly even a little drunk. She reached across the table and placed her hands over his. She entangled her fingers within his and rubbed the inside of his palms with her thumb. "I had a really nice time tonight. I needed this." Clark held his breath as the sensation of her hands and the effects of the mojitos began to settle in. He watched as her eyes were still drawn down to their hands as an intimate moment was exchanged between them. As the server returned, Simi drew her hands back to herself, causing a cool breeze to rob him of his comfort.

Clark was the first to move from the booth. He reached for her coat and held it for her to slip her arms through.

She accepted the gesture as he guided her out of the restaurant. Stepping out into the cool evening air, she tightened her coat around her. Clark walked to the street edge and motioned for a cab. Simi came up from behind. "If you don't mind the walk back, I could use some fresh air. It's not often I can enjoy the city late at night."

"I don't want you to get too cold." Clark began removing his coat to place it over hers. She put her hand on his shoulder to stop him.

"I won't get cold. My coat is not only fashion, but also quite warm." She reached for his arm, and he began to lead her back to her hotel.

"Fashion?"

"Yes, Fashion." Clark chuckled at her stance. "Well, it is a very *fashionable* coat." He purposely corrected. As they stepped over the bridge, Clark stopped at a staircase entrance. "Have you walked along the river walk yet? There is another staircase that leads back up to your hotel along the way." Simi peered down the dark walkway. She cautiously looked back up at Clark. Her hesitation lingered for just a moment longer. "You can say no." Simi arched her eyebrow.

"Why do you think I want to say no?" She questioned.

"It's dark. No one is down there. I can see how you would want to say no." Clark offered, leaning against the bridge wall centered on the stairway entrance.

"Wouldn't that want me to say yes?" Simi challenged; Clark was momentarily taken aback by the question.

"You are dangerous. Perhaps next time. Earlier in the day." Clark pivoted away from the entrance as Simi lingered for a moment.

"Are you scared of me?" Clark turned back slightly, flashing a smile that sent chills down Simi.

"Absolutely." He reached his hand out, inviting her to continue the walk. Simi couldn't hide her smile after Clark's admission. She stopped on the bridge and frowned. She pulled back his hand and turned him to face her.

Simi questioned, "Why are you single?" Her eyes narrowed as she pointed at him. "Unless, of course, you're not, then that's really rotten of you."

"Rotten? That's the best word to describe infidelity you could come up with?"

Simi shrugged, still waiting for him to answer. "Well?"

"Is 'I haven't found the right one' too cliché?"

"Yes."

"Hm. Well, then, I would have to say it's me. I might have too high of expectations. I probably want too much from someone, and well, until I have found someone who satisfies or challenges that notion, I will be single." Clark brought her hand back to rest on his arm as they resumed their walk to her hotel.

Simi took a moment before she asked, "Don't you get lonely?"

"Sure, but that's not an excuse to waste someone's time."

"What if you miss an opportunity?"

Clark chuckled. "I am not celibate, Simi. I go out, I try, I am open. Look, I am out right now with you, aren't I?"

"Me?" Simi questioned. "I don't count. I am sure I don't meet your expectations."

"You don't know what my expectations are."

"No, but I am sure I don't meet them."

"A second date could confirm or deny that," Clark proposed. He looked over to Simi, her gaze off to the distance. "Well, I had a really nice time tonight," he emphasized.

Simi chuckled at his intonation, "I did too."

"Top 10 dates?"

"Definitely. Top 15," Simi laughed.

"Ooo, that hurt." Clark grabbed at his chest. "This is why I don't get a second date?"

"I mean, it doesn't help." Simi pushed against his side.

"How can I redeem a top ten ranking before you go inside?" Clark pulled her to face him. They stood outside of her hotel.

"Before I go inside? Not even going to try?" Simi asked. He was selling himself as the chivalrous type.

"To invite myself up? I am still not convinced there isn't foreign security watching me right now."

"You are funny." Simi smiled. The night was quiet enough that she could hear the lake's waves behind them. "What if I invite you up?"

"I would have to decline. I am old fashioned like that." Slowly, he bent down, watching her eyes close as he pressed his lips against her forehead. He held it there just for a moment, inhaling the scent impressing a memory within him. He pulled back to see a smile spread across her face. She fluttered her lashes to meet his gaze.

"Okay, you just made it to the top 10." She stepped slightly back, stunned, still processing his sincerity before her. Her heart swelled with delight, with desire.

"Next week, then?" Clark offered. He had seen the success of his move. A kiss on the lips would've been too forward. He wanted to entice her as much as she had done to him. He watched Simi's gaze drift over to the doorman.

"Clark, I enjoyed tonight. I just don't think—"

"Why not?" Clark interrupted. "Give it to me straight. Why is next week such a bad idea?"

"It's complicated," Simi honestly answered. "What if—"

"Then let it happen," Clark interrupted again. "At least we can have some fun and companionship on the way there."

Simi looked away from Clark toward the lake. She struggled with her decision. She wanted to see him again; she wanted him to embrace her again. Guilt heavily hit her as she realized how much she enjoyed her evening with him. The kiss was still warm on her skin. She thought of Jane's comment. Delusional.

Simi wasn't delusional; she could enjoy her time with Clark at a safe distance.

"Thank you for dinner, I really had a nice time." Simi continued, "I will see you next week; meet you at Prime?" Simi smiled as Clark nodded, his eyes giving away his excitement at securing a second date. She pressed her lips together and waved a small goodbye as she walked into her hotel.

Clark watched her go, waiting; a look back would guarantee a successful night. She greeted the doorman and continued on her way. No glance, no look back. Just like that. Any power he had wielded by the end of the night, Simi had retaken right out of his grasp. He was once again left with nothing but more questions and a more profound desire to resuscitate happiness in her.

Chapter 6

The following morning Clark was resting across his sofa, unable to sleep. He stayed in his living room, glaring at a six-thousand-piece puzzle he had begun after finishing his white-to-black gradient, which now leaned against the living room wall after securing a sticker backing. He kept studying the box. *Evening Prelude* was a picture of a Market Square outside Paris. He hadn't been able to get past the border since he started late last night. This woman had entranced his mind for weeks, and although he had felt last night was mostly successful, Clark was still in the dark.

He replayed each gaze he received, each smile. The way she would slide her thumb under her fingers as she listened. Her hands, her hands were so soft against him, he barely felt the bandage hiding her injury. His kiss on her forehead required him to hold so much restraint within himself. He began to worry that he had created this fantasy version of Simi that wasn't real.

Suddenly, his front door swung open; he wasn't surprised to see Adam walk into the room. He stopped, not expecting to see Clark fully dressed from a night out.

"Oh, is she here? I can come back!" He whispered, adjusting the grey beanie on his head.

"No one is here." Clark sat up. "Just couldn't sleep last night."

"Did you go out?"

"I did."

Adam smirked. "Was I right?" Clark looked up. "How much did she cost?" Adam joked, resting a black leather duffel next to his puzzle on the table. "Started a new one? Must not have gone all that well."

"I don't believe you are in my place this early because you care about last night." Clark pushed himself up from the sofa, walking toward the kitchen. "You look awful. That only means you had too much fun with Evan yesterday."

"I gotta tell you, he is always a good time." Adam defended. "You should give him another chance. He wants in all the time."

"I am sure he does." Clark couldn't think of a worse human to get involved in business with. "Where are you going?" Clark asked, referencing the duffel.

"We! Amanda is doing girl's weekend, so I thought we should jump on the next shuttle to Vegas today!" Clark turned on his tea kettle and reached into the cabinet for a package of coffee beans.

"Amanda is doing a girls' weekend?" Clark looked over at Adam curiously.

"Well, she's going to see her mom and sister; she left last night." Adam took a seat on a barstool in front of Clark's counter. Adam avoided Clark's gaze, knowing what he was thinking. "We are fine. She is fine."

"Then why Vegas?" Clark asked. "I thought we were done with Vegas for a little while longer?"

"Yeah, no, like I get why you think that, Clark, but . . ." Adam fumbled over his words, trying to avoid the conversation that was bound to happen.

"Listen, honestly, Adam, I am not in the mood for Vegas," Clark admitted; he also was worried about Adam being back in that environment.

"Which is why we should go! I grabbed two seats; we are set at the Palazzo, too, because it's your favorite."

"No, it's not." Clark quipped.

"Well, it's Amanda's favorite, and come on! Kelsey made all the arrangements; we have a lull," Adam exhaled. "Listen, man, I need this."

It was rare for Adam to make any type of confession like that. It stopped Clark for a moment. He looked at Adam. He seemed paler than usual and a bit sweaty on his brow.

Before Adam was married, Vegas was his escape. There were no rules for him here. Amanda closed her eyes to whatever he indulged in while in Vegas. Her only rule was not to bring anything back home, or in nine months. Clark wasn't sure what had sparked Adam to need this weekend. If Clark agreed to go with Adam to Vegas, he would enable an already delicate situation. If he didn't go with Adam to Vegas, there could be a worse outcome.

"Okay, I'll pack up. Just two days, right?"

Adam cheered with excitement. "Like 48/72 hours." Adam paused. "I promise."

"Fine. Turn the water off when it whistles. I will grab my stuff."

"No way! You gotta tell me what happened last night." He followed Clark into his bedroom, sitting on the bed as Clark went into his closet.

"Your shoes better be off!" Clark commented.

"They are," Adam quickly kicked them off, leaning against the headboard. "Now tell me, what is it like to go on a date with an escort?" Clark peeked out of his closet to glare at Adam.

"First of all, you would know better than I."

"Oh no, my friend. I never dated. I paid and left." Adam grabbed one of the many Economists stacked next to Clark's bed. "Did you even get the benefits of her profession?" he asked.

Clark brought out his bag and began to fill it with his selected garment items. He usually packed light for Vegas as if he needed something, it was always easy to buy.

"If you keep referring to her like this, I will not talk to you about it. Until I know for a fact that that is what she is doing, I am not assuming. I won't let you either." Clark was about to speak again but paused.

"Maybe she is a sugar baby, then? I think you would do well with one of those." Adam asked.

"A sugar baby?"

"Yeah, they are there when you want them. Don't expect more than you want. It's very transactional unless you want it to be more."

"You know too much about this." Clark walked into his bathroom to grab his toiletry bag. Clark hadn't mentioned to his friend that he had been casually returning to Prime. He knew better than to share what he had witnessed. Adam would bravely call out all the red flags, and until Clark could figure out her situation fully, he would leave most details close to his chest.

"So, what is her story?" Adam asked.

"I don't know," Clark admitted. "Few interesting things though, she has a tab at Prime, she just casually wears a vintage Patek watch, and . . ."

"And what? Outside of the Patek, which I want to come back to." Adam boosted himself on the counter of the bathroom. He was picking through the assorted colognes Clark had on display.

"She lives at a hotel—I think she has family money." Clark finished filling his toiletry bag and went back to the bedroom with Adam behind him.

"She is Persian, but she doesn't have an accent. Sometimes I hear a twinge of something, but it's more of a French accent, but I don't know. I am still going with an heiress trapped in a bad situation." Clark admitted.

"An heiress? Did you visit your Aunt recently? She always has that Hallmark channel on." Clark couldn't help but laugh. He knew how juvenile it sounded. "Have you asked Patrick about her?"

Clark nodded. "Yeah, that first night. He knows her. Just didn't share much." Clark began zipping up his bag.

"You always liked a challenge." Adam walked into his closet. "I would get a lock for your watch drawer, though." Adam looked around, pulling the sleeves of Clark's hung clothes. "Are you seeing her again?"

"Yeah, next week."

"Well, it all sounds sketchy. Though she was beautiful, so I am not surprised by this with you." Adam shared.

"What does that mean?"

"Simplicity does nothing for you. Of course, you are going to be a dog with a bone over a beautiful, mysterious woman who may or may not be supporting her lifestyle as a lady of the night, or what did you say? Heiress?"

"Arranged marriages are a thing. Maybe she is here escaping some patriarchal situation."

"Uh-huh." Adam wanted to laugh at his friend grasping at

straws. "Whatever her story is, you will get it out of your system eventually. For now, we are going to go to Vegas and do it up as we used to. Now come on, we can talk more in the car. We're going to be late." Adam hurried Clark out of his bedroom.

Clark went into the kitchen, turning off the tea kettle that had been whistling for the past five minutes. He made one last sweep of his apartment before heading out the door with Adam behind him.

They arrived at the private terminal of Midway airport. They made their way up the runway, where a small plane was being loaded. Adam had convinced Clark to buy into a private jet share program. Bougie as it seemed, it ended up being a good idea as they had met other like-minded individuals and made great connections.

As they walked up to the plane, a black SUV pulled beside them. A young, well-dressed man hopped out and held out his hand. Clark did a double-take as he saw Simi come out of the car.

"Isn't that?" Adam asked. Clark stopped. Simi adorned black strappy stilettos and wore another figure-hugging dress. She caught his gaze and froze for a brief moment. Clark reacted to move toward her when she slightly put her hand up and shook her head.

She quickly returned her focus and accepted her companion's arm as they walked toward the plane, followed by her driver, who brought her designer bags to the plane valet. Her hair was in a full braid, and she wore oversized sunglasses. She pulled in close to her younger companion. Younger than himself. She looked back ever so slightly before making her way up the plane stairs.

Clark's chest was tight. He was thinking of all the worst scenarios. Could he not approach her because she was with this man for the weekend? Was this a forced relationship—an arranged marriage in play? What more proof did he need to see that this woman was involved with other men at all different levels?

"That's her." Clark was barely able to get it out. He turned away as she headed into the cabin. Clark struggled to accept it, remembering her pure moments with him last night, her authentic self. This made no sense.

"Well, this shuttle just got more interesting." Adam grinned at Clark. "Weren't you saying there was more than meets the eye about her?" Adam questioned, "Should have paid her and let her go, man."

Adam cackled with a slap on Clark's back. They were both standing at the bottom of the stairs. "Come on, let's go." Clark hesitated as Adam took the first step. "No, come on," Adam pleaded. "Listen, whatever is going on with her, that's on her. You and I were going to Vegas to have some release and fun. Fuck her, man. You don't want that in your life."

Clark cleared his throat and nodded; he began to follow Adam into the plane's cabin. Although Clark hadn't exactly agreed with Adam's address, it was too late to back out now. As they entered the plane, Simi and her companion were already seated next to each other, with another couple facing them. Adam and Clark took the two solo captain's chairs that faced each other. Before Adam could sit, Clark pulled him back. He wanted to see. Clark had to see. He had to believe what he saw and felt—a connection to this woman who was freely living a life like this. Most importantly, ignoring the fact that they had just shared a wonderful evening last night. Her frames were dark; he couldn't see any fade in her eyes.

The flight attendant began passing along champagne to the passengers. Adam took the flute and quickly downed it. He looked over to Clark.

"What happens in Vegas doesn't count," he defended. Clark had been too absorbed in his own situation to realize that he was attending Adam's relapse this weekend. Clark didn't say anything as Adam had expected him to. Clark went against his gut and waved to the attendant for another glass. He would give Adam this weekend. He took the second glass and passed it to Adam.

"I am not being a good friend by allowing this."

"No, you are being my best." Adam raised his glass and set it down on the table. Clark took a deep breath and quickly finished his flute.

The plane sat 12 guests, but only eight seats were filled. Before long, the aircraft started revving up, and he could distinctly hear her voice. She was not speaking in English, nor what he would've thought her native tongue to sound like. He heard French. He was right, she spoke French—and he knew French. He listened to her whisper to her companion, *"We will be there soon; you are safe."* She kissed his hand, holding her palm over his.

"Adam." He turned to look from the window. "Switchback." He couldn't watch this. Less than 12 hours ago, she walked arm in arm with him. She was smiling and laughing with him. What kind of emotional discipline did she have that she could move on to another man so quickly? Clark shook his head. *No,* he thought. *Women want to be loved and protected.* This was all wrong from who he was with last night. She was breaking the story of who she was for him. She was destroying this beautiful image he had created for her, and he couldn't watch her be that close to another man.

Clark stayed focused, reading pitches brought by Adam, and enjoyed the endless champagne the stewardess was providing. Even when waves of her scent lingered around him, he didn't let his concentration break. He made sure she knew he could play the same game as her.

As the jet landed, Clark had finished up with some good prospects, but most importantly, a pleasant buzz entranced his entire self. As they exited, multiple cars awaited their arrival. Adam excitedly ran down the steps toward his last name on the sign for the Palazzo. Clark noticed the car she got into was also for the Palazzo, as if it were fate. Before he entered the vehicle, Simi caught his gaze and shyly waved. She joined her companion in the car, and the door shut.

"Don't say anything," Clark spoke flatly.

"Listen, man, it's Vegas— she's gotta work too." Adam couldn't help but tease Clark.

***

"So, do you want to tell me who that was on the plane?" Daroush entered Simi's room as the last bellman dropped her bags.

"No." Simi handed the bellman a generous tip as he exited the room. "There was no one on the plane."

"Those men knew you. Who were they?" Daroush pressed.

"I don't know what you are talking about, Daroush; maybe we had shared a flight before."

"Simi, the old hipster gave you the evil eye the entire flight." Daroush chuckled. "Who was he?"

"I promise you, I don't know him." Simi wasn't lying; she didn't know who Clark was with.

"Are you ever going to lose these perks?" Daroush opened the curtains of her bedroom. "I think this is the biggest suite you have put us in." His accent had become purely French, with occasional twinges of his American dialect during his time in the states with her. "It's almost been six months?"

"I didn't bring you here to talk about that. I also wanted you to have fun and give you privacy." Simi began unpacking her bag.

"You keep forgetting that I am with someone. Someone you avoid meeting." Daroush responded.

"How am I avoiding meeting her?"

"Come to Paris."

"Daroush, I don't want to fight with you."

"Simi, I am here for you, but you worry me." Daroush came to her side, forcing her to look at him. "You haven't mentioned Rom—"

"Daroush, please stop." Simi broke away from him. Daroush saw how visibly upset he had made his sister. He came over, holding her hands in his. "I just thought you and I could have some fun here before you returned. I felt bad dragging you stateside, but we always had fun in Vegas." Simi urged, "I missed you. I like to spoil my baby brother." Daroush rested his chin above her head. "I needed to get out of Chicago; you have been saying so yourself. So this is good. This is nice." Simi wiped at her eyes. She refused ever to let Daroush see her cry.

"Abji," Daroush softly soothed her. He pulled back, catching her gaze. "Okay, I will let you spoil me," he teased. "I still want to talk, really talk, before going back." He left the door slightly ajar, exiting her room as he shouted, "this place is huge, Simi!" followed by gleeful laughter.

She smiled to herself. She watched the cars pass by on the strip, looking out the window. Her thoughts lingered on seeing Clark. She felt awful for ignoring him, but she didn't know what else to do. She had put Daroush in such a tizzy already. How was she going to explain this to him? She knew Clark had been upset. She counted the drinks he had consumed on the plane and felt his friend's judgment. She noted how it all probably looked from his perspective. Could they cross paths here? Would he give her a chance to explain next week? Would he show up next week?

Simi walked away from the window. She had left Chicago. She was proud of herself. She got on a plane and went, and she could do it. This was cause for celebration. This was progress. She didn't need Jane. Maybe all she needed was her brother. She would celebrate and possibly consider a trip back to Paris. She might not be ready to see her Maman, but her curiosity was getting the best of her regarding Daroush's girlfriend.

***

When Clark returned to his room, he sat on his bed and fell back into the pillows; despite his best efforts, he couldn't get her out of his mind. Sitting in the steam room only left him thinking of her more. He was admittedly fixated on this woman. This was his tick. He knew it, Adam knew it, and even Patrick called him out on it. The emotions evoked when he thought of Simi confused Clark. He had never experienced these feelings of jealousy or betrayal. Here he was, standing in them. He didn't like it. It didn't make sense to feel this way so quickly toward her. He had to stop. He was in Vegas; the world was his oyster, and he had frustrations to release. Tonight, he would succumb to Vegas.

He pulled his usual outfit—jeans, a black shirt, and a jacket—out of the closet and laid it on the bed. Going into his bathroom, he splashed cold water on his face, letting the droplets fall onto his bare chest. He flexed at his reflection. He was mentally preparing himself for the possibilities of tonight.

As Clark entered Tao to meet up with Adam, he was not surprised to find him at a table with three other women. Adam was on a bender, but at least this time, he was with him and not Evan. Clark wouldn't let things get too far with Adam.

"Clark, come join!" Adam was not drunk, but he was getting there. "Ladies, this is my brother!" Adam grandiosely announced. "Now, please, make room, make room!" The girls wiggled out of the booth, giggling in the process. At least Adam had found a diverse group this time. "Clark!" Adam heavily patted his chest. "They are here for a girl's weekend." Adam frowned. "Where did you say you were from again?" He asked one of the girls.

"Jersey." One of the girls leaned into Clark's arm. "I am Jenna." She sweetly smiled. Adam started laughing.

"Right, Jersey Jenna!" Adam announced, nudging Clark in his ribs. Clark smiled at his friend's antics and helped him to the rest of Adam's drink until the server came back to the table. He needed to catch up; otherwise, he wasn't in long for this night out.

Clark wouldn't take the time to try and remember the names of the other women or the few more that joined. He leaned back and let them gaggle amongst each other, fighting for his attention. He needed to be distracted; he needed to be in a black-and-white situation. These were women solely interested in having a good time with no strings attached. Bottles had been opened, and food started to arrive.

As the night drew on, they went to the nearest club. Clark was pretty sure most of his cash was gone. He stood up from the table, slamming one last shot of tequila before staggering his way to the dance floor. This was one of his private pleasures. The vibrations of a good baseline could clear his head from all thoughts, worry, and frustrations.

Adam had convinced him earlier to take a hit, and he felt the effects as he stood on the floor, not to dance, but just to feel the energy. The pulsating beats were so loud that his entire body felt controlled by them. He was drunk, and he was high. He closed his eyes, just focusing on the music when he felt that he was being touched, being pushed back, pushed back until they stopped against the rails. It was dark, the lights kept flashing, and he saw only a black mane of locks.

His shirt was being lifted. She ran her fingers over his abdomen; she pressed hard against him. She was hot; she was soft; she smelled familiar! Rosewater! He finally remembered. The damn lights kept flashing. He tried to search for her face. It was her; it had to be her. He felt her body strain up to kiss him, and he came down and pressed his lips against hers. She tasted as he imagined with remnants of champagne, her hands desperately clung to the back of his neck, and she wanted deeper inside the kiss.

The beat dropped one final time, and the club went black, with cheers cascading through the venue. Then cold. There was no one against him; she was gone. Or was she never there? He quickly looked around, trying to find her. If that wasn't real, Clark was way over his limit. Adam cheered from the DJ booth and motioned him over. His small daydreams of Simi had turned into a drug-induced hallucination. Sorting out his wits, Clark traveled through the throng of people dancing and made his way to Adam . The rest of the night evolved into a blurred memory of entertainment.

The next morning, Clark woke up on the floor of his room. His head was pounding, his mouth dry, and he felt dirty. Two women lay entangled in the sheets, mostly clothed, depending on how Clark wanted to look at the situation. One of the women was shapely with jet-black hair. His memories pushed through; a small wave of sadness reflected over him as he realized it was not Simi. She wouldn't have been in a club if she didn't like festivals. Now he was faced with the part of Vegas he dreaded. He wasn't worried about being an asshole. He just hoped these girls knew that when the shower water turned off, they didn't have to go back to their room, but they should get the hell out of his.

He turned on the water, letting the cold sensation run over his body. He lowered his head to allow the water flow freely down his body. His memories of last night kept bringing him back to a kiss. A kiss that felt so right, so powerful, so mesmerizing.

He inhaled deeply, imagining that scent of rose water. He smelled it frequently during his time in Dubai and Oman. He knew it so well he could taste it. He sighed heavily as the cold water pulsated down his back. Adam and his vices. Clark winced, worried he had let Adam go too far. Adam was his own man, Clark justified, and the reality was that Clark needed a night like last night too. The water began to draw him back to a sense of reality; feeling tight, he knew he needed air. Fresh air and sun. He needed out of this space.

Chapter 7

Simi waited as the server pulled out her chair at Bouchon. She had left a note in Daroush's room to join her for breakfast. She had assumed she would dine alone, as Daroush was still jet-lagged. She rested her menu to the side, leaned back in her chair, and looked toward the fountain she was seated next to. She inhaled happily as a gentle breeze fell over her. Vegas in the morning was a special time. The streets were quiet and clean. The air was still cool. She lived here much shorter than she originally anticipated but had thoroughly enjoyed her time. Happily entranced by the falling droplets, she didn't notice who pulled out the chair next to her.

"I didn't think you would wake up in time to join me." She spoke to him in French, only to match her gaze with Clark. "Oh," Simi laughed. "I am sorry, hi."

"Hello." He took his seat next to her. The server brought an extra menu to Clark and informed them of the specials. Clark continued to look at her as she smiled politely at the server. Simi ignored his gaze, ordering a coffee for herself and Clark. As the server left, Simi smiled back at Clark. "Is this okay that I am here with you?" he asked.

Simi held in her amusement. "I would think it's okay."

"Who are you here with?"

"Who are you here with?" Simi playfully responded.

"A friend." The server came back with coffee and placed the porcelain cups between them. He poured each cup evenly.

Simi looked up at the server and ordered a quiche with bacon and fruit. "The quiches here are excellent. You should try it." Clark growing impatient with Simi, nodded and mimicked her order. "Literally, one of my favorite quiches. Thomas Keller is such a treat. Have you ever been to French Laundry?"

"Simi," Clark's voice was low. "Are you okay?" Hearing the concern in his voice brought back the realization of what he thought Simi was doing here. It was no longer funny.

"I am here with my brother. He is visiting from Paris." Clark, clearly relieved, relaxed his arms resting on the table. "It was suggested to take a little trip, I lived here for a short time after university, and I brought him here hoping to recreate that trip. Unfortunately for me, I have aged, and this morning I find myself a bit hungover." Simi raised her cup, tilting her head to the side.

"Where is your brother this morning?"

"Snuggling his phone, I am sure. He has a girlfriend now in Paris."

Her tone caused Clark to inquire. "You don't like her?"

Simi immediately frowned at Clark's assumption. "I don't know her." Her face softened. She set down her cup and rested her hands on her lap. "I love that my brother is in love. He deserves it more than anyone." Simi swallowed hard. "I just want him only to experience the happiness of love and never know the pain of it." Simi looked toward Clark. "You must understand."

"Probably would have to be in love to understand."

"Sure, when you were last in love and the heartbreak after the relationship ended."

Clark clicked his tongue. "I would have had to have been in love to experience that."

"You have been in love. You are like, what, 40?" Clark hit his chest with his hand with a pained expression.

"You think I look 40?"

"I think you look old enough to have had heartbreak at least once," Simi explained. "That smoking ages you." Clark looked over to Simi curiously. "I can be observant too." She winked at him. "I guess I am protective. He deserves only the best things."

"And you? You don't think you also deserve the best things?"

"I had my shot." Simi pressed her lips tightly. "Lost the game."

"I find it hard to believe a man would leave you unless by brute force." Clark looked over, noticing her quickly blinking; her gaze settled on her lap. Clark watched her features as she held in memory. A realization came over him; the border of Simi's puzzle was near completion.

"Well, I forgive you for how you acted on the plane then," Clark empathized. "It is too soon for us to start meeting family?" he jokingly offered, hoping to bring her back to a positive headspace.

"Do you often speak out declarations?" Simi inquired. "You don't even know me."

"Speak it to the universe; it comes to fruition." Clark could see his antics having a positive influence on Simi until a look of concern came across her face.

"I am sorry if you got the wrong impression."

"In general or just yesterday?" Clark tempted her for an answer.

"Oh, how I imagine you wish I would say both." Simi took a drink of her coffee, setting it back down on the saucer plate before her. "I told you I wouldn't live up to your expectations."

"You still don't know what my expectations are." Clark raised his arms up, resting his hands on the back of his head. He repositioned more comfortably in his seat. "Happy to have our second date tonight."

"What about your friend?"

"He is grown."

"Are you so intrigued with me that you do not care what you may find out about me?" Simi leaned her elbows on the table.

"Yes." Clark's answer was simple, and he moved forward in his chair. "You are playing your bravado too big with me, Simi. There is always a simple explanation, and I have the patience and discipline to find out your story." He leaned in closer to Simi, her fragrance enveloping his senses. He lifted her hand off of her coffee cup. Her palm was healed with a fresh scar. Clark held her hand in his; turning it over, he smiled, looking up to meet her gaze. "Where were you last night?"

"I was with my brother."

"Where were you and your brother last night?"

"Here." Simi smiled, enjoying their exchange. "Where were you last night?"

"I think you know that answer," he said softly; he reached to cup her face and slowly drew her in for a kiss. Their lips lightly touched against each other as Clark held her securely in his grasp. He teased to gently part her lips, wanting another sweet taste of her. A small moan escaped her lips, and Clark encouraged her to invite him in.

"Clark?" Clark blinked, realizing he had fantasized the kiss. He let go of her hands as the server brought their plates to the table. "Where did you go just now?"

"Someplace delightful." Clark took his first bite. "You were right about this quiche. Wow." Clark gestured with his hand.

"I am glad you like it." Simi evoked an amused hum as she took a few bites of her breakfast. She smiled inwardly, watching his mannerisms. Wherever he had drifted off to had made him happy.

Clark frowned, setting his fork down, and pulled his phone from his pocket. His frown deepened at the screen, then he looked over to Simi. "Can I steal you away from your brother tonight?"

"You are really pushing this second date. You don't think I will show up next week?"

"I think when opportunities are in plain sight, you should take advantage as much as possible," Clark answered. "I will wait until next week if that is what you want." He peered over to Simi. "Is that your preference?"

It wasn't. Simi was trying to keep her gaze off his loosely buttoned linen shirt which gave Simi a glimpse of what strength was hidden beneath his clothes. She had caught herself staring a moment too long as he waited for her answer. Simi pursed her lips together, reflecting on her next words. "I am staying in a Chairman's Suite. We can have a quiet dinner, where you can lay out your list of expectations for me." Simi drummed her fingers on the table. "Then I, in turn, can list my expectations for you. How does that sound?"

"I will bring my notebook." Clark smiled. Simi reached into her wallet and handed an extra room key. "How is seven?" Simi smiled and noted that with the time change, seven p.m. was nine p.m. for them.

"Perfect." He lifted her hand and pressed a soft kiss on her knuckles. "I will take care of the check on my way out." Simi smiled in appreciation and watched Clark exit the outdoor dining area. She pulled her coffee cup and rested it between her hands as she leaned back, resuming her watch of the fountain next to her.

Clark opened the door to his suite. He looked down at his text messages from Adam. Where was he? He went into his bedroom and slowly opened the door.

"Ugh, kill me now!" Adam moaned. Clark had found him in worse positions. Adam didn't look up to see his friend. "My body has betrayed me!" Adam declared, lying flat on the back of the bathroom floor.

"Have you taken a shower yet?" Clark asked, throwing a towel over his friend.

"I cannot stand higher than a kneel right now."

"Maybe a bath then." Clark stepped over Adam and turned the water on, trying to get the temperature right.

"How is it that you are okay?"

"I wasn't—I took a shower, went for a walk, had breakfast. We just need to hydrate you up and get some food into you." Clark left Adam in the bathroom—not revealing his interlude with Simi. He found the room service folder; taking a seat on Adam's bed, he reached for the phone, ordering an array of remedies to soothe and get Adam well.

"I think this is what death feels like. If you are shot and bleeding out—this has to be how it feels. Or maybe a sword wound." Adam wallowed from the floor. Clark smiled as he finished up with the dining server over the phone then came back into the bathroom. "You will tell Amanda, I am sorry. You will take care of her, won't you?" Adam raised his hand—"You can marry her, but you can't have sex with her. I want her to continue to think I am the best she ever had."

"Okay, buddy, let's get you into the bathtub. You need to cool down."

"Please don't make me move—please—please, I will do anything." Clark ignored his friend's whimpering request, pulling him up and settling him into the bathtub. He brought a bucket over to the side of the bath.

"Just stay put for a bit. Relax and keep your eyes closed. Food is coming." Clark took a washcloth off the sink and folded it. He ran cold water, soaking the towel entirely. "Keep this over your face. I will be back."

As Clark ordered a hydration IV for Adam, he was relieved by this outcome. It was the best-case scenario for both of them. Adam declared he didn't want to leave the room, leaving Clark free of worry about seeing Simi tonight.

Clark continued to cater to Adam, forcing him to eat and drink as much as he could handle. When his IV treatment was finished, Adam had fallen asleep. Clark grabbed his wallet and left the room. He needed to clear his head—from the morning, and for what could happen tonight.

When he saw her sitting at Bouchon, he waited, looking around to see if she was alone. Entranced with the fountain, in a soft floral dress, he finally saw the version of Simi she was hiding from him with her sultry bravado. When she spoke of her brother, of love, she inadvertently was showing him who she was—enamoring him even more with what she was doing and the reason behind it. Walking through the casino floor, he ended up in the Canal shops.

He looked along the window displays when a jewelry display caught his eye. He looked over the beautifully placed pieces. Nodding to himself, he turned away from the store. He pulled out his phone and began searching. He immediately recognized the images, recalling the necklace Simi had worn the other night. He walked back to the jewelry shop he had passed to obtain the piece that had caught his eye.

When Clark returned to his hotel room, he went to his bedroom before checking on Adam. He placed the small bag off to the side of the dresser and caught his gaze, holding his reflection. His own reflection made him acknowledge a distressing feeling he had been ignoring. How would he accept her truth? Could he accept it?

He looked over to the bag, wondering if the gift was appropriate. Did other men bring her gifts too? Clark walked away from the mirror dresser and rotated his neck, trying to push out the tension building up. After this morning, he found it hard to believe that she would offer herself up to anyone other than a man who loved her.

Or could afford her.

Clark's inner voice broke through his stubbornness. An overwhelming sense of dread came over him. If she was here with her brother, how was she affording this trip? He roughly had an idea of what a Chairman's Suite cost. He knew how much two seats on the shuttle for Vegas were. Frowning, he sat back on his bed, hunched over, his elbows resting on his knees. He swallowed hard, searching for other context clues to explain her lifestyle. He remembered her reaction to his comment at breakfast. That didn't explain her finances.

Clenching his jaw, he shook his head. He never argued with the impulsive logic that came to him. It was his instinct, which is what he followed that led him to all of his success. Now, he struggled. He struggled with this sensation that made him feel uncomfortable and protective of her, of her femininity.

This was the first time he would follow a feeling and push his trusting logic to the side. If he was going to do what he shamed many for, Clark had to be prepared for what could ultimately happen to him. He may finally experience the feeling of heartbreak.

Clark left his bedroom and crossed the space to Adam's door. He tapped quietly and walked into Adam's room.

"How are you feeling?"

"Better," Adam sighed. "Not exactly how I expected today to go. We will make it up tomorrow, though. Sunday day party by the pool. I bet if I am outside, it will be better." Adam set down the remote and lifted himself to sit up from the bed.

"Yeah, we will see how it goes tomorrow," Clark answered.

"You shouldn't stay in on my account. Go out—meet some new friends." Adam insisted. "I need to call Amanda anyway. It might be good to stay on the phone with her tonight."

"It's okay to miss your wife."

"I know. I do miss her," Adam revealed. "No regrets. I still had fun. You seem more pensive than usual. Last night finally caught up with you?"

"I found Simi," Clark admitted, "I went to get breakfast, and she was there. I am going to have dinner with her tonight." Adam hummed, continuing to flip through the channels. "She is here with her brother."

"Oo a brother? She has to share that inheritance fortune now?" He joked, still monotonously flipping through the channels.

"You sure you are going to be okay?"

"Yes—go, but you and I are poolside all day tomorrow." Clark nodded as he left Adam's room.

∗∗∗

Simi stood in front of the mirror in her bedroom. Daroush tapped the door slightly as he walked in. She turned slightly, then back at her reflection, frowning as she smoothed her hands over her dress.

"His name is Clark." She admitted, still facing the mirror. Daroush took a seat on the bed. "The guys from the plane? His name is Clark; he is here with his old hipster friend for the weekend." Simi shared with Daroush. " I didn't know he was going to be here; we recently became new friends ourselves." She faced Daroush leaning back on his elbows.

"You have never been this secretive with me before, Simi. I don't like these half-truths you have been giving me."

"They are not half-truths—I am just sharing what I am ready to share."

"We never had secrets from each other." Simi shifted her eyes away from his. "None that I was aware of," Daroush finished.

"Do you still talk to *him?*" Simi reached out to the dresser picking up a stack of bangles. She raised her eyebrow in question.

"That isn't fair. He is our father." Simi clenched her teeth. Daroush sighed heavily. "He checks in about once a month. He wants to make sure Maman is okay. That you are okay."

"He doesn't ask about me."

"He does. Especially since the passing of—"

"You told him!" Simi dropped the bangles from her hands, furious at her brother. "You had no right to tell him anything about me. Or my life." Daroush stood up against Simi.

"I had to." Daroush kneeled down and began picking up the jewelry at Simi's feet.

"Why did you have to?" Simi folded her arms. Daroush picked

64

up the last of her bracelets and stood back to face her. He pressed his thumb playfully between her eyebrows, smoothing out her frown. Simi was not amused. She swatted at his hand, still waiting for an answer.

"Baba was asked to attend; Baba was going to be there in Paris." Simi felt flush.

Simi shook her head. She refused to believe Daroush's words. Simi took a deep breath, and she let herself remember.

An afterparty for the Knuttle Gallery at the Venetian-Palazzo. Robert, a curator she worked with while she attended NYU, was poached to open the gallery for Knuttle, often referred to as the Irish Picasso. While his work was the main attraction on display, they intended to host many of Europe's up-and-coming artists. Robert offered for Simi to join him as soon as she graduated. He didn't want to lose her. Simi spoke many languages which had increased commissions of their New York gallery by over 35%. Robert intended to keep her as long as he could. Buyers were much quicker to cut a check after Simi charmed them over in their native tongue.

The opening was a successful night. Knuttle had just about every piece sold, with the exception of a piece he titled *Love and Marriage.* Simi found herself drawn to the painting. There was an eerie and uncomfortable resemblance to her own parents' wedding photo. She found herself so distracted that she didn't notice the man who had been watching throughout the party. The man who was behind the funding for the gallery and hosted the afterparty for his dear friend Knuttle's successful opening. The man who would bring her a glass of champagne as she looked toward the door, hoping to discreetly sneak out of the afterparty, and introduce himself as Roman.

"No, Roman wouldn't have done that to me. He knew better. He wouldn't have put me in that situation." Simi wouldn't believe that type of betrayal was possible. "Maman wouldn't have let him invite our Father."

"She encouraged it." Daroush corrected.

"And you?"

"I agreed with them. Maman and I have forgiven him, you need to as well."

"He left us! Momma died, and he left us, Daroush—you needed

a father. I wanted a father, and he left like we didn't matter."

"Abji, you know it was more than that."

"I hate him." Simi hissed. "I don't think about him, I don't say his name because I hate him so much." Simi clenched her fist, wishing the images of her father out of her mind. Quietly she continued. "You know this. Roman knew this."

"What is going on with you?" Daroush frowned. "You are being so ugly. Momma and Maman did better than this."

Simi cringed at her brothers words "I wasn't expecting you to tell me, Roman, was to surprise me with Baba, in Paris." Simi cleared her throat. "That was a lot for me to hear."

Frustrated, Daroush shook his head. "I was coming in here to invite you to an underground DJ set I found happening off of the strip, but it seems you have other plans." Daroush presented Simi with her bangles again. "Clark, was it?" Simi nodded again, accepting the bracelets back. "Where is he taking you?" Daroush asked as he walked into the bathroom. She listened as he ran the water bringing out a glass to her. He sat on the bed again—waiting for her to join him.

"I invited him here. I called for one of the chefs tonight." Simi joined her brother—taking the glass of water. "What?"

"Nothing- I didn't say anything." Daroush insisted. Simi nudged her brother. "It's nothing."

"Tell me."

"I just am curious as to how long you are going to stay in Roman's shadow. This was never your world. The suite is great but come on—a private chef, the private jet?"

"It was a shared jet." Simi corrected.

"You know what I mean. When you first brought me out here, we did dollar shots and shared a room with six people. It was fun. He is gone now; you don't have to keep up with this lifestyle anymore."

"I am not."

"Yes, you are. This isn't you. This isn't us."

"I thought you were growing up, but you are still bratty as ever, Daroush." Simi was hurt by his words. "Maman spoiled you too much." She sat up from the bed and walked back to the mirror. Under her breath in Persian, she uttered. *"Ungrateful."*

"What did you say?" Daroush pressed.

Simi said nothing, keeping her eyes locked on her gaze, looking in the mirror, deciding which earrings to wear for the evening. She was angry and hurt by her brother but refused to engage in a fight. She heard him scoff as he stood up from the bed.

"I'd rather be ungrateful than live blindly in some fantasy land." Daroush spewed back. "Let me know when you are ready to come back to reality." Daroush swung her door open and looked back at his sister. In French, he said the ill-timed word, *"Delusional."*

Simi winced at the word as his footsteps retreated from the suite. Simi swallowed hard, stepping away from the mirror. She noticed the time. She had mere minutes to refocus herself before Clark's arrival. Running through a list of options, she settled on a quick chug of a mini-bar bottle of vodka to calm her down, thinking of a way to smother Daroush in his sleep and have him beg for mercy.

Chapter 8

Clark hesitated before placing the key card over the suite's lock pad. He took a step back away from the door. He was nervous. He couldn't quite believe it. He had been in bigger arenas of intimidation and never broke a sweat. What would happen behind these doors tonight was unknown. Clark always had a plan ready, he could forecast most events flawlessly. He had no estimation of where tonight would go outside of his own wants. Taking one deep breath, Clark was ready to open the door when it was opened for him.

"Hi." Piercing green eyes narrowed at him. Her brother was leaving. "I am here for Simi." He watched Daroush attempt to intimidate him; he hid his smile as her brother glared at him, standing closer to Clark as he walked out the door. He didn't say anything to Clark as he left the door open for him. Turning away, Clark heard a slew of curse words in French; unable to hide his smile; he chuckled and walked into the hall of her suite. He closed the door behind him and called her name. He stepped further into the room as he saw her exit her bedroom.

Clark tensed as she walked toward him in a black full sleeved dress that revealed the beautiful shape of her body. The sound of her heels and the jingle of her bracelets echoed throughout the space. She smiled, lifting her hair over her shoulder. As grand as the suite was, he couldn't take his eyes off of her. Her modest but sexy style had Clark eager to unwrap her like a Christmas present.

"Are these for me?" Simi accepted the favors from Clark. "Thank you." She set them on the table in front of Clark and turned back to him, greeting him with a kiss on the cheek. "You look nice."

"I feel a bit underdressed." Clark pulled the side of his blazer open, his black shirt paired with dark wash jeans."

"You shouldn't. We are just hanging out. It was either this or sweats for me. I rarely have an in-between."

"I liked your dress from this morning." Simi caught his gaze; she smiled, turning back to the table.

"What did you bring for me?" She picked up the bottle of wine and slid off the fabric. She tilted her head in delight. "My favorite. How observant of you." She smiled brightly at him. "Let me get this open for us. Take a seat." He picked up the small bag, not yet opened, and brought it with him to sit on the sofa in front of the fireplace. He removed his jacket, folding it over and laying it off to the side.

Simi brought over two glasses and a decanter for the wine. As Simi looked back to the wet bar, Clark stood up next to her.

"I bought one just in case." Clark removed the wine opener from his pocket. "If you don't mind." He took the bottle from the table and began cutting the aluminum from the top. Simi settled into her seat, crossing her leg over one another, pulling the fabric back to her hips. He refocused his gaze. He was going to slice his hand open. He opened the wine placing the bottle in the decanter before pouring two glasses for them. Simi accepted the glass as Clark took his seat. She leaned forward, peeking down into the jewelry bag. She raised her eyebrow. "I couldn't help myself." Clark placed both their glasses back down and reached for the box inside. He sat next to Simi and handed her a long black velvet box. She opened the box, and her breath caught. She looked quickly at Clark and then back down at the piece. Her fingers danced over the gold bracelet, tracing the red rubies on both ends that indented slightly to form a V. "Do you like it?"

Simi kept her eyes on the piece and nodded quietly. He had hit home with this gift. "This is too much," she began to hand him back the box; her bravado façade had been penetrated.

"It's not." Clark took the bracelet out of the box and reached for her arm. "So technically, the rubies are supposed to signify Phoenix wings, but the Simurgh came first, and I had short notice." Her breath held as Clark secured the bracelet over her gold watch. "It even matches."

"It does," Simi cleared her throat; she touched the bracelet on her arm, then the watch. "This was really thoughtful, Clark. Thank you."

"I am glad you like it. I went down a bit of a rabbit hole on Persian Mythology. Interesting stuff. Very rich culture."

"It is." Simi reached for their wine glasses and handed one to Clark. She had finished her internal dialogue and was ready to begin again with Clark. She reached for his free hand, intertwining her fingers with his. "Clark . . ." She almost sang his name. "Is there another name that follows?"

"Williams." He noted how she moved the conversation off of her back to him.

"Clark Williams." Simi leaned back in her seat. Her leg was still pressed against his. "Well, Clark Williams, I have to admit that what I originally planned for tonight has been discouraged."

"Oh really? You wore the wrong dress, then," Clark retorted.

"I meant regarding our dinner." Simi softly chuckled. "So, how does the idea of ordering some stuff off the room service menu sound?" Clark had assumed that was the original plan.

"What did you want to do instead?"

"There may or may not have been a private chef who was going to come in and cook?" Simi blushed as her voice floated up.

"Room service is the better option . . ." Clark was not interested in any interruptions tonight. Simi nodded and went to retrieve the black binder for them to select their options. Handing off the book to Clark, she sat next to him. She admired her bracelet, adjusting it around her wrist, sliding the watch above and below it. Clark engaged her in options he thought would be good for the evening. She easily agreed, seemingly distracted now by her gift. Taking the lead, he closed the book and picked up the phone behind them.

As Clark returned to sit next to Simi, her mood noticeably altered. "I feel like the bracelet didn't land well with you."

Simi lifted her eyebrows, shaking her head. "No, it's me. Daroush and I exchanged some words. Sibling stuff." Simi posed her wrist out. "Your gift is thoughtful, it has me thinking about some poems related to Simurgh."

"I'd love to hear some," Clark requested.

"Not tonight." Simi smiled softly, resting her arm back down. She shifted in her seat to face Clark. "So what does Clark Williams do?" She lightly began to caress his arm resting at the top of the pillows. "I sold a company a little bit ago and decided to take some of the capital and open a VC where we can house small companies and entrepreneurs," Clark explained. He noticed a frown begin to form across her face. It was the usual face he had been given when he explained his idea.

"That seems risky."

"It is." Simi stayed silent. He could see she had questions but wasn't sure how to form them. "When people often hear this idea, it seems altruistic. The fact is—not a lot of people who look like me get to be success stories, and I want to change that."

"How do you change that?"

"If people didn't have to worry about basic income, childcare, and insurance, so many people would have a chance to start something of their own."

"You mean to say you will pay for all of this?" Simi questioned, trying to understand the philanthropic endeavor. She listened as he explained the challenges many small companies and entrepreneurs face, specifically in non-white communities and among females. He brought up points she had never taken the time to think about. He took the time to educate her and explain his reasoning that his new company could set up a chain reaction where investors would want to focus their money. The familiar cadence was back and Simi felt it in her heart.

"What is it?" She took a moment before she answered. Her eyes were low.

"You just remind me of someone."

"To get you to smile more like that, I will take that as a compliment." Clark took another sip of the wine.

"Well, let's say you get another successful win. Another big idea is produced under your umbrella. What makes you think they will also pay it forward."

"Lead by example," Clark answered. "You repeat what is seen around you."

"I don't know, Clark—I have been around a lot of money, new money too; most don't give back like this." Clark nodded in agreement. "Most go off and buy villas and never visit them." Clark laughed, remembering Adam's eagerness to buy property in Belize. "It leaves me wondering how much you got from selling your company. You need a handsome number to change an industry's eco-system."

"After me for my money?" he pondered aloud.

"Well, the thought never occurred to me until now." She glanced at her bangles on her wrists. "I could use more luxuries in life." She sarcastically replied, waving her hand around the suite they were in.

"We were bought out very well. More than I could ever spend," Clark answered. "This is why I can give back."

"You aren't married yet." She was right. Adam's wife Amanda was burning through cash quicker than Clark thought they should. It was not anything he was personally worried about—both Adam and Amanda had the security of family money—but it caused a level of anxiety still when he witnessed it.

"I will have to find someone in my income bracket then." Clark playfully looked around the suite. "You seem to be in my income bracket. If not above it. What did you do before you moved to Chicago?" The question was purposeful. It was going to extract more from her.

"I sold art. I was an Art History major at NYU. I worked at galleries. I even spent a short time here, opening a gallery."

"And now you are selling art on the black market in Chicago?" Clark teased. "Your secret meetings upstairs—it's just an exchange of priceless artwork?"

Simi hid her smile behind her fingers. "Heiress, black market dealer? Clark, just ask me what you want to ask me."

"Not yet."

Clark took her glass from her hand and set it on the table. He moved closer to Simi, resting his arm on the back of the couch, bringing her body closer to him. He brought his hand to her cheek, caressing her soft skin. Her eyes closed as Clark ran his thumb on the bottom of her lip. Her hand came up to his cheek, and she opened her eyes slightly, meeting his eyes. She leaned in for a kiss, lifting herself up to sit on his lap, her knees resting on each side of his hip. Her dress lifted, allowing Clark to slide his hands all the up her womanly thighs, discovering the lace texture around her bottom. She exhaled at his hands, tensing above him. Her lips parted was an invitation for him. He moved his hands up her hand and treated himself to a taste. Their tongues danced together in a delicate waltz, both beginning to discover one another while she let Clark take the lead. Slowly his hands traveled to softly cup her breasts, gently massaging, looking for a sweet spot to caress. A soft nip came from Simi as he teased her sensitive area. She exhaled his name, pulling back from their kiss. Clark brought his hands up to her head and entangled them in her thick locks. Bringing her back in for a deeper kiss, her sweet sounds of delight were heavenly.

Simi broke the kiss leaving his lips, softly pressing more kisses down his cheek and neck. Lighting raced across his body when she licked right above his collarbone. This wasn't right, Clark had not transferred the power over to her, but she had taken control. He attempted to shift position, but her thigh locked him in place. Her lips pressed against his throat, her fingers playing with the chest hair visible from his v-neck. She traced her hand around his muscles, feeling the heat permeating from his body, his heartbeat noticeable under her fingertips. Clark threw his head back as her hands began to travel lower. "Simi"

The painful ring of the doorbell broke them from their interlude. Simi's eyes were radiant; she was wanton for him. This wasn't a façade; this wasn't bravado. This was her. "Hungry?"

Dinner was quiet; both Simi and Clark were still coming down from their first intimate exchange with each other. They continued to converse politely, both of them still mentally back on the couch.

Simi asked thoughtful questions about CG to Clark, which he was more than happy to answer. After she shared that her brother would be out most of the evening, it was Clark's turn to open up about his family when she asked about his parents.

Clark's parents were still married, but after he sold his company, he bought each of them a separate house in different states. Simi didn't understand why they did not just simply divorce, but Clark understood why; they were his parents, and they loved each other, but after close to fifty years together, they were ready for their own space.

"Are you close with your parents? Your family?" Simi asked.

"They are my parents. I love them, of course." Clark clicked his tongue. "You know I can't recall a time in my life when I haven't been a loner."

Simi didn't quite understand. "You seem very close with Adam after all you have described."

"Right, but Adam is married. He always had a girlfriend. He was rarely ever single."

"And you are mostly single?"

"It has been hard to find the type of partner I need. That I want." Clark leaned back into the dining room chair. The candles had melted a few inches down, and the plates between them spread across the table were near completion.

"Yes, that's right. Your list of expectations." Simi lit up. She grabbed her wine glass and pushed her chair closer to the table. "I am so ready for this. Let's go."

"My expectation of a partner—"

"Wait!" Simi threw her hands up, "I should get a paper and pen."

Clark waved to her, motioning she stay seated. "It is quite simple." Simi smirked, providing Clark with her full attention. "I'd like her to have brown eyes . . ."

"Uh huh . . ."

"Brown hair, a bit of an erratic personality, with a good amount of mystery behind her."

"Well, you are in luck; I have many cousins that need green cards. We are all types of that." She pushed her chair back and stood from her seat. She poured the last of the red wine into her glass. "Join me on the balcony?"

Clark nodded, standing up to follow her as she walked toward the floor-to-ceiling windows; she held her glass back for Clark to grab and pushed the curtain open with her free hand. She opened the door to reveal an expansive balcony with a large inground jacuzzi off to the side. She wasn't going to make this easy. Clark took a seat on the large lounger that gave a great view. Lights illuminated the night sky, but beyond the distance, you could see the bleak darkness of the mountains surrounding this desert paradise. The sounds of the strip were vibrant. She joined him accepting his arm around her shoulders.

"Do you need a green card?" Clark looked at her.

"Nope, I am a proud anchor, baby."

"So you aren't from France? Your accent is muddled, but English dominates it."

"I did most of my schooling in LA; then we went back to Paris for a bit. I wanted to come back to the states and go to university in New York. My brother did most of his schooling in France; that is his home."

"Where do you call home?"

"I don't know. I don't think I am interested in planting permanent roots anymore." Simi gestured.

"So your game is to move around cities, make men fall in love with you, then quietly disappear, leaving them heartbroken in your wake?"

"That was beautiful, Clark." Simi chuckled as she sipped from her wine glass. "I think so." She playfully pushed into Clark. "My brother has been asking me to come to Paris. There is a lot I would need to face up to if I were to go. I am not ready yet." Simi looked down at her arm, the watch and the bracelet taking her attention.

"What happened in Paris?" Clark enclosed his hand around hers. "We don't have to waste this evening playing games. You can tell me." He brought her hand back to his lips and kissed them softly.

Simi believed she could tell him. The bracelet was meaningful. More so than he knew, Clark realized. He inadvertently was making her remember things that she had buried. Things she didn't address because she was busy living her life, focusing mostly on Roman.

"My mom was sick when we left LA. She died shortly before I transferred out to NYU. I have many regrets about how I acted at the end of her life and haven't yet found the courage to go back. I haven't even seen her grave." She began blinking back tears.

"Have you lost anyone before?" she asked Clark.

"No, I haven't," he shared. "I came close once, though. They pulled through, but it was pretty scary for me.

This was not where she wanted the night to go. She found herself in conflict. Her recent revelation went against what her body wanted her to do. She didn't want Clark to leave; she wanted quite the opposite. Clark's hand still engulfed hers. She rested her head on his shoulders, crossing her legs over each other. She had the ability to change the course of the night and decided to do just that. She tilted her head up and reached for his cheek. She wordlessly asked for another kiss. A source of comfort to temporarily cover an open wound.

He leaned in, kissing her again, this time with vigor and urgency he was desperate to control. Simi turned her hips and rested her legs over his lap as she was cradled into his arms. She began to tug at his shirt. She wanted to finally feel him. Clark broke from the kiss allowing Simi to free him of his shirt. Once removed, she lightly scratched her nails from his shoulders down to his belt, jerking ever so slightly to finish her task. Her hands tickled as she traced around his hips, bringing him as close to her. He reached for her hands.

"Bedroom?" Clark proposed. Simi silently agreed.

Clark lifted, securing Simi's legs around his waist. The sensation of her thighs clenching around his waist weakened his knees, attempting to falter his steps. The cool night air swept over both their heated bodies. Clark pushed the balcony door open and continued straight down the long hallway toward the room he had seen her exit. The door was slightly ajar; assisting him, she pushed it open wider.

He gently placed her on the bed as she removed her set of bangles over her dress, tossing them freely to the floor. Clark ran his hands up her thighs until he reached the ends of her dress, pulling it off to reveal her. He stared. He appreciated.

Simi held her breath; elevated on her elbows, she dropped her head back as he ran his fingers down her stomach, hovering at the top of her lace panties. His fingers trailed over the fabric, and her eyes closed as a breath finally escaped her lips in a lustful sound: "Clark."

She ignored the amused hum, letting her elbows fall, relaxing fully on her back as he ran his hands over her panties and around her thighs. She fought the trembles, continuing to urge for the sensations. She gripped the blanket beneath her. *If this was just with his hands . . .*Simi opened her eyes, lifting to sit before him as he stood before her. She looked up to him, his face dark, controlled desire. She tugged at his pants, hooking her fingers inside, bringing him closer to her. His fingers fell into her hair, and she pressed her lips against his stomach, smiling at his audible reaction. She continued to leave a trail of wet licks and kisses. She relieved him from his pants—leaving the thinnest fabric between her lips and him. A part of him she was desperate to taste and experience.

"Simi." Her head was gently jerked back as he still held on to her hair. The look in his eyes impassioned her body. She was wanton. "You still haven't told me where you were last night." His voice was low; his grin had Simi nervous.

He freed his hands, inviting himself over her body on the bed. He leaned down, capturing her eyes as he lightly brushed his lips over hers.

"Please." She said in a whisper, pushing up her body to feel him. She pressed her hands flat on his back. Urging him with her strength to press down—he held back. Staying above her—denying her the sensation of his warm body against hers. "Clark, please." She frowned—her skin was on fire. She was willing to lose and beg just to feel a release. His restraint was infuriating.

Clark gently kissed her furrowed brow—attempting to relax her frustration. "I was dancing last night, and a beautifully exotic, dare I say, tribal woman began kissing me." A sinister chuckle. He brushed his cheek against hers, his hair scratching her skin. She wanted to feel that again. She wanted that over her breasts, that scratch across her nipples.

"I uh . . .I" His lips now lingered lightly over her throat. Her breasts begged to be touched next. He hovered just over her nipples. Simi was at her tipping point. "Please, Clark." His chuckle riled her; she felt his breath above her. He was so close; why was he doing this? He had to be in as much duress as she was. She whimpered as his breath traveled away from her breasts. She gripped his arms. "Why?" She pleaded.

"Tell me where you were last night." Clark hovered above her. He rested on his knees and elbows, emitting his heat but not the satisfaction of his touch. Not yet. "I can wait all night." He lightly blew across her hot flesh.

"This is fucking ridiculous," Simi flippantly declared. She held her breath as she felt his shift, just not in the direction she wanted. "Clark!" She begged. "It was me!" Simi pulled at him forcefully. "I was very drunk at Tao—I saw you, " she near shouted. "It was mean; I shouldn't have done it. I won't do it again." Simi had nothing else left; she breathlessly lay—waiting.

Clark smiled with satisfaction. He released his weight held by his knees and rested above Simi's hips. "No, you won't." The pleasing sounds that escaped her lips had made it all worth it. "You won't tease anymore." Simi nodded. "Because if you do something like that again," he held in his threat. No more needed to be said. He knew—she understood.

Clark restarted his trail of kisses from her lips, down her décolletage to the middle of her breast. She moaned in delight. His kisses brushed over each nipple, hardening, begging for attention.

"Clark." She moaned, squeezing his arms.

"Shh." He kissed her stomach. "I am going to take care of you tonight." He continued to trail his lips down. Her thighs clenching beneath him, he kissed down, inhaling her sweetness, heat, and readiness for him. Slowly removing the small fabric, he revealed a neatly kept triangle of black curls framing her soft, pulsing lips. Bringing her panties down to her ankles, with following trailing kisses, he kneeled beside the bed, bringing all of her to him—all of her wantonness. A soft kiss on the inner thigh; his beard scratched her skin.

"Please." She said above a breath. Her hands reached for his head; she had not gotten used to his hair and the lack of ability to grasp it. She flailed her arms to her sides. Her lower lips were still closed but throbbing; he brought his to hers. A loud moan escaped from her. "Clark, please."

He obliged, sliding his tongue up and down, opening her up for him, just for him. He continued in his repetitive motions, watching and listening for cues of guidance and direction. He wanted to please her; he wanted to show her a desire not achievable by any other means but a connection between two people who shared lust, passion, and feelings for one another. That this was the kind of sexual pleasure she should participate in. One of being taken care of. That she should only welcome men to her bed that want her because they care for her.

Her thighs pressed tightly around his cheeks, and her back arched slightly, forcing his lips and tongue deeper into her. He increased his pace at her request. Simi's pleas for him echoed in the room; he swirled again and over her again, trying to capture memories of this moment, of her sound, being pleased by him, being taken care of by him. He brought his hand around her thigh and placed it on her stomach, slowly making his way up to caress a free breast. She grabbed his hand, helping him find his destination. He held her full, brushing his fingers slightly above her peaked nipple. She breathed out louder this time, covering her eyes with her hands.

She was close. He continued on, feeling another shiver from her body; her arms collapsed to the sides, grasping at the bedding around her. Her breathing was labored, and her pleas louder. Clark grabbed her thighs and pulled her closer to him; keeping with her pace, she arched again, off the bed just slightly her hands just shy of grabbing for him, and she shuddered with a delightful cry. He slowed his pace savoring the moment. Her lips closed with a final kiss from him as her body relaxed around him.

Clark stood from his kneeling position, carefully swinging her legs to lay her on the bed. He paused for a moment, taking in the scene. Her eyes still closed, he stepped into the bathroom for a washcloth. He turned the water on as cold as it could get. Tonight was about her. As pained as he was, this was not how he was going to have her the first time. He soaked the cloth and wiped it over his mouth, splashing cold water on his face, over his head, her pleas still replaying in his head. He reached for a towel to dry off as he mentally began cooling himself down to rejoin her.

He came back out to the bedroom; Simi hadn't moved. He kneeled on the bed to join her, watching her breathe, taking in the beautiful curves of her body bare to him. He could do that to her all day. Her eyes fluttered open as he pulled her in to rest on him. Her smile and glazed expression of satisfaction quickly turned to annoyance. Clark chuckled, bringing her into his arms; he lifted her hand to his vantage point.

"Your stamp from Tao. I saw it this morning," Clark revealed.

Simi groaned, burying her face into Clark's chest to hide her embarrassment. "That was amazingly mean."

"But still amazing," Clark corrected. The steadiness of her breathing calmed him. Her warmth and softness had him succumbing to sleep faster than he had ever fallen. Inhaling deeply with her scent and taste still surrounding his senses, he gave in to sleep with her in his arms.

Chapter 9

He was awoken by Simi stirring. The look of bliss and contentment was no longer present. Instead, she frowned, gripping the pillow tightly under her cheek. Clark wanted to wake her from the dream but debated with himself. He needed to leave before she woke up. A lot had happened between them last night, and he wanted to give her privacy to reflect. To relive the memories and crave to re-create more.

He gently pulled the covers back, quickly replacing them so the warm air did not escape and chill her. He looked about the room to gather his belongings. Simi was still in distress within her dream. He came back to her side and placed his palm over her arm. She softened immediately under him. Clark pulled his hand back as Simi turned over, asleep and calm.

He looked toward the nightstand. He took a pen and leaned over, writing on the small pad a note to Simi, which included his cell, room number, and another dinner request. He folded the paper and rested it next to the lamp. He looked to the bed and gently pulled her hair from her face, leaning down a soft kiss on her temple. He paused right above her ear, "doux reve cher, Simi," *Sweet dreams dear, Simi,* Clark whispered in French.

Clark returned to his hotel room; he was surprised to see Adam awake, dressed, and waiting for him to go golfing. It was an odd request, as neither of them usually played, but Clark went along. He hurried, quickly getting ready for a day out with Adam.

Adam brought Clark to the Las Vegas Puite Golf Course. It was a beautiful day; sparse clouds and a cool breeze surrounded them as they attempted to look like they knew what they were doing.

"So, how long until you tell me about last night?" Adam leaned on the golf cart, wiping the sweat from his brow.

"I mean," Clark smiled confidently. "The performance I gave her last night . . ." He twirled the golf club under his palm. "I left her a note, asking to see her again."

"A note? You don't have her number?"

"She has mine." Clark quipped, trying not to acknowledge that she had not yet texted him.

"And we are going to ignore the fact that she sleeps with men for money?"

"I still don't know the truth," Clark admitted. "Honestly, what is the difference between that or random one-night stands?"

"There is a difference between having sex with random strangers after dinner for fun or for money." Adam looked at his friend with disbelief. "You really are acting wild with this one, Clark."

"You have never been this interested in my personal life before." Clark lifted the club, resting it on his neck. "What's this to you?"

"It's nothing." Adam pushed himself off the cart and began walking toward the tee, Clark closely behind him.

"Adam?" Clark prodded.

Adam threw his head back dramatically and sighed heavily. "I am going to be a dad. Amanda is pregnant." He quickly rushed out.

"Adam! That is fantastic!" Clark hugged Adam, patting his back cheerfully. "This is such great news!"

"I can't have a child." Adam waved his hands; he got up abruptly. "Do you see what I did this weekend?" Adam ran his hands through his hair. "312 days all gone because I got scared." Adam kicked at the table. "What kind of father is that?!"

"A father is human," Clark reminded him, "As for starting again. Today is day one. I selfishly let you fall deeper off the wagon this weekend."

"It wasn't you. It's been a few weeks now." Adam admitted. "That is why Amanda left for the weekend."

"Did you talk last night?" Adam nodded. "After what happened before your wedding, I honestly thought this side of you was done," Clark pressed. "When did this start? The cubs game? Your reconnection with Evan?" Adam didn't answer. "That guy, Adam, that guy just uses people. He is a drifter—in the moment, he is a good time, but when shit hits the fan—he runs. What kind of person can do that?"

"I know you aren't wrong about Evan, but when Amanda told me she," he paused, "that *we* were pregnant, I just wasn't ready for that reality."

"Why?"

"Clark, I can't do this. I don't know how to be a father. I barely had one."

"You had one; you have one." Clark reminded. "Not in the way you may need, but he is there." Adam rolled his eyes with a curt huff. "Listen, I have a father. One I look up to, and the most important thing he gave me was the fortitude to know I was loved and protected. That is all you have to do. I was scared of him, but I knew everything he did was for me to be who I am today. You can do this." Adam stayed quiet. "You have all the financial security; that's most of the battle. You can take the next few months to learn the rest. Adam, this is going to be so great for you. This will ground you," Clark encouraged.

"Clark, my life is about to change."

"It has changed, and I am happy for you." Clark took his hand off Adam's back and gave him space on the green. "To think, I thought you were just losing it on trying to find funding." Clark noticed Adam's nervous laugh, one he knew all too well. "You are still struggling to find capital." Adam didn't make eye contact. "You haven't shared anything about it.

"It's a hard sell. That is a fact; you just have to give me time. I will find the money. I have never let you down. I don't intend to start now."

"And you think you won't be a good father? Listen to you. You have this in the bag." Adam waved him off. "You know I can start attending the pitches with you, Adam," Clark offered. "When is the next one?"

"Spare me the extra leg work of trying to extract charm from you to a board full of old white men. Should I find a capital group run by mysterious heiress brown-eyed beauties, I will just send you." Adam lined up his shot and hit the ball out into the green. He walked over to Clark with a smirk.

"You know, Adam, who knows? Maybe I will join the dad crew soon too?"

"Clark, I can't take you seriously with this," Adam groaned. "It makes no sense how you are acting with this girl."

"This feels different,"

"Feels?" Adam questioned. "Clark, emotions aren't your forte.

This is not something you want to get involved with."

"Emotional education or Simi."

"Both!" Adam dropped his club from his hand.

Clark looked back at his friend, "She is well versed; she is educated. She was a professional. You and I know how people can be misled into crazy situations. Let me just take my time and see this through." Clark popped his club straight and pointed to the green. "Now watch this shot." Clark took his stance before pulling back and hitting the ball clear and clean off the tee. It was his best shot of the day. He looked back at Adam's slow hand clap. "I got this, Adam, and trust me. After last night? She will not be going back upstairs to any rooms after Prime unless it's with me."

"I think this VC should be the biggest chance you are taking this year." Adam reminded.

"It still is—you just have to get to know her."

Adam didn't attempt to hold back his laughter. "You don't know her! What the hell are you talking about?"

"I am getting to know her, and you will see. When you meet her, you will see there is more than meets the eye with her," Clark justified.

"No, I see what I see in plain sight. You used to do the same." Adam took a seat in the cart, waiting for Clark to get in for their next shot.

When they got back to the hotel, Adam felt a need to hit one more table. Clark joined his side, feeling a bit perplexed that he still had not received a message back from Simi. A feeling of dread began to bubble inside of him. He began wondering if she had knocked down the card. Perhaps, she thought Clark had just left. Dread turned into a slight panic. Adam nudged Clark as the dealer was waiting for his signal. Clark laid down the cards.

"I am out." Clark folded. "I am going back to the room to check on something. I will be back down." Curious, Adam nodded and went back to playing with his hand. Clark opened his phone as he walked through the casino—dodging his way through the masses to get to his elevators. She wouldn't have thought he had just left her, not after last night. He checked his phone—emails were updating normally. Texts came and were sent. She might not have been able to read his handwriting—but he left his room number.

Reaching his floor, he quickly opened the door, hearing a scoff under his shoe. An envelope was addressed to him. He pulled the cardstock out to read.

"I'm sorry."

He turned it over, but nothing. It was blank. He felt sick. He went to his room and reached for the phone to call the front desk. He asked to be connected to Simi's room, only to find out she had already checked out. Clark couldn't understand. There was nothing he did that should have caused this reaction.

She was of sound mind, wasn't she? Clark raced through the night, had he pushed her? No, she consented. None of this made sense, and now he had no way to contact her. The only thing left was if she would still show up for their meeting back at Prime. That was too far away. His progress would have rescinded, and she might return to . . .He scowled at the idea. He had to find her and know what had happened. What had he done?

Patrick. Clark remembered how coy Patrick had been, when he had asked about Simi. Clark would get him to talk. He grabbed his phone and texted Patrick.

***

The smell of vodka was heavy on his tongue as he pressed down on her. She continued to count silently backward from one hundred. It would only be a few more minutes. She wouldn't open her eyes. The repetitive motions on top of her matched along with the rhythm of her count. 'Stop.' That is what she wanted to say, but stronger was her need for this punishment. She turned to the side, hoping to inhale a breath not clouded with the scent of vodka. A jolt of pain seared across her cheek.

Simi gasped, waking to find herself alone in her bed. She took in a quick breath, reminding herself she was no longer there. The curtains had been pulled back, but no evidence of Clark remained in her room. She turned to lay on her back, stretching from her fingers to her toes. She pushed back the images of her dream as her hands roamed over her body. Sensations and memories flashed through her mind of the hours earlier. The residue of her pleasure was still sticky on her thighs. Grazed scratches of his beard covered her. She exhaled a curse; a cold sensation struck her. Pulling back her sheets, she left for the bathroom to shower. Her head throbbed; she had indulged in too much last night. She was fighting with herself, remembering the pleasure of a night with Clark, ignoring the dream that had awoken her, and finding herself feeling as if she had betrayed Roman.

Roman. Her breath caught in her throat. She got a chill as she looked at her reflection before darting into the bedroom. She stepped over her bangles and looked for her dress. Finding it on the other side of the bed, she hurriedly shook it out. Her watch fell to the ground. She grabbed the watch and went back into the bathroom. Dampening a washcloth, she began to wipe it down. The reflection of the rubies caught her eye. The bracelet was still adorned on her wrist. How could she have let Clark have her like that, see her like that?

Simi began to tremble. Her thoughts—breaking her mind. Justifications, reasoning. Her date nights were not her. It was an act—a little fantasy play. A punishing exercise that would ensure no other man would want or love her as Roman had. How did she let herself get swept up by Clark?

She pressed her fingers on her forehead vigorously, rubbing to soothe the sharp pains. She clenched her jaw, her heartbeat in her ears. She had to breathe; she squeezed her hands tightly together. She was searching for her poem. What was it? Simi searched—nothing. She squeezed her eyes shut—trying to find a memory of her mother. What did she say? Why couldn't she remember? A distressing sound escaped her lips. She freed her hands and captured her reflection again. A calming moment surrounded her as he saw the memory cross her eyes.

Her mother's gentle caress through her hair. A young Simi, angry at the world.

"Don't get lost in your pain." Her mother's voice echoed. *"Know that one day your pain will become your cure."*

Simi repeated the poem, pacing her breath in a rhythmic style to control her breathing. Still, her body was shaking; the usual calming method was not working. Simi justified hurting herself, hoping the pain would free her of this misery. Of her life of constant loss.

Roman.

She looked down at her wrist and unclasped the bracelet. She cupped the delicate jewelry in her hand, walking to her nightstand, still trembling as she rested the ruby wings down. She saw the tented note. Her throat began to tighten as her heartbeat was louder and louder. She hurried back into the bathroom with the paper in her hand. She opened her makeup bag, searching, digging until she dumped all the contents out on the floor. Kneeling, she sifted through the items; her breathing had become staggered.

What did she do? A weak cry quickly came out of Simi. Finding the lighter, she quickly stood up and reached for Clark's note. She clenched her teeth, her lips trembling as she saw his message. Another whimper as the flame met the bottom of the paper. She dropped it into the sink, watching the flame, silently asking the fire to engulf all evidence of last night. Of Clark.

She could not see Clark again; she could not do this to herself again. Roman was not replaceable.

Looking at her reflection, tears streaming down her face, this was the first time she had truly felt like the whore she was depicted to be.

Simi turned off the lights—she couldn't bear to look at herself a moment longer—and entered the shower. She had to get all of last night off of her; she had to erase it all. Simi grabbed the bar soap, rubbing on her stomach furiously, letting her nails scratch into her skin until she was red. Blood began to appear and dribble down the drain, mixing with the water. Another quiet sob escaped after months of holding it all in. Her body refused to listen. She held her hand against the wall, sliding down as she reached her knees. Her head was down as the water cascaded over her back. She cried out loud at her pain.

***

The flight back to Chicago was quiet; Simi had found a jet that could get her back to Chicago immediately. She didn't care about the cost—she needed to get out of Vegas fast.

After abruptly waking up Daroush in his room, Simi told him that they had to leave immediately without explanation. He tried to talk to her and find out what had happened, but she stayed silent. She was scared that if she shared anything, it would be like a broken tap. Everything would come out and flood. She needed to be closer to Jane before she let anything out. On the plane, she sent a flurry of texts to Jane, securing an appointment first thing tomorrow, apologizing, and admitting that Jane was right. That she needed help, that she was ready for help. Her pain was not curing her.

During the flight, Daroush could see how fragile she was. He tried not to be angry with her, but her refusal to let him in was new. She never hid anything from him. This new Simi was hard for him to be with. Daroush felt rejected; she wasn't trusting him to help. She was intentionally leaving him in the dark. A sentiment of abandonment resurfaced, but Daroush pushed it down. This was not the time. Flying was already difficult for him; fighting with Simi wouldn't make the flight easier. He gave her the space she needed until he could get her safely back to Chicago.

Daroush followed Simi into her room. She didn't have the energy to fight him.

"I am going to shower and change," Simi said quietly.

"I am going to stay; I can order us some food." Daroush stated as she nodded in agreement and then slowly walked into her bedroom.

Daroush had been waiting for this. His older sister always maintained control around him. She had never been this secretive before. Daroush could always tell what was on her mind before she said it. He knew Simi had not grieved for their mother, and she had figuratively buried their father. When Roman died suddenly, Daroush worried about what kind of state he would find Simi.

She was fine. Like nothing had happened. Her reserve and stoic behavior transported him back to when their mother had passed. He couldn't stop crying, but not Simi. She held the same demeanor both times. By the time he had gotten to Chicago, she had already handled what was needed. There was no funeral; there was no body per his wishes to be cremated. Daroush wasn't even sure where his ashes were. His urgency to console his sister was for nothing, as she needed no consoling. She wasn't grieving. Daroush didn't stay long and returned to Paris within a few days. He waited. It was only human that she would eventually need to grieve.

His entire childhood was filled only with happy memories because of how strong she was for him. She protected him from truths he found out later as an adult. He didn't know how to protect her from Paris. He wanted her to come home.

Simi came back to the living room and sat with Daroush.

"I am sorry about today," Simi softy spoke.

"What happened last night?" Daroush felt nervous as Simi swallowed hard; she hadn't met his gaze.

"Daroush, I have to talk to you." Simi exhaled heavily.

"Yes, you do. I do not like what I see, Simi. This isn't you," Daroush explained.

"I know. I am not doing very well; I am struggling with a lot."

"Of course, you are; I can help you through this if you just let me in. Grieving is healthy. It's good for you," Daroush encouraged.

"I have done some awful things recently," she confessed.

Daroush grew concerned. "You are starting to scare me, Simi. What is going on?" Simi drew in a deep breath, delicately sharing what she had been playing in.

A website, an idea that at the time seemed like a good one. Few photos, intro paragraph, interests. It was too easy. She purposefully used the word intimacy as she explained that it wasn't always expected—except when it was. She couldn't look at him as she spoke; she could hardly hear the words herself. She didn't expect her brother to understand her guilt and her shame, but she had to start being honest to rescue herself before she was in too deep.

"Simi! What the hell are you thinking with this? Are you kidding me?" She kept her eyes low. "He didn't want this for you. Why would you do this? Was that guy one of them? He followed you to Vegas?" Daroush squeezed his fists. "I will kill him; I will kill all of them." Daroush was furious with her.

"Please, Daroush, calm down." Simi pleaded, covering her hands over his fists.

"I wouldn't have left you alone with him! You don't do something like this," he shouted. "Not my sister! Did he hurt you last night?" Daroush demanded to know. "I will kill him–he is dead."

"Daroush, please, you have to listen to me," Simi pleaded; his reaction was more intense than she had expected. "I am sorry." She reached for him, bringing him back to sit with her.

"No, no, I am calling Maman, and you are coming back to Paris with me. You aren't well here alone and no, get your things, Simi. We are leaving tomorrow." Daroush sounded angry, but he was terrified. His sister was the epitome of strength. He didn't know anyone stronger than her.

"Daroush, I am not leaving," Simi stated.

"Like hell, you aren't. Roman took care of you, I trusted him, and Maman trusted him. He protected you. You were safe." When Simi had met Roman, Daroush thought the age difference was a bit awkward, but when he saw how much Roman loved his sister, nothing else mattered. Simi had finally found happiness when their world had so much darkness. Daroush hurt for his sister. Out of anything she could have told him, this was not even a consideration. "Simi, you aren't safe. You will be hurt. I will not lose you too!" Daroush squeezed her hands tightly. He was overwhelmed, but it was time for him to be strong for her. "Simi, I am not going to let anything happen to you. I just don't know what has happened to you." He shook his head in disbelief.

"I don't know, but I will fix it. I promise you I will fix it." She held her brother close to her. "I am sorry, I am sorry for so much, but I am sorry I put this on you," she whispered. "I want to get better, and I will."

"You have to come home with me," Daroush demanded. "I am your brother; you have to listen." Simi chuckled as she kissed the top of his head.

"There is nothing for me in Paris, Daroush. You know this. I am just a little broken right now, but I have someone here who can help me." Daroush's eyes were red, fighting back tears.

"I am not leaving you here. We will make arrangements and bring Maman back to the states to be here with you," he decided.

"Daroush, love, neither of you want that." Simi softened his brow with a caress of her thumb.

"Simi, you had a man follow you. You are not safe." Daroush

continued to convince her.

"I promise he has nothing to do with what I told you. He has no idea about what I told you, and frankly, if I see him again, I doubt he will want anything to do with me," Simi announced. "This isn't about him, though, Daroush, I am going to see Jane tomorrow, I will take myself off of the website. I am going to get better." She reached for his hands. "I just," Simi swallowed hard, holding back tears. "I just don't want you to think less of me."

"Abji, I do not presume to know what pain you feel from losing Roman or Momma. I know that broken hearts cause people in our family to do questionable things." Daroush gently nudged Simi. "Momma always said you were like Baba, Maman agrees too."

Simi stayed quiet, relieved to be honest with Daroush finally, and stunned with the realization she had another line item to go over with Jane tomorrow. Like Father like daughter, it seemed.

Chapter 10

The familiar room was dimly lit, and more calming aromatics of lavender filled the air. Simi sat diagonally across from Jane. As any good therapist, when Simi was ready, Jane was there for her. The silence was thick. It was not new for Jane to wait Simi out, but Simi didn't know where to begin. She kept her eyes down. Daroush was in the waiting room. Simi wasn't ready to speak. It was the first time Jane would prompt the discussion.

"Can you start from the beginning?" Jane gently urged.

Simi looked up, her eyes full of tears, her teeth chattering; she inhaled a few breaths quickly and nodded.

"You can cry, Simi. There is no shame in crying. This is therapy; this can feel good." Jane pulled a box of Kleenex from her side table and set it in front of Simi.

"Jane." Simi couldn't stop shaking her legs. "I don't want to be Persia anymore; I don't want to be Simi without Roman. I am scared. I don't know what to do." Simi quickly reached for the Kleenex bringing it in front of her mouth, attempting to suppress her cries.

"Simi, take some breaths," Jane soothingly encouraged. "You are safe here, Simi. Have you been hurt?" Simi finally grabbed her gaze, looking at Jane, her thick bright red glasses matched her pleather belt, and her pixie haircut was styled. She leaned forward, dropping her journal on the glass table between them. "If you have been hurt by one of those men, you need to tell me."

Simi shook her head no and said barely above a whisper, "I

wasn't hurt." Jane exhaled, nodding to Simi, wanting her to continue. "I am here because I finally broke. Yesterday, I had a complete breakdown after I betrayed him. I hurt Roman."

"Simi. "Jane paused. "Roman is dead." Tears rushed to her eyes. She breathed out slowly. Jane had to be direct with her. She had to push her, Simi needed this, but it never was easy. "You can't betray someone who isn't here anymore."

Simi began explaining why she wanted to take Daroush to Vegas, reminding Jane of who Clark was and how he was also there. Jane listened as Simi retold the trip's events, processing what Simi was sharing.

"Okay, Simi, I am not quite able to understand how you feel now that you have betrayed Roman when you have been sexually active in the past."

"It wasn't me with them, Jane. I explained this to you. I was myself with Clark. I let him in. That is how I betrayed Roman."

"I am sorry, Simi. It was always you. If this is truly what has gotten you to the point of self-realization, then you need to understand that this betrayal you feel like you did goes beyond one night with Clark."

"Don't say that to me, Jane." Simi quivered. "Don't tell me that, please." Simi whimpered.

"Simi, can you tell me how we have gotten here, why you started with this website and taking on these dinner dates?"

"There is a Rumi poem. It loosely states that pain can be the cure. When my mother got sick, she often recited it to me. When Roman died, I thought seeking it out would end this misery of loss I seem to find myself in constantly." Simi shared. "Simi and loss go hand in hand, so Persia, she is sexy, she is charming, and she doesn't care about loss because she doesn't—didn't—feel."

"She was always you. You are feeling everything, aren't you?" Jane asked. "We are going to have to start over again. You and I will have to start from the beginning and talk through your grief of your mother and Roman. I am not a poetic scholar, but you should know that art is a form of interpretation, and I am afraid, Simi, you went in the wrong direction with this poem."

"I do not want to experience loss anymore, Jane."

"Loss is life, Simi. It is a part of life for all of us. Some experience it more than others, but we all go through it."

"Jane, I took myself off the website." Simi looked back down. "I saw what I was doing in his eyes; when he saw me, he was frightened. I love my baby brother, and I have hurt him so much." Simi tried to hold back her tears.

"He is outside waiting?" Simi nodded, and Jane looked back at the door. "Do you want me to bring him in?"

"No!" Simi's eyes widened in horror. "No, I have already scared him too much. I told him the truth about everything." Simi regulated her breathing. "I have to get his trust back, and I have to make sure he isn't worried about me."

"Your brother is allowed to be there for you. You both lost your Mom. You can find comfort in each other. He might be the best person for you to confide in." Jane waved her hand. "Outside of me, of course. Have you talked to him about your mother's death?"

"No."

Jane looked at her curiously. "Have you talked to anyone about your mother's death? Roman?"

"Roman, he didn't like talking about things that happened in the past. So it was mentioned, but I never shared with him much." Simi frowned, "Honestly, I spoke about it more with Clark the other night than I think I shared with Roman."

"How did it come up?" Simi rolled up her sleeve, pushed her watch down, and showed Jane the ruby bracelet Clark had given. She shared the backstory of her name and its meaning.

"The bracelet opened the door to start talking about her."

"How did talking about it with Clark make you feel, Simi?"

"Safe," she quickly answered.

Jane nodded; she removed her glasses and set them on the table in front of her.

"You know that you haven't betrayed Roman; you do understand that?" Jane questioned. Simi stayed quiet. "Okay, we can work on that too." Jane smiled tightly, attempting to lighten the mood.

Jane began informing Simi that it was time for her to go home to Houston, to the home she shared with Roman. It was time for her to grieve his death. Simi had to come out of hiding and join society again. The isolation had built up Simi's ability to justify her delusion that she could be two different people in the same body. Jane had hoped Simi would agree to let her brother join her but insisted that it was better for her to do this alone and that she would lean on Daroush when she returned to Paris.

"We are going to go to twice-a-week virtual sessions in the morning," Jane continued to explain, handing Simi additional paperwork to authorize. Simi signed the papers and handed them back to Jane.

"I feel bad about Clark," Simi shared. "I liked him, and I did feel good with him." Simi pressed her lips tightly together.

"I would strongly suggest focusing on you and getting home this week. We can revisit the topic of Clark soon," Jane offered. "I promise I won't forget him." She smiled. "I know you won't let me either." Jane picked up her notebook. "Lastly, Simi, we are going to begin working on you," Jane informed her. "Find out what Simi wants, and how she intends to live out her future. Will you go home to Houston and stay there? Maybe come back to Chicago—try something new. Perhaps you want to go back to Paris?" Simi began to feel uncomfortable thinking of all the options available to her. "In your grieving, there is going to be planning and goals. Healthy achievements to keep track of to ensure that while you are in my care, you will not dive into another date night scenario," Jane stated. "Oh and think about going sober for a while too."

"Wow." Simi laughed. "It sounds like you are about to put me through Therapy Bootcamp."

"Call it what you want. Trauma needs to be addressed in your life, and healing needs to be done. You have too much potential to let yourself drift off in the wind."

Jane couldn't say it out loud, but there was a connection to Simi that hit close to home. She truly cared about Simi and wanted to help her.

Simi felt her heart ache. Jane spoke to her as her therapist, but her words penetrated a maternal authority she hadn't heard in years. Simi wasn't naive to think she was special, but even if it was the same treatment, she gave all her clients, to Simi, this moment of hearing those words was enough to ignite a drive to succeed. To make Jane proud of her.

"Home, huh?" Simi asked.

"Yeah, it's time for you to go home," Jane answered reassuringly.

"I don't even know where to start."

"Let's book your ticket. Then we can call . . ."Jane flipped back to the beginning of her journal, searching for a name Simi wasn't ready to bring back to her lips. "Jackie? She can make sure the house is set up for you. Then"—Jane closed the journal looking toward Simi— "when you are settled, you can call Gregory." A cold rush flew through Simi's body. Instantly, her eyes began to water. Simi was growing exhausted with how quickly she was rushing to tears.

"If I make that call, Jane, it's all real," Simi struggled to say. "If I see Gregory, it all happened." Sorrow hit hard this time. Simi couldn't hold it in. She leaned and covered her hands with her face. Upon hearing the name Gregory again, all the memories, all their memories of laughter, of life together with Roman, rushed back to her mind. She sat in her chair, arms crossed, holding herself tightly as she quietly cried into her hands. Jane waited, not moving from her seat, letting Simi have the privacy of her cry. When Simi finally looked up. Jane took in her breath and said the words.

"Simi, it did happen. Roman is dead." Simi's jaw clenched tightly; she held her breath, nodding excessively, accepting and understanding. Simi continued to let her tears fall freely as the rest of her session was in empathetic silence.

Daroush was scrolling on his phone as she joined him in the waiting area.

"How are you feeling?" he asked, grabbing his coat from the chair next to him. "Your session is over already?"

"It's just the beginning." Simi reached for the door turning back to Daroush. "You need to fly home." Before Daroush could protest. "I won't be able to heal worrying about the effect I am having on you." She reached for his hand. "Go home, you can call every day, but you need to go back to your life."

"You are not safe here alone," Daroush stated.

"I am not alone, and I will stay safe." Simi looked at the door that separated the waiting room from Jane's office. "Jane said I needed to go home. Back to Houston," Simi shared. "She is right; I need to go home." Simi grabbed Daroush's cheeks with her hands. "I am done, I won't ever do something like that again. I promise you."

Returning to the hotel, Daroush began packing. Simi secluded herself in her bedroom, processing her session with Jane. Her heart was heavy, in true acknowledgment of mourning. Laying on her bed, she stared at the ceiling; she closed her eyes. Her mind was unclear as to what sadness she was feeling now. Her thoughts drifted to Clark. She felt awful; she could only imagine his reaction, his confusion. This wasn't a time for her to be involved with anyone else but herself. Jane was right, and it was only now that Simi saw the work, she had to do to obtain some semblance of her life back.

There was a soft knock on the wall. Daroush was holding a stack of books in his hand.

"I brought these for you. I know how much comfort they brought Momma." Daroush sat next to Simi on her bed. Simi recognized the poetry books their mother had memorized. She would read to them constantly. Rumi, Hafez and Shirazi to name a few.

"Do you miss her?" Simi asked softly. Daroush was holding back his own emotions. She held her hand over his. "Thank you for bringing these." Simi saw the time. "You hungry?"

"Sure." Daroush noticed her bracelet. "When did you get this? It is really pretty."

"Clark got it for me," Simi shared.

"You think you will see him again?" Daroush asked.

"I can't focus on that now. I gotta heal." Simi shrugged her shoulders.

"You will rise from those ashes, Simi, then maybe"—he pointed to the bracelet— "you will be ready to see him again."

"You don't even know him." Simi looked at him curiously.

"I saw him before he got to the suite. I heard him talking to himself through the keyhole, I saw him shuffle his steps a bit."

"So?"

"Men only act like that when they really like someone." Daroush smiled. "Roman always looked like a puppy around you. That guy did too." Daroush chuckled. "Bigger puppy, though." Daroush sat up from the bed. "Maybe we go to Prime? I need to see Patrick before I leave."

"Why?"

"Don't frown like that. You didn't give me much choice, I had to make sure someone watched out for you."

"He was one of Roman's favorite GMs," Simi commented.

"I am sure he would like that reflected financially somehow. It probably was a stressful few months —no, I am sure it was a stressful few months you put him through." Daroush chuckled.

"I hear you, Daroush. Get dressed. I will knock on your door when I am ready.".

Daroush left her room as she looked down at the books. Her mother's fingertips always held one of them. She brought them close to her and inhaled. The pages were delicate, and the fragrance of rosewater still lingered. She set them to the side and began sitting in the feeling. Sitting in the sadness and reality that a part of herself was gone, part of her life was gone.

She pulled herself off the bed, walking toward the room's closet. Feeling around for a bag on the top shelf, she felt the familiar strap and pulled it down. Unzipping the black pouch open, she looked down at her keys. Roman's keys, their keys. It was time to go home.

****

When Clark had gotten a hold of Patrick, Patrick insisted on talking to him in person. Clark was embarrassed, angry, and vulnerable. Emotions were flooding him, and he didn't like it. After landing back in Chicago, Clark immediately cabbed to Prime. It was near closing time when Clark reached the bar. Bradley greeted him when he arrived, pouring a generous glass of whiskey for him.

"She went home." Patrick pulled up a seat next to Clark. Bradley nodded and went back to closing up for the night.

Patrick knew the best thing for Clark to do was to let her go. He would not tell Clark that she was still down the street. He would not tell him that if he had arrived here a few hours earlier, their paths would have crossed, and Patrick would have been delighted to no longer be a part of this situation. Still out of respect for Simi, he did what he thought was best.

"So, left for Paris?"

"It's possible." Bradley brought over straight pours for Patrick, himself, and Clark. "Do you know the name Roman Charles?" Patrick continued. "Well, he owned all of this. The entire hospitality group. In the past few years, he took more of a chairman role, but was still pretty present in most things."

"You are speaking of him in the past tense," Clark noted.

"Heart attack almost a year ago. Right out there." Patrick motioned to the lobby. It came as quite a shock—he was in good health. Always at the hotel gym, never overindulged. He didn't look his age at all. He had been here just the night before celebrating our anniversary, and she was with him. I would guess at least five years together. It was awful. It happened so quickly." Patrick paused for a moment, reflecting on that night. "After he passed, she never left."

"Roman Charles," Clark repeated.

Everything began clicking for Clark. It all made sense, and there was indeed more to her story, from her tabs, the watch, and even to her sadness. The border of her puzzle had been solved. Now he wondered why did she flee Vegas? What happened that morning when she woke up? What did he do to not even receive a way to contact her? Did she regret everything between them?

"I appreciate you telling me all this." Clark leaned back.

"I believe I tried to divert you the first night you asked me about her," Patrick insisted. "I know that blonde though, if you are interested."

Clark chuckled. "You might have." Clark finished his drink and reached for the straight pour next to his hand.

"Weren't they getting married too?" Bradley spoke up. Patrick grimaced over to him. "You were going to be there?"

Clark looked curiously to Patrick, glaring over to Bradley before he spoke. "I think there is a case in the back that can be brought to the bar? Can you check on that?" Bradley, realizing his mistake, nodded, leaving Patrick alone with Clark. "Yes, there was supposed to be a wedding, and I was invited. The story goes, Simi isn't a storybook kind of girl." Patrick gestured, "So it took a bit of convincing to get her to walk down the aisle; it was supposed to be in Paris on New Year's Eve, so about six weeks after he died," Patrick continued.

"That is . . ."Clark felt gutted. "That is awful." Clark needed more than just these pours to get him through the rest of the night. "I appreciate all this. I honestly, like, from the bottom of my heart am glad she is safe."

"You sure you are, okay?" Patrick insisted.

"Yeah, it was fun—I have too much coming up for me to get distracted with anything else."

"That's right. Adam was in here with . . ." Patrick furrowed his brows. "I always forget that guy's name."

"Bad tipper," Bradley commented as he walked by.

"Anyway, it sounds like you guys are close to starting something again. That's great!"

"Yeah, still a work in progress." Clark finished the rest of his drink. He stood up, placing the glass back on the marble bar. "Anyway, thanks, thank you, guys. I will be around."

Clark took his time walking home, still reeling from all that was shared with him. There was a knot in his stomach. He realized that he might never see Simi again. It was an empty feeling. She could avoid Chicago altogether. She didn't live here. When Clark finally got home, he went into his office and grabbed his laptop. Pulling up Google, Clark searched for Roman Charles.

Clark guessed that Roman had almost 20 years on her. Though, in Clark's opinion, you couldn't tell. Clark continued to read about how Roman Charles had hit luck with wins on Wall Street before leaving New York and retiring in Texas. He then began investing in hospitality and art ventures local to Texas and New York, expanding his reach slowly throughout the US.

It was in Roman's social media, undoubtedly run by Simi, that he found her. She was by his side professionally in certain events and then beautifully hung on his arm at social events. Everything was coming together. His logic had not failed him; he had known there was more complexity to her. Clark closed his laptop. Stretching back onto his couch, arms straight over his head, he contemplated what to do next.

Nothing immediately came to mind.

Clark lifted himself off the couch and walked to his window. He looked out to his view of Grant Park, illuminated with light.

It could have been nice, he thought to himself, withdrawing from the view of the city, back into the darkness of his apartment.

Chapter 11

Simi was standing on her deck looking out at the field of flowers. August was the most difficult month in Texas. Humidity smothered the state. She pulled her hair back, swiftly securing it into a messy bun. She had finished her morning call with Jane and needed to take a walk. Ten months had passed since Roman died. She stepped down the wooden stairs that led to a stone pathway to the back acres. She walked this path with Roman thousands of times; it was often used as an outlet to recap his day or talk through ideas. Her walk today was silent, leaving only the sounds of nature to keep her company. Simi took her time as she began collecting an assortment of fresh flowers to bring back inside.

She scuffed her feet against the stone path, softly humming until her eyes caught a beautiful selection of flowers. Kneeling, she began sorting through the mallows scattered amongst the poppies; she plucked the brightest ones as she adjusted to sit slightly off the path in the field. She had asked Roman to bring a bench out here, but he insisted on leaving it as natural as it was. They shared intimate moments amongst the flowers, moments that made her heart swell. She had taken for granted how beautiful and special this area was to them. She held the flowers in her hands, adjusting the stems to make a pleasing arrangement. Securing the base of stems together with a thread of twine, she set the bouquet to the side and began pulling for another assortment. A memory brought a smile to her lips. Roman would playfully limit her to only gathering one bouquet at a time. A sudden revelation came to her. She stood up and walked down a little further, where a group of boulders gathered. She pressed her fingers over her lips, hiding a blush from the rest of her memory. It was here that Simi would use her feminine wiles to convince Roman to let her pluck all the flowers she wanted.

She sat on the largest rock, adjusting herself comfortably. Simi thought back on the conversation with Jane this morning. Jane reviewed the stages of grief Simi had been through and where she was now. Jane informed her that in the past few sessions, Simi had shown signs of graduating toward acceptance.

The final step.

Simi brought her knees up to her chest. The past few months had been hard; when she returned to Houston, the depression was hard to push through, but she did it. Jane worked with Simi to create a schedule to stay on track. It included wake-up times, mealtimes, and activities, yoga, and Simi's latest language course. It was simply all Simi had the energy for. Simi poked fun at Jane's Therapy Bootcamp, but today, sitting in the boulders amongst the flowers, she smiled with her heart at the memories she shared with Roman; she had to give Jane's method credit. It was working.

Simi walked back over to the field of flowers, finishing her second bouquet; she tied both bundles of flowers together as she made her way back to the house. She kept her eye on the outdoor dining table under the deck's pergola. Her next memory was more difficult to replay. Coming up to the table, she pulled out a chair. She rested the flowers down and looked toward the head of the table where Roman had sat.

"You know this will stain the furniture." She moved Roman's lemonade glass and placed a coaster underneath. Roman had just finished a call as she brought dinner to the table. She walked along the deck, lighting citronella candles, bringing one back to the table. She looked up to see Roman watching her. He reached his hand out.

"Come sit with me."

"Dinner will get cold," Simi countered.

"Simi, please." She hesitated for a moment before coming to join him. She went to the sofa, moved his laptop and phone from the seat, and joined comfortably next to him. His arms wrapped around her, pulling her in closer. He rested his chin on her head. *"We have to go up to Chicago tomorrow."*

"I know."

"I'd like to spend a bit longer than originally planned there." She pushed back and turned toward him.

"Is everything all right?" His eyes stayed on the sunset. She caressed his cheek. She noticed his mood had become more somber.

"Of course, love, I just was thinking about snow."

"Snow?" She laughed. *"You hate the cold."*

"I think I am starting to miss it."

"Well, we don't need to go to Chicago for snow. Oooh, what about if we finally went back to Zurich and played in Verbier for a bit?" Simi planned. *"We could stop and visit with Maman and Daroush? It has been so long since I've been back in Paris too."* Roman kissed her hand.

"What did you make for dinner?" Roman asked.

"Grilled white fish and dill rice, nothing too fancy." Roman's phone began to vibrate. *"It is dinner time."* She pulled him up from his seat, bringing him to her. She softly kissed him. *"Whatever that is can wait."* She brought him to the table, he took a seat, and she finished serving.

He kept his gaze on her as she went to the outdoor refrigerator and pulled out a bottle of chilled white wine. Bringing it to the table, she poured two glasses for them before setting the bottle in the chiller off of the side. She took her seat beside him, and he reached for her hand.

"You take such good care of me." Simi smiled.

"You make it easy to want to." He brought her hand to his lips. He suddenly inhaled very sharply. Roman began to cough; she reached for the glass of water and brought it to him, assisting him as he drank from it. When he was done, he rested his head back in the chair. She brought a cloth napkin to his lips, searching his eyes.

"I am fine. Just hot." He waved his hands at her. Simi still stood over him feeling his face. He was flushed and clammy. *"You are making too much of a fuss. Sit, sit, I am fine."* Simi frowned at his sudden dismissal.

"After Chicago, we will come home, and you are going to the doctor."

Roman regained his composure, nodding sarcastically.

"Yes, yes, but then we are off to Verbier." Roman began eating. "Then we go to Paris. I think I would like to do some time there." Simi smiled. "It would be nice to be scowled at by Maman again," Roman teased.

"She loves you—she didn't like Houston; she just worries about me."

"Cause we aren't married." Simi avoided his gaze. "Does she know why we aren't married?"

"The food is going to get cold." Simi sighed.

"I will ask you every day until you say yes."

"You have." Simi smiled. "It's silly. There is no reason for it. We are happy as we are." Simi shook her arm. "I wear your watch. You own me. It's done."

"What if I want to marry you?" Roman challenged. He reached for her hand, kissing the inside of her palm. "What if I want to see you in a beautiful white dress and confess my love in front of our friends and family?"

"You have no family."

"I have yours."

"Roman, why are you bringing this up now?" Simi pulled her hand back.

"I want you to reconsider. I want you to be my wife."

"I am—I proclaim to you that I am your wife." Simi smiled. "Tell me where to sign."

"Marry me, wear the white dress, and marry me." His voice was low; Simi noticed an urgency in it. Biting at her lips, she sighed.

"If I say yes—"

"In Paris." Roman quickly interjected. "Next month, we will go see the family, a small ceremony. It's enough time for whom I want to come to arrange everything."

"Roman, it sounds like this is already done." Simi knew him all too well.

"It is. I just needed you to say yes." Roman pushed his chair back and reached for her, pulling her up from her seat. "Simi joon . . ." He reached down for his watch and unclasped it from her wrist. Kneeling in front of her. He looked up with a satisfied grin.

"I would just like to stay—"

"Simi, don't ruin this moment." Roman reached back for her wrist. "Marry me." Roman clasped the watch back around her wrist and stood up. Simi thought he was ridiculous and couldn't help but smile at his antics. "Marry me," Roman whispered, kissing softly on her forehead.

"Yes." Simi finally answered.

The doorbell brought Simi back from memory. She inhaled deeply, acknowledging the emotion that came with the memory. She wiped her eyes and pushed back from the chair. Her heart still heavy, she quickly shifted her focus and regained her composure before going to greet her visitor.

"Simi," Gregory said, taking off his sunglasses. "Look at you. Come here." Simi's jaw tightened as she accepted his hug. He was close to Roman's age and just as tall as he was. Gregory had usually carried more weight than Roman, but Simi could see that was gone. He was dressed for travel in light khakis and a blue shirt with a blazer. He pulled her back. "Still stunning." Simi smiled, stepping aside to let him in.

"I am sorry to make you come down here." Gregory set his bag down by the chair and removed his blazer. Simi took it to hang in the front closet. "I know you were never a fan of Houston."

"It is just too hot here for me," Gregory lamented. "I always felt like Roman had escaped here, so he didn't have to compete with me daily." He flashed a perfectly white veneer smile.

"Speaking of you, you look great." Simi complimented. "Can I get you anything?"

"Water with lemon is fine." He followed her into the great room, where she entered the kitchen. He took a seat and waited for Simi. "When Roman," he spoke loudly so she could hear. "When Roman died, it scared me. I changed everything about my diet and am in the gym as much as possible. Gayle has even noticed an improvement in the bedroom." Simi chuckled as she brought two glasses of water to the coffee table. "Still wearing his watch." Simi dangled it from her wrist.

"It's mine forever." She smiled. "Please extend my apologies to

Gayle. I know she reached out, but I wasn't ready," Simi shared.

"I know." He patted her knee. "I understand how you have been handling this. I get it. Gayle, she will come around." Gregory took a drink of his water.

"I have to thank you for working with Jackie and handling everything. I know I let everything slip, but frankly," Simi waved her hand. "Jackie has been managing Roman's life longer than I knew him."

"There is no need for any more apologies, Simi," Gregory insisted. "Everything is okay, I promise you. Now, there are a bunch of things you need to sign. I was Roman's legal executor so that I could roll everything over to you, but there is a ton of paperwork."

Simi swallowed hard, trying to keep her emotions in check. Her heart pounded loudly as Gregory continued to present her with paperwork. He explained the multiple equity ownerships Roman had in various businesses and assets, and a broad overview of all his financials—Roman's entire career wins in front of her.

Roman worked hard for what he had, though he was more for living in the present. When he did share stories of his life on Wall Street, Simi often had a hard time being able to see Roman as cutthroat as his reputation claimed him to be. Gregory handed her a notarized piece of paper from a company Roman was a board member of in New York. Gregory explained that they were asking for Roman's shares to be paid out according to his will unless there was another person in line to take his place on the board. Simi placed the letter down.

"Okay," Simi cleared her throat. "This is a lot." Simi shook her head. "I appreciate you sharing all this with me, but I just need to know what pertains to me." Gregory looked at her curiously. "I mean, I just want to ensure I know what I have spent since his passing. It shouldn't take me long to pay it all back."

When Simi began living with Roman, he took the money that she had and diversified it—she had an idea of how much she had. She also knew that she would be able to sell the house.

"Simi, this all pertains to you. What do you think I am here for?" Gregory asked.

"I don't want to be crass about it. I just need to know what his will says. What he left me, what I owe his estate."

Gregory reached around behind him handing her a copy of Roman's will. "Simi, you don't owe anything. *You own everything.*"

Simi's heart began to race, and a cold feeling rushed through her; she didn't accept the papers in front of her. Simi quickly shook her head; she felt flushed. This wasn't right. "No, he left me everything we shared. Everything he earned on his own was his," Simi explained.

"He isn't here anymore." Simi's breath became labored. "Everything he earned, he owned, is yours. Did you never talk about this?" Gregory waited.

"We did—I told him what was his was his. I always told him that."

"That is if you had separated. You never talked about what would happen in the event if he—"

"Gregory!" Simi hushed. "He wasn't supposed to die! We didn't talk about it because it wasn't supposed to happen!" Simi pushed herself off the couch and walked to the windows, looking out to the outdoor dining table, further out to the flowers, to the field, to the boulders. Tears freely fell from her eyes. She pressed her forehead against the window, holding her arms tightly around her. She couldn't comprehend what Gregory said. Why would Roman do this?

"We never married. It's not mine." Simi softly spoke as Gregory came to join her. He rested his hand on her back, hoping to soothe her. "You have to do something else with it, Gregory. This is too big for me."

Simi was the definition of poise; he never saw her waiver in emotion, similar to Roman. Seeing the tears, he knew he had to get her out of here. "Let me take you to lunch."

"I don't think having me out in public is the best thing right now." Simi wiped her eyes. "I'm sorry, Gregory this is just not what I was expecting."

"I know that now and should have realized it before I got here." Gregory sincerely spoke. "Is that Boxster still in the garage? Let's dust her off a bit and go for a drive. Can I persuade you just to take a drive?" Gregory proposed. "Isn't there an In & Out around here?"

"It's like an hour away," Simi answered.

"That's perfect. All this health stuff—I need some good junk food." Gregory chuckled. "You know you can't drive in the east coast like you can down here. What do you think?" he coaxed.

Gregory settled two bags of In & Out in front of Simi as she sat on a picnic table shaded by a large oak tree. Simi let her gaze drift to a reflection pond where kids were kicking around a soccer ball. She noticed how quiet Gregory had been. He was usually a mile a minute, very extroverted and the life of the party. One of her and Roman's private games with each other would be to see how long Gregory could talk without taking a breath.

"I remember when Roman called me and told me about you." He broke the silence. "I thought it was a phase, maybe a fun, flirty fling. Then when you guys came to New York and I met you, I understood. I never saw Roman relax. So . . ." Gregory looked up. "You took really good care of him."

Simi smiled, appreciating his words.

"Do you remember that trip? You guys came over to our place for dinner. We had a few other friends over too." Simi nodded politely, searching through her memories. "Roman wasn't always the best around new people. Gayle had invited a new couple and I didn't mention it to Roman." Simi grinned at his truthful statement. "I don't remember the exchange exactly, but Roman didn't like something they had said, and you remember how direct he can be."

"Oh, yes, I do." Simi finally found the memory, recalling the events with Gregory that night.

"You didn't miss a beat when the table went silent. You came right in with a cheerful diversion, something I would have done for him to alleviate the tension. You delivered it brilliantly, and as the table was laughing along, I saw you tilt your head at Roman, and the look you gave him hit my chest. You caressed his hand and drew it back into your lap." Gregory leaned back. "Simi, that's when I knew. You didn't know any of us. You didn't care who sat at the table. You were there with Roman, and that was your entire focus." Simi had given up on holding back her tears. Letting them freely fall. Gregory handed her a napkin. "Any doubt I had about you vanished immediately. I never saw anyone protect him other than me like that."

"I never cared about what he had, Gregory," Simi shared. "I am not naïve. I knew what it looked like." She said dryly. "I loved him."

"I know. I should have known today would have surprised you. This is how Roman operated." Gregory sighed heavily. "Did Roman ever tell you I was married before Gayle?"

Simi looked up to Gregory, surprised. She shook her head as Gregory chuckled. He wasn't surprised by that either. Gregory rested his elbows on the table and told Simi about his first wife. She had died in the towers on 9/11. They had only been married two years, and she was also a lawyer. Gregory removed his sunglasses, setting them off to the side. Simi captured his gaze, feeling the pain as he explained the tragedy. The feeling of being robbed. The unexplainable grief that he fell into until Gayle had come into his life, slowly bringing Gregory back from the darkness of isolation and heartbreak.

"Earlier, when I spoke about trauma—I've had my fair share too." Gregory's voice cracked in the end.

"Gregory, I am so sorry," Simi said. "I can't imagine what you went through." Simi shared.

"Yes, you can, Simi; you are in it." Gregory corrected. "From what I heard; it was very sudden with Roman?"

"It was." Simi blinked back tears. "We were getting ready to leave and return to the hotel, and it was less than five steps. Roman went limp against me; it happened so fast." Simi frowned. "I was worried about his head on the floor. I didn't know what to do. People were yelling to call 911, someone pushed me aside. When the medics came and moved him into the ambulance, they had him on oxygen, and I could see his eyes. He couldn't talk, but I felt . . ." Simi lowered her gaze, that memory in the forefront of her mind. "It's silly."

"Tell me." Gregory urged.

"Before he closed his eyes, he looked at me, and everything slowed. He was telling me he loved me." Simi sniffled, she exhaled and swallowed. She gestured as she continued. "By the time I blinked, his eyes had closed; they never opened back up." Simi swallowed. "When they took him out of the ambulance, I just knew. It was the same feeling before I lost my mother."

"What did you know?" Gregory asked.

"He was gone. The feeling washed all over me. All my breath left my body, and it was minutes before I inhaled again. I sat in the waiting room at least an hour before they let me see him before they took . . ." Simi choked back on her words. She brought her hands back to her face, hiding the sobs escaping her mouth with her palms. Gregory came to the side of the picnic table and embraced her, holding her tightly, and she returned his hug.

"Thank you for sharing that with me." Gregory smiled tightly, tears brimming from his eyes. "I don't know about you, but I could use a drink now." Both Simi and Gregory chuckled. "You are going to get through this. You will love again, too." Simi looked at him curiously. "You and Roman were loners. I get it, but Simi, you cannot mourn alone."

"I know," Simi admitted. "I am working with someone, and my brother calls every day, and look, I finally called you back, and here we are, crying in the middle of this park," Simi smirked. "You coming here was nice. I have been scared to see you."

"Same," Gregory confessed. "I knew seeing you without Roman would make it real."

Simi nodded, truly understanding the meaning of those words. It was real, Roman was gone, and all that remained was the beginning of a closer friendship between them.

When they got home, Gregory went to Roman's office, where the urn was placed in the middle of his desk. While Simi had not yet ventured into that space, she invited Gregory to have his moment with his friend. Simi waited for Gregory outside with two glasses of white wine.

"Thank you for that." Gregory joined her outside. Simi handed a glass over to him as he sat in the armchair next to her. "I take it you haven't gone in there yet?" Simi shook her head. "I understand."

"Can I ask how long it took before you felt normal again? After your first wife?" Simi looked over to Gregory. His eyes were red; he was coming down from a moment heavy in emotion. He sipped from his glass.

"I don't know if I ever did. I think I more or less evolved into another version of myself," Gregory admitted. "Simi, there is no guidebook for moving on after death. I did what was best for me. I encourage you to do the same." Gregory leaned closer to Simi. "This place is a version of who you were. You have been given an amazing blessing. The world is yours; Roman would not want you here living in the ghost-like shell of a past life. You know that."

Simi knew Gregory was right. Figuring out her next steps was going to be a daunting task, but she felt much more capable than she did a few months ago.

"We will have to sign a few things before I go. How were you liking Chicago?" Gregory walked along the deck railing turning back to Simi, still seated.

"I mean, I won't lie. I spent months in that room. I met with Jane, a therapist I found when I realized I needed one, as you said. I have been a bit of a ghost in a shell of a life."

"I could see you in Chicago. Actually," Gregory said, "There is a building we both bought in at a pre-build price to flip. It's done now, and one of the things I wanted to talk to you about. If you wanted to see it—"

"Are you going to sell yours?" Simi asked.

"More than likely—but that doesn't mean you have to. Think about it. Maybe Chicago is the next evolution of Simi?" Gregory emphasized.

Gregory walked inside, with Simi following. At the coffee table, he lifted the highlighted pages, and Simi signed her name in the appropriate spaces. No words were exchanged between them as she signed page after page. Emotions began to well up inside Simi again; every stroke of her pen was a confirmation of her new reality. She clenched her jaw tightly as she signed, attempting to spare Gregory another round of emotional wailing.

"Last one, Simi," Gregory said hardly above a whisper. She signed the final page and gripped the pen in her hand tightly. "You are going to answer all my phone calls now, right?"

"Every single one." Simi nodded. "I will reach out to Gayle as well."

"Thank you," he echoed with relief. "She does miss you." He began putting the paperwork in his folders, sliding them back into his bag. "Let's meet soon in Chicago to check out the property?"

Simi immediately thought of Clark. She had been resilient in not reaching out after finding his profiles through social media platforms. She was unsure of where Jane would stand with the idea of her coming back to Chicago but nodded in agreement with Gregory.

"Thank you for today, Simi."

"I should be thanking you. I realize I needed this." Simi and Gregory embraced each other in a comforting hug. She exhaled as Gregory gave her an extra squeeze of reassurance.

"I will touch base with you soon. Again, no pressure on anything, but think about what you want to do now." Gregory kissed her on the cheek.

Simi slowly closed the door in front of her. She took a deep breath. A day of revelations and mourning. She hadn't been prepared for all that was going to be revealed. There was so much she had to sit with. To think about and plan out. She walked out of the foyer and into the living room. She leaned against the wall, looking around the space, replaying all the words exchanged and all the emotions shared. Her heart was heavy as she was coming to terms with everything.

She walked back to the windows and stared out at the field of flowers.

"So, what do you want to do now?" Simi softly said to herself, thinking of Chicago. Thinking of Clark. Gregory had found support in his mourning that had turned into something beautiful. Should she be so lucky to have met someone she could lean on as she built herself back up again?

Chapter 12

The sun rudely beamed over Clark's eyes before opening them. He inhaled deeply, turning over on his bed. A warm body next to him snuggled closer as he lifted his head up, adjusting his face above her hair. He gently scooted off the bed, trying not to disturb her. He tucked the covers back and quietly headed to his bedroom closet.

Shortly after Vegas, Adam suggested reaching out to Rachel. A sorority sister of Amanda's whom Clark had shared a few dances with at their wedding. Bruting in Chicago— the average summer lasted a slim 93 days—didn't seem ideal as Clark knew what the rest of the year looked like. Taking Adam's advice, he reached out to Rachel, and he began seeing her frequently.

Standing in the closet, he looked around for his gym bag. He hadn't anticipated her spending the night, but he didn't really ask her to leave. Clark decided to change and shower at the gym, sneaking out of his own apartment. In the elevator, he sent her a text.

Late to a meeting! Sorry I couldn't make you breakfast. Next time for sure.

It had been a busy summer for Clark. Adam secured funding, they leased out a floor at the Merchandise Mart, and began setting things up for Cottage Growth. Clark was happy that his former retired executive team had been itching to come back to work. He was motivated, and everyone eagerly supported his idea and wanted to work with him again. As difficult as he perceived himself to be, he must have done something right.

Cottage Growth currently housed four small companies and

six individual entrepreneurs, and a rotation of ten Chicago Public School interns. It was the highlight of his week when he would pass out their paychecks, reminding them to open a bank account. He only had two students left that hadn't done so, and he scheduled a time to take them. He wanted to ingrain financial acumen as early as he could with his interns. Word began spreading around what CG was, and the response for pitches tripled every week. He wanted to say yes to as many deserving candidates as possible, but he had to keep current clients on track and ensure their success before bringing more on board. This was the momentum that he needed to stay focused and not drift back to memories that caused him to retreat into a world of fantasy. A fantasy where Simi hadn't ghosted after Vegas.

Clark had removed his Instagram app from his phone after discovering Simi's page. One night during a weak moment, he looked up Roman's profile just to see her, and on one of the photos found a tag. Finding her page dated back to the beginning of Instagram, where people mainly took photos of inane objects, he remembered every post. Her first photo—eating a cheeseburger outside NYU. She had become less active in her later years, with her page mainly focused on what Clark assumed had to be her years at college in New York. His favorite post was a video. Simi was at a bar surrounded by friends, having a battle of languages. He couldn't follow it all, but it seemed she had to keep up with each person's conversation in their native tongue, and if she faltered, she had to take a shot. She laughed through conversations, cringing when she had made a mistake and throwing back what he would guess was tequila. He was curious, how many languages did Simi know?

Her last post in Houston. In a field of flowers. She had a small smirk as she was looking away from the camera, her hands full of flowers he assumed she had picked around her. This image spoke to him. Clark believed this image was her true self, the small slivers that he would see come out when he could break her wall down. The hardest thing for Clark to accept was not knowing if he had been culpable. He still had her note hidden away in the drawer of his nightstand.

Kelsey, Clark and Adam's longtime assistant, came to the door of his office.

"Hey, Clark, Adam will meet you straight at Prime tonight." Kelsey leaned against the door. "Do you need help with any of this?"

"No, no, I got it." Kelsey didn't listen and stood next to Clark, looking down at what he knew was a mess to her. Half Clark's height, Kelsey was a spitfire. She held her own flawlessly against Clark. He never had to worry about hurting her feelings; she was tough, and Clark was sure she would beat him in a fight. Pulling her blonde hair back into a tight ponytail, she moved Clark out of the way. It only took her moments to reorganize the paperwork to get Clark through the next few hours.

"That is better, thanks." Kelsey reached behind Clark and grabbed a bottle of water.

"Adam told me you guys were going to self-sponsor the holiday party. You know you can get away with not doing one this year. We are brand new, and I don't think anyone is expecting it."

"Which is why we should do it. Morale sets expectations. Bring everyone together."

"I get it. Just looking out. You will have to expect it to be in January—most of the large spaces are already booked up by August."

"That's fine. Kick off the year with a party." Clark nodded. "You coming tonight?"

"Oh no, that is all you guys." Kelsey blocked her hands up, smiling.

"I feel like I am being heavily left out of the loop with Demkov."

Kelsey removed the water cap and quickly took a drink, shaking her head. "I haven't seen the Mrs. a lot I am always eager to get home."

Clark knew Kelsey would share anything if it were a cause for concern. Clark motioned for Kelsey to take a seat as she reviewed his schedule with him over the next week, reminding Clark of press interviews and encouraging him to re-sign with their old PR firm. Clark nodded in agreement, allowing Kelsey to take the initiative to move forward. As Kelsey continued her overview of updates, Clark's phone vibrated—a few messages from Rachel, sending him reminders of what he was missing back at his apartment. He inwardly smiled as he turned his phone over, returning his attention to Kelsey.

Clark arrived at Prime later than he knew Adam preferred him to. Making his way into the restaurant, he avoided looking at the bar. No distractions. He patted Patrick's shoulder at the host stand; looking across the room, Adam waved him over. He approached the table to see a large older man sitting gleefully, his suit coat open with a graphic t-shirt in what Clark presumed to be from Eastern Europe. Demkov stood and looked Clark up and down with a satisfied grin and piercing blue eyes. His salt and pepper goatee stretched along smoke-stained teeth.

"Finally, get to meet this amazing man!" Demkov announced in this thick accent. "You do quite well hiding, leaving Adam to hustle. I admire that. Don't let them know who is in charge." This was not who Clark was expecting to sit with tonight. He looked over to Adam, who waved his hand in encouragement. "Sit, sit." Clark opened the button of his blazer and took a seat.

"I apologize it has taken me so long to meet with you, but," Clark motioned over to Adam, "we are 50/50 partnership. If anything, I work for Adam." Demkov laughed without hesitation.

"No disrespect to Adam, but you and I know that is not true." Clark stayed silent, looking over to Adam, who gestured for Clark to go along with it.

Viktor Demkov was formerly into real estate development until he shifted focus on US-based investments for his international clients. Not only was he interested in the collective Clark and Adam were creating, but he was most intrigued by the firm's integrity.

As they were seated at a large round table in the back of the restaurant, Demkov led the conversation regaling his tales of when he first came to the US, starting in New York until he found a home and better opportunity in Chicago. After the mortgage crisis, he was done with real estate and returned to Russia. He found that friends and friends of friends were eager to get their money out of Russia, and he happily brought their money back to the states, investing it as he saw fit. Demkov seemed to be keeping them happy as the number he represented was higher than what Clark would have assumed.

A server opened a bottle of wine and began to pour. Adam quickly waved his hand over his glass.

"Not drinking tonight, Adam?" Demkov questioned in his thick accent, shooting a perplexed look Clark had picked up on.

"In support of Amanda's pregnancy." Adam casually mentioned.

"That is very good of you." Demkov waved his hand, gesturing his question. "How much longer must you wait?"

"She is due in November," Adam shared. Demkov raised his glass in front of him.

"Then I wish you a son for peace of mind and pray for you should a daughter come instead." With a hearty chuckle, Demkov took a drink as Clark followed suit. Adam maintained a smile. Demkov was old-school through and through. "And you, Clark? Do you have a wife?"

"No, not yet." Clark leaned back in the chair.

This was the part that got under Clark's skin. He hated having to connect on a personal level. It should be simple, invest money, and be happy with the returns. Not happy with returns, take the money back.

"Well, why not? You are handsome enough." Demkov chortled. He sat back in his black suit coat, pulling out his phone. "I can get you a fresh girl from Russia in two weeks." He grinned.

"Actually, he has been seeing someone. It sounds like it could be it," Adam intervened. Demkov smiled and looked over to Clark.

"Yeah, its new. We will see where it goes." Clark looked over to Adam, who motioned for him to continue. "Just trying to catch up with Adam." Clark was bad at this.

"Well for men like us, it's important to find them good as mothers. You can play with the other women out there, but it's important that you find one whom you can trust to raise your kids," Demkov shared. Clark held in another laugh.

"I will keep that in mind." Clark nodded.

"I just want to say, my involvement in Cottage Growth is appreciated—"

"We should be thanking you," Adam chimed in. Demkov raised his hand.

"I have my hands in many things, but the utopian aspect of this company it tops everything. This community you are building can change so many lives and give so much opportunity. This is why I wanted to be involved," Demkov announced. "Even if you don't have the next Twitter under your roof, you never know how close it could become. Then boys"—Clark flinched at the reference— "you and I can truly retire anywhere in the world," Demkov ended.

Walking out of Prime, Demkov turned to look at both Adam and Clark and stopped before a large black SUV pulled up behind him. He removed his coat, pulling out a cigar from its case. In a swift moment, he cut and lit the cigar, taking a long inhale before turning slightly away to exhale.

"Well, boys, I had a wonderful night." Demkov clapped his hands together with the cigar fitted on the left side of his teeth. "I will see you in a few months—maybe sooner if you are interested, Clark. I expect you to work hard but also play a bit too. Adam will bring you out next time." He paused, looking up at the tower above them. "I love this place. Good pick." He chuckled to himself as he jumped into the back of his car.

As soon as Demkov turned the corner, Clark shot a look to Adam. "You just stopped telling me things altogether."

"I knew everything you thought. I knew everything you were going to think before you arrived. The fact remains we are funded and funded well," Adam defended.

"How did you even meet someone like this?" Clark and Adam began to walk.

Adam knew that if he told Clark that Evan was involved, it would be the largest betrayal in their friendship. He didn't like it, but he knew that he had to keep this close to his chest.

"I don't think you know how hard it was for me to find the money for this project, Clark. I had to find eccentric people who didn't laugh at the idea," Adam explained. "Given my current situation, I think you better get used to being a buddy to him. He likes to have a good time. I've had a night or two out with him. It can get intense."

"I don't want you putting yourself in these positions, Adam."

"Clark, I got it handled," Adam quickly snapped.

Clark tensed at Adam's reaction. "I have all the Demkov meetings, outings, whatever you want to call it from now on." Clark took

Adam's glare in stride. He knew Adam had been working on his sobriety, but how well he was doing changed by the day. Today, he was irritable, but finally able to relax now that their dinner was finished. "How is Amanda doing?"

"She is fine; things are good." Adam continued to be short.

"Are you taking the El home or a cab? We can split one." Clark continued to gauge Adam, nervous that he was struggling again.

"I'll walk to the El. I want to stretch my legs a bit."

"Adam, are you good?" Adam patted Clark on the back, and with a short nod, he began walking in the direction of the train station. Halfway down the block, Adam turned back to see that Clark was out of sight. He quickly turned the corner and headed away from the El stop.

Clark reached into his pocket and pulled out a pack of cigarettes. It was still warm; the city was still active. He thought back to Demkov and his assaulting persona. There was something familiar about Demkov that pestered Clark all night. Despite that distraction, Clark could see past this ethnic façade. There was intelligence and calculations within Demkov. He understood upward mobility and was unorthodox enough not to be intimidated by the gamble Cottage Growth possessed. Clark was so involved within CG that he didn't take the time to understand how crazy it sounded to the average investor. This was not how things worked here. It made sense that Adam had difficulty selling this idea and it made even more sense that it would take an unconventional character like Demkov to support it.

He brought the cigarette to his lips and let it hang loosely as he reached into his pockets, looking for a lighter. He turned to the side as a cab pulled up, bringing the flame to his lips; he almost burned himself when he heard her voice.

"Clark." He turned, stunned. Her expression was bright and hopeful. "Clark," Simi breathed out as she came closer to him. He stood speechless as his eyes narrowed on the man who came up behind her. "I can't believe you are here." Simi watched Clark's face transition from disbelief to a serious stare. Simi turned back. "Oh, this is Evan, he is—"

"Hey Clark." Evan cut in. "My firm is handling a property for

Simi." Evan came closer to Simi, brazenly placing his hand on her outside shoulder, bringing her closer to his side. Simi smiled politely as she sidestepped out of his reach. Evan retracted his hand flawlessly as if it was his choice, gesturing in confusion. "How do you know each other? I thought this was your first time in Chicago?" Evan looked over to Simi.

Simi had flown to Chicago earlier in the day to view the condos Roman and Gregory had purchased. She spent most of the afternoon discussing options with Gregory, still unsure what she should do. Gregory encouraged her to take her time deciding, opening the day for Evan to invite himself to show her the city, as Gregory had to return to New York. Simi accepted Evan's offer but found herself learning more about himself, not the neighborhood or the property.

"Your father finally gave you a chance, huh?" Clark smartly retorted, purposely insulting Evan. "We've met." He answered shortly.

"Clark, I . . ." Simi reached for his arm. A breath escaped her lips, and she frowned, desperately searching for the words—something to say other than his name.

"I was just dropping Simi off after our dinner. We were about to have a nightcap; would you like to join us? I have been dying to hear how CG is going, and oh, I heard about Rachel—nice," Evan emphasized, clicking his tongue.

Clark looked over to Simi, unaware of anything between them. Her eyes were hopeful until Evan said another woman's name. She quickly removed her hand from his arm and then looked away.

"Maybe next time." His gaze was still on Simi. "Good luck with your property. It was nice to see you again." The words cut his tongue as they escaped his mouth. His stomach was knotting, twisting in discomfort. He saw Simi's disappointment, but she nodded in understanding. He turned away from them and began walking away, heading home.

Simi was crushed. After what she did, what other type of response did she expect from him? He acted as cruelly as she did.

"You ready?" Evan asked, gesturing toward the bar.

"Umm, would you mind a rain check? It's been a long day." Simi noticed an obvious annoyance from Evan.

"Are you sure? It looks like you need some cheering up. I happen to be quite masterful at making women smile." Evan attempted to sway her. "Amongst other things, of course. The night is still young."

Simi smiled politely at Adam. "Thank you, no; I think that is all I need from you tonight."

"Yeah, of course; I was meeting a friend nearby anyway. Listen," he pulled out his wallet and brought out his card. "I am free all day tomorrow if you want to see anything else or maybe see the space again." Simi took the card and nodded. "Or if you want me to cheer you up. You can call anytime." Evan grinned.

Simi took a step back from Evan; she waved the card in her hand. Evan turned away to hop in the cab off the curb. As the cab pulled away, Simi stuffed the card in her pocket and looked in the direction Clark had headed.

Chapter 13

Out of all the scenarios Clark had imagined, seeing Simi with Evan was not one of them. He was enraged and confused. Simi didn't know their history; she didn't know they knew each other. She looked too happy to see him. Why! So many questions. The way she had left things, Clark would have assumed she would never want to see him again. That is not how she acted. In her eyes, there was hope, and there was . . . longing. Her smile. She wanted to see him. She could have seen him anytime she wanted! Furious at this point, he flicked the cigarette out of his hand as he trudged back home. He was going to need to calm down. He tensed up as he felt a pull on his arm. Who would try to mess with him tonight?

He turned quickly to a taken aback Simi. Clark immediately softened. "Sorry, I–"

"No, it's okay; I came up on you." Simi stepped back. "I didn't know what to say before." She frowned. "I guess I still don't know, but I . . ." Gentle thunder began to growl in the background. Simi didn't seem to notice. "Is there any way we could talk?" Simi pressed her lips together. "Would you—would you want to talk to me?" she asked unsurely.

Clark was struggling to communicate also.

"I am sorry, this is silly. I didn't mean to bother you." Simi turned to walk away.

"I'd like to talk," Clark finally managed to say. "It's really late, though– "

"Right, well, I am in town for a—" Simi interrupted.

"*Since* it's so late," Clark spoke over her, "my place is a few blocks away."

Simi thought for a moment.

"I don't want to cause a problem for you." Simi waved back at the hotel. "Umm, if you are in a relationship now or something. Maybe we should just have lunch, so I can apologize and clarify some things." Simi struggled to maintain eye contact with Clark. A penetrating sting still lingered when Evan mentioned another woman.

"Simi, if I was in a relationship, I would know better than to invite you back to my place. That is not my style." The attraction, the spark, on both sides was still vibrant, enticing, and special. She was afraid to look into his eyes—would she see the same desire she had for him? Clark reached for her hand. "We are just talking." Simi nodded, accepting his embrace as he pulled her in his direction. "It's nice to see you again." She smiled. "Let's go before it really starts to pour."

The rain started to fall as they both rushed inside. Clark greeted his doorman, who opened the elevator for them. Pressing his floor number fifty-seven, Simi viewed her reflection, wiping away the raindrops that had landed on her. She tried to temper her heartbeat. She was ready to talk to Jane about possibly reaching out. To see him today so quickly—could this be a purposeful coincidence?

"Nice building." She broke the silence in the elevator.

"It was always my favorite building in the city. Great views. I always wanted to buy here." They reached his floor, and Simi followed him to his unit. Opening the door, he invited her in. "There is a washroom to your right if you want to grab a towel." Simi smiled in appreciation and went into the powder room. Hanging his blazer up, he quickly tried to straighten up his living room, organizing papers in a stack, and picking up glasses. Clark kept his home pretty clean, but a few things would occasionally be left behind. He went to the kitchen and pulled out a wine glass and a short glass. The lightning struck again over the lake, followed by thunder.

"Wow," she breathed, "This view—it's the entire lake and park." Simi had found her way to his kitchen. She had removed her blouse and wore only a black tank top with jeans that fit her curves so well that Clark had to refocus his gaze. She walked right to his windows, taking in the view, the lights of the city muffled in the clouds in contrast to the black abyss of the water. Clark came to join her, handing her a glass of red wine.

"You have a beautiful place. It feels like you." Clark's home was designed with contemporary furniture and simple neutral colors that brightened the space. Each piece had been chosen with great consideration. This was his first home purchase, and he was proud of it. "This kitchen is amazing too. She ran her hands across the marble. Do you cook?"

"I *can* cook," he emphasized. She nodded in understanding. Clark watched as she nervously walked around his kitchen.

"Do you want to go outside? The balconies are covered, and I have heat lamps too."

"Please."

Clark guided her outside. The rain had begun to pour heavier. Simi set her glass down on the table and moved toward the railing. The wind had picked up, blowing some rain onto her. She held onto the rails and inhaled deeply.

"This is amazing." Clark was still by the table, only feet away from her. He watched the wind dance in her hair; the droplets fall on her skin, following them as they ran down her arms, across her face, and down her neck. She stood there for a few moments, eyes closed, letting the rain pulsate on her skin before she shook off a chill. Clark had now taken a seat as she turned back to him.

"So, Simi." Her time was up. She joined Clark, sitting on the other side of the small terrace table. She smiled nervously at Clark, her heartbeat still heavy and rapid. She was so happy to be sitting here with him but so nervous about how this was going to end. Perhaps, she shouldn't have followed him.

"I am so sorry for how I left things in Vegas." Simi sighed heavily. She was going to share. No more hiding behind half-truths. She was going to communicate honestly. "I had a tragic loss, I have had losses and was kind of, well, I wasn't doing well. When we met, I got swept up and confused." Simi cleared her throat. "One may say I was in a state of delusion." Slowly talking, she tried to articulate as clearly as she could. "Our night together in Vegas, though quite nice, and please don't take this the wrong way," Simi shyly laughed, "created a much-needed breakdown for me to have." Simi uncomfortably smiled. "So, thank you?" Her voice cascaded up. "I am so sorry for leading you on or being dishonest with you."

"I accept your apology." Clark smiled. "It's going to take me a minute to process the whole cause of your breakdown." Simi dropped her head, pressing her lips as she looked down at her lap.

"I said not to take it the wrong way," she insisted, hiding a blush, remembering their night. If there had not been so much baggage with Simi, she would bravely admit that night was one of the most exciting and sensual experiences she had ever had. The control Clark took over her, the anticipation and slow tease to get what he wanted out of her. All drama aside, it was a memorable night. "Were you very mad?"

"I wasn't happy, Simi." Clark inhaled, clearing his throat. "I felt hurt—yeah, that was new, and scared too? I thought maybe I had taken advantage of an already delicate situation. Which I didn't like myself for."

"Nothing I did had anything to do with you."

"I get it—obviously." Clark agreed. "I can say it now to you. During our period of nonverbal exchanges, I let myself get wrapped up in a fantasy version of you." He caught her gaze; she was intently listening to his words. Her eyes worried, he reached out to comfort her, gently pressing his hand against her arm.

"I didn't mean to—"

"I pursued you, Simi." Clark reassured. "It's on me too." Pulling his hand away, lifting his whiskey glass, he said the following into his cup before taking a sip. "I did leave my number, though; you could have said more than I am sorry." Clark chuckled as Simi's eyes widened. "That was mean. Sorry, I am trying my best not to be overly petty."

"Are you really trying your best?" Simi shot a glance; she pressed her lips together. "I couldn't reach out because, in a moment of haste, let's call it, I burned your number."

"You burned my number?" Clark chuckled. "Jesus."

"It was an intense moment of haste." Simi lowered her head, focusing on the jewelry displayed on her arm. "I found your LinkedIn profile. When the time was right, I was going to reach out."

"Is the time right now?" Clark asked, nervous about her answer.

"Honestly?" Simi returned her gaze to Clark. She softly smiled then broke her gaze from him, shaking her head. "I don't know."

Clark made no reaction. His chest throbbed; a searing source of discomfort cramped throughout his body. He nodded, settling deeper back into his seat. The rain had intensified. He wasn't ready to look over to her. Inviting her back inside could lead to him finding himself in the same position he was in Vegas. If she wasn't ready, if she wasn't healed, then what the hell was he doing? What could he do? He knew what he wanted to do.

"I should probably go."

Clark looked at Simi and dismissed her statement. "Come inside, let me pour you another glass; wait until the rain dies down a bit." Clark stood up from his seat. He waited for her to stand as she contemplated his request. Simi exhaled shortly and grabbed her glass as she stood, following Clark into his apartment toward the kitchen. Clark circled the island, bringing both bottles off to the side to where Simi stood. As she slid her glass toward Clark, her caught her arm.

"I like your bracelet." She wore his gift. Her watch was still loosely clasped on her wrist. She wore both pieces together. For Roman and for Clark? Simi looked down at her wrist, adjusting both pieces, bringing them to rest closer together.

"It was thoughtful, a meaningful gift. More than you probably realize." Simi pulled the freshly poured glass closer to her.

"I have thought a lot about what to say to you if I were to see you again."

"Yeah?" She was unsure of his comment. "Maybe I should go, Clark."

"You don't need to go; I am just thinking out loud. I would have shown up at the hotel tomorrow to talk to you."

"You would have?" Simi furrowed her eyebrows. "You were so dismissive; I wouldn't have assumed that."

"I was in shock." Clark motioned to the living room, leading her to sit with him. "Shock mixed with rage."

"Rage?" Simi grew more concerned.

"Seeing you with Evan—was a trigger." Clark rubbed his chin with the underside of his hand. "It was short-lived once he mentioned why he was with you."

"We are mostly working with Maxim."

"Yeah, that's his dad," Clark informed Simi. "Who is we?"

"Gregory—he is . . ." Simi exhaled, leaned forward, and set her wine glass on the table. She sat back and turned to face him. "Clark," she began to explain. "The tragic loss I mentioned, what happened was–"

"I know about Roman," Clark interrupted. Simi settled herself slightly away from him. "After Vegas, I talked to Patrick. He told me what had happened."

"Oh," Simi processed what he said. "What else did Patrick tell you?"

Clark was unsure what else she wanted to hear. In his hesitation, she asked, "Did he tell you about the wedding?" Clark nodded; Simi, visibly uncomfortable, leaned forward and grabbed her wine glass, taking another drink. She leaned her elbows on her thighs, her glass between her hand. "Did he tell you anything else?"

"Simi," Clark moved closer to her. He brought his hand to her back, trying to provide some comfort to her. "Whatever you think you may need to explain to me, you don't. If you are healthy and no longer a part of that, then everything is fine. You don't need to tell me anything more than that." Clark began rubbing his hand in circular motions; he could feel her heartbeat begin to slow down.

"Thank you, Clark." Simi sat up; Clark pulled his hand away. Seeing her this close, feeling her this close, he slowly adjusted in his seat, creating a smaller space between them. "Gregory is a friend, he and Roman bought condos in a building in West Loop. That is why I am here. To decide what to do with the unit," Simi explained. "Maxim is the developer."

"I gathered." Curiosity tugged at Clark. He never had this opportunity before and didn't resist the urge to ask.

"What did you think of Evan?" Simi looked unsure. "General first impressions," he elaborated.

"Um," Simi frowned, looked up to the ceiling, and scrunched her nose. "I mean, I wasn't impressed?" Simi chuckled nervously.

"He seems a bit egocentric." She shrugged. "He talked a lot, actually, he talked most of the time at dinner, but, you know, harmless. I will give him points for taking his shot."

"He hit on you?"

"I don't know if I should be offended by how surprised you are by that." Simi gestured. "What is the friction between you too? How do you know each other?"

"Silly, thinking he would be a professional." Clark leaned back into his couch. "He is a fraternity brother of Adam's. We all went to college together. We just never jived well. He is all smoke and mirrors. His egocentrism, as you mentioned, he is inauthentic, manipulative, and not trustworthy." Seeing the look on Simi's face, Clark interjected. "Don't worry; Maxim is legit. I am surprised Evan is working with his father. Maxim must have had a recent change of heart."

"What happened?"

"Evan misled some big people in Chicago about a charity thing—myself included. It didn't end well, and Maxim still is trying to manage his reputation after it."

"I liked Maxim if you were interested in that too." Clark chuckled softly at her statement. A lull fell upon them, unsure what to say next to each other. Simi motioned to the coffee table; another puzzle almost finished. "Is this your meditation?" He looked at her curiously. Simi stood up to view the puzzle better. "What you do to settle yourself?"

Clark was a bit impressed by her insightfulness. "Yeah," he gestured his hand to the stack of puzzles on the other side of the love seat; Simi walked to them, kneeling and lifting up each completed and secured puzzle. "I can thank you for all those."

"Me?" She looked back at him.

"Yes, otherwise, I might have flown to Houston." Clark tried to keep his gaze away from Simi as she walked about his apartment. He recalled what her body felt like beneath him, how soft and warm she was. Memories he thought he had buried away were very present and distracting. He adjusted in his seat as Simi returned to the couch.

"I am flattered, but I saw your press on Cottage Growth. I am sure a few of those are my fault; I wouldn't say all."

"You have been stalking me online?" Clark teased playfully.

"Observing." Simi said, "I would love to hear about it."

Clark happily updated Simi's on CG and bringing the executive team back together. Clark shared the companies under their support and his fearless, determined entrepreneurs. She listened as contently to him as she did five months ago. Clark wondered, if she hadn't fled, what would have happened. Could he have healed her quicker, brought her back into his life faster? Such a short time with her, but it meant so much to him. Clark was happy to see that he hadn't diluted himself from reality too much. His feelings for Simi hadn't faded, but had hers?

"I had a thought after you first told me about Cottage Growth."

"What was that?"

The storm was vibrant over Chicago. His last glance at his phone was a bit before midnight. He listened as Simi described her time working in art galleries, the deals artist have to make to get shown and the complicated relationship and loss of profit for the artists when working for the dealers. She had an interest in making it easier. She wanted to know if something could be created where the artist could sell their work for their true price and not have to be robbed in the process.

"Don't get me wrong, galleries do a lot of work, and there is a delicate game with them because they have to manipulate demand and exclusivity to the art world to heighten interest and increase sales," Simi continued. "But honestly, Clark, if you are new or young, you might be broke for years until you catch your break if it ever comes. It's similar to what you said about entrepreneurs starting their own businesses. The privilege gets a leg up—same in the art world." Simi pushed one last point. "Think about what art is being withheld from us because of rent and college debt." Simi's voice became impassioned. "If we don't have art, poetry, or music, we might as well be a bunch of apes," Simi boastfully ended.

"Marry me." Clark shook his head in disbelief. He came to his knees, kneeled in front of Simi, he took her hands. "Let's go—city hall, we will deal with everything else later. Just marry me, Simi." She got it. People understood his goals and his purpose for Cottage

Growth, but she got it. She felt it just like he did. He chuckled along with her laughter; Simi playfully nudged him against his knee.

"I was being serious, Clark."

So was he. He rested back on his legs and pulled his hands back on his lap. "I don't know much about the art space; I would need some time and more information from you on how this all works. Nevertheless, I am more than happy to assist you with this." Clark pushed himself up to stand. "Probably could help you better if you were local."

"Is that right?" She peered up at him; Clark eagerly nodded with a raised brow. Simi stood to join him. "I will considerate it."

"I'd love to show you around. I promise not to talk as much, but as a true Chicagoan, I must ensure you know all this city has to offer."

"I know you have your plate full." Simi tried to discourage him.

"I can take a day; it would be nice to step away and turn everything off. You would be doing me a favor. A little recharge." Simi looked away, stifling a yawn.

"It's late, I should get back to my hotel, but can I reach out tomorrow?"

"I have a guest bedroom," Clark quickly offered—grimacing at the urgency. He didn't want her to go.

"No, that's silly. I am like a five-minute cab ride away." Simi paused. "However, I think this is a good time to take your number?" She smiled.

"I will take yours." Clark entered the digits into his phone, calling to ensure it was authentic.

"Wow, with the trust?" Simi laughed, holding her phone in her hand. She rose from the couch, stretching her limbs.

"Do you blame me?" Simi couldn't. "If you don't want to stay here, I will ride back with you." Clark insisted. "It is late, Simi." He came closer to her. She was considering it.

"I know, but my stuff is there," Simi spoke softly as Clark neared. She looked up at him; his hand cupped her cheek, and her eyes closed at the sensation. His thumb traveled lightly around her cheek, barely touching her lips.

The day had been long; she was tired, so tired that she knew she wasn't thinking clearly. Her heart wanted her to say yes, but her brain, which was in constant repair mode, made her hesitant. Would Jane approve of this? In the moment, it didn't matter. Her body did.

"Maybe you are right." Clark began to retreat. "Let me get you back."

Simi grabbed his wrist at the first feeling of withdrawal, with an ask in her eyes. One she hoped he could read.

Clark read it, received it, and delivered it. He brought Simi in, deep for a kiss. She clung against him, accepting him. His arms wrapped around her, just as he remembered, just as he dreamed. He began to step backward, leading her intentionally into the guest bedroom. Their kiss was passionate and desperate. He found the bed behind his legs and brought her down with him. She straddled over him quickly, pressing her body against his, resuming their kiss with ferocity. So many guarded feelings were forgotten as they fell into the pure instinct of want and desire. She tugged on his clothes, her impatience showing through. Clark wrapped his hands around hers, slowing down the kiss, finding restraint for himself. Simi slightly pulled back, pressing her forehead against his, her eyes low, nervously chuckling.

"I'm sorry for that," she whispered, but didn't pull back. "I am probably doing everything wrong again." She sighed.

"There is nothing to be sorry about. You have done nothing wrong." He lifted her chin to meet his eyes. "I have hoped for this since I left you that night in Vegas."

"Why did you leave that morning?" Simi asked; Clark often thought back to what would have happened if he had stayed.

"I thought it was the right thing to do." Simi processed the statement and pulled herself off of Clark, sitting beside him on the bed.

"Probably was." Simi looked around the room; she saw the clock display the time.

"Stay." Clark pressed one more time. Simi agreed.

Simi took the clothes Clark had given her to refresh in the bathroom across the hall. Her body was still cooling down from their kiss. She might have gone a little too far, but it would be the farthest she would go. She worried about what Jane's opinion would be about tonight, if Jane would have thought Simi going after Clark tonight was a good idea. Returning to the room, she nervously fidgeted with her watch. Looking down, she rubbed her thumb over the face of the watch. There was no reactive emotion; a more peaceful feeling began to flow through her. She unclasped the piece and set it on the nightstand. She kept her ruby bracelet on.

"Thank you," Simi said as Clark handed her a glass of water.

"Is there anything else you need?" She smiled, looking away from Clark, "What is it?"

"Would you lay in here with me? Just until I fall asleep?" Simi stood up from the bed. "It has been a crazy day—I, um, I don't want to just stare at the ceiling for the next few hours. Would you mind?"

"In what world, Simi, do you think I would decline an invite into your bed?" Clark chuckled. "However, I will stay above the covers for my self-preservation."

Simi smiled; she pulled back the covers and settled into the bed. "Comfy."

"This is probably the second time someone has used this room." Clark sat on the bed and settled on the pillow next to Simi. He reached for the lamp.

"You can leave it on," Simi suggested. "Sorry—just ignore me." Simi fumbled nervously.

Clark took a deep breath, turning over on his side. He reached his arm over Simi and pulled her into his body. He rested his head over hers and kept his hand over hers as it was positioned on her stomach.

"Relax, Simi," Clark soothed deeply. He felt her deep breathing, and she adjusted beneath his arms.

Clark admitted he didn't know how long someone needed to grieve. That was the question he was not ready to ask. Had she moved on? Did she still pine for Roman, or was tonight a revelation that she was ready? Clark knew it was going to be a year soon. He didn't know if that was enough time for her. Did she still love Roman? Was she able to love someone else? He didn't know how long he could wait for her to finish grieving.

Yet, at this moment, listening to her soft breaths, feeling her weight against him, he felt euphoric. He stayed with her until he felt her body completely relax against his. He began to pull away when—"No," she reached out for his arm. "Don't go." Clark obliged. He lifted himself slightly to slide under the cover with Simi. She pulled him into the bed, wrapping herself back into his embrace. Simi rested her head back on his chest, holding on to him tightly as his arms were secured around her. It had been a pleasant surprise to be asked to stay, whether she consciously realized it or not. Clark continued to savor the moment.

Chapter 14

"Simurgh, can you recite it for me?" Simi walked over to her mother's bedside, her hand reaching for hers. A young Simi bravely held back her tears. "Try your best."

"I don't have your cadence. I won't do it well." Simi enclosed her hand around her mothers and sat next to her on the bed.

"Just a little so that I may sleep better. In English if you would like." Her mother pulled her to lay beside her and began to stroke her hair. Simi closed her eyes tightly, trying to ignore the sounds of the room, the incessant beeps coming from the monitors. She wanted to go home. She wanted to take her mother home. "Please." Her mother's voice whispered above her.

Simi forced a gulp down her throat and recited her mother's request, a poem by Rumi—"Even after all this time the sun never says to the earth 'you owe me'. Look what happens with a love like that, it lights up the whole sky."

"That was beautiful, Simurgh. I will always be your sun, even when I am no longer here, I will always find a way to provide you warmth and love. I promise you this."

"Simi, shh, hey . . . wake up," Clark soothed her. "You are safe." He was awoken by her sounds of whimpering in his arms. He began to rub her arm gently and turn her toward him. Simi finally opened her eyes, her dream visibly causing her distress. "You, ok?" She reset herself instead of confiding in him.

"Just a dream."

"Do you have nightmares often?" Clark was two for two, with Simi having upsetting dreams in his arms. Perhaps that is why she asked for him to stay. Maybe since Roman's passing, she struggled with sleep.

"It wasn't a nightmare, but I have active dreams." She pushed her head deeper into her pillow, looking up to the ceiling, remembering. Clark didn't press further. He reached for his phone on the nightstand. After a few moments, Simi peered at him.

"What are you doing?" She asked, peeking at his screen.

"Checking on a few things. You want some breakfast? I make really good pancakes," Clark offered.

"Yeah, but I can grab something on the way back to the hotel." Simi sat herself up on the bed. "What time is it? Don't you have to get into the office?"

Clark, still lying, looked up at Simi. "You agreed to spend the day with me. If something comes up, they know they can call."

"That's silly. I am not going to take up your day. I am here for a few days," Simi insisted.

"You don't want to spend the day with me?" Clark faked a pained expression. "I think you will like what I have planned today." He sat up from the bed. "I ordered an uber for you downstairs. I will come to get you from your hotel."

"Are you sure?"

"I am. Let me take you downstairs."

Clark favored Chicago among the best cities in the world, and he wanted Simi to understand why. There was everything he could ever need. He was fortunate to have been brought downtown and exposed to the cultural arts in his youth. His mother introduced him to art, symphonies, and opera. At first, he would usually attend as her guest out of obligation, then he started to understand what she was trying to impart to him—education across all scopes. She wanted him always to be able to carry a conversation at any level to any interest.

Clark had usually flexed his ability when attempting to woo a woman but subsequently found that after he thought he had a connection with someone interesting, they fell short. He had learned that even if a woman knew about something, it was more surface knowledge. Trying to go the extra mile and teach them was an even worse move as they either became disinterested or insulted. He quickly had to learn to temper his intelligence. People had fragile egos.

Clark never understood the act of needing to be the smartest person in the room. While he ran his company, he hired the best he could. Regardless of their age and education, if they knew the area better than Clark, they had the job—with the extra responsibility of teaching him everything they knew along the way. There was something to be said about the company leader sitting side by side desk pods of interns and associates, absorbing all he could. It was important to Clark to bring back his former environment to Cottage Growth. To evoke the same community building and hope, people across companies and fields pool together and learn from each other.

Clark met Simi in her lobby, offering her the option of his favorite doughnuts from the Donut Vault with a cup of coffee. The rain had stopped, leaving a dreary overcast above the city. A perfect backdrop, in Clark's opinion. He toured Simi down Michigan Ave before stopping outside the art museum, the first stop he had planned for the day.

There was a noticeable difference within Simi. She spoke without hesitative pauses and answered Clark's questions naturally. She was different. She was open. He was learning as much as he could— her passion for art and her impressive linguist skills captivated him.

Clark quickly realized he would have to make a day exclusively at the art museum with Simi. She excitedly walked through the halls, educating Clark on the artists' background and the paintings' secret meanings. It was an entire world he didn't know—it was the first time he had been placed in the "surface knowledge" pool. Clark stopped in front of a painting.

Resting by Antonio Mancini, depicted a beautiful woman illustrated in bed. Her long brown hair swept across the white pillowcase, matching sheets that barely covered her naked body as her eyes stared out into the distance, leaving the viewer to contemplate what she was resting from. Clark was partial to believing it was from a moment of shared passion. "You know, I've seen this before," he mused.

"The painting?" Simi asked. Clark clicked his tongue.

"No, more like the image." He gave a side smile. Looking at Simi, then back at the painting, to Simi, then back at the painting, causing Simi to envelop into a smile.

"What are you doing?" she laughed.

"May I?" With his free hand, Clark tilted her chin slightly to the side. "Now look off into the distance with elated passion." Simi rolled her eyes. "Yep, yes, this moment, though painted in 1887, has happened in the present time—in Vegas."

"Cute—but this painting is mistitled," Simi noted. "That woman is not resting. She is restless," Simi pointed out. Clark observed the painting.

"You think so?" he asked.

"Despite her outward beauty, you can see she is not able to rest. She has a story behind that gaze; there is a pain in her eyes. She is *attempting* to rest. She is not resting," she finished.

"Well, not to disagree with an expert," Clark stated, "I will continue to think she is resting after a beautiful night of passion. Gazing back at her lover, wanting him to join her back in bed."

"Such the romantic." Simi rolled her eyes at Clark.

"Maybe just a sucker for a beautiful brunette woman in bed." Clark, still focused on the painting, saw from the corner of his eye a slight smile form across Simi's face. "I hate to take you away from here, but it's a bit of a trek to where we have to head next. Are you still game?"

Clark quickly rushed Simi down Michigan Ave to the Millennium Station South Shore Line.

"Where are we going?" Simi asked, holding his hand as he hurried her through the station.

"Hyde Park, I am taking you to lunch at my favorite diner." Clark quickly stepped aside, helping Simi into the train car.

"Is that still Chicago?" Simi took an open seat.

"My dear, Hyde Park might be the best part of Chicago." Clark sat next to her.

Hopping off the 57th street station, Clark walked the familiar path to Salonica's. He held the door open for Simi and walked in behind her. He motioned for a table and followed the server down. Simi slid into the booth, removing her jacket and setting it off to the side. She pursed her lips together, amused.

"What is it?" Clark inquired.

"It sounds so awful in my head that if I say it out loud, it might make me have to apologize to my brother." Simi chuckled—shaking her head no. "It's really awful."

"Now you got to say it."

"I couldn't tell you the last time I was on public transit or in a diner. Things that were so normal to me, especially while I lived in Paris and New York." Simi shyly looked away. "LA and Houston, it's a bit isolating. You have to drive everywhere; everyone has a big house. You don't really cross class communities. I got lost in that bubble. The walk and train ride were nice—I think I have been missing the urban setting." Simi accepted the coffee from the server, and Clark did the same. "Thanks for bringing me out today."

"The day isn't done."

"I know, but you could have kept me where we were. You are bringing me to what you find special in Chicago; it's genuine. It's appreciated." Simi reached for his hand, interlocking her fingers with his. Clark's phone began to vibrate, and a flurry of text messages with Rachel's name popping on the screen caught Simi's attention. She loosened her grip and pulled her hand back to her lap. Clark internally cursed, turning his phone over.

"Simi," Clark began to explain.

Simi excused herself to the ladies' room before Clark could speak. While she was away, he turned his phone back over, answering Rachel to clear up any confusion she may be having with his sudden lack of availability.

When Simi returned to the table, her mood was noticeably different. "I thought if you need to go. We can just take some food to go; I should probably head back to my hotel too. I have an early day tomorrow."

"It's not what you think, Simi." Clark again tried to explain. "No one is rushing us through this day." He reached for her hand. "I am not in a relationship . . ." He brought her hands to his lips. "Yet."

Simi shyly smiled, feeling a blush rise to her cheeks. She relaxed immediately under his kiss, accepting his truth. "You are doing all this to be in a relationship with me?"

"I am doing all this to spend time with you. If you would like a relationship, you would need to move here."

Simi chuckled, "What's your history with this spot? The food smells amazing."

"This is how my mom got me out of bed for school. If I woke up early enough, I could get a hot Salonica's breakfast instead of cold cereal. I was never late once."

After leaving Salonica's, Clark gave Simi a tour of his favorite Greystones and Red Brick houses throughout the path to Promontory Point. The sun was fighting through the thick overcast, attempting to break through and warm their walk toward the lake.

"You would do well in New York," Simi nudged. "Have you ever lived outside of Chicago?"

"No, but I can't live in New York. Adolescent angst," Clark stated seriously.

"What does that mean?"

"I am Chicago, south side born and raised. Chicago was always second to New York, and it just got under my skin. I didn't get it then." Clark leaned in and whispered the following, "but as an adult, I get it, and New York is awesome." He straightened back up. "But no. I won't leave Chicago."

"You are silly." Simi laughed as they walked through below Lake Shore Drive toward the Point. Simi paused, taking in the skyline of Chicago. "Wow, look at that." Simi breathed.

"We aren't even there yet. Come on," Clark urged. Arriving at the top of the hill, Clark saw most of the firepits in use, hosting gatherings. He walked Simi around the curve and brought her to sit at the ledge on the rocks. "Watch your step; here, I got you." He held Simi's hand as she found a comfortable space.

"The skyline view from the south is amazing. The city needs to commercialize this image more. This is great, and those firepits? How neat is that? I am a sucker for a good fire pit."

"Yeah? Why is that?"

"It's the Persian in me. We are obsessed with fire. Even now, I am just fighting the urge to run over there and jump over the flames," Simi joked. "Fire was the essence of life and existence. Persians gave sacrifices only to the Gods of Water and Fire. For fire, they would offer a sacrifice by adding dry wood without bark, then placing fat on top of it. After that, they would pour oil and light it from below." Simi shook her hand. "They would never blow with their breath, only fan it. Anyone who would use their breath or taint the fire with something dirty or dead would be put to death." Simi realized she had spoken a moment too long, shyly apologizing.

"No, I love this. I love learning about new things."

"You are just being nice."

"I am not that nice of a guy," Clark admitted.

Simi didn't quite believe him but understood that for Clark to be where he was in life, it was probably true. Clark brought his arm around her, bringing her closer into his arms as the wind began to pick up. He turned his head so that his lips slightly touched Simi's ear. She closed her eyes at the sensation.

"I think we should uber back," Clark offered. "But I am not ready for our time to end." Clark reached for Simi, bringing her to face him. "When we get to the uber, I will invite you to come back to my place, and then you are going to tell me you need to back to the hotel." Before Simi could protest, Clark pressed his finger against her lips. "So, I was thinking, before we go back and forth with us accidentally ending up in separate places for the rest of the evening, do you think we could just go ahead and head back to my place?"

Simi contemplated her options. She didn't want to return to a lonely hotel room. She was enjoying her time with him. She was enjoying him. A small smile formed on her lips. "On one condition," Simi countered.

"Anything."

"We eat in tonight, I would like to cook for you," she offered.

"Done."

"Great." She began to climb her fingers up his chest. "I will show you how a real Persian woman takes care of a man." She tapped his nose with her pointer finger with a cheerful giggle as she quickly sat up from the rocks, hurrying her way up the grass back toward the pathway.

"You are moving to Chicago, Simi!" he playfully shouted after her, catching up with her down the stairs.

***

Simi tapped the tips of her fingers on her Starbucks cup. She sat in Jane's waiting room, collecting her thoughts for the session. Simi straightened as the door opened from Jane's office. Usually, the first client of the day, Simi was surprised to see someone else leave her office. Simi relaxed back into her chair, taking notice of the woman's full-sleeve tattoo of music notes. She smiled, slightly taken aback by her striking looks. She slammed the door sharply behind her. Realizing she was not alone in the waiting room, she smiled apologetically.

"Sorry." She spoke with a British accent. She looked back toward the door. "You feel like she works for you?" Simi took a moment with the question.

"Actually, it feels like I work for her," Simi dryly commented.

"Dunno, I don't like it," she shared.

"That's how I knew she was working," Simi responded. The woman looked at her, taking a moment to think about what Simi had said.

"It's all a bit silly if you ask me," she rebuffed.

"I guess it depends on what you are in for?" Simi shrugged. The woman crossed her arms in front of Simi.

"What are you in for?" Her grey eyes narrowed curiously. Simi chuckled softly and waved her hand.

"My entire life." The woman smiled, shaking her head in agreement.

"Me too." She puffed out a large breath. "Good luck." She waved her hand toward Simi and walked out the door.

It was only a few moments until Jane opened her office door, greeting Simi with a warm smile.

"I think I might need sunglasses," Jane commented as Simi sat down curiously. "I haven't seen you this bright, maybe ever? Welcome back to Chicago."

Simi tried to hide her smile as she made herself comfortable in

141

Jane's office. Not much had changed except different inspirationally focused art.

"Thank you. There is plenty to share." Simi took a breath.

She updated Jane about her run-in and time spent with Clark over the past few days. She spoke honestly of all the conversations and interactions, stressing that there had been no lovemaking despite their nights together.

"How fortunate that worked out for you, Simi."

"You mean that?" Simi took Jane's puzzled expression. "I guess I just was expecting you to be a little more 'hold your horses' on the matter."

"It seems like you are doing that yourself. Like the therapy is working?" Jane emphasized.

"Ha. I guess so." Simi momentarily relaxed deeper into her chair. "It is nice being back here. In your office."

"I try to make this a place you want to return to."

"You achieved that."

"What are the key issues you want to talk through today?" Jane had Simi come up with specific topics for each session, ensuring positive progress in each work. It was a bit intense at the beginning for Simi, but she had grown to appreciate the organization of it all.

"First, the question on everyone's mind, where am I living? Second, what I think I want to do when I leave Houston, and lastly, if we have time. My last dream was of my mother. I think we should talk through that."

Jane continued to write in her journal, nodding along. When she was finished, she looked up at Simi. "I'd like to start with the dream about your mother today. There is time for the rest after that." Often Jane would change Simi's preference, finding Simi would purposely put the more pertinent item last.

"I assumed." Simi reached for one of the water bottles available to her on the glass table. Simi relayed the dream that was a memory, the poem she recited to her mom while at the hospital for the last time. She noticed Jane's smile. "What is it?"

"You said this dream happened the first night you slept at Clark's?" Jane made a face that caused Simi to chuckle.

"If Chicago has something going for it, it's full of romantics."

Simi shook her head. "It's very pretty, I'd like to think my mother was talking to me from the heavens, but it was probably more so the poems I read on the plane that day."

"You are uncomfortable with these types of things, even when you shared with me Roman's proposal. You don't like affection."

"That's not true. I know Roman loved me; obviously, my mother did too. Clear-headed, I am surrounded by love."

"Yes, but do you believe you deserve it?" Jane sharply delivered.

Simi held her breath. The aftermath of Jane's message reverberated through her body. The painful truth that Simi knew about was how she thought about herself. Jane's reaction said it all.

"Right—so let's begin talking through that."

Chapter 15

Clark looked at the empty seat in the conference room. He was trying to pay attention to his colleagues and their weekly update. Adam's seat remained empty. Clark hadn't seen or heard from him since their dinner with Demkov. It was Kelsey who had told him he had jumped off the grid, as Amanda hadn't heard from him either. This wasn't the first time Adam had disappeared, but it was the first time in quite a while. Clark touched base with Amanda daily to make sure she was okay. Clark was frustrated that he had missed what was going on. Adam was short after the Demkov dinner, but Clark didn't press him. He should have. Clark assumed Adam was sober again until Amanda told him otherwise. He couldn't understand what Adam was doing or why he was doing it—slowly destroying everything good in his life. For what? Because of what? Fear was too simple of an answer.

Clark refocused on the meeting as he noticed the conversation stop, and all eyes were on him.

"So, when can we expect Adam back, Clark?" Rashid was the first to ask. Clark had been in this position with the group before. The energy was the same—distrust and annoyance.

"When he comes back, everything else can go through Kelsey and me." Clark quickly rebuffed. "If there is anything pressing you to need Adam for, Rashid—let's talk after this." Glances amongst the 5 other individuals in the room were exchanged. Clark grabbed his phone from the table and abruptly left the meeting, not entirely sure if the meeting was indeed over.

He kept his head down as he entered his office, closing the door swiftly behind him. Clark walked directly to the window, taking a moment. Inhaling deeply and recollected his thoughts. Clark knew he was in a delicate situation with the rest of his executive team, one he had to manage quickly because losing any one of them would be a devastating blow.

He pinched the bridge of his nose. He hated everything about this situation and was losing every logical battle within himself regarding what to do with Adam. He woke up today hopeful that Adam would be in when Amanda informed him that he had returned to their house last night. There was more going on than fear about being a father, and Clark would have to figure it out quickly.

His phone vibrated with a text from Simi. She was back tomorrow, and Clark was eager to see her. He felt awful that he had not been able to see her before she left. She didn't seem bothered by his absence which irked him even more. Quickly replying to her, he took a seat on his side table and began working through a plan of action for the leadership team and what it looked like without Adam. He slid a puzzle piece across the glass table, fighting the sickening feeling penetrating his gut.

In the late afternoon, there was a faint knock on Clark's door. It opened slightly, and to Clark's surprise, Kelsey walked through with Adam behind her. With one look from Kelsey, Clark realized they had been here before.

"Hey," Adam said, still standing near the door. "You got a second?" Clark waved him in as Kelsey quietly closed the door behind them. His eyes were low, and he looked tired and whiter than usual.

"Where have you been?" Clark asked.

"I need to step away for a bit." Adam continued, "Not too long, just two weeks."

"Arizona?"

"Yeah," Adam answered. Clark knew he didn't need to press further than that. Adam had gone away for two weeks before and had success on that trip.

"Can I do anything for Amanda while you are gone?" Adam finally looked up to see Clark and smiled.

"Thanks for asking, but her mom is going to be with her." Adam tried hard not to fidget in his seat. "I am sorry that I have to do this again." There was a long silence between the two friends before Clark spoke again.

"Adam, you can take all the time you need. You can stay longer than two weeks and when the baby comes, you are taking your pat leave, and you can return on your own time. That is what being the boss is about. I got things here."

"You sound like you are getting ready to fire me." Adam sighed. He planted his face in his hands. Clark didn't acknowledge his statement.

"This was my retirement; it was never yours. I knew that, but I feel like you think you had to do this with me. While I appreciate that you are here, I want you to know you are free. You are free to sit back and reap the rewards," Clark sincerely offered.

"I know that."

"When do you leave?"

"Tomorrow night." Adam sighed heavily. "Clark, there is some stuff I really need to talk to you about."

"Me too. Do you have time for a bite? A detox smoothie?" Clark smirked, and Adam rolled his eyes. "Too soon?" Clark chuckled as he held the door open for them to leave.

Clark and Adam took their usual table at Meli's down the street from the office. As the server finished pouring their coffees, Clark pulled his cup toward him.

"Where have you been staying?" Clark knew the answer.

"Evan's," Adam admitted.

"Just alcohol or more?"

"More." Clark nodded.

"This is going to be good for you."

"I know." Silence lingered between them. Adam tapped his spoon on each side of the coffee cup. "I need to tell you something, Clark."

"Yeah, I know it's coming," Clark replied.

Adam exhaled heavily at Clark's statement. He knew he couldn't keep it a secret forever.

"But you know I always respected Maxim, so Simi working with him is fine. Evan—I will deal with it. I handle it with you, don't I?"

Clark reminded him.

Adam paused before he spoke, unaware of what Clark was referring to. He chickened out and held in his confession.

"Simi and Evan?" Adam stumbled out. "Simi?" He repeated again, surprised to hear that name, even more surprised to hear her name attached to Evan's.

"Their building on Madison? Evan didn't mention?" Clark spoke flatly, "That's pretty shocking."

It was at that moment that Clark held back, noting that Evan probably had told Adam everything, but he wasn't able to remember. He took a sip of his coffee, trying to eliminate his logic from this conversation where he needed to be Adam's friend and nothing else.

"Are you happy that she is back in Chicago?" Adam asked, piecing together the information.

"'I think so. I mean, I guess we are about to start something."

"You guess? What about Rachel?" It was Clark's turn to avoid Adam's gaze. He wouldn't further explain what happened with her.

"Rachel was good for you. Simi, she was . . . you know?" Adam instantly regretted the comment, aware that their friendship was not in a place to have their usual banter.

"I told you about Roman Charles."

"Right, but you didn't provide any clarity on anything else."

"Do I need to?" Clark was as uncomfortable as Adam was. As the food was brought in front of them, their conversation died. Both were deep in thought, trying to make it through the meal.

"I am not one to judge anyone, Clark. So, you know, she's captured your interest. That's hard enough to do. Make the most of it. I hope to meet her when I get back."

"You will. She is back tomorrow; she's been wrapping things up in Houston the past few days."

"Holidays are coming up. No one likes to be alone during them."

"That's right, you might have a Thanksgiving baby," Clark commented. "I can just see you have a son born on Thanksgiving. A feast every year for the Prince of King Adam." Clark chuckled.

"We don't know the gender yet." Adam diverted his gaze to the side.

"I know you are scared, but it's okay to be hopeful for the future." Clark noticed Adam clenching and releasing his right fist throughout the meal. He saw the discomfort and sweat on his brow. "Just two weeks. You are going to feel so much better."

***

Simi gripped the sheets underneath her. She tried to catch her breath, inhaling only his scent. She reached up, grasping his arms, the warm muscle beneath her fingertips. His lips pressed down at the top of her shoulders. His beard softly grazed along the sensitive area of her neck.

"Clark." She breathed out, digging her fingers deeper into him. She opened her eyes, his smile above her. He pressed into her again, and waves of sensation spiked through her body. "Please." She urgently begged.

"Not yet, Simi." Her eyes furrowed at him. "Shh." Clark returned her attention back to his eyes. "Focus on me. We both have waited a long time for this." Simi closed her eyes, nodding in agreement. She wanted to remember every moment. Every touch. "Do you like when I do this?" Clark whispered into her ear, his hands lightly trailing above her breast. "What if I kiss here?" He shifted, bringing his lips right above where she desperately wanted him to do more than kiss. She held her breath in anticipation, feeling the warmth of his lips right above her. Her body tensed, waiting, wanting until finally he . . .

Simi woke up and took a deep breath; with a sigh, she closed her eyes again. She was alone, in her hotel room, at the Woodlands in Houston. This wasn't the first dream she had about being intimate again with Clark, it was closer to the twelfth, but she wasn't keeping count.

One month ago, she flew to Chicago, and tomorrow, she was moving there. She was scared and excited all at once. Jane supported this move, but her opinions on Clark? She strongly encouraged Simi to take her time. Which she was. Painfully was.

Her original three-day trip turned into a bit over two weeks. Evenings were mostly spent with Clark as she was reintroducing herself to Chicago, but by the end of her visit, Clark had gotten very busy. Though she didn't see him in person the last few days before she left, he had been communicating very actively with her. She could tell he was having difficulty balancing his time and made sure not to make any expectations of him. She was moving to Chicago for her opportunity for a fresh start. Having a friend or more already established was an added bonus, but not the focus.

Simi flipped back her sheets and headed toward the bathroom. She ran the water from the sink, splashing her face before turning on the shower. Stepping in, she let the water fall on her back. It had been a whirlwind, deciding to move and finalizing the condo. She also began viewing white spaces with Maxim, with Evan lurking behind. Simi had made a mental note to follow up with the language center as she wanted to enroll in the upcoming Japanese session but had to test first. She leaned her head back under the shower stream, running her fingers through her hair. She heard the faint sounds of her phone in the bedroom.

She knew it was Daroush—he had been religiously checking in on her every morning. He wasn't the most excited when she told him about her move to Chicago; his preference was still for her to come to Paris. Reluctantly, she agreed that if Chicago didn't work out, she would return with no protest.

After toweling off, she walked back into the bedroom and viewed the messages that were indeed from Daroush. She held a smile, her heart heavy. Today was a day she had been preparing for with Jane. Mentally she felt ready, but her emotions were still on edge. Simi sat on the bed and reached for Roman's watch resting on her nightstand. She rubbed the face of the watch under her thumb, thinking of all the things she had prepared to say. What she was preparing to do. Understanding that she wasn't numb but in the stage of acceptance. Having the courage to confront the reality of her life, her new life was the next and near-final step to closing out her chapter of grieving Roman. She set the watch back on the nightstand and went to get dressed.

Before sunset, Simi walked into the house. Jackie had draped most of the furniture with covers. Boxes were stacked alongside the wall of the foyer. Movers were enroute. While Simi still hadn't decided what to do with the house, the idea of selling it felt wrong. No lights were on as her heels clicked against the wood floors. The sunlight illuminated the living room, brightly directing her to the hallway that led to Roman's office. Taking a deep breath, she walked until she reached his door.

"Simi? Is that you?" Simi's eyes closed in the memory of his voice. This memory.

"I didn't want to bother you. I heard you were on the phone."

"My door is always open for you, Simi joon, always walk in to see me."

Simi paused with a slight tremble in front of the French doors to Roman's office. She pressed her lips tightly together as she pushed the doors open. She took a moment to gaze around before continuing into the room, rich mahogany bookshelves, now empty, oversized desk and leather furniture she would rest in while he worked, now gone. All that was left was the box with an urn filled with his ashes. Simi caught a reflection of herself in the window. She had dressed up for this, taking the time to style her hair and makeup, and adorned a white and blue sundress that Roman often complimented her on. She sat cross-legged in front of the box and slowly began to lift the tops of the cardboard panel, letting them stand straight up. Simi closed her eyes as she rose to her knees to peer down into the box. The red urn sat in the middle. She slowly reached in and winced at the cool sensation of the piece. Securing it fully in her hands, she brought it out, placing it on the floor in front of her. She sat there for a moment staring at the urn. Her heart pounded in her ears.

She was nervous, sad, and shy. She tilted her head, looking for some connection. Anything from this item that contained all that was left of Roman. All that was left of their life together. She extended her arms and picked up the urn to bring it closer to her.

"Hi," she said softly to herself with a half-smile. Tears began to well up in her eyes. "Hi, Roman." Simi swallowed hard. "This is silly." She nodded to herself, placing the urn back on the floor. She sat back on her legs. Tears freely fell. She missed him. She knew she did, but at this moment, she felt the painful weight of how much she missed him. "I hope you know I miss you so much—I still kind of don't feel like it happened. Though, I know it did. I, like right now, am having a hard time processing you are gone." Simi paused. There was so much she had prepared to say but now felt unable to properly express it. "Our time together feels like a beautiful movie I had the privilege of watching." Her voice was shaky as she continued. "I made a few mistakes this year, really bad ones, but the one I am most sorry for is leaving you here alone. I didn't know how to do this yet." She looked at the urn, imagining instead Roman sitting across from her. His bright green eyes gazed forgivingly as she stuttered through this speech. "I have been with a painfully great therapist. She has been helping me process your death and my mother's death. It's hard, but even on the worst sessions, I feel a little less heavy." Simi dabbed at her eyes with the back of her hand. "There is so much I want to say to you. I want to talk to you again about everything and anything. Would you even want to listen? Or are you lounging on a cloud up there just taking it all in?" Simi smiled to herself. "I hope you are happy, though. Wherever you are, I hope you are at peace."

Her chest was tight as she became overwhelmed with emotion. Opening herself up to talk to Roman was the catharsis she didn't know she needed. Simi went quiet again, letting memories of their time together flood into her head. She rested back on her bottom and pulled her knees in. Resting her head on her knees, she continued to cry. Her mind drifted back to the comfort she felt in Clark's arms. She inhaled sharply. She needed to keep those thoughts away. This was Roman's time. She squeezed her eyes tightly as the memory of Clark's kisses penetrated her. The same security Roman provided her. She shook her head and let out a frustrated sigh. Glancing at the urn, she then looked up at the ceiling and clicked her tongue.

"I met someone too," Simi continued to share. The corner of her lips felt heavy, a sad frown forming. "Roman, did you send someone for me? Did you see what I was doing? Were you mad? Tears again welled up; this time, she had no control. Sobs escaped from her. She held her hands over her mouth, freely letting herself mourn and find forgiveness for all that had transpired. Lying down on her side, slightly curling her body up, she stared at the urn for what felt like hours, tracing the gold etchings over and over.

"I'm sorry, Roman." The words blurted out. "I am sorry that I fought you on the wedding and that I didn't force you to go to the doctor immediately. I am sorry for so much." She sniffled. "I am sorry for this—sniffling like a baby." She wiped her eyes. "You weren't supposed to leave me with all this, you know. This was supposed to be for you. You worked so hard for all of this, and at the first test of responsibility, I conducted myself in such a broken manner." Simi shook her head. "I want to make you proud—I want to honor your generosity. I am going to." Simi reached out her arm and stroked the urn with the tip of her fingers. "I miss you so much. I loved you so hard," she whispered softly.

The sun was due to set soon, and she did not want to miss one moment. Simi cradled the urn gently against her breast.

Stepping out of the office, she walked through the hollow home. She pulled the sliding door open as she journeyed to the spot she had prepared earlier in the day in the back fields. The spot she knew was the right place for her to say goodbye to Roman.

A small hole had been dug around a bloom of flowers next to a boulder rock. She could hear his voice commenting that she was disturbing what nature had created for them. She smiled and lifted the skirt of her dress as she knelt on the grass. Sitting off to the side, she slowly unscrewed the top of the urn. She reached inside and felt the grainy yet soft texture of the ashes. She pulled her hand out, looking at the faded stain. Her heart swelled. Despite what anyone thought, despite what it looked like, she did love him. She would always love him, but now it was time for her to say goodbye. Reaching in again, she pulled out a light handful of the ashes, sprinkling it on the flowers surrounding the hole. The sun shone the last bit over the skyline before it sank into the night. She reached into her pocket and pulled out the watch, which she had wrapped in a linen cloth. She covered the cloth with her ash-stained hands letting the residue be absorbed inside the material. She sat the urn close by, off to the side. Roman's journey did not end here. Simi closed her eyes as the sounds of nature began to play a melody to her mood. She leaned against the boulder, smearing ashes over the rock where they had shared intimate moments. She looked towards the petals of the flowers, the delicate pieces often crushed by the antics of their love. She looked back to the linen cloth and began smoothing more dirt over the light fabric beneath her palm.

Simi leaned her back against the boulder, blinking tears freely falling to the ground. She exhaled as she felt a warm breeze surround her. A soft sensation of imagination or memory was warm against her forehead. Simi smiled inwardly and silently thanked Roman.

***

"How did it go?" Gregory pulled out a chair for Simi at the outdoor table by the pool. Twinkling lights sparkled above them as the sound of soft conversation of other patrons filled the air. She rested the wooden engraved box which held the urn on the chair next to her. Simi gave Gregory a half smile. He nodded, seeing the strain in her eyes, the exhaustion she exuded. "He is going to love being back in New York." Gregory tapped the chair. He reached for the bottle of wine in the chiller at the front of the table and poured some in Simi's glass.

Simi gratefully accepted the glass. She brought it toward her lips and finished the pour in one drink. The sensations of the wine calmed her heightened nerves throughout her body. "Another, please." She wiped at her lips.

"Glass or bottle?"

"Bottle."

Gregory waved to the server for her attention.

"You going to be good on your own in Chicago?" Gregory asked.

"I'm not on my own. Not really." Simi smiled, resting her hand on Gregory's arm. "If it doesn't work out, get your guest room ready."

"It has been ready." Gregory winked.

"I miss him so much." Simi looked up at Gregory, teary-eyed. She locked her thumb around his hand, still resting on top of her.

"Me too." Gregory smiled softly. "Do you remember the trip we took to Sobczak's wedding in Park City?" Simi started to chuckle at the memories of the most eccentric event in all of their lives. Gregory also chuckled as they continued to reminisce about their memories together with Roman.

The restaurant became half empty, and both their gazes focused on the pool. Words didn't need to be exchanged between them. Simi knew at this moment that he was Roman's friend and confident first. Gregory was hers now.

Chapter 16

"And then the guys put all my stuff on a truck. I met up with Gregory and drank a wine bottle with him, then a bottle in my room and fell asleep. I took the first flight out, and now here I sit. Officially moved to Chicago." Simi ended after sharing how she finally said goodbye to Roman and came to be back in Jane's office.

"Are you hungover?"

"Oddly enough, no, I didn't get drunk. I think I am running on endorphins, sadness, and excitement. I feel weirdly peaceful. Does that make sense?"

"You went through a lot in the past few days. It might take you a bit to digest everything. So let's get as much done during this session so you can relax the rest of the day." Jane watched Simi's lips lift. "You intend to rest today?"

"Yes, I do. After this, shower and sleep," Simi declared. "I am seeing Clark for dinner tonight. He has been making a big deal about taking me on a proper date. I am unsure what that means to him, but I am a bit excited." Simi drifted her gaze. "A bit hopeful too." Hopeful for something she wasn't ready to say out loud. "Before we start, if you have earlier appointments, I will take them. The language center has a ten a.m. I want to try to get into."

"I will do my best. I have someone before you on Tuesdays, and we are still sorting her schedule consistently. I will see how I can rework it for both of you."

Simi continued to share with Jane. She wanted to get as much off her chest as was needed to enjoy tonight. In her responsibility to do right by Roman, she had also come to enjoy her time spent with Clark. The feeling of loneliness was smaller, even with text conversations. The acceptance phase was real. She was able to talk about Roman with happiness and pride. Her memories did not bear as much painful weight as they used to. Healing was a long process, but with her friendly interactions with Clark, she felt more surefooted walking on the earth again. She appreciated him for that.

After she had left Jane's office, she headed back to the LaSalle Street Hotel, silently hoping this would be her last hotel stay for a while. She was excited to make a home, decorate her space, and begin her life again. Daroush's words back in Vegas never left her consciousness about being her authentic self again.

During the months working with Jane, Simi was looking in the mirror, finally recognizing the gaze in the reflection. A gaze that often clenched her stomach when she saw a resemblance to her mother. This was something Simi had avoided acknowledging often but recently began enjoying the moment and memory to follow when it occurred.

Settling into her room, she sent a text to Clark. She was excited to see him. She was curious to see what he had planned. She opened her suitcase and pulled out a garment bag, a favorite black dress of hers that had been in her closet in Houston for far too long. She was happy to be reunited with it and even more excited to see how Clark liked it.

She hung it in the closet, playing with it as it gently swayed. Smiling to herself, she went back to her suitcase and finished unpacking.

***

Clark grabbed a seat at the bar of Prime. He gave a sincere nod to Bradley, who slid Clark a short glass of whiskey. He needed to mentally decompress. He had stopped by the front desk where Simi had left a key for him. It was burning inside his jacket pocket. He wanted to get upstairs to her as fast as he could, but not with this weight of the concern of the structure and environment of Cottage Growth. He was looking at the challenge of a friendship that may not survive through what Clark needed CG to achieve. What would

CG , or even his life, look like if Adam did not come out on the other side of this? What about Amanda and their future baby? Clark shook his head. This is not what he needed to be thinking about now. Upstairs, Simi was waiting for him.

Clark invited Simi for a classic date. One he had hoped to do before she had left, but with the chaos of Adam's disappearance, he had to focus and be present at the office. He waved to Bradley as he quickly finished his glass, left cash on the bar, and headed toward the elevator. Exiting on the fifteenth floor, he checked that the numbers matched what was on the key card. He smiled as he stood in front of double doors. Another suite. He knocked lightly before sliding the key into the slot and entering the main room.

The fireplace was turned on with soft ambient music playing from the television. He tapped again on the hallway wall before entering the living room. He looked toward the bedroom door, which was slightly ajar.

He laid a bouquet of flowers on an end table against the marble top. Clark heard her call for him from the bedroom. He made his way toward her; turning into the bedroom, she was standing in front of a full-length mirror. She turned, struggling with the top of her dress.

"This is not how I wanted to say hi, but can you secure my top button?" She chuckled, coming to where he stood.

She held her hair to one side, holding her breath as she felt Clark come up against her. His fingers burned as he touched her skin. His body radiated warmth just inches away from her. Clark leaned into her exposed neck, laying a gentle kiss at the base as he forced the button around a small black thread. She closed her eyes, feeling the impression of his lips on her skin.

"You look beautiful, Simi," Clark rasped.

"Thank you." She donned her black dress with a low front v-cut. Gold necklaces filled the space between her breasts. "I should just be a few more minutes. Do you want to pour us a drink before we go? I ordered a whiskey and wine; it could be in the wet bar area. Fresh ice too." She noticed Clark's hesitation. "Too much? Is this too fancy?" She looked down at her appearance.

"No, no, not at all." He stepped back slightly. "Just very hard to look away."

Clark left Simi in her room to pour their drinks. Simi took in her reflection, smoothing out the wrinkles in her dress. She took a moment to appreciate her appearance and very proudly acknowledged that she was looking at herself and not some version of herself. She walked out to join Clark in the living area of her room. Clark handed her a glass of wine as he noticeably poured himself water. Simi, curious, smiled through accepting the glass.

"I've missed you," Clark was the first to say. He watched her smile open up. "I know I said it before, but I am really sorry how you left."

"I wish you could know that I truly understand. Did everything get resolved? You were a bit vague with what was going on." Simi took a seat on the couch near the fireplace. Her eyes followed his descent to join her. "I apologize; that really isn't my business."

"It's all getting resolved." Clark mentioned, "Thank you for asking." At that moment, Clark wanted to share everything with Simi, but her quick rebuff placed a barrier between them.

"Clark?" Simi gently touched his leg. Her eyes were concerned. "We can reschedule tonight. I am moving here. I moved here. Just waiting for the truck to arrive with my stuff." Simi chuckled, trying to ease the tension ruminating from Clark.

Clark took Simi's hand and enclosed his around hers. The distractions of the day melted away as he looked into her eyes. When he looked at her, he felt blind with trust and another emotion he wasn't used to having. Clark knew he wouldn't be single forever, but he never thought he was going to be able to find someone who evoked emotion from him. He wasn't against love, he just wasn't sure he knew how to do it. Clark resisted the urge to ask her about Houston, wondering if she was finally free of her past, free of Roman.

"I have been looking forward to your return since you left. We are not canceling tonight." Clark brought her hand up for a gentle kiss. "I am ready when you are."

"Wait, I got something for you." Simi took her hand back and walked into the bedroom. He heard her rummage through her bags, and she returned with a box. "Here you go." Clark cautiously took the small box from her quickly recognizing the cover. He looked back at Simi, who was brightly smiling. "I thought it could be fun to do this one together?" She took a seat next to him.

"It is the Restless painting," Clark commented.

"Right. There is a site where you can make anything a puzzle, and I thought maybe I could keep this one at my place, and you would help me. You know, a bottle of wine, working together trying to figure out how to disrupt the gallery industry, respectfully, of course." Simi laughed.

"I love it." Clark genuinely did. He loved the idea, he loved the thought and effort, and that feeling he wasn't able to identify earlier was becoming clearer by the moment.

Clark brought Simi to a small intimate French bistro he had frequented a few times and knew she would enjoy it for its authenticity. It was one of the first restaurants in her new neighborhood before it became the place to live in the city. They were taken to their table, a cozy booth tucked in the back with additional privacy. As Simi scooted into the booth, the hostess laid out the menus, and Clark moved in to join her.

"This is nice." She took the menu into her hands and looked around the restaurant. It was illuminated in red and gold; it had the charm of a real Parisian bistro one could find in Paris.

Their server approached the table, introducing himself for the evening. He listed off the specials of the evening. Simi moved closer to Clark; she wanted to be as close to him as possible. Her dreams of what could transpire between them were on the forefront of her mind tonight.

"What may I bring you to drink?" the waiter asked.

"Could we do the Domain de Chevalier, Pessac-Leognan Bordeaux, please?" A bit of a French accent came through the request. Simi was caught off guard. His accent had come through perfectly. She handed off her menu and looked suspiciously at Clark.

"Do you speak French?" Clark reached for his glass of water and shook his head no.

"Not at all. I know how to read Simi," he chided.

"No, you hit every word almost perfectly. You are lying."

"Better than you, it seems." Clark winked. "I spent some time in

France in a study abroad program. Learned the important phrases to get the ladies and order the right wines. Outside of that, Average American. English only."

"I don't believe you." Simi leaned in toward Clark; she softly pressed a kiss off the side of his lips, grazing her cheek against the sharp stubble of his beard. She tenderly placed her hand on his thigh, lightly rubbing. She smiled as she spoke just above a whisper in French. "J'ai rêvé de ce que ça ferait de vous sentir au plus profond de moi." *I dreamed of what it would feel like to have you deep inside me.*

Clark clenched his jaw as she started speaking mentally, translating what she was saying. Yes. He understood. Yes, he wanted to drag her out of this restaurant and take her home. He wanted to get lost in her hair, cover her with kisses, and bring her to the brink of ecstasy over and over until she pleaded for him to stop. Clearing his throat, she pulled back, very pleased with herself.

"You wanted to order the duck instead? It's been so long, Simi. Lost it all." Clark was saved by the arrival of the wine on the table. Clark had been hopeful to keep his knowledge of French a secret until the right time. If he could eavesdrop in the meantime to learn more about Simi to his advantage, it was an added bonus. Simi pulled her hands back from the top of the table but didn't take her eyes off him. They both remained silent until the waiter left. Her eyes narrowed at him. He chuckled lightly. "Let's just enjoy tonight." He raised his glass toward hers.

They continued with light conversation throughout their dinner. Clark did his best to remain present but kept thinking about her dirty French words. What she confessed, what she wanted, what he wanted. He got lost in thoughts of where tonight could go. Where should they go at the end of the night? Clark wanted to bring her back to his place immediately. He would keep her there, take off tomorrow and keep her through the weekend; maybe, he would let her leave on Monday. Clark cleared his throat. He was getting ahead of himself. Tonight was her first night back. Anything happening would be moving too fast. Wouldn't it? Too fast for them? He was aware that the Simi who left him in Vegas had grown and healed since, and that maybe tonight wasn't off the table.

After dinner, Clark brought Simi to a small speakeasy not too far from his side of the city. They were seated at a small circular booth illuminated by candlelight. On a small stage sat a vocalist with a pianist and bassist. The singer was a young woman whose voice had the husk of Billie Holiday. The music had been fantastic all night. The vocalist brought Simi to near tears with her tonal angst and passion. She was so consumed by the performance that she hadn't noticed how intently Clark had been watching her. She reached for his hand and brought his arm around her, bringing herself closer. She laid her hand on this thigh, gently rubbing up and down, hoping to bring the tension out she could feel in his body. Her hand still held on to his which was wrapped around her. With a glance she noticed his eyes were lowered.

The singer again captivated Simi's attention, announcing she would surprise the audience with a cover song. The beginning chords for "Creep" by Radiohead emanated from the piano. The most covered song in the world and a favorite of Simi's, she looked at Clark excitedly. She brushed her lips across his fingers over her shoulder and rested her own hand as the song continued. Simi was entranced by the singer's power. She felt chills rush up and down her body. It was a brilliant performance.

"I feel like I need to catch my breath." Simi smiled. The audience applauded around her. "This music was fantastic. What a treat." Simi was still wrapped in his arms.

"I'm glad you liked it. She was really good."

"The best teenage angst song of all times. It's an all time favorite of mine." Simi was still reeling from the performance. The band announced they were going on a break and the house lights rose. "I didn't know what you meant by classic date, but I am here for it. Did you want to stay?" Simi brought Clark's hand resting in hers down from her shoulder and placed it on her breast. "I am ready to go."

Clark held his breath at her admission, feeling the supple, round warmth beneath his fingertips, her hand above his, slowly guiding him around her body. "Let's go." Simi chuckled as she released Clark's hand free. He signaled to the server reaching for his jacket, and pulled his wallet out with his phone. He began frowning.

"What is it?" Simi asked.

"Can you take care of this? I will meet you outside." Simi watched as Clark quickly left, holding his phone to his ear. She chuckled at the server with a nervous smile. She handed over her card and looked back toward the door.

By the time Simi had joined him outside, Clark was standing against the wall clenching his fists. Simi slowly walked toward him.

"Is everything ok?" She searched his face for clues.

"I am going to kill him myself." He exhaled. "He wants to die so badly. I will just do it for him."

"Clark?" Simi reached her hand toward his cheek, and he jerked away.

"I am sorry to do this to you tonight. I have to go." Clark began walking toward the sidewalk's edge, looking for a cab.

"Wait, what happened?" Simi reached for his arm.

"I just got off the phone with Amanda. That's Adam's wife." Simi was trying to follow. "I just gotta get to Northwestern."

"Hospital?"

"Simi, just text me when you get to the hotel. This is not how I want you to see me right now." Clark extended his arm out for a cab that was down the street. Simi stood right before Clark and held her hands on his arms.

"That's not fair. You don't get to see me at my worst doing my worst and then hide your worst from me. That is not how the game is played. Let me come with you."

"No," Clark cut her off. "This is not for you to see."

"I don't need to see anything, Clark. Something, though . . ." Simi paused, pressing her lips together. "When you are at a hospital, it's nice to have someone in the waiting room." She shrugged her shoulders.

Clark opened up the taxi door and took in her words, the depth and meaning of what she said. He climbed in the car and defeatedly slid down the bench, leaving the door open for her to join.

Chapter 17

Arriving at the hospital, they headed to Adam's floor. Simi kept up with Clark's quick pace as he glanced through the waiting room area before going to the reception desk. Simi controlled her breath as the familiarity of everything began returning to her memory, to her senses. It smelled the same, but it was less muted. It was less personal. Simi stepped to the side, waiting for Clark to find whom he was looking for.

"Ms. Simi," came a voice from behind. "Wow, just look at you. Where did you come from?" Simi turned to see Evan standing there. Before she could speak, Clark's voice boomed.

"Don't talk to her, don't look at her. You need to leave." He stepped in front of Simi, standing face-to-face with Evan. "I have dealt with you for almost twenty years, preying on Adam; it's done. He is about to be a father, and you what? Just enable him. Destroy him because you didn't live up to your potential!" Clark felt Simi touch his arm. He controlled his breathing. He wasn't going to give Evan the satisfaction of a lawsuit.

"Oh, I just destroyed him? Who did he go to Vegas with?" Evan countered. "You treat him like your sidekick and abuse him too. Don't act like you are better than me."

"That's not true," Clark said clearly and slowly, refusing to admit any fault to Evan.

A nurse walked around from behind the desk, coming closer to their interaction. Simi quickly assured her there was no problem and came between Clark and Evan.

"You two are making a scene. Take this outside, or one of you needs to leave." Simi tried to temper both men down.

"You need to leave," Clark quickly announced.

"Fine," Evan agreed. Light bruising was fresh around his face. "You know Clark, you stand here like you and Adam are brothers, and you don't even realize how much he keeps from you. When you find out the truth, when you get to know who he is like I do, let's see how quickly you keep coming to his rescue." Evan was baiting Clark, and he knew it. Evan looked over to Simi.

"Don't worry, this little accident won't interfere with our viewings." Clark's temper flared.

"Considered them canceled. Tell your father she is taking her business elsewhere," Clark growled. Simi found herself momentarily perplexed by his words.

"Is that what I should tell him, Simi?" Evan dug deeper, keeping his eyes on Clark. "Does Clark now speak for you?"

"I think my business isn't what we are all here for," Simi informed both men. Evan finally broke Clark's gaze and smirked at Simi.

"See you soon." He smiled tauntingly and walked out of the waiting room through the double doors. Simi was surprised by the look Clark was giving her.

"You are not seeing him again," he demanded. Simi smiled, attempting to hold in her amusement. Clark was visibly hurting and lashing out.

"Sit down, Clark. You need a minute."

Silence engulfed the waiting room. People bored with waiting were interested in the drama—something to spice up the night instead of what was playing on the television. Clark was fuming. He wanted to scream. He wanted to punch something. He was so angry he couldn't look at Simi. She offered him a cup of water as she sat cross-legged in the chair next to him, saying nothing. He felt even more enraged. Simi reached to the side table and began flipping through a magazine.

"Really?" Clark finally scoffed.

"Can't do anything else while you sit there like a toddler," Simi announced. She smirked as she saw Clark's fist clench. She genuinely felt bad for him, but that didn't give him the right to act as he did.

"Simi," Clark exhaled. "Before you left—Adam went MIA. It's why I couldn't continue to see you as often before you left. He struggles with addiction. Evan's not wrong. I don't pay attention to what Adam does not because I don't care, but simply because he is an adult, and I just figured that he would figure all this out on his own." Clark began to feel so much weight release as he confided in Simi. He didn't look at her but felt her gaze, her hands on his forearm gently caressing as he spoke. "There is something else going on with him. I don't know what it is. This is not all because he is about to be a father. It's something more than that."

"Have you asked him?"

"No," Clark stated. Although confiding in Simi had been cathartic, he was not ready to tell her he was afraid. He had no idea what Adam was holding in, which scared him.

"Picking up on context clues, I can tell you that whatever drives Adam to act in such a manner is deeper than you realize. When someone is broken, the most irrational decisions seem like the best because we are in control. We make them despite anyone else's opinion and for someone like Adam or me, that power isn't often felt within ourselves." Clark looked at Simi. "No one is perfect in this world. Some people are just better at coping with trauma than others."

"You stopped, though."

"Sure, but I hit rock bottom first."

"He has hit rock bottom before."

"Maybe you think he has, but only that person knows when they do it," Simi explained. "My rock bottom was having to tell my brother what I was doing. I had to look my little brother in the eyes and admit that I was hurting myself." Simi exhaled, taking a moment before she continued. "Daroush is my life. I scared my baby brother. I failed as a sister. That was my rock bottom," Simi admitted. "It was not my dinner dates." She nudged him.

The fluorescent hum echoed loudly above them. Simi grabbed Clark's hand, holding it within hers, rubbing the top of his palms with her thumb. Providing comfort the best way she knew how.

Clark turned to her and smiled. "Having someone in the waiting room does help," Clark admitted. "This is not how I wanted the night to go, by the way?"

"No? I thought it was perfectly orchestrated."

"Any other sound advice?" Clark stood up, adjusting his jacket before her. Simi stood up with him and held her hands over his chest. She looked up at him, feeling so much emotion toward him. She resisted the urge to kiss him. Her body wouldn't be able to stop once she started. She pulled at his jacket, smoothing out the fabric.

Softly, she spoke, "Anything you want to say to him, he already knows." She met Clark's gaze. "Tell him something he doesn't."

Clark was escorted by a nurse to Adam's room; walking behind her, he focused on keeping his breathing regulated. Simi's words lingered in his mind. Clark knew his anger was fueled by fear more than anything.

The sound of Amanda's voice had been eerily calm when Clark had spoken with her. Like she had been expecting this to happen. This wasn't the first time Clark missed the cues of distress from Adam. There was similar chaos from Adam before his wedding. Clark just attributed it to nerves and the undue stress of their company. In all the times he had been teased by Adam for lacking emotional insight, maybe this was his wake-up call to listen.

The nurse opened the door, and Clark walked in to see Adam lying there, connected to an IV, eyes closed. His face was bruised, and his right arm was fitted in a sling. Clark smiled kindly at the nurse. She informed him that Adam had refused painkillers, so he could be a bit irritable. Clark pulled the guest chair from the wall and placed it beside the bed. He removed his jacket and folded it over his lap as he sat down. Adam began to wake up.

"Hey man." Adam shifted in his bed, finally seeing that Clark was with him. "You look good." Clark smiled tightly and leaned back in his chair. Adam looked away. "I know."

"Why didn't you just go to Arizona?" The words escaped Clark's lips before he remembered Simi's advice. Clark looked off to the side. "Are you okay, Adam?"

"Yeah," Adam answered swiftly. Clark pressed his lips together. He knew what he wanted to say but was trying to figure out what he needed to say.

"Do you know what happened?"

"It was an accident. Evan was driving, it shouldn't have happened, but it did." Adam continued to look down at the blankets. "You don't need to worry. Evan's Dad is going to handle everything. I wasn't screened—it's all on lockdown." Clark laughed despite himself.

"You think that is my first worry? How will this make us look?" Clark had a sad realization wash over him. "Adam, talk to me. What have I been missing?"

"I don't know what you mean."

"I am asking what is going on with you?"

"I don't know." Adam frustratedly sighed.

"Does Amanda?" Clark urged. Adam stayed quiet. "It's not an ask anymore, Adam. You are going to have to go to Arizona, and you are going to stay home with Amanda until the baby comes, and then you and I will re-evaluate if you want to be actively back at work," Clark conceded. "I never meant to pressure you about anything or overwhelm you."

"I don't want out," Adam protested. He leaned back into the pillows pushing the heels of his hands against his eyes. "I am about to lose my wife and now our friendship." Clark pressed his lips together.

"Amanda is not going to leave you. The love she has for you, you don't find a partnership like that. She's going to need you more than ever now." Adam stayed quiet.

He thought of Simi's words about her rock bottom moment with her brother. Clark took time to formulate the right words, but he was at a loss. The man in front of him was not the same one as before. In their evolution of growth, Adam had gotten sidetracked, and Clark, blinded by his own ambitions, missed crucial cues. He allowed Adam to stray down a path as long as it didn't affect their business. His nonchalant attitude toward Adam's extracurriculars now resulted in a life almost lost twice.

"I am going to be better, Clark. I am." Adam tucked his hands beneath his covers.

"Me too," Clark admitted. Adam turned to him. "I am going to pay attention better, and I am going to be a better friend. I haven't been." Adam didn't often hear Clark admit anything negative about himself. "I know I am wired differently. I know I can bulldoze right over anything personally hard with you and only celebrate the good. I have not been there for you the way you have been for me, and I am sorry." Clark held the back of his jaw tightly. "I am sorry, Adam."

"I am not here because of you."

"No, but you could not be here because of me too."

Adam worked hard to stay as polished and professional as Clark. Friends or not, he learned very early that Clark wouldn't stand for weakness. His high expectations and demands are how they achieved their success. He admired Clark, and he wanted to be more like him. His own personal demons fought him, his fear of his inadequacies. He could never admit that out loud to Clark. He was fearful of rejection or disappointment. The concessions Clark had just made with him, and the apology, was overwhelming. Adam was embarrassed to do so but had nothing left in him. Tears began to fall from his eyes freely.

Clark stood up from his seat and moved to the edge of the bed to pull Adam into a hug. He closed his eyes, letting his friend cry against his shoulder. He frowned as Adam released heavy sobs, holding in his own feelings, recognizing the pain in his stomach and the tightness of his chest. The true realization was that he could have lost his friend tonight. He felt Adam pull back and kept his hand on his shoulder.

"You are going to get better. You are going to be a great father, too." Clark squeezed the top of his shoulder and sat back on the chair next to the bed. They both sat in silence, watching the images displayed on the overhead TV. Nothing else needed to be said.

Simi had become engrossed with a National Geographic article on "The Secret Sounds of the Whale" while she waited for Clark. Getting lost in the details of a family pod of orcas off the coast of New Zealand, she noticed a very slow-moving pregnant woman enter the waiting room. She was looking for someone. Sitting up in her seat, Simi set the magazine aside.

"Are you looking for Clark?" Simi walked over to her. "Amanda, right?" Simi smiled brightly. She had never met Adam formally nor his wife but knew she was pregnant. The woman looked up with tear-stained eyes curiously. "Sorry, hi, I am Simi. I am a friend of Clark's," Simi rambled nervously.

"Oh, wow, Simi?" Amanda realized her quick faux paux and waved her hand over her belly. "Pregnancy brain."

"Clark is in with him. Do you want me to call him?"

"No." Amanda rushed out. "No." She laughed uncomfortably.

"Do you want to sit for a bit?" Amanda nodded, still holding her belly; she walked with Simi and took a seat. "How far along are you?"

"Third trimester," she shared.

"You look beautiful." Simi smiled, and Amanda laughed out loud, wiping her eyes with her sleeves.

"Thank you, but I know better." Amanda waved her hand toward Simi. "I am sorry I had to call Clark. He is usually always with Adam during these types of things and watches out for him." She cleared her throat as tears began to well up in her eyes again. "I am sorry. Pregnancy hormones."

"You don't have to apologize." Simi walked over to grab tissues from the registration desk and brought them to Amanda.

"I just can't believe it. I don't know what else to do. I don't know how to help." Amanda wiped tears from her eyes and looked over to Simi, who was seated, holding a small smile toward her. "You don't even know me." Amanda shook her head.

"How about we put a pin in this moment? We can come back to it in a bit." Simi was worried about Amanda being in stress. In the third trimester, Simi thought you weren't supposed to leave the house. "Are you hungry, thirsty? We can go to the cafeteria or walk around in general?" Simi suggested. "Maybe you can share some things about your pregnancy? Get your mind off of what's happening right now?"

"Well, now you have made it impossible to hate you." Amanda chuckled. "I know it's not your fault about Rachel. Clark is just . . . bah, there I go again." Simi took a moment to process what Amanda was saying. "I could go for a walk and a snack. Baby is always hungry."

They began to walk down the halls as Amanda spoke about her pregnancy. Simi was trying to ignore her comment about Rachel.

Who was she to Amanda and had Clark not been truthful about Rachel?

Clark read the text message from Simi. She was with Amanda. Clark glanced at Adam, who was resting. The bruising, the gauze, the noise from the monitors. It was real, but difficult for Clark to comprehend that this was where they both had ended up. Adam was lucky, but Clark was going to pay attention. The next time Adam would be at the hospital would be for the birth of his new baby. Clark would make sure of it. No matter what Adam needed. Clark would work to be a better partner, friend and brother to Adam.

"Amanda is here." Adam lifted his eyes slowly, a distressed look crossing his face. "She is not here because she is going to leave you, Adam," Clark reassured. "I am going to go so she can come in." He nodded. "You look a bit uncomfortable. If you are in pain, I can get the nurse."

"No, I need to feel this." Adam lowered his eyes again. "Thank you for saying everything you did tonight."

"It needed to be said." Clark patted the edge of the bed, Adam's eyes still closed. He grabbed his jacket and reached for the door. He looked back at Adam one last time. Clark needed to feel this too.

Simi and Amanda had just returned from their walk as Clark entered the waiting area. Amanda quickly rushed over to embrace him.

"Thank you so much for coming." Amanda held Clark tightly, despite the discomfort of her pregnant belly against him, she squeezed him extra hard. Her emotions at eight months pregnant were overwhelming tonight. She was a wreck.

"Look at you, Amanda. So beautiful." Clark hadn't seen her since she had gotten pregnant. "May I?" She smiled as she took Clark's hand to her belly.

"No movement right now, but around early evenings, whoever's in there is having a party."

"I am so happy for you, Amanda." Clark pulled back his hand. "He is in room 327." Clark handed her the visitor's pass. "Do you want to come back to my place? It's not comfortable here."

"No, I need to stay with him." She inhaled heavily. "He is still currently my husband." She smiled through gritted teeth.

"Whatever you need, Amanda, I am here for you." Clark pulled her in for another hug, his chin above her head. "You guys are my family. I am so excited to be an Uncle."

"We know." She took the pass and grabbed his hand. "We are excited too." Amanda looked toward Simi, "I like her too." Amanda leaned in to kiss him on the cheek. She turned fully toward Simi and waved before slowly walking through the double doors leading to the patient's room. Clark turned to see Simi leaning against the wall, her hands stuffed in her jacket pockets.

"Thank you for keeping her company. That was nice. How did you know who she was?" Clark stood next to Simi.

"A sad, very pregnant woman walked in." Simi motioned. "I am not Sherlock Holmes, but I took a guess," she chuckled.

"How are you doing?" Clark realized too late that being in a hospital could be difficult for Simi. "Are you okay?"

"Yeah, you know. Hospitals and I, we just can't get enough of each other." She shuffled her feet. "I still remembered how to get to the cafeteria?" She read Clark's expression of concern. "It's okay; I am okay, but um, ready to go." Simi looked at the door toward the hallway of rooms. "Are you going to stay?"

"No, they will sort this out," Clark expressed.

Clark appreciated how Simi insisted on coming with him, how she advised him, and ultimately how she was there for him. No longer strangers but not yet committed to each other, she knew how to be selfless in a moment despite her comfort or wants.

"Did you get anything good?"

Simi reached into her pocket and pulled out two Rice Krispy treat bars.

"You are lucky I got one for you," Simi quipped, walking toward the elevators.

"Why don't I deserve a treat? I didn't do anything wrong," Clark defended.

"The jury is still out on that." Simi smirked, pressing the elevator button for them to leave the hospital.

Chapter 18

Leaving the hospital, Clark insisted on dropping off Simi at her hotel. She didn't protest. The night had not gone as planned, but something deeper had transpired; an intimate exchange of words depicting weakness, knowledge, growth, and sincerity. Their hands remained interlocked the entire ride from the hospital to the curb of her hotel.

Simi looked out the window, feeling slightly unsure of herself. She wanted to forget the conversation with Amanda, just for to-night. She wanted to be selfish and continue the night the way she had hoped it would end. Refusing to hit Pause just one time couldn't hurt? Simi shyly glanced toward Clark, watching the road behind the driver. Light rain began to fall, tampering on the roof of the cab.

"You want to stay with me tonight?" she offered. Simi caught his gaze as the cab stopped. She noted his hesitation.

Clark pulled out cash, exited his door, and came around to open the door for Simi. She took his hand and joined him outside. The cab drove off, and in the stillness of the night, they stood alone on the dimly lit city street.

"Simi . . ." Clark slowly spoke. He brought her hand to his lips, lightly brushing her knuckles with kisses. "If I go inside with you, I am going to want to kiss you." Simi held in her smile. Clark leaned in, speaking closer to her ear. "If you let me kiss you, I will not want to stop." The vibrations of his voice sent tingles down her body. She exhaled, light rain falling over them. "I don't want to be put in the position you left me in Vegas." She understood his concerns.

"It would be awkward if I ghosted you in the same city we both live in." Simi pulled at his hands. "Plus, Chicago seems to be very small. I run into you; I do business with your arch nemesis. It's all a bit convenient if you think about it." She smirked. "But I understand your caution."

Clark accepted her words and stepped back from Simi, motioning for another cab, when he felt her tug at his hand, bringing it back down to his side.

"What happened in Vegas won't happen again." Simi pulled at his hands and wrapped them around her waist, inviting Clark into the hotel with her.

The ride in the elevator was quiet. Simi was still secure in his embrace. Her mind raced with excitement and desire. Memories of her dreams heightened her senses more with each ding of the elevator. As the doors opened, she left his embrace, walking at a matching pace with him until she reached her door. Waving her key, the sound of the lock released, and they walked into her hotel suite.

Clark followed Simi into the bedroom. She paused and pulled her hair to the side, waiting for him to unclasp the top button he had secured earlier. Slowly, he began to pull the zipper down until it stopped at the bottom of her back. Simi released her hair to fall over her skin and pulled the fabric off her shoulders. The dress fell from her body and hit the floor. Clark placed his hands on her waist, gently turning her to face him. Clark imprinted the memory of her beautiful image in front of him, inhaling her intoxicating scent of rosewater. He reached in, pulling her for a kiss, pressing his lips against hers.

The bedroom was dimly lit by the light of the fireplace in the living room. Clark ran his hands down her back, resting them slightly over her lower back, bringing her in fully to him. He flicked at the silk fabric of her panties against her bottom. Her hands pulled at his jacket ends, bunching the fabric inside her palms.

Simi's invitation was hers. Clark had been prepared to leave, ready to handle the day's events with cigarettes and whiskey on his balcony—alone. The emotional stress of the evening wore on both of them. They needed a release. They were choosing the comfort and security of each other.

Simi pulled back from the kiss, softly catching her breath. She brought her fingers up to caress the swelling of her lips. Clark became entranced as she moved her fingers from her lips to his, pressing her pointer finger against his bottom lip, softly gliding it back and forth before cupping his check into her palm and bringing him down for another kiss. A deeper one, where she invited him in. She pressed her body into Clark, guiding him as he walked back to sit on the bed. She pushed off his jacket first, tossing it to the side. Simi then pulled his shirt over his head, dropping it to the floor. A soft laugh escaped her lips.

"Yes?" He pulled her in close, placing small kisses on her tummy. She reached up, releasing the chain of gold necklaces to fall to the floor.

"Fighting through some shyness," she flustered out, bringing her hand over her eyes.

"You should never feel shy with me, Simi." He spoke, his lips lightly touching her stomach. "And I have seen here before." He placed a kiss on the silk fabric covering her. "I'd like to see you again," he growled. His hands traveled from her hips to her backside, which had been tormenting him,

"I haven't yet, seen you." Simi expressed, her shyness quietly diminished to confidence. Seeing him below her and feeling his arms around her was blissful. She wanted to make him feel as good as she was feeling. Leaning to kiss the top of his head, she swiftly pushed him onto his back, straddling and feeling all of him beneath the thin material, the enormity of his passion seeking her attention and care. She trailed kisses across the top of his garment. Her breasts brushed over him. She kissed him over the fabric, causing a deep moan to escape Clark's lips. He had been resting on his elbows and now fully collapsed on the bed. She tucked her fingers into his bottoms and slowly brought them down off his thighs, over his knees, and down to the floor. Running her hands back up his legs, she came up over him. Clark lifted his head up to see her tracing him with her eyes. She brought her hands back to him. She glided her fingers along his throbbing shaft and pulled him back, followed by a soft kiss.

Clark exhaled harshly.

"Shh." She reached for a pillow and handed it to Clark to prop himself up. She smiled inwardly, returning the favor from Vegas. "Tu voulais sentir ma langue?" *Did you want to feel my tongue?*

"That's not fair." Clark painfully chuckled.

"En Français s'il vous plaît, je ne sais pas quoi faire ensuite." *In French please, I am unsure what to do next.* Simi continued to tease. "Devrais-je embrasser comme ça? Should I kiss like this? Simi pressed another wet kiss, letting him feel just the slightest sensation of her tongue. "Non? vous n'aimez pas ça? Peut-être cela?" *No? You don't like this? Maybe this?*

"Simi . . ." Clark threw his head back deep into the pillow. Simi wrapped her fingers around the base and opened her mouth over him. He gripped her hair, attempting to keep her mouth around him as she was able to push herself against him, releasing him from her mouth. Clark gripped the sheets for life.

Simi sat up back on her knees, tapping at her lips, very amused with herself. "Non, il ne semble pas que vous aimiez ça non plus." *No, it doesn't look like you enjoy that either.* She brought her hands back to Clark, delicately dancing them around his shaft up to his head.

Clark winced her thumb wiped across his head. She leaned forward, looking devilishly innocent into his eyes, her brows furrowed as she asked.

"Préférez-vous une femme qui avale?" *Do you prefer a woman who swallows?* She licked the residue off of her thumb, savoring the taste above him.

Clark continued to remain quiet, pacing himself. He wouldn't break beneath her tonight. He held her gaze as a small smile spread across her face. A smile he wasn't sure was positive for him. Simi positioned herself back down before him. She took him in her mouth as deep as she could before a convulsion of a gag emerged. Simi slid up, dragging her tongue wide at the bottom, and inhaled deeply to go down again, working to reach his base. He reached down and grabbed her hair, guiding her at the pace he wanted, but Simi controlled the situation. She reared back and slowed down, releasing him from her mouth and kissing his base, lower and lower, until he had felt her tongue below him, bringing in one and then the other. His entire body tensed. She came back up to him and submerged him again more profoundly, deepest this time. His hand still buried in her hair. She allowed him to continue his wanted pace. Clark exhaled, enjoying the domination, enjoying the sensation. His breath began to quicken as he was on the brink of release until he felt her push back against him. He fought against the urge to overpower her, painfully releasing her as she sat up before him.

"Vouliez-vous que je continue?" *Did you want me to continue?* She won.

Clark swallowed, his body reacting against him, not understanding what was happening nor why the pleasure had stopped. " S'il vous plaît, continuez s'il vous plaît." *Please, please continue.* Clark opened his eyes, looking ahead at Simi, her beautiful brown eyes gleaming with delight. He was almost out of breath looking at her. She was beautiful before him, masterful at teasing him. She was a match for him.

Satisfied with his confession, Simi, continued to press kisses down his stomach until she reached Clark again, taking him all in and fully releasing her control. Clark held her beneath him, feeling the sensations slowly intensify again, building up until she could get him right back where he was. Her tongue, her lips and mouth, greedily enjoying all of him. Soft moans escaped her lips as she continued, pushing Clark over the edge. His grip slipped into the silky locks of her hair, holding her down against him, feeling her take him all in. He shuddered as she removed her lips, continuing to trail her sweet kisses above his stomach. She cuddled to his side, smacking her lips next to his ear. "Now, we are even for Vegas," she whispered gleefully.

"Même pas près." *Not even close.* Clark secured his arm around her waist before flipping her to her backside, covering her with his body. He kissed each nipple with a lick and suckled to follow. Simi dug into his arms.

"Why didn't you want me to know you spoke French?" Simi's question escaped her lips breathlessly.

"I was hoping to use it to my advantage," Clark spoke over her breasts. "Your little display tonight, does not make us even from Vegas either."

"What does that mean?" Simi caressed his shoulders.

"It means, Simi, that this year, you have haunted my dreams, distracted me, and nearly destroyed my sanity with a mere sampling of all you have to offer, and I imagine it will be quite a long time until I feel fully satiated by you." Simi smiled as his words cascaded over her body.

"How long of a time?" Simi coyly asked. Clark paused his kisses and brought his eyes to meet her gaze.

"That, my dear Simi, is entirely up to you." He reached his hand down and removed her bottoms from his way. He brought his lips back up and pressed them against her cheek. Clark positioned himself between her thighs. Kissing from the inside of her knee to the warmth of her. Simi sighed, closing her eyes at the sensations.

Clark grazed a section of her thigh with his beard. He lightly lifted his two fingers and dragged them along her skin. Clark placed a kiss as Simi held a breath. He was learning about her body. Studying her reactions, her likes and dislikes. Finding the sensitive spots. She was receptive, not wanting him to stop. Clark continued to trace around her thigh and over to her stomach.

"Clark." Simi was close to shaking beneath him. Each caress was beginning to feel like too much.

"Are you enjoying this?" Clark glided his fingers above her black curls, feeling the slickness and readiness of her lips. "This frustration you are feeling—it will pass. I won't make you wait months between intimate engagements." Clark lightly caressed her lips. Simi lifted her hips up. "Or should I?" He teased.

"Okay, Clark." She was growing impatient.

"Relax, Simi, I wouldn't do that to myself." Clark kissed her forehead softly. "I am just taking my time in learning everything I can."

Clark rose to his knees and leaned over her body. Simi, beneath him, was a beautiful sight. She adjusted her legs around him. She reached down, finding him, guiding him. Her eyes closed as he pressed in. She inhaled harshly, furrowing her brows at the sensation. Clark quickly pressed a kiss down, refocusing her attention from the overwhelming fullness she was experiencing. She adjusted her hips beneath him, every movement causing Clark great restraint. Simi exhaled slowly, slowly lifting her gaze to meet his. "Better than the dreams." She smiled.

He pressed down above her, Simi trailed her fingers into his back, and they began to match a steady rhythm between each other. He kissed her as he continued his pace. He kissed each breast, bringing himself to watch her lie beneath him, hair entangled over the pillows, as vivid as the Restless painting. Her eyes closed shut with deep gasps escaping from her mouth. Her hands slid around from his back, holding on to his arms. He felt her begin to tighten around him. Her breath began to hold, as her nails dug deeper into his skin. Clark reached for her leg, pushing it up, opening her more to let him in deeper. She repeated his name over and over as he continued. Small sensations intensified around him, but he wanted more. He wanted to take her as long as she could. He didn't want any of this to end. Not the intimacy, not the banter; he didn't want this night to end. This woman had captivated him in a way he had never experienced before. How she did it, he couldn't understand.

"Please, Clark." Her lips released her final plea as she held him tight, finally giving in to her orgasm. Clark, feeling her pleasure all around him, let go, relaxing his entire body as they both came to an end together. Her body shuddered. She was satiated. Biting her lips, still rubbing her hands around his body, she squeezed her thighs against him. Clark had not yet retreated. He took in her pleasure. He placed another kiss on her chest, causing a giggle and shudder.

"Too much," she said.

"No such thing." Clark withdrew from her and rolled to his side. She turned to join him, resting her thigh over his. She reached to feel and hold him again.

"Prove it," she challenged him. Simi wanted more.

"You sure?" Clark smiled; he had hoped to achieve this. To have her crave and desire him as he did her. Their intimacy together was continuing to grow. Clark reached for her again, proving there was no such thing as too much between them. He claimed her every way she let him, her body begging and pleading for more. He was intoxicated by her, with her. She felt right in his arms. The way she said his name, the more she begged for him, was different from anyone else. He felt his entire self within her, and he wanted to keep her in his arms. He didn't want her out of his sight. Perhaps a life with love was possible for Clark to obtain.

Chapter 19

"Hey, Clark?" Kelsey peaked through. "Demkov is here," Clark looked at her questioningly. "He is walking the floor, talking with the staff pod leaders. You didn't have anything with him today." Clark walked over to her.

"All right, thanks for letting me know. Can you set up in here?" Clark put his hand on the door. "Bring in the liquor cart too." Kelsey nodded.

Clark quickly finished his third espresso of the morning. His mind was still in a languid state of bliss. Leaving Simi this morning was awful. She kept assuring him that she was here now, but still, the thought was taunting his mind. Clark had wanted to be remote but was thankful to Simi for pushing him out of bed. It would not have been good optics for them if Clark and Adam, both were not in the office.

Clark walked toward Demkov, who was sitting at the table of interns, engrossed in what one of the students was sharing. Clark took his time making his way toward him, wanting the natural exchange to continue without his presence being a disruption. He saw Demkov's eyes light up and clapped his hands. He enthusiastically shouted, "that's brilliant!" He caught Clark's gaze and acknowledged him. He waved at the intern, urging him to continue and show him more of what he was speaking to.

Clark stayed at Demkov's side as he visited each company and staff member on board. He greeted them with hearty handshakes and seemed truly engaged with each person when they spoke. If Demkov wanted to run for office, he wouldn't have to make much effort. When Demkov was satisfied with his tour, he walked back with Clark to his office.

"The energy here is fantastic. Those kids in the beginning, that Avery? Oh, he is going places. You should start scholarships for these kids too."

"That's the plan. Access is the goal. It's open to everyone." Clark motioned to the round table with a small spread of cookies and fruit. "Can I get you something to drink?"

"Libation sounds perfect. Ice and vodka if you please." Demkov walked along the windows of Clark's office before standing in front of the whiteboard, deciphering the text and scribbles before him. "I am sorry to have come by unannounced. I just had some concerns." Clark walked over, handing Demkov his glass; while Clark's held water and ice in his glass.

"Sure, let's talk them out." Demkov turned away from the whiteboard and sat on the leather sofa. Clark took his seat across from him. "I think involved investors are a great addition. Sometimes when you are too deep into something, you can miss things. Outside perspectives are really helpful." Clark's response, though canned, sounded sincere.

"It's funny how you say that. When you are too involved with something, you can be blinded. I agree very much with that." Demkov took a drink and rested the glass on the table. He leaned forward. "I am not one to tell you how to run your business, even with my money, I should be fair, our money," Demkov laughed. Clark smiled uncomfortably. "Still, it is yours, but I want to ensure success here as well."

"Thank you," Clark responded. "Just tell me how you would like to be more involved here."

"No, no, I appreciated this little visit, but that is not what I am talking about." Demkov pressed the tips of his fingers together. "I have concerns over your partner and how his lifestyle may not fit what your goals are here. Now listen"—Demkov raised his hands—

"I am no innocent. I have my spot reserved and ready for me in hell. I have accepted that. But, it would behoove you to think about something else for your friend," Demkov finished.

Clark smiled through his teeth. "I understand, and thank you for your sage advice. I will take my time in determining the next steps." Demkov finished his drink.

"People will judge you for everything—especially those whose company you seek. " Demkov patted his knees before standing. Clark stood with him. "No, please, I have taken enough time. I will see myself out. I may stop by Avery's desk again."

Clark followed Demkov out of his office and stood by Kelsey's desk as Demkov re-engaged with Avery before leaving.

"My office," Clark directed Kelsey, following behind. He picked up Demkov's glass. He was tempted to throw it at the wall. "Shut the door," Clark spoke sternly. "Who knows about Adam?" Clark asked Kelsey. She raised her eyebrows, motioning with her finger between them. "Where did Adam get this meeting with Demkov, Kelsey? How was he introduced?" Clark maintained his tone, but he was angry.

"Clark, what is the issue?" Kelsey snapped back. "What did Demkov say to you?"

"He knows—Demkov, who brought in all the other money, knows. I need to find out how, and I need you to tell me how Adam was introduced to Demkov. This is not negotiable, Kelsey; you need to tell me the connection to Demkov now." Clark waited patiently as Kelsey processed her thoughts. She took a seat in front of Clark. She was embarrassed to admit the truth.

"Clark, I don't know."

"What do you mean you don't know?" Clark took a seat across from Kelsey. She shook her head. "Tell me what you do know."

"I don't know what to tell you, Clark. Adam had been trying to find investors since last fall. He was trying to secure money before all the budgets were done for the year. He hustled hard, but every-thing came up short. He went to Money2020 and had a few nibbles but no bites." What Kelsey was sharing wasn't new. "Then, you know, Adam said we had funding. He said someone from Mon-ey2020 finally bit, but Clark . . ." Kelsey hesitated.

"What is it?"

"Demkov wasn't there. He didn't attend. Honestly, I thought it was strange that Adam said it was from Money2020 when it wasn't." Kelsey noticed his grip tighten around the glass before he slammed it down.

"That motherfucker lied." Clark rarely lost his temper, and never had done so at work. He exhaled, stepping back from Kelsey with his hand up in apologies.

"It's okay, Clark—but what is it?" Kelsey stood from her seat, worried by Clark's reaction.

"I need you to write up that Adam is going to be on pat leave. I want Rashid and Cynthia in my office by the time I get back. We will have a bit of a structure change until I sort things out," Clark quickly rattled off as he reached for his bag and jacket.

"Of course—but where are you going?" Clark didn't answer, leaving Kelsey to watch the door close on her as he left the office. "Looks like we are finding new capital," Kelsey muttered as she cleared the beverage cart and plates from Clark's office.

When Clark returned to the office, he had his meetings with his CTO and CFO—updating them on his plans moving forward. Getting Demkov's money out by next year was the new goal, but Clark needed to do it quietly. He didn't trust Demkov and believed he would pull funding randomly. His funds may have been legitimate, but not his character.

Clark brought Kelsey back into his office, apologizing again for his outburst. Kelsey waved it off, ready and waiting for instructions.

"I want you to book me at least weekly. I need to sit in front of these guys, give them the pitch and collect. It has to be in and out and under the radar," Clark explained. "Use my personal card, send the gatekeepers what you think is best to get on the calendar starting as soon as possible, and keep making appointments until new funding is secured." Clark stared intently at Kelsey. "Adam cannot know about any of this. I need you on my side for this."

" I don't play favorites between you guys. I do my job," Kelsey defended.

"You are right—I didn't mean for it to come across that way. You do an excellent job."

"You can't let this overtake the rest of the year with Adam gone. You gotta be the face now too. The floor needs to see more of you and be happy."

"I hear you. I will be here every day; I am not traveling."

"Clark, we have been through worse—we will be fine," Kelsey encouraged.

"We went through worse before we had the taste of success and a win," Clark reminded her.

"You did it before, and you will do it again. That is why your entire C-suite is back. We trust and believe in you. Remember that." Kelsey stood from her seat and left Clark alone in his office, hoping he absorbed her words.

***

"I think I am ready to go to weekly sessions now." Simi crossed her legs and placed her hands on her knee. "I feel like once a week can get me a clearer schedule. This Japanese class has been the hardest one yet." Simi nervously maintained Jane's gaze. "I think once a week will give me more opportunity to practice what we talk about instead of me holding it in and waiting to discuss situations with you."

"I think that is fine, Simi." Simi exhaled, butterflies were in her stomach thinking of how to ask the question. "So, catch me up with where everything stands."

"I expected you to be a bit more saddened by the ask," Simi smirked. Simi was close to her second full month in Chicago. She enjoyed making her place home and exploring the city.

"This ask makes me excited, makes me proud. It reinforces that I am good at my job if you feel strong enough to pull back," Jane explained. Simi had not thought of that point of view before. It made sense.

"About eighty percent of my stuff has been unpacked. It has been nice setting things up for my home. I never felt like a stranger in Roman's home, but I didn't change anything either. This place is all mine. I have never had that before. Most of the furniture is in, too. So, it's just situating and settling every day. Oh, and I am hopefully getting that white space. I will know for sure before Thanksgiving."

"What are your plans for Thanksgiving and the holidays? I know visiting Paris is still on your to-do list."

"It's pretty up in the air still. I don't think I am ready to go to Paris yet, but it will be soon."

"Will Clark join you if you go to Paris?"

"Um," Simi faltered.

"Are you two still dancing around each other?" Jane pierced.

"It's not dancing. He is busy, and he is self-sufficient. He doesn't need me to take care of him, I think," Simi responded. "I am still figuring out how he works and what he needs."

"Did you think you would start caring for him early in a relationship?" Jane tilted her hand.

"I know that I tend to do that. It's just in my nature," Simi shared. "I don't think it is a bad thing."

"Did you feel equal in your relationship with Roman?" Simi frowned at the question; an impulsive defense was beginning to form.

"I have made clear that my relationship with Roman is off-limits. He isn't here to defend or course correct any issues that we may have had."

"I respect that, Simi. I do. I am asking you, though, to think about your relationship with him and how he drew you right away into his world, his home. Where now you are saying this is the first time you feel like you?"

"I don't understand what your point is, Jane. I wasn't unhappy with him."

"I didn't say you were. I want to make sure and don't misunderstand this Simi. I do support your relationship with Clark." Jane adjusted. "I want to make sure you stay visible in it. You have things to complete this year, may I remind you." Simi nodded, "I am excited for you. You are dating Clark, just dating. That's healthy. This doesn't mean you aren't able to grow to another level of intimacy with him, but it does mean you are taking some time for yourself. You have not been absorbed into his life, into his world. This is a positive conversation, and you should be proud of it."

Proud was not how Simi felt. After the first night they had spent together, Simi did assume they would fall into a familiar situation as she had experienced before. She understood that Clark wasn't Roman but was naïve to the new type of relationship she was entering. Clark had begun to close up and internalize everything he was going through at work. There was a substantial shift in his energy, in his focus. He made every effort to entertain her, but seemed relieved when she would insist on the low key night. She didn't want to pry, but he wasn't sharing. Her urge to ask, to get invited into his private world, was blocked by her feeling of inadequacy. She had never had to ask to be a part of someone's life. Clark's actions toward her, with her, all led to a path where she just assumed it would happen naturally.

To Jane's point, she was dating Clark. She was living an independent life of her own where her life was on her terms and no one else's. Now she had to get used to it and enjoy it. Simi thought through the idea as she left Jane's office.

"Oy! Hang on a moment." Simi turned to see a familiar face. The woman quickly threw on a sweatshirt covering her sleeve tattoo of music notes. "I didn't think it would be so cold today, but I hoped I'd catch you."

"Sorry—I haven't caught your name."

"Zella." Simi had noticed her sessions had been after Zella's for a while now. However, their original small talk had faded within the past few visits. "Do you know where we could grab a drink?" Simi looked at her curiously. It was just a few minutes after eleven on a Tuesday.

"Umm, I was going to head to the Soho house for a bit?" Simi shared.

"Yeah, yeah, that would be great. It's so bloody cold today. Are you up for some company?" Simi nodded her head 'yes'. She wasn't truly in the right head space to think otherwise. The sheer ask of this stranger to hang out, though, was a welcomed distraction to avoid her need to replay her session with Jane for the next few hours.

They had shared minimal words in their ride over. Settling at Soho House, it seemed Zella had something on her mind. Grabbing a spot on a u-shaped booth, Zella immediately waved down a server. Simi was still disrobing from her layers as Zella's ordered.

"Two short glasses, one with room temp gin and one with cold gin. Shaken with ice, but poured without. Straight. Double pours each." The server looked over at Simi curiously. "Oh, and chips? I mean fries? A plate of fries." Zella looked over to Simi, "I will Venmo you."

Simi waved her hand dismissively. "I guess I will do vodka rocks."

"There we are! I knew we would get off," Zella exclaimed. The server nodded hesitantly. "I know you might think I am a bit mad. I wasn't stalking you. I just felt like I could talk with you—connect with you." Simi nodded.

"I get it. It's a welcomed distraction—"

"She broke your soul today too?" Zella referenced. "She does that! Why do you go back to her? Why does she do this? Why do we let her!" The drinks arrived, sliding across the wood table between them. Before Simi could reach for her glass, Zella immediately downed the warm gin. Simi clenched her teeth at the sight and was unable to politely hide her face of distress. "I know—the first one is for the nerves. Second I will savor."

"I don't mean to look horrified. That was just a lot." Simi tapped her fingertips along her glass. "So, Zella—"

"Right, right—I know," she interrupted. "I just need the gin to settle in a bit. Can you keep talking?" Zella pleaded. "Like, what's your story? How did you end up here?"

"I won't chug my vodka this early." Simi laughed. "I lost someone here. I got too scared to do anything about it. I stayed here until I broke, and now am trying something new. To recap."

"Lover, brother? Who did you lose?" Zella was looking for comfort, Simi realized.

"People. First my mother, years back, and then my fiance—Roman. I was in a relationship with a man named Roman," Simi shared, taking her first sip.

"Sorry."

"Thank you." Silence hung between them. Simi could see she was nervous. She wasn't sure exactly how old she was, but already Simi felt a sisterly connection with her. She continued to offer more,

"I like Jane because she keeps me honest about my reality. I need that."

"I don't." Zella clenched her hands together. "I mean—I suppose I do need it, but I don't want it."

Simi understood exactly what she meant. She wasn't sure if she and Zella were able to socialize with each other, but today she didn't care. It was nice to have a conversation with another individual. Not to be dissected, but just to be. Simi glanced at her phone and noticed a few text messages from Clark had popped through. She turned her phone face-side down.

After a few hours, Simi had formed a bond with Zella. Despite their individual trauma, there was a spice to Zella that spoke to Simi. She was funny and outspoken, and the brutal honesty of British humor had Simi laughing so hard that her cheeks hurt. She had made a friend, and for someone in their thirties, that was something to celebrate.

"So you just moved here? But you have been with Jane for almost a year?" Zella had made herself more comfortable in the booth.

"Yeah, I was living out of a suitcase," Simi shared.

"Shelter to SoHo house?" Zella asked, surprised. "Cheers to that." Simi waved her hand to clarify.

"No, no—was in a hotel. Just in a state of limbo."

"My misunderstanding. You didn't fit that profile, honestly," Zella retorted.

"What's my profile?"

"Dunno yet—still trying to sort it out. You seem normal, travelled. You have some money, just not sure if you are dripping in it," Zella teased; she drummed her fingers on the table. "I know you have enough to cover this tab, though."

"I'll pick this up—if you tell me about the song on your arm." Simi felt the energy change immediately. Zella kept her eyes low, sitting up and resting her arms on the table. Simi rested her hand over Zella's. "I'll tell you my dark secrets if you tell me yours." Zella grabbed her gaze, her eyes straining to hold back emotions.

She listened intently as Zella shared her story about what brought her to Jane, to Chicago. Simi let her speak freely, keeping her reactions empathetic on the surface as her anger for Zella's situation grew on the inside. Learning about where Zella was now in her life and how she was trying to heal allowed Simi to share her mistakes without fear of judgment. Zella listened as supportively as Simi had. Both understood that they each were on a journey to self-betterment.

***

When Simi arrived at Clark's, he was surprised to see her with two large bags of food. Her giddy embarrassment caused her to admit that she had been day drinking and was hungry when she put in the order. Clark smiled, taking the bags from her and heading to the kitchen. He excused himself to wrap up one more email as Simi opened the containers of Indian food in the kitchen. She inhaled the aromas and eagerly popped a piece of chicken pakora into her mouth. This would sober her up quickly. She had begun to move the items into the dining room when Clark returned.

"Eating in the dining room again?" Clark spoke from behind.

"This is what it is for? Hurry before it gets cold. It smells great." Simi took a seat, adding serving cutlery to the dishes.

"I order from them at least once a month." Clark sat next to her. He was still distracted from the day but wanted to enjoy his time with her. He wanted to know where she was today and who she was with.

"So, how long are you going to internalize?" Simi tilted her head, handing him a plate of portioned options from their order.

"At least an hour longer." Clark accepted the plate. "It's just investor relation stuff. Things Adam was better at than me."

"How is Adam?" Simi was curious but had waited for an opportunity to ask.

"He is good. Amanda says he will be back soon. He has been extending his time. Hopefully, back before the baby comes." Clark spooned a clump of rice together, mixing in some of the curry before taking a bite.

"You shouldn't worry so much, Clark." She lightly grazed her fingers over his cheek and moved closer to him; she began to laugh instead of continuing to be sensual. "This doesn't work with curry oil dripping off my fingers."

"How much did you drink this afternoon?" Clark asked.

"I think we started at eleven?"

"Eleven? Where were you?"

"SoHo house." Simi reached over for a samosa pulling apart the fried dough. She looked over to Clark, who was patiently waiting. "I made a friend!" Simi shared excitedly.

"So you mentioned," Clark said dryly, realizing Simi was unaware of his curiosity masking as jealousy.

"She is so pretty. I don't think we can be friends, which makes it a bit naughty too," Simi delighted. "She also goes to Jane, and we would make small talk, but today she invited me out, and it was a lot of fun." Simi brightened up at her next idea. "You should meet her! I have her number, we can go out and get some more drinks!" Simi cheesed at Clark. "I know you will love her." Simi began annoyingly poking at Clark.

"Stop." Clark's jaw tightened as he swatted her hand away. "Maybe another time. You need some water." Clark left the dining room table and went into the kitchen, opening the refrigerator for a water bottle for Simi.

"You aren't being nice tonight." Simi frowned as he placed the water in front of her. She wiped her hands clean and stood from her seat, swinging her legs over Clark to straddle him.

"Simi," Clark exhaled as he held her waist above him. Simi leaned in for a kiss as Clark shifted his hand away. "Come on, up, up, up. We aren't doing this." Clark patted her, pushing her off of him as he stood. "Can you just give me a second?"

Simi's brightness faded to embarrassment. Taking a step back, she returned to her seat and grabbed the water.

Clark left the dining room, retreating to his bathroom. He wet a small towel with cold water and rubbed it over his face. Clark stared back at his reflection, frustrated with himself.

Simi didn't do anything wrong, his frustrations were not from her. The complications at work were not because of Simi. Clark spoke to himself, encouraging himself to get it together. Simi was here for him, to be with him, to play with him. Resetting himself, he headed back to the dining room. He ran his hand over his head as he walked down his hallway.

"I'm sorry, Simi, work has—" Clark realized he was talking to no one. He walked into the kitchen and living room and looked on the balcony. She left. Coming back into the kitchen, he saw a torn piece of the take-out bag.

"Call me tomorrow—Simi xoxo."

Clark exhaled sharply as he crumpled the letter beneath his hand; with a clenched jaw, he grabbed his laptop and phone and headed into his office, the food still out and untouched in the dining room.

Chapter 20

Thanksgiving had finally arrived. Simi was looking forward to it since she had not seen much of Clark. He had abruptly started taking day trips out of the city, sometimes leaving within hours' notice. Plans were shuffled around or canceled, but luckily, Simi had enough to keep her busy. She had secured her white space and began reconnecting with old contacts for new artist recommendations, and if that hadn't been filling her time, her Japanese teacher was making her not to confident of passing her.

Simi had been working hard to follow Jane's advice and focus on herself and her needs. Simi was beginning to understand how much her life had been enmeshed in Roman's. This realization didn't upset her, but it made her realize that even though she enjoyed her newfound independence, she missed being needed in a relationship.

Zella recently mentioned that Simi didn't have a lot of relationship experience. She had never thought about it before, but it was accurate. Before Roman, it was the typical youthful hook-up, but no long-term relationships. Perhaps Roman and hers was just a special one? Maybe relationships were supposed to be this difficult in the beginning before two people fell in sync. Simi felt even more foolish trying to ask Daroush about his relationship, her baby brother seemingly having more expertise than her.

Simi wanted Clark to need her as Roman had. Simi reflected on her conversation with Amanda about Clark starting a relationship while he was dating someone else was a dick move, but Amanda wasn't surprised. Clark rarely thought about other people before himself, Amanda had shared, surmising that women often feel like they are with Clark, but his heart lies with his success.

Simi understood what that comment meant. Roman was already established; he had nothing left to prove. He worked because he enjoyed it, but Clark . . . Clark was fighting for change, for recognition, and clearly for himself. Simi didn't want to challenge that—or compete with it.

She forced herself not to spiral and decided to see how this weekend went. She would spoil him and enjoy doing so this weekend, and if by Monday morning he left her bed and she felt that pit of rejection in her stomach, then she would bring this up with Jane. Simi exhaled at the thought. The last thing she wanted to hear Jane relay was that rebound relationships often fail.

Standing in the kitchen, food surrounded her counter. She had ingredients portioned out for a Thanksgiving meal to feed a family of ten. She had been excited to cook, but this wasn't how she envisioned the day. Clark was still in her office. He had come over late last night and slept in bed for a few hours, but by the time she woke up, he was back in front of his computer. Simi rubbed the back of her calf with her foot. She looked out the window. It was unseasonably warm today, almost hot, with the temperatures hanging around the mid-sixties. Khoreshes were simmering on the stove, and the Cornish hen was baking nicely. It would be a few hours before everything was ready.

She bit at her lip and pulled out a small container from her drawer. She slid open the metal tin and rolled her finger over the tightly rolled paper of a joint. Simi held the metal tin in her hand and found a pack of matches. She entered her bedroom and grabbed a blanket folding it over her arm. She softly walked to the office where she found Clark leaning back in his chair, jaw clenched and frowning at his phone. When he noticed her in the doorway, his features softened immediately.

"Hey, beautiful." Clark hadn't wanted to be isolated in the office, but the rest of the world was open, even if the US wasn't.

"Have I shown you the roof yet?" Simi smiled. "It's been rather warm, and it's not furnished or even finished, but I think you and I could use some air." Simi motioned the blanket forward. "If you can step away?"

Clark was intrigued. "I can step away." Clark sat up from his chair and pulled Simi in for a soft kiss. She smiled softly into his eyes and reached for his hand. She pulled him down the hallway into her laundry space which revealed an access door, which she pushed with her shoulder, and they walked up a staircase that led to an open-space roof. Clark took a moment as he stepped onto the rooftop. It was the entire view of the city skyline from the west. "Wow, Simi, this is awesome!" Clark walked the space of the roof, peering down of the side of the building. A mid-height brick wall blocked them from the building maintenance on the other side of the roof.

"Yeah, I have plans for it." Simi flipped out the blanket, resting it in the middle of the wood planks. "Hopefully, I will have everything done to enjoy the summer." Clark joined her on the blanket. "Not the most comfortable, but I needed some air." Simi stretched out her legs and leaned back on her arms.

Silence lingered between them. Clark had so much he wanted to tell her but couldn't. He wasn't sure why. Simi caught his gaze and reached over for him.

"Come, lay. Rest your head. I can smooth out the tension." It was an intimate invitation, and though laying on the blanket provided some comfort, the floor was hard. Clark obliged and looked up to see Simi peering down at him. Softly, she began to stroke his eyebrows with her thumb. "Changing the world takes a lot out of you." She brushed lightly over his lips.

"I am sorry." Clark kept his eyes closed as she caressed his face. "I am here with you. This is going to pass."

"Don't be sorry. I wish I could help you."

"You are, more than you know." Clark reached for her wrist and kissed her lightly. Simi wiggled beneath him, retrieving something from her pocket. Eyes still closed, he curiously used his other senses to figure out what she was doing. A familiar odor swept across his nose; he looked up to see a cheesing Simi wiggling a joint in her fingers.

"It's legal now," she chuckled. Clark smiled as he took the joint from her and placed it between his fingers.

"I know I have been distracted, but not enough not to notice you have been too?" Clark took the book of matches Simi offered in her hand. "Having regrets?"

"Regrets?" Simi asked as Clark struck the match on fire and pulled in the first drag. He inhaled, holding his breath briefly before exhaling. "That's an odd question." Simi mimicked Clark's actions on the joint, except her exhale was less graceful, with Simi cupping her mouth and coughing. "Don't laugh. I don't smoke like you." Simi swallowed hard, adjusting to the sensation in her throat. She wiped at her eyes. She took the joint back into her fingers, inhaling much slower this time, returning it to Clark.

"I don't smoke," Clark defended. Simi shot him a questioning look. "Okay, sometimes, yes, does it bother you?"

"I am not the biggest fan," Simi scrunched her nose.

Clark offered her another hit, as Simi waved in declined. "You never said anything." Clark felt embarrassed by her admission. Simi laid back down on the blanket. "I'll do better." Clark positioned next to her, laying shoulder to shoulder. The sky was blue, with white clouds moving above them. Clark intertwined his fingers with hers. "Wild weather for Thanksgiving."

"Reminds me of Houston." Simi turned to Clark. "I have no regrets. I am adjusting to this life, my new reality. Sometimes it feels comfortable. Sometimes I feel scared." Simi studied Clark's face as he stared at the sky.

"Why are you scared?"

Simi held her breath; the question was simple. Her mind was more relaxed, the lines on her face no longer tense. "I guess I just always have this worry at the back of my head that stages in my life are temporary," Simi shared. "Like my consciousness telling me 'don't get too comfortable,' that is scary."

"Do you feel like this is temporary?"

"No, but it's not really up to me, is it?" Simi nudged Clark with a light chuckle.

"What does that mean?" Clark looked up curiously, unsure how she meant that.

"I was just being silly. Did I tell you about the white space?" Simi changed subjects. She hadn't meant to imply that she was worried about her longevity with Clark. "It's all done. Hopefully, I can get some shows on the schedule after the holidays."

"That's great news, Simi."

"Thanks. Is it hitting you yet?"

"Yeah, this is nice. This is the most relaxed I have felt in some time." Clark inhaled again, closing his eyes with a strong exhale. Simi turned on her side and rested her arm on his chest. "I am sorry I have been so busy. It seems that since you have come back, life has just intensified for me."

"Do you want to talk about it?"

"No," Clark laughed.

Simi sat up. She looked around the rooftop and then back to Clark. "Let's go back inside. I can't get comfortable." Clark pulled Simi, bringing her to rest on him.

"Better?" He grinned. "How does this feel so good right now?" Clark gripped his hands on Simi's thighs.

"It's been a bit." Simi shortly stated. Clark frowned, realizing she was right.

"Simi." He frowned. "What else are you keeping from me? You don't like smoking; I am not taking care of you as I should. You need to tell me." Clark sat up, keeping Simi in his lap. He wrapped his arms around her body.

"I don't want you to worry about me. I just try to have a fun time while I have you." The words sent chills down his body.

"Fun? This is just fun for you?" Clark immediately felt a rush of negativity and foolishness clatter into his mind.

"I think this has been fun for you. No?" The look in Clark's eyes made Simi nervous. She didn't want to start an argument. "No, I mean, it's more than fun, obviously." Simi gestured. "What I mean is that it's not just you. This timing is just weird. You're busy and—"

"So you do have regrets. Moving here," Clark interrupted. "Being with me. Is this just fun? It's why you left my place that night. You aren't invested in this, in us."

"Slow down. What are you talking about?" Simi held her hands on his face, searching his eyes. "Clark—do you get paranoid when you get high?" She softened the frown lines on his forehead. "I have no regrets, Clark." Simi drew him in for a kiss. A slow and magical kiss where nerves and senses were elongated. She needed to slow down his racing thoughts. She felt the warmth and strength of his hands on her body embedded into her. It had been longer than Simi had wanted without intimacy between them. She hadn't kissed while high since college, and this one was exceptionally better. Slowly breaking the kiss, Simi squeezed her thighs around Clark's waist as she sat in his lap.

"Simi . . ." She smiled, still cupping his face. "That kiss was amazing. Can we try it again?" Clark felt another squeeze of her thighs around him. "Please?" She batted her lashes up at him.

He couldn't resist this. He couldn't resist her. "Bedroom?"

"Bedroom."

Simi held her hand against the bottom of her throat. Her whole body tingled. Every touch and caress intensified her mental state. His kisses against her skin, his tongue against her. His tongue. She clenched her eyes. He was making up for the lost time. He was saying he was sorry for not being available, for being distracted. He was not distracted now. His tongue again, Simi stretched out her arms. Clark brought her legs down, pulling her hips against his lips again.

"Now, together. Please." Simi reached for him. "I need you inside me." It was all too much. Her body felt waves of pleasure. She felt like she could see them, and her entire body responded to Clark. He leaned down, pressing a kiss on the base of her neck, traveling up to her lips. His weight settled above hers. Simi was overwhelmed with sensations. Her nerves endings amplifying ever caress, she felt out of control. Unable to breath but the blissful pleasure she was experiencing. She felt every single movement. She heard every single sound, and her fingertips hovered over Clark. Simi felt like she would shatter beneath him. When Clark entered Simi had patience left, despite her wants to extend the moment her entire body erupted under him. Simi held tightly to his arms as she buried her cries of pleasure into his shoulder. "Clark." She exhaled. She was embarrassed. She felt his smile against her temple. She finished without him; his smug chuckle didn't make her feel better.

"No, no, come on, it's fine." Simi pulled a pillow over her face, groaning. "It happens to all of us." Clark now erupted in his own laughter. Simi hit the pillow against him. He took it happily, relishing in this moment.

"You can't do that again," she exhaled. "That was too much. You can't do that to me high."

"Oh, this might be the only way I do it now." Clark softly ran his fingers over her bare skin. She shrieked and gathered the blankets over her to protect herself from him. "That probably was the best head I have ever given."

"You are going to be on this all day, aren't you."

"You would too." He was right. Simi would be delighted had she mastered his body as he had just done hers. She ignored the fact that they both needed showers and pulled the blanket over them. She snuggled into Clark's arms, listening to his heartbeat as she drifted to sleep.

Simi woke up to the sound of her oven timer. She frowned, not wanting to move from his side. As she began to pull away, Clark shook his head disapprovingly.

"The food will burn." Simi explained.

"We can order a pizza," Clark offered.

Simi rolled her eyes, pushing the blankets down, and went to the kitchen to check on her food. Returning to the bedroom, she smiled seeing Clark resting peacefully before entering her bathroom to shower.

Clark opened his eyes as he heard the water from the shower turn on. He grabbed his jeans and slid them on as he went into the kitchen. The food smelled great. Trying to focus on the fruit tray, he couldn't help but sneak over to the stove to lift off the covers and spoon a few of the dishes that were simmering. Everything tasted so good and flavorful. He was in his own trance of multiple spoon dips into one of the khoreshes when Simi cleared her throat in the kitchen.

"Well, it's nice to see that you like it." Her hair was wrapped up in a towel and she wore a thin black dress over her body. Clark dipped the spoon into the pot and brought it out for Simi to taste. She looked at him as she blew softly over the eggplant and tomato stew. She nodded, taking a bite. She wiped the side of her mouth. "Wow, that is good."

"It really is." As Clark set the spoon down, he heard his phone go off from the office. He hadn't realized it was the first time he had been separated from his phone for hours in weeks. He caught Simi's gaze like a boy asking permission from his mother. She couldn't help but laugh.

"Get your phone, Clark." He kissed her on the cheek before rushing past her into the office. Simi checked the temperature of the hens in the oven. She pulled serving ware and plates out to bring to her wooden dining table. She had made too much food, though at this moment, she felt confident she could finish it herself. Walking back from the table, she slowed as Clark returned to the kitchen, rubbing his hand over his head. She wasn't able to decipher his mood.

"Um, weird question, but do you have to-go containers?" Clark half chuckled.

"That is a weird question." Simi waited for an explanation as Clark looked around the kitchen.

"I mean, you did cook for like six people." She frowned, watching Clark. "I bet I could get some containers and come back?"

"Clark?" Simi asked. "What's going on?"

"That was Adam on the phone. They had a baby girl a few days ago. They didn't tell anyone and don't want to yet," Clark shared, still processing the news. "Can we?" Clark was flustered. "Would you mind?" He drummed his fingers on the table. "I can order something."

"Let's go meet your niece, Clark." Simi came to his side and placed her hand on his shoulder. "There is a Chinese food place around the corner that's probably open. I am sure you can buy some containers from them and some plastic wrap. I have boxes."

"Really?" Clark asked.

"Of course." He hugged Simi; she once again showed him the flexibility that he knew he needed in his life.

"I hate to use Uber on holiday, though." Clark looked at his phone.

"I can drive." Simi noticed Clark's expression. "I am good to drive. That nap was the rest of my high." Simi began turning the burners off the stove.

"You have a car? When did you get a car?"

"I brought it from Houston. I think it can fit a box in the trunk. I think." Simi chuckled; that car was so small. "I will go change if you want to get the containers." Clark followed Simi out of the kitchen into her bedroom.

"What kind of car is it?"

"It's a Porsche. An old one, nothing fancy." Simi began quickly making the bed.

"Roman's?" Clark asked. He didn't mean it to be accusatory, but it had come out that way. Simi slowed her making of the bed and turned her head.

"Does it matter?" She folded her arm against her chest and stepped back from the bed. Suddenly feeling a fire of frustration rush through her cheeks. "Is there an issue?"

"No, but . . ." Clark tensed. Jealousy—he hated it.

"But what?" Simi waited.

"Is anything else of his going to show up?" Clark aggressively spoke.

Simi narrowed her eyes. She was almost in disbelief at Clark's words. "I don't even know how to answer that." She took a deep breath. Roman was gone; the car was hers now. She was working on this with Jane. She already felt the guilt of his generosity, but to hear Clark rudely question her had her seeing red. "This passive-aggressive nonsense seems a bit out of character for you. Why don't you just say what is on your mind, Clark?"

"I just think it would be better to understand what is his," Clark explained. "The car, this condo? You?"

"Me?" Simi laughed, "Wow, Clark, you come at me with that? Like I am still in a relationship with Roman? Who is dead? After I have been so polite about everything with you?"

"Polite about what?" Clark seemingly curious.

"You lied to me about your relationship with Rachel."

"I didn't lie."

"You did—Amanda told me you were dating all summer. That your interns are thanks to Rachel."

"So?"

"So? How can you say that so flatly?" Simi was exasperated. "You were in a relationship with her! You dropped her like she was nothing. That is awful. You just randomly disappear on people?” Simi was gutted; she was heated and afraid of his answer.

“No, that’s you with your damn notes,” Clark snapped back.

“Not the same!” Simi groaned in frustration.

“If Rachel thought we were in an exclusive relationship, the fault was on her. That discussion never took place,” Clark defended as he walked over to Simi. He lowered his gaze to meet her eyes. “I was always leaving the door open for you.”

Simi took a moment to understand. She held his gaze, her anger penetrating all of her emotions. Her skin was hot; her throat was tight. She barely held back the tears as she spoke. “Well, Clark, the door is closed with Roman. I know. I watched him die, and I buried his ashes. I held them in my hands.” Her voice trembled at the end, but she held her power. She walked away from him to calm herself down, finding solace in looking out the window, focusing on whatever she could to keep the tears at bay.

“Did I use Rachel to try to move on from you? I will admit it, yeah, okay, it was an asshole way to end things.” Clark spoke from the same spot. “Were you . . .” Clark cleared his throat. “Are you using me to get over Roman?”

Simi turned to face him, immediately softening toward Clark’s composure. She took a breath and began to walk back toward him. “To be fair, I was using men, in general, to get over Roman, but I didn’t lead anyone on.”

“What do you think Vegas was to me, Simi?”

“I wasn’t leading you on! I was delusional—I was in grief; I didn’t know what I was doing.” Simi realized they were in a stalemate. Taking a pause she inhaled before speaking, “Okay, this is not going to be resolved now, and I want you to get to meet your niece. Let’s pin this moment. We can settle everything else later.”

Chapter 21

The ride out to Oak Park was quiet. Clark was frustrated by their argument. Clark wouldn't admit he was scared. He wouldn't tell her that the idea of talking about real things with Simi weighed heavily on him. It was too early to bring up the real stuff. They should still be enjoying the honeymoon phase—the excitement of new lovers. Clark knew he was not handling his pressure well. Did she judge him for that? Roman didn't seem like the type to reveal any errors in his life.

This was the first time he wanted to share with someone, even ask for insight into his situation. That was the scariest realization of all. He wanted to be free of all barriers and reveal himself to her. Still, he couldn't bring himself to do it. Roman was a constant presence in her life, whether she admitted it or not, and Clark wasn't sure how to handle or ignore it. The icy tinge of jealousy hit him every time he thought of Roman, understanding that even though she was acting like she had moved on, her heart hadn't. Maybe she was still not ready to open herself up to him. Even if her bed was open, it was clear now that her heart was not. Clark internally frowned, pushing himself deeper into the back seat of the uber.

Simi caught his gaze and smiled softly. She reached for his hand over the box that sat between them.

"I think it's pretty cool they had the baby and didn't tell anyone," Simi commented, hoping to bring Clark back from his spiral of thoughts. Clark stayed quiet. "You know, despite the aftermath, I did quite enjoy the morning. It was pretty out of this world." Simi attempted to ease a smile from Clark, but was unsuccessful.

Simi was unsure how to resolve this fixation Clark seemed to have with Roman. Hearing it for the first time today, she was uncertain how Clark could be jealous or threatened by someone who didn't exist.

She held his hand until the car pulled up to a beautiful brick colonial. They exited the car and stood in front of Adam's home. Clark adjusted the box full of food in his arms as Simi followed behind with two additional bags. Stepping up on the porch, Clark turned to Simi before knocking on the door. "Thank you."

Adam slowly opened the door dressed in wrinkled pajamas, his hair disheveled. He pressed his fingers against his lips and shushed as they walked in. He took the bags from Simi and brought them into his kitchen, thanking them for coming and formally introducing himself to Simi.

Clark helped Simi in the kitchen, unpacking and setting up for dinner. Adam had told Amanda they were coming with food, but she was not expecting a home-cooked meal. Amanda was brought to tears when she introduced Clark's new niece Abigale. He nervously took her into his arms, rocking her as he introduced himself. Clark's heart melted feeling this warm perfection in his arms. Adam had the world, and Clark would make sure he knew it from now on.

Simi sat with Amanda as Clark walked around the house with Abigale. Amanda smiled at Simi.

"He is going to be a great dad one day." Simi had been feeding the hollow pit in her stomach with multiple spoonful of rice and Khoresh. "I want to apologize about over-speaking at the hospital. I said a lot of things that I shouldn't have, and I hope it didn't upset you," Amanda apologized.

Amanda looked tired but had the prideful glow of a new mom.

"No need to worry, I hardly remember what you said," Simi politely lied.

Satisfied, Amanda poured herself a glass of iced tea and served herself another helping of Tachin. Amanda continued to talk about all the amazing things Abigale had done over the past few days. Adam came to join them, complimenting the food, then engaged in more stories of Abigale.

Simi looked over to Clark in the next room. He was sitting with Abigale in his arms, softly talking to her as he rocked in a blue lounger. She couldn't ignore the tug at her heart. Amanda excused herself from the table, moving to sit next to Clark, excitedly repeating the stories she had already shared with Simi. She looked around the kitchen, hoping a bottle of wine would be opened, flinching at her mistake. Grabbing a few more bites, she picked up a Dolma and moved from the table. Simi walked to the back door, glanced over to Amanda and Clark, still occupied, and quietly slid the door open as she snuck outside.

Multicolored leaves crunched beneath her feet as she regained control of her thoughts. She walked along the fence line, disappointed. The first day of her holiday weekend was not going according to plan. She pulled out her phone. The urge to text Daroush for comfort, to get a laugh from Zella presented in her mind. She wasn't sure how much longer Clark wanted to stay with them tonight, but Simi found herself ready to go.

She heard the door open from behind, expecting Clark, only to see Adam come up to the side offering her a cup of coffee.

"Thank you for bringing everything. This means the world to us." She took the mug from his hands. He clinked the glass together and took a sip.

"It's no problem. I know Clark couldn't wait to come by. Happy to do it." Adam nodded. Simi wasn't looking at anything special, but Adam watched out in the distance with her. The dark sky glowed with hidden stars muted by the light pollution of the city. Thirty minutes outside of Chicago, they fought for their presence in the sky. "How are you doing?"

Adam glanced over to Simi as she asked the question. "Recovery is a bitch." Adam smiled alongside Simi's chuckle. "Experience?" he asked.

"Recovery for an addiction or trauma, it's all recovery, and it all sucks," Simi stated. "I have only general clichés in my head, so instead, I will just congratulate you on your baby. I'm happy that you were able to be here for Abigale's arrival." Adam appreciated her honesty.

"You know, Simi, that night in the hospital, Clark said some pretty powerful things to me." Adam sat on the outdoor dining table. He adjusted his glasses, shifting his eyes to catch her gaze. "Knowing Clark too long, I imagine you had something to do with that?" Simi hummed amusingly.

"I am learning that Clark needs help with human emotion, the complexities of it all." Simi chuckled. "He should have worn a warning sign," Simi joked. "Then again, so should I."

"You want to talk about it?" Adam offered.

"Not really." Simi shifted in her stance.

"Do you want me to tell you how babies come from women's bodies? Cause that shit is wild," Adam emphasized.

Simi rolled her eyes toward Adam. She shifted around him, keeping her eyes low, focusing on the colors under her shoes. "Do we look like we just fought?"

"No, Clark looks exactly how I expect him to."

"So it's me then?"

"You kind of look like you could cut his throat." Simi's guard began to lighten with Adam. "I just wanted to share." Adam half turned to look back at the house. "What Clark said to me that night was something I didn't know I needed. I know it's because of you. The fact that he listened and that you were able to humble him to get there. It's in my selfish interest to keep you around."

"So you need me?"

"If you could stick around, it would be greatly appreciated." Adam chuckled.

"I think you know better than I, that my presence in Clark's life isn't up to me," Simi curtly responded.

Adam nodded, understanding what Simi was insinuating. "You might think that, but I can tell you with great confidence your longevity with Clark has outlasted everyone, and you weren't even with him for most of it. In life, Clark is a beast—but for this?" Adam placed his hand over his heart. "Something like love? Clark is as fresh of a pup as Abigale in there. A Pup Beast if you will," Adam joked. "Give him time."

Simi inhaled, frowning as Adam's words reached her. He made sense.

Adam turned to the door, seeing Clark beginning to come toward them. Their time was up. "I hope it's okay for me to say this—I am sorry about Roman."

"Thanks," Simi answered softly.

The sliding door opened as Clark exited the house to join them. Simi smiled tightly as Adam departed from her. Adam patted Clark on the shoulder as he walked back in. Clark came around Simi, embracing her into his arms and resting his chin on the top of her head. She took in his embrace, moving along as he swayed with her.

"You were incredibly patient and generous today. Thank you." Clark pressed his cheek against her temple.

"If you are ready to go, there is something I want to show you."

"Yeah, we can wrap up. Adam wanted to touch base for a bit, though. I'll be in his office for a few minutes. If I take longer than ten minutes, though, come get me."

"I'll wait for you to be finished." Simi began walking back toward the house.

"You are trying to avoid talking to me tonight, aren't you?" Clark questioned.

"Quite the opposite, you will see." Simi reached for his hand and walked him into the house.

The ride back to the city was as quiet as their journey outbound. She didn't attempt to engage in conversation. Clark was deep in thought. When the uber stopped, he was so focused that he didn't realize they were not at either of their homes. Simi stood outside typing in the four-digit code Maxim had texted her for access to the white space. She looked back at Clark as the lock detached and pushed the door open.

Their footsteps echoed in the cavernous space as she looked for the lights, flicking them on. Clark strolled into the space.

"Here you are. I am thinking about calling it Shaadi after my mother," Simi remarked. "What do you think?"

"It's white."

"Clark," she sighed heavily. "I brought you here to invite you a little into my world. What I do while you are away. I feel like I am alone in this relationship with you."

"You feel like you are alone while you are with me?" Clark was clearly concerned.

"I do." Simi answered. "I get why you don't trust me but–"

"It's not that I don't trust you, Simi," Clark quickly interjected then held his comment.

They stood in the middle of the floor of the white space, both full of words, unable to speak them aloud to each other.

"Just tell me what it is, Clark," Simi asked.

"It's Roman."

"Oh my god!" Simi let her head drop backward as she covered her face with her palms.

"This is why I didn't want to bring it up! You aren't ready to talk about the real things yet! I know if I push this too much that you will—" Clark cut himself off.

"I will what?" Simi raised her eyebrows. A sudden realization came over her. "You think I am just going to leave again?" Simi sighed, shaking her head. Walking away from Clark she leaned her back against the painted concrete sliding down the wall with a hard thump on the ground. Simi brought her knees up and rested her elbows on them. Simi did not look up as she felt Clark's footsteps approach her taking a seat beside her.

"Simi—" Clark began.

"I just need a moment, Clark." Simi hated the tremble she heard in her voice. She hated the sadness within her. She hadn't been able to look at him yet. She rubbed her hands together, trying to collect her thoughts when she reached her wrist. She caught her breath and finally looked over to Clark. She reached her arm out, pushing her sleeve back. "Clark, when I told you I buried Roman's ashes, I buried his watch as well," Simi spoke softly; she reached for his hand and put it over her wrist, on top of the ruby-flamed wings of Simurgh. "Clark, I didn't move here just for you, but you were a bonus. I don't know how to do this style of dating very well. I was enmeshed in Roman's life. He was open and shared everything with me. I understand you want your privacy, and I will get used to that, but if we do progress, if we continue to date and learn more about each other, I do hope you have the ability to one day want me and need me as I want you to." Simi finished, unsure how Clark would respond to a raw declaration. He held her gaze until it was too much for Simi, and she had to look away, looking down at his hand resting above her wrist.

"Simi," he lifted his hand from her wrist and brought her chin up with his finger. "I am sorry." Simi pressed her lips tightly. She began blinking quickly, hoping to hold back her emotions. She was preparing to handle a negative response. "I am sorry that I have put you in this position. I am sorry that I haven't been able to express myself to you clearly." Simi nodded, hoping this ending would be quick so she could go home. "When you walked back into my life, I was excited. You have this fire, this energy I want to be around every day." Clark removed his hand and leaned deeper into the wall. He rested his head back and took a breath. "Simi," he cleared his throat. "I think my company got funded with bad money, and I am terrified that I am about to lose CG . Then today happened, our heated exchanged, and now I realize that I am even more terrified about losing you." Simi's eyes lit up, and her heart lightened. She wasn't sure she had heard him right. "Tonight, in Adam's office, he finally came clean to me. Recently, I found out that Evan was the reason we had funding through a contact connected to him. This was something Adam hid from me. I was just waiting for him to tell me. As soon as he did, I wasn't upset or even disappointed. I know the stress I put him through and the expectations he feels he has to show me. So it's on me. We talked about that for maybe five minutes. I will figure out a way to fix Cottage Growth, I know I will." Clark lifted his head off the wall. "I was sitting in his office talking about you. Trying to figure out how to do this. It's very clear you don't think I want or need you, and that is the complete opposite of what I want, Simi."

"What is holding you back?"

"I haven't let Roman go." Clark gave an aggressive exhale followed by an embarrassed chuckle. "I am sorry, Simi, I am trying here." Simi rose to her knees and came closer to him. "You loved him hard, Simi. I realize that."

"You mentioned you almost lost someone before." Simi rested back on her legs, she reached for his hands. "Who was it?"

"Adam."

"Today, you held his baby. You spent a holiday with Adam and his family. Your family." Simi smiled, holding a steady tone in her trembling voice. "He survived. He is here with you today and tomorrow." Simi cleared her throat. "I don't have that. Roman is gone. He isn't coming back. He didn't survive." Simi quickly inhaled. "My Momma," she sniffled, blinking back tears. "I won't ever feel her hugs again. It's been so long that I almost forgot how her embrace felt. She can't recite poetry to me to calm me down. She can't tease my cooking—" Simi's voice cracked, tears freely falling, She won't know her grandchildren, she won't hold them in her arms on a family holiday." Simi took in a shaky breath. "All I have are my memories, mementos of people I loved and lost. That's it." Simi pressed her lips tightly, "But then, we met, and when I am with you, I don't feel lonely. When you are present with me, the coldness of the world doesn't penetrate as deep as it did before."

She didn't resist when Clark pulled her into his arms, holding her tightly into his embrace as he tenderly kissed her head.

"Gregory lost his first wife, tragically." Simi looked back up at Clark. "When he told me about her, I could clearly see he still loved her. I understood it very well, but he is remarried with two sons. He is happy, and he loves his wife, like he really loves her." Simi chuckled. "In Houston, he gave me hope." Simi exhaled. "I love Roman, Clark. I will always love him," Simi confessed. "That doesn't mean I am incapable of loving again." Simi brought Clark's hand to her wrist. "I only wear this bracelet now." Simi looked up to Clark, hoping he understood her sentiment.

"Simi, I am so sorry. I feel foolish that I hadn't noticed," Clark admitted. "I feel awful about this entire day." He took her wrist and placed a kiss above the ruby wings.

"You shouldn't. I think we both learned a lot today about each other, and I hear that is what you do while you are dating." Simi attempted to lighten the mood. She positioned herself next to Clark and rested her head on his shoulder.

"I think Shaadi's is a great name for this space."
Simi smiled, still resting on Clark.
"I think so too."
Returning to Simi's, Clark helped Simi clean up as she arranged small bites for them to snack on. Both hungry and exhausted from the highs and lows between each other, hoping to save what they could of the last few hours of Thanksgiving.

"Thanks," Clark accepted the tea from Simi as she set a board on the coffee table. Clark opened his arm to invite her to sit with him. Keeping her cup in her hand, she sat next to him.

"Would you want to share with me why you think Cottage Growth funding is at risk?" Simi hesitantly asked.

Clark shared the details of the charity scam Evan had run through Chicago. She was shocked to hear the amount of money swindled and even more shocked that charges weren't brought against him.

"I have had my CFO triple check, and the money is legal and legit, but there are multiple factors in play that leave me no choice but to quickly raise the same amount of capital and return the funds to the investment group."

"If capital was sparse to find in the first place, and you can't find it—what happens then?" Simi inquired.

"I will self-fund before I close doors."

"Self-fund? Is that something you can do?"

"It is what I wanted to do from the beginning; everyone discouraged it."

"Why?"

"If I self-fund, it's everything I have."

"Oh."

"I will figure all this out; I know I can do this," Clark assured Simi. "I will also figure out how to make things better between us. I am asking you for patience and guidance."

"Of course, Clark," Simi answered genuinely. She wanted to offer support; she wanted to offer help and introductions to people Clark and Adam may not know, but Roman had. Simi restrained herself.

"Can I ask you how much you need?"

"I need twenty-five million to buy out the investors. I want to raise fifty million from reputable investors, and if I can't, I can self-fund."

"You have that kind of money?"

"No, I have enough to buy out the investors and then float us for maybe two years if we could flip a profit," Clark assured her. "If I had that money, I would have funded this myself from the beginning, no matter what my financial advisor told me to do. That would have been more than enough for me to work with."

"What if I had that kind of money?" Simi smiled; Clark looked at her seriously for a moment and then chuckled.

"Simi, if you had that kind of money, you wouldn't be here."

"Oh?"

"Not at all. I can see you just setting out, traveling, using all your language skills to break the hearts of men worldwide."

"You seem to forget how you met me."

"You were not who you were now. Luckily, I got you in before you realized all your power."

"You got me?"

"Yep, and well, the fact you also aren't sitting on fifty million." Clark reached for Simi, bringing her to sit closer to him. He brought his hand over her shoulder snuggling her in close. "I can get us there. I was close enough once; who knows what comes out of CG. Clark turned to Simi. " Je t'achèterais le monde entier si je savais que c'est ce que tu voulais." *I'd buy you the whole world if I knew that is what you wanted.* Simi hummed in amusement. "You are going to have to teach me Persian now."

"I am?"

"We will want our children to know Persian as well?" Simi raised her eyebrows. "fantasmer avec moi?" *Fantasize with me.*

"This is what you want to fantasize about?"

"I don't have to fantasize about anything else." Clark took her tea and placed it on the table alongside his. He turned to her, leaning in for a kiss. She immediately accepted him, pushing him back on the couch as she lay above him. No teasing was allowed tonight, just elated passion of intimacy and promise of the day. Clark paused Simi, motioning to the bedroom. Simi smiled, confirming her answer with a kiss as she pulled herself up and drew his hands in hers to her bedroom.

Clark took his time in pleasuring Simi, speaking through the body language of intimacy between two lovers. Two lovers who had reached a deeper connection with trust and honesty. Clark was falling in love with Simi. There wasn't a shred of doubt left in his mind that this is what it could feel like to be loved, to have a partner who is committed to helping achieve the best version of oneself.

Clark growled in satisfaction as Simi begged for him, wanting him closer and deeper in her, to her. He kissed her deeply before an accidental love confession slipped off of his tongue.

"Mmm" Simi stretched beneath him, still indulging in Clark. "We should have emotional breakdowns every day," she teased.

"I don't think I can handle that." Clark lay beside Simi, keeping her body close to his as he rested on his elbow. "But I can definitely do this every day." He gently ran his hands across her stomach. "Christmas will be a better holiday; I will take you someplace nice."

"I've always been away for Christmas; it would be nice to spend it here. See what this Chicago has to offer. Plus, I'd like to have a small Yalda celebration." Simi chuckled. "Small meaning me and you."

"Yalda?"

"Winter Solstice—oldest Persian holiday. It's fun," Simi continued. "We stay up all night reading poetry, eat watermelon, pomegranates, and so on."

"I would love to spend Yalda with you, and if you insist on staying in for Christmas, then you will host."

"Why?" Simi laughed, surprised by his demand.

"I am not dealing with pine needles fifty-seven floors up in the elevator. You have six floors and a private elevator."

"Okay—but you have to get me a tree."

"Done."

Chapter 22

Three weeks, five cities, fifteen video sessions, and over fifty phone conversations. Clark was exhausted. The only thing keeping him going was the nights he could spend with Simi in bed. Her presence was a source of calmness and serenity. He waved Simi's fob at the entrance of the elevator. Clark had been living mostly out of Simi's place with his travel and office schedule. Any spare time he had, he wanted to be with her. Clark wanted to ensure she felt as important as she was to him.

As the elevator opened, he hadn't expected to see her there as she had become recently focused on her white space. The smells from the kitchen wafted into his senses. She was home, pots simmered on the stove while her fireplace was lit, and a spread of red fruits displayed on her coffee table. Pillows and blankets were layered on the floor, and a stack of books was placed squarely in the middle. Clark pulled his bag over his head and pushed his carry-on toward the side of the wall. Tired from San Francisco, he had forgotten about her celebration of the winter solstice, her Yalda night.

"Oh hey, I didn't hear you come in." Simi's hair, wet and fresh from the shower, came toward Clark and embraced him with a light kiss. She pressed her hand to his cheek. "So cold. I wasn't expecting you so early. I figured you would head home first."

"And be late for all this? I am starved."

"Go take a shower; get the travel off of you. You texted that you had good news from San Fran, I want to hear how it went."

As Clark returned to her bedroom and walked into Simi's closet, he looked for the bag he had left from an earlier trip. He noticed it was empty, and clothes were neatly folded and hung for him above where his bag had been stored. He smiled inwardly.

Clark turned on the shower and walked back into the bedroom closet. Kneeling, he opened the weekender and pulled out two black jewelry boxes. He opened both in front of him. Stunning blue sapphire gems sparkled before him.

The longer box revealed a bracelet wrapped in blue and white sapphires in a fine white gold setting. Clark shifted his gaze to the smaller square box holding the ring, the favored and ridiculous choice to present to Simi.

It was not intended to be an engagement ring, but when he had gone to the jeweler, he was presented with the ring as a matching set. He was easily sold. He wanted something special for her. He had read that in ancient Persia, they called sapphires *lazvard*, the color of the clear sky. Ancient Persians believed the earth was leaning on a huge sapphire whose reflection gave the sky its blue color. They also called sapphires 'eye of the sky'.

He pulled the ring out of the box, a solitary stone sitting in a platinum band.

It's a set. Give her both.

Simi returned to the kitchen and turned off the burners as she heard the shower begin. She was excited to share this Yalda night with him. Out of all the holidays, she favored this one the most. Persian New Year, Nowruz, was fun, but there was something about Yalda that was intimate and special.

Yalda, which translates to *the rebirth of the sun*, was a celebration of light triumphing over darkness. Fires were built at sunset, on the last day of fall, and would be kept burning throughout the night until sunrise the following day. During this night, people would gather with family and friends. Eating, drinking, singing songs, and reading poetry. Simi's preference, of course, was Rumi, though she had a few favorites from Hafez as well.

Simi had spent the day cooking and setting up her table for the evening. She brought out her red linens and Persian decorations, setting up the coffee table by the fireplace with her ornate display.

Her table was adorned with a small watermelon, pomegranates, apples, and red pears. There was an ancient myth that eating watermelon on Yalda would make them immune to cold weather. Simi desperately needed this to come to fruition now that she had chosen to live in Chicago. Daroush had sent photos of Maman with his future fiancée at the gathering they were attending. The idea that maybe next Yalda, they could all be together played in her mind. This holiday was always hard because she was away from her grandmother. Typically, the eldest relative would host this night. Simi remembered the best stories Maman would share and how excited she was to stay up all night. Though she never successfully made it to sunrise, it was still fun to be up late as a little kid.

Simi walked over to her couch and settled in front of the fireplace. Earlier in the day, she had a pretty good session with Jane. Since Thanksgiving, she had felt a weight lifted from her relationship with Clark. The idea that Roman's ghost presence was so involved on Clark's side had opened Simi's eyes to the type of affection from her he needed. Everyone was different, and she unknowingly used the same tactics with a completely different person. Clark was similar, but needed other things from Simi. Their relationship was progressing positively. Simi wanted to bring Clark into more of her life, of who she was. She wanted Gregory to meet him, and she even was trying to figure out when he could join her to visit Maman and Daroush in Paris. Going home for Nowruz was ideal as it would be after his first board meeting, and she hoped he could take an extended trip.

When Clark came into the living room, Simi was seated amongst the pillows, flipping and folding the pages of the poems she wanted to read to Clark tonight—her mother's favorites and ones Simi recently discovered on her own. He joined her, the fireplace keeping them warm as soft instrumental music played in the background. He picked up one of the books scattered around Simi.

"That one is in English. It is by Hafez." Clark began flipping through the pages. "If you see one you like, read it out loud," Simi urged. She scooted closer to him, still running her fingers through a book of Rumi.

"You will have to teach me to read Persian too." Clark took the book. "I want to make sure what you are reading is accurate."

"You need to make time for my lessons." Simi smiled seductively.

"My free time is coming, just you wait. Then you will be begging me to go back to the office," Clark prompted.

"We will see."

Clark smiled, continuing to peruse the book below him. "San Fran might bite, but if it doesn't, I feel hopeful about my New York meetings."

"Yes, about New York. Could I jump along with you? There are some old gallery contacts I want to meet with, and if your schedule allows, maybe we could have dinner with Gregory and his wife?" Simi watched as Clark kept his eyes focused on the book. She had noticed that his jaw would drop slightly to avoid a smile, and he would push his tongue against his cheek before pressing his lips together when Simi had made him happy.

"I will make sure I fit it in. I'll have Kelsey get you a ticket."

"No, I can do it—just send me the details."

"I think I will lead tonight with his one." Clark ignored Simi's ask and continued to read. "The woman I love." Clark read aloud. Simi paused, cautiously looking at Clark, who had his left hand holding the book outward as if he was presenting this poem to an audience. "Because the woman I love, lives inside of you, I lean as close to your body with my words as I can, And I think of you all the time, dear pilgrim," Clark raised his eyebrows, curious at the word and the reliability of this English translation. "Because the One I love goes with you, where you go, Hafez will always be near if you sat before me, wayfarer, with your aura bright from your many charms. My lips could resist rushing to you and needing to befriend your blushed cheek. But"—Clark expressed with a raise of his other hand—"my eyes can no longer hide the wondrous fact of who you really are." Clark captured her gaze. "The beautiful one whom I adore has pitched his royal tent inside of you, so I will always lean my heart as close to your soul as I can." As Clark lowered the book, Simi was hiding a smile. "How was that?" Clark asked.

"That was an interesting choice," she answered slowly.

"It's impressive. I don't think I could even write a sentence that impassioned. That is an art. It's like poetry," Clark added dryly.

"You are in a good mood," Simi commented.

"Am I usually that sour?"

"Not sour. Serious—heavily occupied as of late."

"You were supposed to say something if you were upset," Clark reminded.

"I am not, trust me. This is nice, you being silly, you being more comfortable around me."

"Silly? I confessed love for the first time, and you call it silly." Clark pressed his hand on his chest with a pained expression.

"Uh huh—you don't know what love is." Simi brought her knees to her chest. "Or if you do—you are too stubborn to recognize it." Simi playfully pushed her fingers above his forehead.

"Describe it. Poetry runs through your veins. What is love?" Clark rested his arm on the sofa holding his head up with his hand. He watched her eyes lower as she processed what she wanted to say.

"Love is reckless; not reason. Reason seeks a profit. Love comes on strong, consuming oneself unabashed." Simi paused. She had memorized this Rumi poem from an early age. Her mother often read this to her as a young girl in place of fairy tales. "Yet, in the midst of suffering, love proceeds like a millstone, hard surfaced and straightforward." Simi still had her gaze lowered but felt Clark's eyes. "Having died of self-interest, she risks everything and asks for nothing. Love gambles away every gift God bestows, without cause God gave us being, without cause, give it back again."

"Original words from the Persian poet Simi?"

"Rumi—from his *Mathanwi IV* book. It was one of my mother's favorites," she shared.

"It was beautiful." Clark reached into his pocket. "I have something for you." Clark revealed the box and placed it on her lap. Simi looked curiously at it.

"You didn't have to get me a gift, Clark."

"Open it," he urged. She paused for a moment, then opened the box. Words gathered at the tip of her tongue, but she was speechless. "It's lazvard, or as may be better known as, cheshm-e âsemân." *Eye of the sky.* Clark attempted in Persian. Simi caught his gaze with a smile at his pronunciation.

"It's beautiful, Clark. " She pulled the delicate jewels from the box, and Clark clasped it around her wrist; it fit beautifully next to the ruby bracelet.

"Do you like it?"

"Very much. You are giving me quite the gemstone collection, I love it." Simi leaned in for a kiss, noticing Clark's hesitation. "What?"

"I have something else, but I want to ensure you don't take it the wrong way." Simi smiled, gently raising her eyebrows in curiosity. Clark reached into his pocket, as Simi shifted in front of him.

Simi reached for the box, and upon opening it, she smiled. She pulled out the ring and held it close. She traced her fingers around the sapphire and then slid it on her right-hand ring finger. "This is beautiful. Thank you." Simi reached for him, placing a soft kiss against his lips. "I have nothing for you."

"Simi, how you have been supporting me and taking care of me this past month, it's all I want." Clark pulled Simi closer to him. She adjusted to sit above him. "Are you happy, Simi?"

"Very much." Simi reached for the bottom of her shirt and brought it over her head. She reached for the clasp on her back until Clark's hands covered hers. She smiled shyly and let him take the lead.

It was after midnight when Simi brought out a chilled bottle of champagne with two flutes. After making love, they had stayed embraced amongst the blankets and pillows, watching the fire glimmer against the darkness.

Clark stretched out on her carpet, a blanket barely covering his naked body. She sat down next to him, placing the bottle and glasses aside on the table. He pulled her over his body, her hair cascading over him to one side.

"This was the best Yalda."

"This was your only Yalda," Simi answered dryly.

"The way you have things set up here, I can see how you enjoyed those firepits at Promontory Point. Maybe next year we can do a Persian celebration there?"

"Perhaps, but I was thinking maybe next Yalda would be in Paris? My Maman cooks better and reads better than I do."

"As lovely as that sounds, it will get awkward when I suddenly begin to make love to you on the carpet," Clark teased, unwrapping the foil from the champagne bottle. Holding the cork, he slowly twisted the top off with a soft pop. Simi held the flutes steady as he poured. "You want me to come to Paris?" Clark set the bottle to the side.

"I would." Simi handed the crystal flute to Clark. "For Norooz, to start. In March? It's the first day of spring. I have to see if you will get an invite back for Yalda." Simi teased.

"I will be there, Simi." With a tilt of the glass, the two edges' clinking sound echoed through the room. "I suppose if I am to meet your Maman, it will only be natural to introduce you to my side of the family. I think there is a family reunion this year."

"A family reunion? I mean, dinner with parents might be a good start."

"Nervous?" Clark nudged against her. "There is nothing to worry about, Simi. They will love you." Clark pulled Simi back into his arms and leaned his back against the sofa. She leaned her head back. If there was a time to share his feelings with her, it was now. She kissed the top of each finger before softly biting the tip of his pointer. He freed his hand and cupped her face gently. Their gaze locked, her eyes dazzling with affection and adoration of him, for him.

"I love you." He turned her to face him as he confessed. His heartbeat pounded in his ears until he saw her start to smile. "I love—" She pressed her thumb against his lips.

"I love you too," she matched. Clark held her tight in his arms. He reached for her hands; he wanted her to feel his heartbeat, the loud pulsating beats of lust, love, loyalty, and dedication they were sharing at this moment.

Simi with Clark, him with her, embracing each other into one solid bond. Silence surrounded both of them, slowly breathing inches away from each other. He was making this moment a memory, a memory where he told her he loved her, and she accepted. He pulled her into a kiss, sealing their exchanged words.

***

"Simi?" Jane peered over her glasses. "Last session of the year.

218

How are you feeling?"

"It's been a wild year." Simi kept her gaze on the window. Light flurries were falling from the sky.

"Can you expand on that comment?"

"I mean, from where I was last New Year's Eve to now. It's a bit wild."

"Do you feel proud of where you were to where you are?"

"I guess—I mean, yes, of course."

"Are you hopeful for the future? For your goals?"

"Yes."

"You are distracted. What is on your mind, Simi."

Simi had hoped today's session would be easy.

"Roman." Simi smiled hard. "After Yalda, my dreams have come back. Roman is in them, and he doesn't say anything. He is just watching. I am trying to talk to him and it's like a statue."

"Is it the same dream every time?"

"No, last night," Simi frowned, "this morning or whatever, he waved."

"Waved?"

"Yes, no words. Just a wave. Waving hello, like, hey, remember me? Or waving bye, like, okay you are good now. I don't know."

"What do you want to believe?" Jane twirled her pen within her finger. "Do you want to believe he is letting you go?"

"I don't know," Simi admitted. "I thought this was all okay."

"Why do you think something is not okay? What specifically?"

"If Roman is waving to remind me of his presence, then I have to understand that it's something deeper, something I am not addressing. " Simi swallowed hard. "If it's Roman waving bye, then he is happy and proud of me?" Simi slightly trembled. She had not been emotional with Jane about Roman for a while now.

"That was good, Simi. The way you were able to rationalize both sides." Jane smiled, truly impressed.

"What do you want it to be: hello or goodbye."

"I don't want to say it out loud," Simi confessed.

"Can you tell me why?"

"If I say it out loud, it's so awful sounding. If I say I want him to confirm with me that he is happy and saying good bye, my heart breaks, but I am happy. Clark is making me very happy. This life I have started, I wake up happy," Simi earnestly explained. "If I say he is saying hello, remember who Roman is, then I am scared about what that means in my reality. I would not have healed as I thought I had."

"It sounds like you want Roman to be saying goodbye," Jane insisted.

Simi winced at her statement.

"It's okay to let him go."

"I have!" Simi insisted. "I thought I was past this, I don't understand, Jane." Simi was growing frustrated.

"Simi, dreams don't always have to mean something."

"To me, they do,"

"Okay, I usually like to end year-end sessions positively. Seeing how this is truly upsetting you, let's try this. I want you to close your eyes."

Simi inhaled, resting her head back on the chair and closing her eyes.

"I want you to think about Shaadi's, your white space. It's your first gallery show, the event is sold out, and everyone is excited by this unknown artist and her new conceptual," Jane hesitated, causing Simi to squint one eye open. Jane's course corrected. "She is raw talent, and you discovered her. Everything is selling, and you are about to change this new artist's life. The night is over, and your feet are tired, but the euphoric feeling of success pulsates through your body. What is the first thing you want to do?"

"Call my mom." Simi's eyes flew open. Her hand quickly covered her lips as she was confused by her answer. She looked to Jane, "I don't . . . I wasn't expecting to say that."

Jane nodded, orchestrating her next question. "Simi, you mourned and grieved for Roman, but have you for your mother yet?" Jane pursed her lips. "Am I correct in that you never visited her grave? Back in Paris?"

"No, I didn't. I haven't"

"I think we should get ready to prepare for that trip. Having your family and now Clark, I think you will feel better secured in visiting your Mother? This is something we can dig a bit deeper into this after the New Year."

Simi nodded in agreement as she rubbed her hands back and forth over her legs, still coming down from shock. "Any plans for the New Year?"

"A quiet night home with the husband."

"I didn't realize you were married."

"You aren't my therapist," Jane cracked.

"This is true."

"I hope you have a great holiday season, Simi. I am looking forward to your new year."

Chapter 23

Simi rubbed the side of her plate nervously. Clark wasn't going to make it. She felt it before he left the hotel this morning. Simi knew she shouldn't have mentioned Clark possibly joining at all, but a bit of her was hopeful. Simi looked out the window. It was raining in New York, melting the snow off the streets. Chicago was still buried after a three-day storm stayed over the city after New Years' weekend.

Sitting across from Gayle and Gregory, she did her best to stay present with them. Gregory clearly noticed that Simi was embarrassed by Clark appearing as a no-show, worried about how it reflected on her. Gayle hardly seemed to notice as she had been so excited to unload all of her life updates with Simi. Gregory cocked his head toward Simi, offering a sign that she could relax.

"Well, it's not any different from Roman. He didn't care about anyone's time other than his own," Gayle stated sharply, bringing both Simi and Gregory's attention back to her as she picked up her phone, noting the time.

"Simi wasn't sure her friend could join to begin with. I insisted on this," Gregory responded curtly, annoyed with his wife. "It's nice having you in New York again, even for a short time."

"Of course, she knows what I meant. Right, Simi?"

"Yeah, plus this has just been nice to catch up with you, both of you," Simi replied. "Being back in New York, I almost forgot that I used to live here. How I survived university here—I will never know."

"I told Gregory Chicago was the wrong choice. You belong here, and you are even closer to your Grandmother. I didn't understand why you chose Chicago."

"Fresh start," Simi quickly defended. "Something new, and well, it never is forever for me anyway. I might be back here before you know it."

"Hope so." Gayle reached for Simi's hand. "Chicago . . . honey, this is New York!"

As their dinner wrapped, Gregory opened the car door for his wife when the valet pulled up. He kissed her cheek as she laid her head back on the seat pillow. She had been overserved and over-chatty. He closed the door turning to Simi. Gregory grinned as he stuck out his leather gloved hand. Droplets of rain had begun forming into light whimsical flurries of snow.

"Thanks for bringing some of the snow our way." Gregory chuckled. "Sorry I wasn't able to meet Clark tonight," Gregory said.

"Me too. This was still fun. Gayle is a firecracker. I always loved that about her. Just took me a bit to get into cadence with her."

"Are you sure you have to leave tonight?" Simi answered with a nod.

"I will be back out more often, I promise. Get Gayle home." Simi hugged Gregory tightly. "You have to come to Chicago soon."

"I want to. I want to meet Clark too. I think if you want to move forward, you should," Gregory encouraged.

"We are taking it slow. No need to rush anything."

"I meant about the other ask. Which, you know, you don't need my permission to do." Simi stayed silent, not ready to answer Gregory back.

"It was just a thought. I don't want to make anything more complicated than I already have."

"I respect that. Still, I want you to know I support it, and I think Roman would too." Gregory pulled Simi close for a hug. "Text me when you land back home." Gregory winked, verifying Chicago was Simi's new home.

Simi stood back as Gregory entered the driver's side of his car, slowly rolling onto the street to take Gayle home. She took in a deep breath and inhaled the vibrant city around her. New York was special. There was no denying that, but Simi only had memories of tight living spaces, exhausted rides on the subway, and running from working long hours then booking it to class. It was a time in her life on which she rarely reflected. It was mostly a blur now, but walking the crowded streets, overwhelmed by the noise of a busy Friday night, Simi took her time. Her phone vibrated, and she was surprised to see it was her brother.

"What are you doing in New York?"

"How do you know I am in New York?" she quickly texted back. Daroush didn't wait and called her through WhatsApp.

"I asked you first." Simi smiled hearing his voice, feeling relaxed.

"Just a quick trip. I just finished dinner with Gregory and Gayle. What are you doing up?"

"I am about to go to bed, went out, same stuff. I just saw you in New York and got excited."

"Why?"

"Thought you might be coming home, you know, like you said you were going to." Simi sighed.

"I know, I promise I will be visiting soon."

"If you come, you better give yourself at least a month. Maman isn't going to let you make a quick trip."

"I don't want to make a quick trip either. So that is why I need to find a good time to come." Simi realized the time and looked out on the street for a cab. "How is she?"

"She is good. No need for you to worry."

"And you?"

"Living life the best way I know how." Daroush chuckled. "You know you are stalling my engagement. I believe purposefully."

"You can propose without me meeting her. You don't need my approval. If Maman has said yes, I am merely an excuse for you to stall." Simi opened the door and informed her driver of her destination. "Did you get a ring yet? Send me a photo." There was noticeable silence.

"I am using Moms." Daroush shared. "I was going to talk to you about it."

"No need. It's yours to use." Simi wasn't upset, but she was surprised he would use a token of love originally gifted from their father.

"You don't think I should."

"I didn't say that, Daroush, and if it feels right to you, then it's right."

"Momma loved the ring. I want to keep it alive, give it a new home like it's her blessing."

"Well, if it begins to singe your beloved's skin, you have your answer from above," Simi smartly rebuffed. Daroush was silent again. "Bad joke."

"I thought you being in love again would soften you a bit." It was Simi's turn to be quiet. " You are still in love?"

"When you say it like that, it sounds so silly, but to answer your question, I am still with Clark. Which, again, is why I am in New York."

"So where is he?"

"I'd imagine already at the airport. He left his meetings and went directly there."

"You should share your location with him."

"Did you do that when you were here last with my phone?"

"Can you blame me?" Simi couldn't. "I don't spend all day tracking you, I just happened to tonight."

"Uh-huh."

"I have better things to do."

"Sure."

"You are just being annoying now."

"I am."

"Good night Abji." Daroush exhaled.

"Good night." Simi grinned as the call ended with a glow from her phone.

Clark was deep in thought, scribbling into his leather notebook. He was reciting his pitch which he had memorized when a small cup of espresso rested on his journal. He looked up to see Simi smiling at him. He had felt awful that he couldn't meet Gregory and keep his commitment to her.

"How did it go?" she asked.

"Really well, I think." Simi took a seat next to him, and he reached for her hand, kissing it softly. "Thank you, and I am so sorry."

"It's okay. I am actually glad you weren't there. Gayle was a little sharp-tongued tonight. I think she is still bothered how I kind of dropped off and needs a more elaborate statement of, I don't know, maybe forgiveness from me?"

"That sounds stressful."

"It was, and it wasn't. You would have to know her. I did, though, walk a few galleries and get a few artists' names, so it wasn't a waste for me." Simi realized she was talking to herself as Clark absorbed his notes. Simi sat back in her chair and waited until he was available again.

"I'm sorry, I'm sorry, I'm sorry." Clark closed his notebook. "All I want to do is get back home and lie with you for the next two days. Please tell me we can do that. I need one win." Clark sincerely asked.

"My place or yours?"

"Always yours." He took a sip from his espresso. "I am sorry I didn't make it to dinner."

"It's ok. I just wish there was a way I could help."

"I appreciate that—and I will ask you if I need it. Right now, it's just conversations with other angel investors. I might have to make a few changes to get the support right now. I have time, so I am not too stressed." Clark felt the tension permeating from Simi. He reached for her hand, bringing it to his lips. She looked up and smiled. He turned her hand around, noticing her wrist bared only her ruby bracelet and no ring resting on her finger. A tinge of jealousy went through him. Simi was still quiet, and Clark realized he might have missed something important tonight. "Was the dinner hard?"

"I don't know if hard is the right word. Being at dinner with them without Roman was different. Being here in New York right now is different."

"You weren't here today," Clark corrected. "In a few weeks, everything will get settled for me. I will bring you back properly."

The flight attendant greeted them, preparing for the flight.

"I've never had two empty shuttles back to back before," Clark commented. "It's nice." Clark settled in closer to Simi.

"I didn't book us on shuttles. Kelsey sent me a note, but I took care of it and booked the planes," Simi shared.

"What? Simi, that's ridiculous! Why did you pay for this?"

"It's a non-issue, Clark. Don't worry about it. Aren't you happy we are alone?"

Clark felt a mix of emotions—confusion, frustration, but mostly exhaustion. He would discuss budgeting with Simi later, but tonight, he was grateful to be alone with her.

"So what happened today?"

"Simi, they let me talk, but I knew it was a 'no' when I walked in. This is why Cottage Growth is important. I want twenty-year-old me to walk into a meeting and see two forty-year-old mes and then two sixty-year-old mes. I have made real money, and still," Clark sighed. "Still, I can walk into a room, and I fight through the feeling of being a small kid from the South Side. It never leaves you. I need to make this work."

"Clark, you will make this work. I know you will. Just keep being you, and someone will see the potential in what you are trying to achieve. Trust yourself that this will all be resolved soon."

***

Clark had been sitting at the table in his office for two hours. He had picked up a quick puzzle and dumped it out, focused on just finishing it that morning. It had been weeks of trying to find funding. Not one 'yes'. Bloated budgets, unrealistic goals—no one saw the vision of the long game.

He fought with Marcus earlier in the day, preparing to pull his own money, readying himself to infuse CG with his own capital and push everyone out. He didn't care about the fines or the taxes placed on him. Finishing the entire border, he continued to replay his options in his head. The door was closed today—Kelsey knew to gatekeep.

He kept the office lights off. The sun over the lake was perfect brightness for Clark. The warmth on his skin was comforting as it reminded him of Simi and her touch, her body against him this morning while he held her close. He missed her even though he had her.

Clark knew he messed up in New York. He didn't want to admit it, but since they had gotten back, he felt like Simi was pulling away. He knew she was busy hoping to get the gallery open before spring. He just wasn't expecting a sudden drop-off as she had. It was only a month ago they were lying naked on her floor, in love.

Clark clenched his teeth, spinning a puzzle piece under his finger, remembering she didn't wear his tokens of love in front of her friends. He didn't ask her about it because he didn't want to know her answer. The next morning, both sapphire pieces were back on. Clark didn't ask because Simi had shown him the answer. Clark was beginning to spiral. He didn't make mistakes. He thought everything carefully through. Now, he was questioning every single decision he had made.

Had Cottage Growth been a pipe dream, and had he blindly ignored all the red flags and pressed on because that's all he knew how to do? Was it the same with Simi? Was he ignoring flags with her as well?

After finishing a full corner of the coral reef picture, he decided he would sell his apartment. That would free up money for salaries for at least a year. Tonight, he would tell Simi his plan, and prepare her for what his future might look like in the upcoming months.

"I know you said no visitors, but . . ." Kelsey interrupted, pushing the door open to reveal Abigale in her arms, followed by Adam with a stroller.

"Abigale is not a visitor. She is a Queen." Kelsey pouted as Clark came to pick her up from her arms.

"I'll get her back when you guys are done." Kelsey waved, closing the door behind her. Adam tossed his bag and laid out on the couch. Clark greeted him as he continued to bounce Abigale in his arms.

"How are you? I can't believe how big she has gotten, Adam!" Clark paused, noticing Adam's appearance. He gained weight, and though he was tired, Clark was sure he hadn't seen him this healthy looking in a long time.

"You were right. Babies change everything." Adam sounded happy in his delivery. "She is my entire world. Don't drop her." Clark shook his head.

"These eyes. You are going to have so much trouble on your

hands." Adam chuckled in response. "I will be there to answer the door to any boy who picks you up, though." Clark continued to coo Abigale. "Where is Amanda?"

"I got us a hotel for the weekend. She and her sister are getting massages, and then her sister will watch the baby during the holiday party. Honestly, though, I might hide here for an hour with her and try to get some sleep."

"I didn't know if you guys would make it at all."

"Of course. Abigale's going to know her father and uncle were game changers." Clark stilled only for a moment before continuing to rock. Adam continued, "Saw you were just in New York. What was that about?"

"Just went in quickly. Simi had to check on some stuff."

"In New York? I thought she lived in Texas?"

"She did—I told you about the white space she got in West Loop. She wants to charge commission-free gallery shows for artists."

"Philanthropic souls you are."

"I think I messed up in New York. I will see her tonight and fix it," Clark declared. "This was the worst time in my life to fall in love."

"But for you to have found love. How nice is that?" Adam continued to gaze adoringly at his daughter, still being rocked by Clark. "Have you learned how much Roman left her?" Clark looked at him curiously.

"I don't think that is any of my business."

"Sure—but you aren't curious? She could have more to her name than you?" Abigale began to fuss in Clark's arms. Adam swooped up from the couch, bringing her back into his arms.

"If she does, it doesn't matter. Plus, he could have had a wife and kids—you don't know. She isn't acting like someone who inherited mass wealth like that. She doesn't talk about money, so I assume she is settled enough." Clark reflected on his statement, remembering that she had chartered a private jet for their trip to New York. He quickly pushed the notion out of his mind.

"Does she know how much you have?"

"No, I mean, maybe. She knows what I don't have."

"Well then, why would she tell you anything?" Clark took in those words. Reflecting back on the entire conversation with himself earlier. The verbal exchange of 'I love you' was still not enough. "When you guys are talking openly about money, then you know you are at the next stage of trust."

"That is ridiculous."

"Unfortunately, it's not. She could be sitting on wealth or months away from being broke. You should know, and she should know the truth about you, too. If you think this is it."

"Enough about my stuff. How has it been? You look good. I don't think I have seen you with this much weight in a bit." Clark shifted the conversation.

Clark pushed the digits to Simi's white space door lock and quietly entered. He was out early, ready to take her out to dinner and bring her back to his place. Simi had her airpods in, sitting on a barstool next to the white counter. Clark paused as he heard the aggressive intonation of her usually gentle voice.

"Yes, no, I understand that. It's not going to happen again. The money will be in your account. I am advising that you do not do anything until then." Simi tapped her fingers on the table. "That doesn't matter. Things change, and I am telling you this will be settled on Monday." Simi spoke assertively into the phone. "You chose to do this after hours on a Friday." Simi paused. "Yes—thank you. Wire is fine. Just send me the details. Right—I will round it to fifty thousand because this will not happen again. Fine, yes, thank you." Simi tapped her iPhone then clenched her hands together. She quickly grabbed her phone and began texting furiously. She slammed down the phone. "That bastard. Fuck." She exhaled.

Clark took a moment to try and process what he had heard. He reached back and grabbed the doorknob, pretending to open it, and walked in. Simi perked up to see him.

"Oh hey! I wasn't expecting you." Simi scooted off her chair as Clark came closer, resting his bag on the table.

"I was done early and wanted to take you to dinner." Clark tried not to let his gaze linger over the paperwork on her table.

"Oh, umm, could we rain check? I know your party is tomorrow, and I wanted to make sure I got everything done here to enjoy tomorrow night with you and, of course, Sunday." Simi spoke brightly. Clark tried his best not to harden his face.

"Is everything okay? Maybe we can order in here, and I can help."

"No, I have it under control. If you have a night free, you should catch up on some sleep. Tomorrow night is going to be a lot of fun." The daggers in his heart were being pushed deeper. "You okay?" She reached up and soothed his brow. He grabbed her hand, moving it off of his face.

"I am good. I'll see you tomorrow." Clark quickly composed himself. He still held her hand and kissed her fingers softly. "I love you."

"Love you." Clark closed his eyes at her words, desperately trying to believe her.

Clark left the space and walked down the street. She sighed heavily and turned behind her.

"He is gone," Simi announced to a teary-eyed Zella coming out of the bathroom. She immediately embraced her in a hug, and Zella continued to cry in her arms. "It's done; it's going to be okay. I promise nothing is going to happen." Zella nodded, continuing to sniffle in her arms.

"You didn't tell me how handsome he was," Zella said muffled. "You know he heard it all."

"Probably, but I will deal with that after his party." Simi pulled Zella back. "You are going to stay with me, okay? Tonight and tomorrow, you will come to the party with me too."

"Simi, I don't know how to thank you for all this."

"Don't worry about it. Everyone deserves a second chance, including you. But you must tell Jane about this, and we must come clean with her about our friendship as well."

Chapter 24

Clark was crushed. What had she gotten herself into? She was able to lie to him plainly. A missed dinner led to this? He didn't know how to feel. He picked up his cell and quickly explained the situation to Adam.

"Clark, this is where communication is key. There is probably a super simple explanation, and you just need to be patient and wait. Do not jump to conclusions."

"Adam, she is wiring fifty thousand dollars like it's nothing! Where do you think that money is coming from?"

"Maybe she didn't bury that Patek? Have you checked your watch drawer?" Adam chuckled, hoping to lighten Clark's mood. "Bad joke. Listen, give her tonight. Let her come to you, and don't spiral. She wants you to get through tomorrow."

"When did you two become best friends?"

"Listen, Clark, let her come to you. Trust me on this." Clark, even more infuriated, hung up the phone.

Clark did his best to follow Adam's advice and not spiral. When he got home, he dumped a puzzle on his table and began blaring music. He poured himself a heavy whiskey and sat. As he flipped the pieces over, he realized it was the Restless puzzle she had gifted him. Festering, he didn't even want to look at the pieces strewn across the table. How was he going to get through this night? Quickly finishing his drink, he stepped away from the table to sit on his balcony. The cold didn't matter, and the number of cigarettes he was about to consume was needed.

Clark immediately regretted his decision. Drinking too fast and unable to finish his second cigarette, he stumbled back inside, making his way into the shower. Resting his head against the marble, he watched the water trail around his feet. His heart was still heavy, but he at least felt calmer. In the distance, he thought he had heard his doorbell. It was nearly midnight now. He turned the water off, waiting to hear if it would go off again. It did. Confused, he grabbed a towel and wrapped it around his waist. A quick rush of worry went through him. Maybe something with Adam. He opened his door to find Simi standing before him.

"Hi," Clark mumbled out. Simi smiled suggestively at him. He took in her image. Her hair styled, her makeup dark with bright red lips. He hadn't seen her this done up in quite some time. She looked beautiful. "Come in." As she entered his apartment, he noticed her stilettos and the sheer hosiery on her legs. He hadn't seen those before at all.

She turned to face him, slowly unbuttoning her wool coat to reveal a beautiful black lace lingerie set. "Simi, wow. I was not expecting this." Clark adjusted his towel. Simi stayed quiet and pulled out a stock piece of cardstock from her pocket. Clark took the paper from her and read the note.

"There is a lot to discuss, but now isn't the time. So tonight—no words, just love."

Clark looked up from the note and nodded. Satisfied, Simi dropped her coat and turned for his bedroom. Clark, swallowed, mesmerized by the sway of her hips as she strutted down the hallway out of his line of site. He took a deep breath, dropped his towel alongside her coat and turned to follow.

***

Clark tried not to focus on the hotel lobby while socializing at his party, but his gaze couldn't help but linger until he saw Simi step out with her friend Zella. Clark excused himself from the group and met them at the entrance of Prime. Patrick had graciously allowed them the entire space to celebrate.

"You look beautiful. Thanks for coming." Clark leaned down and kissed Simi's cheek. "And it's so great to meet you, Zella."

"Thanks for letting me crash this. I have heard so much about this place." Zella nudged Simi.

"Go mingle—I will come to find you later." Simi encouraged Zella.

"Yeah, no, um, I am good. You do you." She kissed Simi on the cheek and waved at Clark.

"You didn't tell me she was British. Or a model."

"She is a cellist, very talented. She knows French so watch your mouth around her."

Clark laughed, wrapping his arms around her. "Last night was incredible." Simi smiled shyly, still feeling the sensations of their night together. "After we get through this tonight, I want to talk." He pressed his forehead to hers. "We have a lot to catch up on."

"Tonight, Clark. I promise." Simi softly kissed his lips.

The night was vibrant. She'd never seen Clark this at ease. Something had changed, and his happiness was exuding through his stories. She couldn't imagine that last night shifted his personality this much. Simi had a chance to meet founders of startups housed under Cottage Growth , and their excitement for possibilities matched Clark's. It was endearing how much potential she was surrounded with.

Clark introduced Simi to Kelsey, who entertained her with stories of Clark—finding similarities between himself at the office and his home life.

"But in all fairness, Clark has to be the most kind, generous, self -focused person I have worked for. Even if he refuses to believe he is on the spectrum. Right boss?" Kelsey ribbed.

Clark laughed, happily taking shots from Kelsey. "Remind me to schedule your bonus review next week, Kelsey."

Kelsey raised her glass with a wink as she stepped off to find her wife.

Clark stayed by Simi's side throughout the night until she found Amanda. They sat at a side cocktail table. Simi listened as Amanda shared how she had been doing as a new mother. She was undoubtedly glowing, not just as a new mom. She was proud of Adam for staying honest and true to his recovery for Abigale.

Simi had found herself alone when Amanda excused herself

to pump. Simi had no eyes on Zella, and she couldn't seem to find Clark's tall frame in the crowd. She was about to leave her table when she felt a warm hand press against her back. Her assumption of her visitor was wrong as she locked eyes to a man she was sure she would never see again. Fear washed over Simi.

"I didn't know if I would see you again, and yet here you are." His eyes narrowed toward her neck as he raised his hand to caress her with the front of his fingers gently. "Persia."

Simi immediately pulled away from him, bumping into Clark.

"Hey, you okay?" Clark steadied her. "Demkov, thank you for coming. Simi, this is the man who made CG a reality." Clark shook his hand. Demkov nodded and reached for Simi's hand.

"Such a pleasure, Simi, was it?" Demkov pressed his lips against her hand. Simi paused herself, taking in the moment. Understanding what was in front of her, she regained her composure.

"Thank you, yes." Simi pulled her hand back.

"Simi, if you don't mind." Simi looked at Clark, unaware of any discomfort, unaware of her hesitation. Understanding their need for privacy, she turned on her heel and quickly began to look for Zella. Simi couldn't believe that man was Clark's investor. She cringed at the memories quickly flashing through her mind. She continued to look for Zella, not finding her on the main floor or in the ladies' room. Coming out of the hallway, she saw Adam.

"Hey, I haven't been able to talk to you yet tonight." Adam could see she was visibly flushed. "You ok?"

"Yeah, just was looking for my friend."

"Zella? I like her—I think she made a friend at the bar." Simi relaxed immediately, realizing Zella was safe. Simi wasn't sure why, but she wouldn't have put it past that man to try and make a pass with Zella. Simi had to relax, this was not the time to panic. "Do you need a drink?"

"Water." Simi was able to spit out. Adam handed her his glass, she looked curiously.

"Seltzer water with lime, looks like a drink—isn't a drink." Simi nodded, understanding Adam's confession. "I see Demkov made an appearance." Adam stood by Simi's side as she watched the pair talking. "I will be so happy when this is all over, Simi." As if Clark had heard them, he looked over and back to Demkov to excuse himself. Simi kept her eyes on Demkov, who raised his glass in her direction and motioned toward the elevator bank beyond Clark's view. She wasn't sure, if Adam had seen Demkov's signal and understood it was for her.

"I am sorry about that. He was the last person I had to talk to. Are you ready to go?" Simi didn't have a chance to object.

"Go? It's nine; come on—Amanda and I can at least do another two hours. We will even go listen to live music." Clark chuckled at Adam's plea—he glanced at Simi's gaze.

"Can you just hold that thought? I need to talk to Zella. I will be right back." Simi elusively rattled off before leaving them.

Simi headed toward the elevator lobby. Her heart was racing. What was she going to do? How would Clark take it that Demkov was someone she was previously with? What would that do to him, especially under the circumstances in which it happened? She found Demkov waiting, leaning against the wall. Before she could say anything, he put his hand up.

"I don't want to talk here. I will give you an hour. Meet me in this room." He handed her a key. "I will be waiting and we can discuss how to proceed after tonight's interesting revelation." Demkov hit the elevator button and the door opened for him to enter. He gave a sharp grin as the doors closed.

Simi turned her heel and went back to the restaurant. She kept her composure as Clark and Adam continued banter between them, occasionally stopping to say goodbyes and walk some of their employees out. Zella was still at the bar conversing between Patrick and Bradley. Simi counted the minutes and sorted out how to handle her situation.

"All right, I think that is it! Do we know what we are doing next?" Clark waved over to Kelsey. He needed her to close the night out for them. "Adam is buying for the rest of the night," Clark teased.

Simi gently pulled him to the side.

"Something isn't sitting right with me. I am going to head home." Simi softly spoke to Clark.

"I can come home with you."

"No, Adam and Amanda deserve a night out. You haven't been with them in a bit. " She stroked his cheek.

"I will come by later tonight then." Clark looked into her eyes. "Simi, are you sure you are okay?"

"Yes, please come by tonight." Simi reached up and pressed a deeply meaningful kiss against his lips. One that caused sarcastic awe from Adam.

"In a coat?" Clark smiled devilishly.

"Only a coat." Simi smiled. "I am so proud of you, talking to everyone here tonight. CG is special. " Simi leaned up for one more quick kiss before stepping back and waving bye to Adam.

Clark waited for a moment before turning to Adam. "That sounded . . . I don't know."

"You don't take compliments well. Let's go find Amanda. I think I saw her with Kelsey."

Clark still felt unsettled as he followed Adam. He pulled out his phone, tempted to call Simi to request she wait for him. He didn't like her leaving like this. He would spend a few more hours out and then get back to Simi.

Simi stopped by the bar. She made sure Zella had her key and that Patrick would ensure she got back to her place tonight. Simi's stomach was tight, and she was scared. She would make this quick. Whatever he wanted, she would figure out a way to resolve this without Clark's involvement. Taking a moment, she hit the elevator button and went to meet with Demkov.

"There she is. I remember you beautiful, but tonight, even more so. I still dream of you. You have become the woman of my dreams," Demkov announced as Simi opened the door to his hotel room. She regretted letting the door close behind her.

"I am not the woman of your dreams," she answered sharply.

"It seems you are not interested in recreating our past times tonight." Demkov leaned back, rolling his arms in front of his chest. "Can I offer you a drink?" He made his way to the small wet bar and poured two glasses from a dark bottle. She stayed by the door. "Come, take off your coat. Relax a little bit." She didn't move. "Where have you been, my darling? Weeks of delighting in your pleasurable arms, then nothing? Not even a goodbye?" He took a seat on the sofa. "Come join me on the couch. I won't bite."

"I am not what you think I am." Simi kept her stance and her distance. "We met, we had our time together, and it was done. There is nothing more to discuss."

"But there is so much more we need to discuss," he instigated. "Tell me. Does he know?"

"He knows enough." Demkov took a sip from his glass.

"Does he know that his newfound love has been had by me? The man who made his dream a reality?"

"I will tell him," she declared.

Demkov was impressed.

"You think he will keep you? Still be able to look at you?" Demkov rose up, glass still in his hand. "I am not a cruel man, Persia, though I like Simi more. So much more authentic." He walked toward her. "Tell me how a man like Clark could handle this. I will sit in every board meeting where he has to answer to me. He has to look me in the eye, knowing where he lies at night is where I have been." He picked up a tress of her hair. "That I have touched where he touches, I have had what he has. No?" He clicked his tongue. "A man like Clark has fought too hard to be taunted by that image every time he and I meet." Simi couldn't argue with Demkov's point. It would not be possible for Clark to unsee it.

"I will tell him. How and what he chooses to do with that information will be up to him." Simi kept her eyes focused, not letting him waiver her at all.

"If you think so." Simi was suspicious of his easy surrender. "I know that boy, and he will not risk his success on you. Then I, still happily invested, will not only be right, but your availability will be wide open. It's a win-win. He will break your heart, and that's exactly how I came to enjoy you."

"Chto by ni sluchilos', ya bol'she ne budu dostupna dlya tebya." *Whatever happens, I will not be available for you again,* Simi declared perfectly in Russian. Demkov paused, a slow smile spread across his face. He came closer to Simi, his eyes looking deep into hers. He sucked in a breath from his teeth and walked away from her.

"When you confess to Clark, and he leaves you, you will be broken again, and who knows. Perhaps you will find your way back to me." He returned back in his native tongue.

"No." She answered.

"Well, then, I guess we are done here." Simi turned for the door. "Oh, and Persia? When you deactivated everything, my money was returned. I am not a cruel man. As you have come to find, I am quite generous." He moved closer to her, holding a white envelope. "For my sessions with you, plus additional pay should you decide to change your mind."

"I don't need your money." Simi refused the envelope.

"But does Clark?" Simi wanted to tell Demkov, that Clark didn't. "I suggest you take it. Maybe you know someone else who can benefit from your back-breaking labor." Demkov viciously laughed.

Simi begrudgingly took the envelope. She, at this point, would do anything just to leave. She began to blink back tears as she turned for the door and exited the room as fast as she could. She heard faint laughter come from beyond the door as it closed, and she hurried to the elevator. She felt flushed. Her skin was on fire.

She counted down the floors, just wanting to get home and take comfort in her covers. She would have to tell Clark tonight. Her hands trembled with the envelope in her hand. She kept trying to find a moment to pause and catch her breath. She couldn't. She had to keep it together. She was only twenty minutes from home. In twenty minutes, she would be safe. She had to get a cab right away. Watching the floors count down, she eagerly anticipated the door opening. Simi rushed out of the elevator, her breath caught, eyes widened.

She froze. His eyes were dark, and Simi felt the rage. She immediately came to him. "No, no, it's not what you think."

"Do not touch me." He grabbed the envelope—he didn't have to look. He felt what was inside. He grabbed her wrist. "Last night? Was I a practice round for you?"

"Clark—"

"I heard your call yesterday—why didn't you tell me? You–" Clark's face hardened. "How could you do this again?" He asked in an accusatory tone. The lobby was empty; no one yet had come by.

"Clark, you are hurting me."

"I am hurting you?!" he snarled. His temper was gone. He

quickly released her from his grip. Simi tried to hold in her tears. "I saw you enter the elevator, and I waited, wondered, refused to believe that you were doing this again." Breathless, he leaned back against the wall. "I waited because I didn't believe it. But here it is— the final piece of the puzzle with you."

"Clark, please," Simi's mind was racing. "It is not what you think. I was up there for less than ten minutes. You know this. Let me take you home and tell you what happened," Simi pleaded.

"If Roman didn't give you what you needed, you didn't have to do this. I would have helped you," Clark admitted.

"What? No, you need to listen. Just come back home with me. We need to talk," Simi continued to plead. "I am able to fix everything, Clark. Please, just pause. Take a breath. Come home with me so I can explain everything to you," Simi urged.

"I am not going home with you, Simi. I can't." Simi reached for Clark, but he pushed her hands away and pressed the envelope against her chest. "I don't even know how to look at you now." Clark gave a disgusted scoff. "Is that your game? You wait them out until they die on you? Did you think I was older?" Clark angled his jaw. "How did you really meet Roman?"

Simi snapped as she slapped her hand across his cheek. Clark, stunned, took a moment to realize the impact and the searing pain across his face. She narrowed her eyes at him, her heart breaking at his cruel words, that he could speak to her this way.

"You warned me that you wouldn't meet my expectations. I was never expecting this." Clark pressed his hand on his cheek, and looked down at his fingers.

Simi knew Clark couldn't know what transpired between her and Demkov. Clark's refusal to listen and jump to conclusions was his own fault. She expected much more trust from Clark. She wouldn't fix this.

Simi raised her chin, fire inside of her—convinced now that Demkov and Clark were perfect business partners for each other, Simi let him leave, let him assume the worst of her. This was how it had to be. Now, he had no other choice but to stay indebted to Demkov.

***

Jane had propped the Kleenex box next to Simi. "Start from the beginning." This time she did not open her journal or reach for her pen. She leaned forward in her seat and waited for Simi.

"It's over," Simi said in a whisper. Her voice had been raw and sore for a few days now. "Clark and I, we, um, aren't together anymore." Jane nodded. Simi tried to find the irony that in less than two years, she was sitting in Jane's office crying over the loss of another love. Simi sat stoically in her seat. Her eyes were red from crying, and she was exhausted.

Simi started from the beginning, informing Jane of her friendship with Zella and how she had come to her aide. She continued to explain who Demkov was to Simi and who he was to Clark. She paused, remaining somber in her recitation of Clark's attacks.

"He didn't even give me a chance, Jane." Simi looked off to the side, her arms crossed over her chest. "I just needed him to hear me. He couldn't even look at me." Simi sighed in disgust.

Simi rarely saw Jane have to take a moment to process. She always had the right thing queued up, ready to go. "So Clark has no idea about the connection between you and Demkov? He assumed you had sex for money that night, because he thinks you need it? The money he heard you were sending for Zella."

"Yes," Simi answered. Jane took another pause.

"Is Zella okay?" Jane put her hand up. "Don't answer that." Shaking her head, correcting herself. "Simi, people can say awful things when they are scared and angry."

"Not an excuse," Simi defended. "He wouldn't even listen to me. He didn't give me a chance to explain."

"People also *do* awful things when they are scared and angry," Jane gently reminded.

Simi shook her head. "No, if this year taught me anything . . ." Simi frowned. "You—you helped me realize I am not damaged, I am able to be loved. I have come to accept these things. I believe this. Clark doesn't know how to trust, he doesn't truly know how to love."

Simi looked away, rotating her ankle of her leg resting over her knee. "This doesn't matter. This is what it is right now. If Clark can't take a moment to hear me out, he won't forgive me for sleeping with Demkov. I fell into another delusion with Clark. I was excited but it wasn't real. This life, the past few months, was another delusion," Simi declared.

"Simi, your relationship with Clark was real. Your gallery is about to be real. Your friendship with Zella is real."

Simi ignored Jane's comments. "You told me before that I have never taken time for myself. Now is the time, I need to go back to Paris. I need to be with my family, I need to visit my mother's grave and finally mourn for her."

Jane hesitantly smiled. "So you are going into hiding again?"

"No, I will be back. He doesn't own Chicago. Neither of them do," Simi announced. "I will come back. I will get the gallery off the ground. Pass my Japanese class if it kills me. Whether or not I continue to do it here and be a resident of Chicago, that will be up in the air."

"It sounds as if you don't need me anymore." Simi laughed. That was the furthest from the truth.

"I would like to see if we can continue to talk virtually."

Jane nodded. "Of course."

When Simi left Jane's office that morning, she had a laundry list of items to complete before her departure to Paris. Starting with breaking the news to Zella, to dropping the keys of Shaadi's with Patrick, who had agreed to keep an eye on it until she returned, whenever that would be.

First, she had to make a call. The Chicago wind that she had found to be so brutal felt good around her body today. She found herself running hot, still distraught and heartbroken. Had she acted better when Roman passed? Had she immediately returned to Houston or Paris to mourn, had she done things differently, would her path have crossed Clark's? Is she only capable of seasonal love? Scuffing her boots before her, she pulled out her cell phone. She tucked in her airpods and secured them with her black and white knitted cap. Listening to the line trill, a warm and comforting voice answered.

"Salam, Maman joon." Tears began to well up in her eyes as she heard the happiness in her grandmother's voice. It was time to go home.

Chapter 25

Nearly three months later the night he walked out on Simi still felt as raw as yesterday. Clark stalled everything, much to Marcus's delight. He stopped pulling his money and continued to work with Demkov, who, since the holiday party, had started to visit weekly—focusing on one startup of brothers who had just come in from Philadelphia. They were focusing on black-owned restaurants with their delivery app, keeping commissions low and providing living wages for their drivers. It was the only thing keeping Clark motivated and distracted enough to ignore Demkov's hovering.

He spent nights in his office, unable to go home. Smoking replaced meals, and drinking replaced coffee. The pain he felt had been unbearable, so he numbed it the best way he knew. There had been a noticeable difference at the office, which brought Adam back to view. Clark was no longer perceived as approachable and attached as he had originally seemed.

Adam had attempted to get Clark to open up about what transpired between him and Simi, but he wouldn't. Clark began to distance himself from Adam and hadn't visited with Abigale. Clark would stay in his office even when she was brought to the Cottage Growth site.

On nights he did make it home, he took comfort in silence and whiskey. He was sulking, and he hated it.

He half-expected to see if Simi would reach out for her to try to explain, to make him listen. Convince him that he got it wrong. She never did. By the time Clark had come around to reach out himself, he was blocked, stopping by her white space to see it dark and locked up. He wouldn't go back to Prime. Not trusting Patrick would keep his confidence.

He switched gears back to work. His numbers were good—not great. Projections were the same. Clark had successfully pushed two app launches, one of which was the Philly brothers, the other a fashion retail launch. Both were out on the market, doing well. Clark pushed the marketing team to find more creative ways to gain exposure for more wins.

Today was the first board meeting of the year. Clark had no choice but to stand there and assure a Demkov and team that his dream of encapsulating a slightly utopic working environment wasn't crazy. That their considered bloat benefits had meaning to the staff, which then would deliver excellent results. His staff was delivering excellent results—there wasn't one person he could call out as inferior; other than himself. They deserved better, and he needed to be better again. He would be better again.

Clark had arrived first at the office, before the sun had risen. He walked around the floor, looking at the desks, the marker scribble on the glass walls and white boards. Even though he wasn't in it— there was still excitement in the air.

"I wasn't expecting to see you here this early." Adam opened the main door. Clark turned to look at him.

"Just want to get today done—so I can focus on getting better results for the next one." Clark picked up a marker from the desk and dropped it. "Why are you here so early?"

"Four a.m. wakes ups are my life now. Plus, I wanted to double-check a few things and review them with legal before we start."

"Anything I should be concerned about?" Clark noticed Adam take a moment with his answer.

"No, I don't think so."

"I'll be in my office then." Clark walked away from Adam and headed toward his office. He threw his bag on the couch and walked toward the window. The tension in his chest hadn't dissipated in three months. He had to focus; this was not the time to show weakness. He turned to see Adam as he heard his office door open.

"Clark—we need to talk," Adam started.

"Unless it's about the meeting today, I don't want to talk about anything." He turned away, focusing on the skyline across the river.

"I hate seeing you like this. I have never seen you like this. Even at our lowest of lows you never—"

"I never what? Lost my cool? Showed emotion? Yes I know, I am an asshole."

"There is another way, there may be an investor who can help us. We can swap out funds after this board meeting."

"Something is going on isn't there?" Clark turned back to him and clenched his jaw. "This is why legal is involved. The capital is compromised! Adam! Damn it!" Clark near yelled.

"No, that isn't it."

"This is on you! You weren't honest; you went to fucking Evan, after everything, after he almost destroyed his father and you let him do that to us! To me!" Clark exhaled aggressively. "Just tell me what it is now before I make a fool of myself today."

Clark waited as Adam stood firmly against him. Adam scoffed and looked off to the side.

"Again, Clark, there is nothing wrong with the money other than the source of it." Adam cleared his throat, his tone calm and collected. "I just wanted to offer you another solution since Demkov—" Adam attempted to explain further.

"No, I don't want any money from anyone else. I am going to get us out of this. I am going to profit and buy Demkov out within the year. There isn't going to be a single dollar in this company that isn't in my control."

"What does that mean?" Adam furrowed his eyebrows. "You aren't self-funding this—you don't have the cash or assets." Adam tried to warn Clark, "You will lose everything if you do this. Including CG."

"I don't have to answer you."

"Actually, you do," Adam reminded.

Clark walked closer to Adam, standing toe to toe.

"You going to throw me out of your life too, Clark?" Adam challenged.

"I think you need to leave. I'd hate for you to get on another bender, now that Abigale is here. You push me on this anymore, your fragile ego will want to end it all."

"Fuck you, Clark." Adam stepped back, heading for the door. He turned back, his hand tightly gripping the doorknob. "Evan might have been the connect, but the funding was always going to be temporary. You told me that. You told me to find the capital and we were going to buy out the board with the profits. I did exactly what you asked. So Clark—excuse me if it's your fucking ego, too blind to see what you had. This is now on you."

"Get out." Clark lowered his voice.

"Don't worry, Clark. I am gone." Adam slammed the door behind him.

Clark momentarily felt a panic. He pushed it deep inside. Adam wasn't going to leave, he wasn't going to abandon Clark today, but that didn't mean he hadn't threatened Clark to leave. Especially when Clark had threatened him first. They had fought before, but Clark had never fought with Adam in such a raw way. The tension in his body was surging, every nerve pulsating to the max. Clark closed his eyes and moved to the side table. He looked down at an unfinished puzzle. Hurt. Clark was wounded, almost defeated. He couldn't settle into this feeling. He looked over to the clock. Get through today. Stick to the plan. He had this.

When the meeting began, Clark cautiously eyed the stenographer next to their General Council. He pushed the concern deeper down and focused on the agenda. Adam and he flew through the meeting as fluidly as if their fight hadn't occurred earlier that morning.

After a long and strenuous day with pushback from Demkov and his team members, frustrations, and a laundry list of expectations by the next quarter, Clark was in no mood to attend the dinner he had committed to or be in the same room with anyone, especially Demkov, who had been particularly difficult. Clark felt he was being played with, and he didn't like it.

As the dinner started, the flow of alcohol helped alleviate the tension of the day. Conversations were softer, and interest and willingness to listen seemed easier.

Demkov had been the most talkative throughout the evening, discussing matters of his investments in other parts of the world

and their successes. His Russian accent had become more prom-
inent as the night went on. Clark continued to indulge Demkov
throughout the night until it was just them two together. He had
convinced Clark to join him at a local cigar lounge.

Demkov's driver had dropped them off in front of a butcher
shop on the city's far west side. Four heavy knocks on the door
gained them entrance; they were led through a simple market to the
back. A door opened to a dimly red-hewed lit room. Clark faint-
ly heard bass coming through the walls until they finally passed
through the last door leading to a speakeasy strip club.

"My friend, you will have a good time here with me tonight." He
noticed that this was very much a local and Eastern European-on-
ly environment. Half-dressed women straddled men on couches.
Drugs and the smell of straight vodka were prevalent as they walked
to a private room for Demkov. Clark took a seat opposite the couch
where Demkov sat. At a snap of his thumb, women and vodka had
come out, timed as a cliché movie. Demkov lit his cigar, offering one
to Clark, which he accepted.

The music was softer in this room, he could still hear Demkov.
"This is my favorite investment." He laughed. "This is where the
money is, Clark. You figure out how to make this sell legally, and
you will never have to work again in your life."

Two women came, and each sat on the arms of his chair. He lit
the cigar and picked up a poured shot of vodka. He raised his glass
toward Demkov.

"To many more successes," Clark toasted, throwing back the
shot. The burn flowed through his throat more sharply than he had
been used to.

Demkov joined Clark at his side in an empty sofa chair next to
him. They both were quiet, watching the women continue to dance
for them.

"I have to say, when Evan brought Adam to me about you both,
I wasn't convinced." He reached for another shot glass of vodka.
"Then, Adam showed me your prior success, and I was so im-
pressed." He took a sip. "How someone like you could create what
you did. Fascinating." Clark felt the tension start to rise in his jaw.
He heard exactly what Demkov implied. "I know I was hard on you

guys today. You handled everything well." He patted Clark on the back.

"How did you meet Evan?"

"You don't know? He is my nephew. Sure, sure, my brother and I don't talk a lot. Who do you think gave Maxim a leg up? He gets to be legit and respected while I am his older brother. I will do any-thing for him, for Evan too." Demkov nudged Clark. "I have had to save both Evan and Maxim many times. I am happy to do it. Fami-ly—understand?" Demkov took another drink. "I'd say Evan is more like me than his old man anyway." Demkov pulled a drag of his cigar. "You know we share a lot of mutual people—you and me."

Clark was forcing himself to sober up as quickly as possible. He wanted to leave.

"Persia is what she went by. She told you, Simi. I was quite surprised to see her again. I hadn't been able to find her." An over-whelming feeling of rage surged through Clark. He turned to face Demkov taking a puff from his cigar. "Ah, so she never told you about our little conversation that night? Rightly so, it seems she is out of the picture now, yes?" Clark didn't respond. He wasn't going to give Demkov any indication of distress. "She claimed you knew about her lifestyle choices, which is noble, my friend. To still lay with that kind of woman." He waved his hand about. "I, of course, had to educate her on who I was, how important I was for you, and it seems she understood and left you alone." He leaned in close to Clark so he could clearly state, "You only bed those type of women, boy; you don't marry them."

Clark continued to regulate his breathing. He had to keep his temper in check. He was not on an even or safe playing field. His fists were clenched as he processed this information.

"She was a favorite of mine, I gotta tell you. Evan showed me that site. It was just something fun. Try a new flavor of woman." Demkov rested his head back on the chair. "She sold herself decent-ly, but I saw she was a bit broken. I loved that. Whatever got her to that point, so sad." Demkov shook his head. "But, I couldn't resist; you just gotta love that power beneath you." He laughed smugly again. "She would take it too. There was one night where I—"

"Enough!" Clark bolted up from his chair and grabbed Demkov by his shirt, pulling him to his face. Clark had about five inches on him. The women gasped, and men began to approach from the door. Demkov waved them back, speaking in Russian.

He looked at Clark and laughed. "Relax, easy, just take your hands off me, Clark." Jaw tight, he released Demkov's clothing. "We are just talking."

"We are done talking. We aren't talking about anything ever again." Clark reached for his coat, slung on the back of his chair.

"Come on, come, Clark, now relax. You are going to disrespect me over some woman? You are smarter than that." Clark made his way for the exit.

"You are right Demkov, I am smarter than that." Clark stepped back toward him. "I don't need your fucking money." Clark turned back and made his way out the exit. He knew he just had to keep walking quickly and straight to get out of there. He heard Demkov yell in the distance, but didn't care.

As the door shut behind him, Clark rushed through the market out to the street. He kept walking. Reaching for his phone, he dialed Simi.

He had been so wrong. He had never been this wrong about anything. He pressed the phone up to his ear. He was still blocked. Finally, feeling a safe distance, he leaned against a building catching his breath. It was three a.m.

He started connecting the dots of that night, imagining Simi being approached by that bastard. He was threatening her and Simi protected him, his business at a sacrifice to herself. An overwhelming wave of nausea fell over him. He felt his keys in his pocket. He never returned her fob. After everything, he learned tonight, he needed to see her. He couldn't wait.

Clark entered Simi's apartment quietly. Not fully accepting he was breaking into her apartment, invading her home, until he was halfway toward her bedroom. She would understand that he had to come immediately and fix this. He pushed her bedroom door open and held his breath. She wasn't alone. Clark immediately walked back into the door frame, muffling a curse that woke them up.

"What the hell? Who are you?!" Clark went back toward the

elevator, hoping it was still on her floor, hearing a man yelling from the bedroom. The other voice wasn't Simi. She stormed out of the bedroom, holding the sheet around her. Zella.

"What the fuck do you think you are doing?! Are you drunk?!" Zella began throwing pillows at Clark.

"I'm sorry—I am sorry. I just need to talk to Simi. Just tell me where I can find her."

"How did you get in?" Zella yelled. The man she was with stepped out of the bedroom only to quickly rush back in. "Well?" She looked at Clark.

"I still have her fob. Zella, please. I need to talk to her."

"Give me the fob and anything else you have." Clark complied with her request and tossed it on the counter. "That it?"

"Yes."

"All right then, get out." She went toward the elevator and pressed the button. The door opened immediately.

"Zella, please, where is she?" Clark held the door of the elevator open.

"I will let her know that you need to talk to her. She can decide if she wants to call you." Zella began pushing against Clark. "You realize this is illegal? I should call the cops! You need to go."

"Zella, please."

"I live here now. She doesn't. I *will* call the cops next time." Zella angrily pushed Clark back fully into the elevator. "Oh." Zella reached for a black bag Clark immediately recognized as his weekender. "She thought you might come back for it." Zella threw it at him. "Jewelry is in there, so don't be daft. And don't come here again!"

Clark walked out of the elevator holding his bag and took a seat on the steps in the lobby. He opened up the bag. Both sapphire pieces were present. He dug his hand around and looked through his things. Frustrated, he dumped the entire contents of the bag, relieved not to have found what he was looking for. Clark heard the elevator door behind him open and began repacking the items discarded on the ground. He looked up to see Zella, dressed, kneeling to help as she handed him the jewelry boxes.

"Sorry about that." Clark stood up. "I just wanted to talk to her."

"She is back in Paris," Zella volunteered. She sighed heavily and sat on the same stair Clark had been resting on, inviting him to join her. "You really messed up."

"I know."

"That money you heard her wire, she was doing that for me. She was protecting and helping me out." Zella sighed heavily. "You don't know the guilt I have had about what happened between you two. Maybe if you hadn't heard that call, you wouldn't have jumped to conclusions."

"The only person at fault here is me."

"Oh no, this mess is entirely your fault. I just have a tiny bit of guilt." Zella squeezed her pointer finger and thumb together.

"How is she?"

"She is at home. I was expecting her back by now. She is letting me stay here."

"Are you okay?" Clark asked. "I know you two haven't known each other long, so it must have been something for Simi to help you like that."

"I am much better now. The past two months have been rough; I am still healing and up to my old tricks." Zella motioned upstairs. "Eventually, I will smarten up. Or Jane will start making me come in every day."

"I am starting to think I need Jane in my life too." Clark was still holding the jewelry box. "What do you think my chances are if I show up in Paris?" Zella broke out in laughter.

"If you plan on breaking and entering, well, I don't know much about her grandma, but I would prepare for a shoe to your head." Clark chuckled alongside Zella. "She is coming back. Maybe I'll throw you a bone and let you know when she does."

"I broke her trust. I said awful things to her. She won't forgive me."

"Maybe, maybe not."

"Are you telling me I might still have a chance?" Clark looked at Zella curiously.

"I wouldn't give you a chance. Especially if you insinuated I was some type of Lifetime Black Widow," Zella curtly responded. "She blocked you for a reason."

"How do you know she blocked me?"

"Mate, you literally just broke into her flat. You obviously have been blocked." Zella amusingly shook her head at him.

"Why are you down here?" he questioned as Zella shot him a glance of annoyance.

"Simi deserves to be happy. I know we haven't been friends long, but in our own trauma, we have shared, we are close. I have never had a friend like this. Hell, I have never had someone treat me like this without demanding anything in return. She has given me hope again. I wake up in the morning and play. I hadn't touched my cello in a long time. She is my big sister now." Zella cleared her throat. "So despite my personal hatred of you and how daft you are, you made her happy after Roman. You helped her break a dark cycle as she did for me."

Clark took in all that Zella had shared with him. "You going to put in a good word for me? Maybe get me unblocked?"

"No!" Zella quickly snapped.

"You going to tell her what happened tonight?"

"Oh yes, but it's going to be extra dramatic. Boo hoo tears, ripped shirt in the raining screaming 'Simi!' . . ." Clark grabbed the handles of his weekender and stood up from the stairs. He looked toward the door then back at Zella.

"Tell Patrick I said hi." Clark winked at Zella, who did not confirm if that was whom Clark saw upstairs.

"Good luck, mate." He smiled tightly and pushed the lobby door open, walking out to the dark streets. Zella stood up, watching until he was out of plain view. She retrieved her phone from her pocket to see a text from Simi. She smiled as she responded, waving the fob against the elevator doors and heading back upstairs.

Chapter 26

Simi inhaled, the sun shining brightly over her. She sat on a blanket, and her mother's poetry books surrounded her as she sat in front of her grave in Pere Lachaise Cemetery. A small headstone was surrounded by flowers, and Simi would light a few candles as she recited poems. After her first trip to visit her mother's grave, the peace she had felt speaking to her again was addictive. She returned every day, recited poetry, and sat with her mother.

Simi opened a book by Hafez and looked toward the gravestone. She had begun imagining her mother sitting with her as she read.

"Today, I wanted to read this one with you." Simi opened the pages and quietly spoke the following poem to her mother. "I have learned so much. I have learned so much from God, that I no longer call myself a Christian, a Hindu, a Muslim, a Buddhist, a Jew. The truth has shared so much with me, that I can no longer call myself a man, a woman, an angel, or even a pure soul. Love has befriended Hafiz so completely it has turned into ash and freed me of every concept and image my mind has ever known." Simi exhaled as she recited the last words. She closed her eyes and lifted her face toward the sun. Pausing in a moment of reflection, choosing to believe it was her mother's hand stroke against her cheek in place of the warm sun.

She regretted waiting so long to visit her mother's grave, to visit Paris, but was grateful to be back now. The love from Maman and Daroush was what she needed after the disappointing ending of her relationship with Clark. The pain of loss always kept her running away from comfort. Afraid to experience what life was like when the one you love isn't there anymore, but you still are left roaming the earth without them. Maman and Daroush were always there to support her, and she realized she had been selfish in not opening herself up to her family's love. She felt the warmth around her, she connected to her mother again, and though she hadn't noticed it before, she felt a fullness replace emptiness inside of her.

She thumbed through another poetry book as she heard the familiar footsteps of her brother making her way toward her.

"You are here early today." Daroush took a seat on the blanket next to her.

"Yeah, I didn't sleep well." Simi kept her eyes low.

"You seemed very sad after your talk with Jane. You barely ate at dinner." Daroush picked up the poetry book, finally getting Simi to look at him. "Is everything okay?"

"Yeah, I am fine, Daroush," Simi insisted.

"You know, if you lie to me on Momma's grave, lighting can strike you," Daroush chided. Simi pushed at his shoulder. "Fine, okay, when you are ready to share. I am happy to listen."

"Just thinking through things, Daroush, really trying to take my time and make smart choices. A bit tired of mistakes." Simi exhaled.

Simi appreciated Daroush letting her words settle in the air. The wind began to pick up around them, and Daroush started telling a story from when they all lived in Los Angeles. Simi smiled, listening to his version of the story of when they lived with their auntie. Simi and Daroush spent the morning sharing stories of their youth. Daroush insisted Simi was old now and hadn't remembered facts correctly. By the end of the last story, Simi was wiping tears from her eyes, her stomach aching from laughter.

"That is not true. That never happened. Daroush, you imagined that."

"On Momma's grave it's true, Simi!" Daroush insisted, trying to calm his own laughter down. "You want to gather your things, Simi. It will rain soon." Simi looked up at the beautiful blue sky. Daroush motioned behind her, where dark rain clouds hovered. Daroush began helping Simi gather her things.

"Do you want a moment alone before we leave?" Simi motioned

toward the headstone.

"I have been here quite often, and I talk to Momma all day." Daroush winked at the headstone. He stood up and offered his hand to Simi to stand. "I am her favorite son."

"You are her only son," Simi dryly stated. "I am still surprised that she is buried here. It's such a beautiful area. So much history, and I mean, it's just perfect for her." They began their walk home.

"You know, that is all Baba," Daroush shared; Simi raised an eyebrow. "Baba's mentor through medical school was the Shah's doctor. He is still alive and lives here in Paris, you know."

"No, I didn't know."

"I believe he still cares for Shahbanu, Farah, who lives here too." Daroush waved his hand. "When Momma passed, Baba made a few calls here and there et, voila. He got Momma a beautiful resting spot in the city she loved."

"Why did you wait so long to tell me all this?"

"I didn't know where your head was with our father. I didn't know if you would have a tantrum and demand that she be buried someplace else," Daroush argued.

Simi smiled and nodded. "I have been a little dramatic in the past." Simi looked back toward her mother's grave. "He did love her," Simi stated.

"Yeah, but I understand you aren't ready to forgive him. He did leave us." Daroush grabbed Simi's hand. "Honestly, I think he knew what he was and wasn't capable of. I appreciate that." Daroush took a large step away from Simi before he spoke again. "You know, you both are very much alike."

Simi frowned, looking at her brother's purposeful distance. "Who?"

"You and Baba." Daroush braced for her reaction.

Simi shook her head—"I am not going to hit you, Daroush, don't be afraid." Simi laughed as he came back to join her. "You are wrong, though."

"I don't think I am, Abji." Daroush quickly stepped to the side playfully. As Simi rolled her eyes, he returned to walk with her. "Both of you are runners."

Simi glanced sharply at Daroush. "That's not true."

"Isn't it?" Daroush insisted. Noticing her silence, he began to tease. "Ahh, you're thinking about it, you know I am right."

"It's not the same. He is our father. He wasn't supposed to leave us when Momma died."

"Perhaps not, but Father or not, he is still human. No one is perfect, and there isn't anyone standing on this earth that doesn't regret a mistake or two in their life." Daroush glanced back at Simi.

Simi frowned, understanding Daroush's intent. She looked ahead down the paved street, silent during the rest of their walk to Maman's home.

Sitting in her room, Simi looked out the window. Simi had been enjoying Paris, but knew she had to return to Chicago. Last night's session with Jane revealed to Simi that it was time for her to return. She owed it to herself to finish what she had started. She had so many things in motion that had come to an abrupt stop. She had artists ready to show, and she wanted to keep her promise to them. She also was a bit scared about returning to Chicago, but she had Jane and now had Zella. Simi knew she had the freedom to come and go from Chicago as she pleased. She could avoid any accidental run-ins quite easily.

She understood where Clark's behavior stemmed from. She could even let him apologize for what he said to her, but she wasn't sure if Clark could ever truly forgive her and move on. She had fantasized about their relationship had they met in normal situations. Well, as normal as possible. Maybe before she had the idea to sign up for the website, he would have seen her at Prime, in a hoodie, hair disheveled, tear-stained, consumed by a bottle of wine. He could have swooped in then. Would they have been more successful together? Or still crash and burn?

Simi would leave those thoughts before the tinge of sadness crept into her consciousness. She was still annoyed about how she missed him and how she may actually still love him.

That idea, that thought, is what weighed heavy on Simi last night. She wasn't sure how it was possible to feel anything toward Clark. Last night, with Jane, Simi opened up about missing him, that she had been thinking about reaching out, just to check in. She felt uncomfortable all week that something was wrong. It wasn't from Zella or anything with her in Paris. The only other person she had grown to care about was Clark.

Simi had mainly stayed to herself for the rest of the day, unable to shake the worry from her consciousness. She looked up as Maman came into the room with a cup of tea. Simi adjusted on her bed to let her sit beside her. Her Maman, rested the tea on her bedside and grabbed Simi's head, kissing above her hair very tightly and around her face. In the slow cadence of Persian, she spoke to Simi.

""In keh injâ hasti, delamo az khoshhâli be dard avorde." *You being here has made my heart ache with happiness.* Maman smiled shakily. "Hame jâ to khone mibinamet, va nafasam ghat' mishe—chun kheili shabih-e Shaadi jooni." *I have been seeing you throughout the home, and my breath catches because you look so much like my Shaadi joon.* Tears began to well up in Maman's eyes. "Zibâyi-esh ro dari… va del-e oun ro ham." *You have her beauty and her heart. Maman grabbed Simi's hand.* "Âtashesh ro dari, ghodrat-esh ro ham. Mesle man." *You have her fire, her strength. Just like me."*

Simi didn't try to hold back the tears, and she embraced this moment with her Maman.

"Delet barâsh tang shodeh?" Do you miss her? Simi kept the conversation in Persian.

"Har rooz, bâlesh tang misham. Vali in keh injâ hasti, delamo kheili arâm karde, Simi joonam." *Every day, but you being here. It has helped my heart heal so much, my Simi joonam.* Simi moved into Maman's open arms and settled her head on her lap. She closed her eyes as Maman began stroking her hair. Simi's eyes felt heavy. She gave into the maternal comfort of her maman and let her eyes close, giving in to sleep.

"My blushing bride." Simi turned to face Roman. "We made it to Paris at last." Simi didn't hesitate. She rushed into Roman's embrace. She buried her face deeper into his chest, holding him tightly.

"You left me," Simi murmured against his chest. "Why did you leave me?" Roman pulled Simi away from him. He took her hand and spun her around. Simi looked down to see herself in a simple white wedding dress. She looked back up at Roman. He was in an elegant black tuxedo. He flicked his arm, revealing his cherished Patek watch

on his wrist. "Roman." Simi caught her breath and embraced him again.

"Simi joon, you have the world. Why are you so sad?" Roman whispered into her ear.

"I never asked for the world."

"You didn't ask me for anything, Simi. That's why I gave you everything." Roman lifted her chin.

"I miss you."

"I know," Roman gently kissed her cheek. "I miss you too."

"Let me stay here with you," Simi quietly asked.

"You have so much life left to live Simi. You have so much love left," Roman encouraged.

Simi shook her head. "No, I–"

"You do. There are people that need you more than I do. I was so lucky you chose me and let me love you until the end of my days."

"No, Roman, I was . . ." Simi's eyes began to tear up, she felt his embrace begin to loosen. "Wait, please."

"Simi joon, I love you." Roman began to turn away from her. "It was worth the wait to see you in that white dress." Simi felt her legs, unable to move, follow him.

"Roman . . ." Her voice cracked as she pleaded for him. He stopped momentarily, glancing slightly back at her.

"Don't wait too long to wear one again."

Simi's eyes slowly opened the wetness of her tears on her cheeks. Simi slowly lifted herself from the bed. Her heart beat rapidly. Catching her breath Simi looked around her room before laying back down. She slowly took a deep breath, one at a time, hoping to ease the thoughts racing in her head. Peering over to the clock it was before two a.m. Maybe Jane was still working.

***

Simi was lucky last night to get in touch with Jane. She quickly rushed out the details of her dream, attempting to keep her emotions at bay. The realness of the dream, the closure she thought she felt, she was still confused by it all but so grateful for the dream. Jane listened to Simi's interpretations, and her expressed emotions, finding clarity in what she was ready to do next.

Simi was in the kitchen with Maman, watching her as she quickly chopped the parsley for the Gormeh Sabzi. She was distracted as Maman was talking to her about her friend's grandson who was graduating medical school in Los Angeles this spring. Simi smiled and listened to all his great attributes, not ready to reveal to her maman that he was probably not interested in a bride eight to ten years older than him.

Daroush came into the kitchen. "Why aren't you dressed?"

"What do you mean?" Simi asked, confused. Maman looked at the clock, worried about the time. She began to push Simi out of the kitchen. "Why do I have to dress for dinner?" Simi's stomach dropped as she looked back at Daroush. "Maman did not bring that med student here, did she?" Simi quietly asked.

Daroush chuckled, pushing his sister down the hallway. "No we just have some relative who is visiting from Tehran tonight. Don't worry, it's not a match date." Daroush opened the door to his sister's room. "But wear something nice. Maribelle will be coming tonight."

Simi stood in the mirror, smoothing out her grey skirt. She adjusted her necklace over her turtleneck and began brushing her hair. She heard the doorbell ring from her room. Daroush's footsteps quickly rushed to the door. Maribelle, Daroush's fiancée, had already arrived, which meant Simi was late. She should have already been in the living room, helping Maman host.

Simi sighed. Her head wasn't where it needed to be to entertain. She inhaled another deep breath and looked at the top of the dresser where many photos of her momma were on display. She smiled softly, nodding to herself as she left her bedroom.

Slowly, she walked down the hallway through the kitchen, the conversation in the family room slowing, becoming quieter with each step. Entering the room, Simi looked at Maman, standing with her hands on her cheeks, her eyes hopeful. She looked over to Daroush, confused. Simi focused to the sitting chair and blinked, shocked.

Tears immediately formed in her eyes; she pressed her lips tightly together as she swallowed, continuing to blink back tears.

Her father rose from his seat, removing his grey hat from his head. He held a bouquet of flowers.

"Salam, Simi."

The room was silent. No one took a breath. Simi looked at his suit and saw the effort. The flowers lightly shook in his hand. His eyes—unsure. Simi unsure as well. Simi looked back at Daroush, unable to read his face before looking back at her father.

She slowly crossed the room and stood in front of her father.

"Salam, Baba." Simi's voice broke.

Her father dropped the flowers from his hand and immediately embraced her. Simi closed her eyes, returning the hug. Maman clapped her hands in celebration. Simi smiled. Simi was finally done running.

Simi sat next to her father as they ate. As if a dream, Simi found herself at a table full of family and full of love. Her father held her hand, possibly afraid to let it go. Simi wasn't sure, but she didn't mind. It was an evening of stories, laughter and a welcome for Daroush's future bride.

Simi's phone began to ring from the kitchen. She ignored it, listening to Maribelle share a story. Daroush frowned at her as it kept ringing. Simi nodded, she put her other hand over her Baba's reassuringly. She excused herself from the table and went into the kitchen.

She frowned as text messages and calls began pushing through. She silenced her phone, trying to figure out what was happening in Chicago.

"Simi are you serious right now?" Daroush came into the kitchen. "Turn off your phone."

"Sorry, I know." Simi shook her head. "I am coming. I just need to make one call."

"Simi, it can wait."

Simi looked back curiously at Daroush, his tone urgent. He reached into his pocket, pulling out Momma's engagement ring.

"It has been a perfect night, this is the perfect night to do this." Simi caressed the side of Daroush's cheek, smiling. She nodded.

"You are right." Simi put the phone down. "That can wait." Simi hugged her brother. "This cannot. I am very proud of you."

Simi followed Daroush back into the dining room, elated to

enjoy the rest of the evening with her family. She sat back down and reached for her father's hand. Feeling her father's give an extra squeeze, she captured a sincerity in his eyes that transported her back to Knuttle's painting. Simi tilted her head gently to her father. He leaned in pressing a soft kiss against her cheek. Simi hoped that in this moment her Momma was happily watching in the clouds as her family was together. As it should have always been, home in Paris.

Chapter 27

Clark was still in bed when the insistent ringing of his doorbell started going off. He pulled the pillow over his head and squeezed his eyes shut. Clark had just been able to fall asleep after the events of the hours prior.

He would go away

He didn't.

He heard Adam open the door, calling for him until he reached the bedroom.

"Are you okay?" Adam asked. He came over and pulled off the pillow. "Did you get hurt?" Clark was surprised to see Adam so concerned.

"I am fine. Nothing happened," Clark dismissed. He pushed himself from the bed. "Except everything that did happen." Clark rubbed his hands over his face. "I didn't think I would see you today."

"You always showed up for me, Clark. One fight doesn't end twenty years."

"No, but I guess one fight can end *one* year relationships." Clark sarcastically chuckled.

"On that note, be proud that you actually did end one relationship in your life. Even though I think it was the wrong thing to do."

"It was," Clark admitted.

Adam looked at him curiously, surprised at Clark's admission. "What happened last night?"

Clark told Adam the events with Demkov, what he realized Simi had done for him, and then how he heroically broke into Simi's apartment to beg for forgiveness.

"Yeah, I heard that part. Did you really cry, though?" Adam teased.

"How did you hear about that?" Clark had a sudden thought— "Are you still talking to Simi? Adam?" Clark asked with urgency.

"Before Simi left, she asked me to be available for Zella. She was worried about Zella and knew that I could be trusted." Adam put his hands up. "I am not talking to Simi, Clark. Zella called me after you left because she was worried about you. She had a more entertaining recount than you shared, my friend."

"What is the story with that girl?" Clark inquired.

"It's not my story to tell." Adam came to sit on the bed with Clark. "I just wanted to make sure you were okay."

Clark nodded nervously. "I am, I will be. I have to pull my money out today."

"Okay," Adam agreed.

"No fight?"

"No fight. I have been at the office with Cynthia most of the morning." Adam shrugged.

He updated Clark that Cynthia had been working on reorganizing budgets and getting the original capital investment back to Demkov. He shared that the entire C-suite, including Kelsey, took paycheck holds until Clark's money was in CG's accounts.

"Thank you, Adam."

"It's fine. Can you just do me one favor?" Adam stood up from the bed. "Since we have a small cushion until you become broke. Can you just do one more meeting with potential investors? This Friday, ten thirty a.m. with Mr. Donahue. It will be the last one, and I will not stand in the way of you going penniless for this."

"Adam..."

"Clark—I am asking you to hold the call to Marcus and give me until Friday." Adam cleared his throat. "I took the shortcut with Demkov; we both had our hand in how we got here. Just give me one last chance to fulfill my obligation and job to find a proper source of capital."

Clark looked out the window. Taking this meeting, giving Adam one last chance to prove himself, was more important than what Clark wanted.

Adam woke up and left his new daughter to clean up the mess Clark had made after all the awful things he had said to him. Clark felt small, and if this is how Adam had always felt around Clark, then he was beginning to understand their dynamic more deeply, and Clark never wanted Adam to feel this way again.

"Okay, Adam. One more."

When Adam left, Clark remained in his bed. Still decompressing from everything. He turned over, facing his windows, and looked up to the side wall. The Restless puzzle painting was finished and hung on his bedside. It was a cruel reminder of what he no longer had next to him. If had just listened, breathed. If he just trusted. Clark sighed heavily, turning over again to lay on his stomach, forcing the pillow over his head, hoping sleep would resolve all the pain he was in.

Clark walked into his office on Friday; he had been working remotely since the board meeting. Walking on the floor, he felt strong, positive energy surround him. No stress was in the air; people were happy to see him. The feeling of euphoria was similar to when they had first opened. He walked over to Kelsey, who followed him into his office.

"I wasn't expecting you to be late."

Clark looked at Kelsey. "What do you mean? We meet with this group at ten thirty."

"Nine thirty, Clark."

"Kelsey, I swear Adam told me ten thirty." Clark quickly dropped his things.

"Come on. You can catch the end. I think Adam is almost done." Clark followed Kelsey to the conference room. Clark needed to be in there, he wanted to show Adam his support.

"Excuse me, Adam, Clark is here."

"Thanks, Kelsey," Adam stood at the front of the conference room table and motioned for Clark to join them. "Apologies, Mr. Donahue, our CEO had a delay this morning that couldn't be ignored."

Clark remained still. He felt a slight push from Kelsey to get him through the door as Mr. Donahue rose from his seat.

"Clark, so great to meet you." He smiled with a firm handshake. "Please, call me Gregory."

"Gregory Donahue." Clark repeated returning the shake.

"Then, of course, you know Ms. Ghorbani," Adam gestured with glee.

Gregory stepped off to the side, and Simi's hand came forward, her ruby bracelet securely fitted on her wrist.

"Good to see you again, Clark." Simi smiled brightly at him.

"Same." Clark breathed as their hand embrace was much shorter than he wanted.

Clark, confused, finally exhaled and refocused. He apologized for his late arrival, walking toward the front of the room, and took a seat at the top of the conference table. Adam smiled and nodded toward him before he continued.

Clark's heart was beating so loudly, he wasn't even sure what Adam was saying. He focused on each slide, making sure not to glance down at the end of the table. How was she here? Why was she here? Clark had to endure twenty more minutes of this cruel moment as Adam continued his presentation.

Clark noticed Gregory lean into Simi, quietly talking, while Simi nodded her head in agreement. His stomach dropped as it clicked. Simi was the investor. He looked at Adam, remembering his push to get Clark to talk to Simi about money, to find out how much Roman had left her. Pieces of the puzzle fell into place in front of him.

The night Clark told her he was worried about the funding, she had indirectly told him that she had the money, and Clark ignored her. He frowned. Why did he ignore her? Why didn't he just ask?

Clark couldn't let her do this. Could he?

"That concludes the concept of Cottage Growth, our goals, mission, and ability, if properly funded." Adam clapped his hands together. "Do you have any questions?"

"I just would like some clarity." Clarks gaze moved over to Simi as she adjusted her chair closer to the table. "You mentioned the culture a lot, the positive environment you are promoting to establish change."

"Yes," Adam stood, moving closer to where Simi sat next to Gregory.

"I wonder what happens when an employee or a company underperforms. You know, umm . . ." Simi drummed her fingers on the table searching for the correct word before turning her gaze to Clark. "When someone doesn't meet your expectations, how do you handle that?" Simi grinned at Clark before turning her attention back to Adam. "Do you just fire them? Is there a performance evaluation plan?"

"Fire them? No, not here. Cottage Growth is all about reaffirming confidence. We," Adam motioned to Clark, "take time to figure out what isn't working. If we were quick to look at a situation and made a poor decision, then we are simply not living up to our mission statement. Right, Clark?" Adam smiled brightly. "Is there anything you want to add to Ms. Ghorbani's question?"

Clark's jaw clenched as he realized what both Simi and Adam were doing. He wasn't sure if Gregory was in on the joke, but he seemed very interested in what Clark had to say.

"Along with what Adam said, we do not want to make the mistake of overlooking someone's or a company's potential. If there is an underperformer in our midst, even in the C-Suite—"

"Or the CEO's office?" Adam added.

Clark cleared his throat, seeing Simi gleefully smile larger as he finished his answer. "Yes, even in my office, we come together as a community to figure out how to make it work."

Simi nodded, her smile slowly vanishing. She leaned over and spoke softly to Gregory. Clark maintained his composure, trying to get Adam's attention.

"Do you think we could have the room to ourselves for a few moments?" Gregory asked.

Clark quietly exited the room behind Adam, avoiding eye contact with Simi.

He quickly followed Adam into his office and closed the door behind him. "Adam? Care to explain?!"

"Have a seat before you give yourself a stroke. Do you need some water? You look a little pale." Adam tried to contain his amusement. He came around to lean on his desk as Clark took a seat. Adam brought both his hands together, pressing the tips of his fingers tightly before continuing. "Roman Charles wasn't married before. Roman had no children, and Roman had no family outside of Simi." Clark began to feel nauseous, recalling what Roman's estimated net worth was on the internet. "I don't know what happened in New York, but when you both came back, she reached out to me. She offered to replace the money."

"That was in January."

"Yeah, and that conversation you heard. That was for Zella. Simi had to delay moving that much money while Cynthia was in the review process. It was going to raise flags. She smartly gave herself a buffer of a weekend so that it could be properly justified in the financials for us."

"Then the holiday party." Clark finally took a seat.

"Yeah," Adam leaned against his desk in front of Clark. "I, of course, understood that Simi was no longer wanting to replace the funds at that moment. So, we canceled the deal."

Clark leaned his head back in frustration. "The fuck, Adam."

"So, you know, time passes on until the board meeting and I wake up to a call from Evan who tells me what happens with Demkov," Adam smacked his lips. "Not surprisingly, Demkov wants his money back immediately. I get a call from Zella, and she tells me your heartbreaking story. So, I go back to my phone and scroll down to Mr. Donahue. He is Simi's lawyer, also Roman's old BFF. If Zella made me feel sorry for you, man, how would Simi feel?" Adam shrugged. "So, I made the call."

"She is offering to fund us exclusively?"

"That was the original ask, but" Adam leaned forward, with an enthusiastic whisper, "did you know, your ex-girlfriend is also a board member of OMC Capital?" Adam smiled; teeth clenched. "Surprise!" He exaggerated with his hands.

"What? That's not possible. I met with OMC in New York."

"Did you happen to tell her who you were meeting with while in New York?" Adam asked. Clark looked down, still processing. "Roman was a board member of OMC, and well, his seat goes to next of kin."

"I get it, Adam."

"So like I said, Roman didn't have—"

"I got it."

"No other wife"

"Adam—"

"Zero kids—like none. Zero offspring." Clark glared at Adam. "Roman's next of kin is Simi." Adam smiled.

"I said I got it."

"Simi—your ex-girlfriend Simi," Adam emphasized. "So, we are clear? Do you understand?"

"Adam, Clark," Kelsey tapped on the glass. "They are ready."

Adam nodded and looked back over to Clark. "Ready?"

Clark allowed Adam to take the lead, following him into the conference room. Simi and Gregory were standing, laughing alongside each other with Cynthia in the room.

"Clark, I must say, it has been a real treat to see what you have done here. When Simi first told me about it, I knew it was special. I am happy we were finally able to close this deal," Gregory announced. "I appreciate you both going through today. I wanted to make sure I clearly understood what you guys had going on here. I have a few ideas who will want in on this concept back in New York too."

Kelsey returned to the room, handing Cynthia four folders of contracts.

"I updated the new numbers as requested in these contracts," Cynthia said.

"New numbers?" Adam looked at Cynthia.

"Just a few adjustments," Gregory announced. "Let's run through it one more time."

Clark and Adam took their seats on the opposite side. Gregory began speaking, Clark hoping Cynthia and Adam were listening because he wasn't. He was entranced with Simi.

"Simi, are you sure?" Adam asked, bringing Clark back to attention.

Simi nodded. "Yes."

Adam shifted the contract to Clark, circling the new capital investment amount Simi was bringing in with OMC Capital. It was twice what Clark needed; it was double what Clark had told her he wanted.

He looked over at Simi, at a loss for words. She smiled softly, with a tilt of her head.

All four parties in the room continued to follow Cynthia's instructions for signatures and initials on their contract. She collected each folder and began to go over the process of next steps with Gregory and Simi. Cynthia invited Gregory to follow her to her office, leaving Simi alone in the conference room with Clark and Adam.

"So how awkward is this?" Adam gleamed a full-toothed grin. "Simi, while we were in my office, I updated Clark on what our plans were, before he betrayed your trust and broke your heart, cruelly if I might add, and then had you jet off to Paris, alone to wallow in the painful fact, that you, Simi, may never love again."

Simi raised her eyebrows, smiling ear to ear, completely entranced by Adam's description. "That was beautiful, Adam. Wow."

Clark was still not amused, but he still wasn't able to come up with any words.

"So before I leave you two alone, Clark," Adam turned to him, "Simi's money will be in our accounts by Monday. No one was taking a paycheck hold, but it's really cute that you think people like you that much that you thought they would." Adam laughed. "Am I forgetting anything else, hmm?"

"Adam, I think Clark and I need to talk," Simi suggested.

"We are all set!" Gregory came back into the room. He walked to Simi and kissed her cheek. "Proud of you." He addressed Clark, "Looking forward to seeing you more, too! We have a great spot in the Hamptons; we would love to host you this summer." Gregory extended his hand and firmly shook Clark's.

"Let me walk you out," Adam offered, fulfilling Simi's ask and leaving Simi and Clark alone.

"Hi, Clark."

"Simi." Clark sat next to her, fighting his urge to kiss her. He had no idea where she stood. Was she simply here to fund him, or was it more? "I honestly don't know what to say."

"You look a bit stunned. I had an idea about Adam's fun, but he really left you in the dark about everything, didn't he?"

"Yeah," Clark answered. "So did you."

"Not intentionally," Simi calmly responded.

"You didn't have to do this for me." Clark finally had the courage to look at her. To stay in her gaze, his jaw locked as the excitement and intensity for her resurfaced.

"I didn't do this for you. I did this for them, and the ones after them." Simi pointed out to Clark's staff on the floor. Simi brought her chair closer to Clark. "You okay?" Simi reached for his hand.

Clark swallowed hard at her touch. "Simi, I am so sorry, about everything."

"I know."

"I regret everything I said, everything I did, how I treated—"

"Clark," Simi softly caressed his cheek. "I missed you."

Clark did not pause, holding her hand on his cheek and pulling her in for a kiss, barely taking a breath, pressing his lips against hers, keeping her securely in his grasp. His passionate urgency was interrupted by a giggle from Simi as she pulled back from the kiss, hiding her embarrassment.

"So, I gather that you missed me too." Simi smiled.

"Simi, do you forgive me? Can you forgive me?" Clark pressed another kiss on her forehead. "I will start seeing Jane, I will tell you everything, no secrets. I will blindly trust you if you can just forgive me for hurting you," Clark exhaled.

"Clark, I wouldn't be here if I hadn't forgiven you."

"But you said—"

"Well, yes, the money is for them, but I came back for you." Simi held his hands in hers. "Any man willing to wail on his knees, screaming my name, ripping his shirt to pieces on Madison Ave at three a.m. in the rain deserves a second chance," Simi playfully teased.

"Zella . . ." Clark scoffed. "You are back?"

Simi cupped Clark's cheek in her palm. "Yeah, I am." Clark closed his eyes at her words, rubbing her arm.

"Let me take you home. We can finish everything from there."

"As lovely as that sounds, I have to leave in a bit, but I will need to stay at your place when I get back. Zella has made that place her home."

"Where are you going?"

"Jackson Hole."

"Wyoming?"

"Yep."

"Why?"

＊＊＊

Entangled in the sheets of their hotel suite, the sun shone brightly across the mountain views as Clark rested his head on Simi's belly, splaying soft kisses. He leaned on his elbow and drew his fingers around Simi's wrist and kissed around her ruby bracelet. There was no denying each other; leaving Cottage Growth and flying out to Jackson, it was a deep conversation and discussion between them, listening to each other's viewpoints, apologies, needs, and wants for the future. The rawness of hurt healing quickly between them with every vulnerable exchange. Once the hotel room's door closed, no words were left between them, just the need to finally show each other the affection they missed. The desire still held between the matured love that had forgiven and grown between them.

"Why did you only give back the sapphires? Did you not like them?"

"I liked this one more. I didn't want to give this one back, but felt like I should give the others back."

"They are yours if you want them." Simi pushed Clark back and brought her leg over his waist, straddling his hips. He began massaging her thighs. "I keep thinking about what would have happened if I hadn't fucked up that night."

"I am glad you did. I needed to go back to Paris. It was great that I did. If you hadn't, who knows what kind of situation we would be in today." Simi lowered herself, softly pressing a kiss on Clark's lips. "Now there should be nothing left but for us to love, be in love, and make love."

"You promise the rest of this is going to be easy?" Clark gently brushed her hair back.

"I don't know if easy is the right word, but it's possible the worst is behind us?" Simi shrugged. "We know so much more about each other now than we did."

"I want to go to Jane with you."

"Why?'

"I don't want any more weeks or months of us being apart. If that means I have to sit in therapy every week for the rest of my life, I will do what I need to do to keep you right here. Always in my arms."

Simi smiled, kissing his lips before relaxing on top of him, resting her head on his chest as he stroked her hair.

Softly and very slowly, he started to speak in Persian to Simi. A poem by Rumi, which he listened to repeatedly to ensure proper intonation.

"Hengâm-i keh rooh bar giyâh mi'oftad, donyâ por az hesse bâzgasht ast—harf bimonad." *When the soul lies down in that grass, the world is too full to talk about.*

Clark held the moment mentally between them. Feeling Simi smile on his chest as he recited the words. When he finished, Simi pressed a kiss above his heart. With his eyes closed he paused the time between them.

Epilogue

Shaadi's Gallery, Chicago

"Simi, you don't understand. These children playing string instruments should be illegal."

Zella cringed dramatically as she stirred honey into her tea, wincing again at the memory of a particularly heinous violin shriek. "There ought to be laws. Fines. Noise ordinances."

"You're being ridiculous," Simi called from across the gallery.

She was mid-conversation with a canvas, stepping back to take in the other pieces arranged along the walls. Securing this artist had been difficult getting her out of Wyoming had been even harder. "This is good for you. They warm your heart. Don't you love it when they giggle?"

Zella raised a brow.

"I hate it. I never should've said yes to this." She took a bitter sip of tea. "How long 'til summer's over?"

"Zella, it just started," Simi chuckled. "I can't wait for their little recital. I'll be front row, watching from backstage."

"This is my penance. Your philanthropic tendencies are rubbing off on me and it must stop."

"You're not paying a penance. You're rediscovering your joy."

"I could do that on a beach in Ibiza."

"You're doing it right here—with children who adore you, and a cello you actually touch again." Simi grinned as she joined her. "Admit it. You're starting to feel like yourself again."

Zella leaned against the counter. "Fine. But just so we're clear—I still believe one of my students is both tone-deaf and possessed."

"Be nice."

"I am nice," Zella muttered.

"No. You're British. And chronically unimpressed."

Zella's phone buzzed on the counter. She glanced down and subtly turned the screen toward herself, suppressing the smile that crept onto her face. A short, sweet message glowed back at her.

Simi didn't miss it. "Was that him?"

Zella sniffed. "None of your business."

Before Simi could prod, the door chimed.

Clark entered, juggling two coffees and a large bakery bag. "Morning, ladies."

"Clark," Zella replied dryly. He kissed her cheek. She tolerated it with the same expression one might reserve for slightly sour milk. "I brought you a cinnamon roll. Truce?"

She snatched the bag. "Temporarily."

He passed Simi her coffee and pressed a kiss to her temple. "You ready?"

"Almost. Our new artist is stopping by later. Zella, she's got a little... Wyoming energy."

Zella narrowed her eyes. "Is that a real phrase?"

"You'll see." Simi grabbed her bag. "Be nice."

"I am always nice."

Clark smirked. "You've been suspiciously soft lately. Is that the mystery man's doing?"

Zella gave him a glacial look. She appreciated that he hadn't said Patrick's name aloud she still wasn't ready to bring it up with Simi. "You can take your cinnamon roll back."

"That's enough," Simi said, cutting in. "I'll be back—hopefully before she arrives. Thanks for holding down the fort."

She walked out with Clark, the door shutting gently behind them. Silence settled back over the gallery.

Zella turned to the painting propped in the center. Women—

full-bodied, mid-dance, mid-laughter, unapologetically alive. She frowned. She'd seen this artist's work online. She hadn't expected to like it. But this one... this one sang.

She stepped closer, tracing the curve of a spine, the tilt of a head, the belly that jiggled mid-laughter. Her breath caught.

Moments later, she emerged from the back room with her cello in hand. She dragged a chair into the gallery, sat, and placed the instrument between her knees. Fingers on strings. Listening.

A pulse. A minor chord.

The weight of everything she'd carried—the scandal, the silence, the shame sat with her. But so did something new. Something raw and possible.

She played.

Not flawlessly. But honestly. And when she finally stopped, she exhaled and rested the cello on her lap.

"That's a damn good painting," she murmured.

She grabbed a pencil and scribbled on the back of a torn envelope.

"Round Women in E Minor," she whispered, grinning.

The door chimed again. Zella froze. Early delivery? No. Not a delivery.

The woman who stepped inside was tall, with wild black curls and piercing green eyes. Her denim overalls were spattered with clay and cobalt paint. She moved like someone who hadn't apologized in years.

Zella was surprised to see a woman who looked like her, dressed like that.

The woman scanned the gallery once, then locked eyes with Zella.

"You must be the musician."

Zella blinked. "And you must be the artist."

"I hope you like round women. I've got twenty more on the way." She dropped her bag by the door and extended her hand, henna winding across her skin like a secret. "I'm—"

Zella raised a brow. "Let's keep it mysterious, shall we?"

The woman grinned, retracting her hand. "Sure."

Her gaze dropped to the cello. "Do you play anything less...

intense?"

"No."

"Perfect."

"Honestly, you aren't what I expected to walk in today," Zella said, giving her a long look before turning back to the painting.

"I'm not surprised by that."

"Why do you just draw pudgy women?"

"Does it make you uncomfortable?"

"No, but I bet there's a story behind it."

"Isn't there always?"

"Well, it's too early for a drink. Simi will be back soon."

"I don't drink."

"Oh," Zella furrowed her brow.

"But I saw a weed shop round the corner. Might pair nicely with those baked goods while I wait."

Zella looked toward the counter. Then back at the artist. "Yeah," she said, cracking a smile. "We'll get along just fine."

www.ingramcontent.com/pod-product-compliance
Lightning Source LLC
Chambersburg PA
CBHW032235310726

48973CB00008B/2139